D0680983

Books by Kathryn Lynn Davis

AT THE WIND'S EDGE

THE ENDLESS SKY

Published by Zebra Books

THE ENDLESS SKY

Kathryn Lynn Davis

ZEBRA BOOKS
Kensington Publishing Corp.
http://www.zebrabooks.com

ZEBRA BOOKS are published by

Kensington Publishing Corp.
850 Third Avenue
New York, NY 10022

All Kensington titles, imprints and distributed lines are available
at special quantity discounts for bulk purchases for sales pro-
motion, premiums, fund-raising, educational or institutional
use.

Special book excerpts or customized printings can also be created to fit specific needs. For details, write or phone the office
of the Kensington Special Sales Manager: Kensington Publishing Corp., 850 Third Avenue, New York, NY 10022. Attn. Special Sales Department. Phone: 1-800-221-2647.

Zebra and the Z logo Reg. U.S. Pat. & TM Off.

First Pinnacle Printing: 1984
First Zebra Printing: May, 2001
10 9 8 7 6 5 4 3

Printed in the United States of America

PROLOGUE

Tunisia:
June, 1897

Antoine de Vallombrosa, Marquis de Mores, glanced up, instantly alert when he heard a noise outside. He rose abruptly, kicking the chair aside, and flung back the tent flaps.

"What is it?" he demanded, forgetting, in his haste, that the Touareg guard could not understand him.

"It's nothing, sir. Just one of the men checking the camels."

Mores was surprised to hear the man speak in perfect French, and he turned to peer through the darkness until he located the vague outline of the guard, his rifle grasped in his hand. "Jean?" he said.

"No, sir. Henri."

"You should be asleep, Henri. You've worked all day; there's certainly no need for you to take guard duty as well. Why don't you find one of the Touaregs to do the job?"

Henri shifted uneasily, then lowered his voice. "With respect, sir, I just feel better with one of our own out here at night. I can't quite bring myself to trust those Arabs, you see. Besides, Jean is sleeping now, but he'll take over for me soon."

By now Mores could make out the expression on

Henri's face and he saw that it was grimly determined. "I just feel safer," the man repeated.

The Marquis started to protest, but before he could speak, the cry of a jackal surprised him into turning back to stare out at the blackness beyond the tent. The mournful wail sliced through the night silence like a flash of light in a deep black hole—the only force strong enough to penetrate the heavy darkness. Odd that the sound should have intruded on his thoughts, Mores mused, unconsciously running his hand through his curly dark hair, which recently had begun to turn gray at the edges. He had become accustomed to the jackal's howl in the past three weeks; it had transformed itself into a disturbing lullaby that urged him toward sleep every night.

But just now he was as nervous as Henri. Perhaps it was the hot desert wind that whipped through the languid darkness, touching the skin with warm gritty fingers. Or perhaps the darkness itself, which hovered before him just out of reach—deep and black, like a threat or a warning.

"I'd best get back inside," he said abruptly. "Good night, Henri. And be sure you get some sleep before the night is over."

"Good night, sir," the other man replied. "Sleep safely."

When the tent flaps were firmly closed behind him, Mores sat down at the table on which he had left the half-finished letter to his wife. He saw at once that, despite the wavering light of the lantern, the tent was draped in darkness. The Marquis stared blankly at the canvas walls of the tent for a moment before he turned back to the reassuring vision of his own handwriting scrawled across the page before him. As he sat there unmoving, Mores found himself wondering, for the first time, what had really brought him here.

What had caused him to leave his native France, his

wife and children, and come to this godforsaken Tunisian desert? Ostensibly, he was here to attempt to unite the Moslems and the French in northern Africa in order to force the British off the upper reaches of the continent. His purpose was quite clearly to rid the French government of a rival which had long been a painful thorn in his country's tender flesh.

But Mores knew that his real purpose was much more complex than that. Some force beyond political necessity had drawn him here—the same force that had led him to the North Dakota Badlands to try to revolutionize the meat packing industry. The same force that had sent him to build a railroad across the desolate North China Plain. All his life he had been motivated by a power he could not name to achieve some final, impressive victory over nature and man. He believed he had been born to conquer a wilderness.

Now, at forty-four, he was still handsome, still vigorous, still every inch the French aristocrat he had been in his youth, and still obsessed with the same restless dissatisfaction that had been his constant companion since childhood. Mores twirled the waxed end of his graceful mustache, staring blindly into the murky corners of the tent. Maybe he had not changed because somehow his endeavors had always failed.

Time and again he had struggled with his enemies—both the land he chose to conquer and the men who opposed him—right to the end, only to find that they were stronger than he. Despite his constant efforts to assuage the gnawing ache inside him, he was still a man in pain, though it was not of a physical kind. He was, forever, intensely aware of his own dramatic failures. It was true that he had given his enemies a good show, but the final victory had always been theirs.

The Marquis' glance fell on the half-covered sheet of

paper on the table before him, and the shadow of self-recrimination lifted from his black eyes for a moment.

Dearest Medora,
     I write with your American portrait before me, and with a very tender sentiment for you.

He smiled. The thought of his wife never failed to give him comfort, regardless of the depth of his distress. Because with Medora he had not failed. She was the only unchanging, dependable force in his life. . . .

. . . . *May, 1897—"Is our marriage everything you hoped it would be, even after fourteen years?" Medora asked.*

The Marquis looked up to where she stood perfectly still on the balcony, her hand resting on the open door. Her back was turned to him, and at her feet, the city of Tunis spread like an intricately patterned stone carpet. The only movement came from the subtle shifting of her flowing gown and the rise and fall of the strands of her long, red hair. The thin, silky curtains danced languidly in the sighing wind, drawing an occasional veil over the spires, minarets, mosques, and ancient ruins which, in Mores' eyes, made Tunis an enchanted place.

"It's more than I hoped for, much more," he murmured, afraid to break the spell that held her poised before him, framed by silk and solid stone. "Are you happy to be here?" the Marquis added, moving toward the open doors. "I thought you might have preferred to celebrate our anniversary in Cannes, where we were married."

Medora turned then, slowly, as if she too were aware of the fragility of the moment. "No," she assured him. "It's lovely here."

She was smiling, just as she had smiled since they began the voyage to northern Africa, but he sensed a current of unease beneath her mask of calm contentment. Even the sparkle in her piercing green eyes had begun to waver in the past few days.

Medora read her husband's thoughts in his eyes, and she smiled more brightly and moved toward him, tossing her thick hair back over her shoulder.

In spite of his doubts, the Marquis answered her smile. His wife had not changed much in their many years of marriage, he realized. Her skin was still as smooth and unmarred, although the slender curves of her petite body had softened somewhat, as had the harsh lines of her thin nose and high cheekbones. The softness had given Medora a new dimension as she matured, and even today she was a woman to remember—the kind of woman whose eyes looked beyond the thin exterior of things and plunged directly to the heart.

"Stop thinking," Medora warned as she slid her arms around Mores' waist. "Your thoughts are keeping you apart from me."

Although he was so much taller than she, their bodies fit together easily, as if they had been formed to meet as they did now, skin to skin, as their robes fell open.

But it had not always been so, the Marquis remembered, resting his chin on top of Medora's head. Once he had nearly lost her. Mores' hand tightened convulsively on Medora's shoulders. It did not matter now, he told himself. It had all happened a very long time ago.

But Medora raised her head just then until her eyes met his. This time she could not hide the sadness that touched her face, and all at once the Marquis felt the pain of separation as keenly as he had so many years before. It was as if suddenly his wife were slipping away from him all over again.

Medora twined her arms around the Marquis' neck, pulling his head down until their lips met, and the warmth that flared between them was as sudden and unexpected as a brief but devastating summer storm. "Don't go," she whispered raggedly.

Mores looked up in surprise. "What?"

"Don't go on this trip through the desert."

"I've already told you, I have to do this."

"It's too dangerous," Medora insisted.

The Marquis sighed as he buried his fingers in her hair. "For me, danger is everywhere, my dear. And much more in France than elsewhere, with the powerful and obstinate enemies I have made. I shall feel safe only in the desert," he told her.

Medora gazed levelly at her husband for a moment, her eyes veiled to hide her troubled thoughts, but when he drew her closer, she did not resist.

God, but she was something special, Mores mused. There had never been another to equal her. Not for him anyway. Even the memory of the long-lost Nicole had become vague and unrecognizable over the years.

"I love you, Antoine," Medora whispered. "You, and no other."

The Marquis was disturbed by the desperation with which she echoed his own thoughts. *And as their lips met and they clung together, Mores realized at last that where her skin touched his, Medora had begun to shiver violently. . . .*

. . . . A dry, hot gust of wind brushed the back of the Marquis' neck and rattled the papers beneath his hand. He would not soon forget the expression of dread on his wife's face when she had drawn away from him that night. There was no doubt about it—Medora, who feared nothing, had been afraid for him in Tunis.

And she was not the only one. Neither Henri nor Jean had bothered to hide their own trepidation. But Mores would not listen to them; he could not. He knew very well that his only real strength was his unfailing courage and abiding belief that someday, if he kept up the battle and never gave in, he would win.

But his enemies were determined to see that he did not. He knew the French government itself was against him, though he had come here to help them. The ministers could never forgive him for his socialist sentiments, for the support he had received from the French people, and for his violent campaign to clear the government of corrupt officials. He had spent the last several years in and out of jail, fighting battles against an opponent a hundred times his own size, and he knew now that the opponent had finally had enough. That was another reason he had left France. He sensed that he was no longer safe there.

So he had come to Africa and lost himself in the desert, where he traveled from town to town, tribe to tribe, and hoped his past would not follow him here. But, once again, he had miscalculated. He had recognized an enemy in Rebillet—the French military attaché—from the first moment they met. The man had reluctantly agreed to sign a document insuring that the French government would not interfere with the Marquis' expedition, but Rebillet had refused point-blank to issue a safe conduct.

Less than an hour earlier, Mores had written to Medora:

The best I can do now is to succeed. I see daily more and more the importance of my object, and feel that I am watched on all sides by people ready to take advantage of any mistakes or weaknesses. My enemies are around and in back of me, and in Paris, but not in front.

The desert had become his refuge, and he knew that he had to win this time, regardless of the odds. Because his own countrymen had turned against him, because his family waited in France, hoping for his victorious return, because their safety as well as his own depended on the outcome of this project. Now, more than ever, he was aware of the presence of the force that had guided his life. It had driven him, challenged him, tempted him, nearly destroyed him, and, finally, it had brought him here.

He felt now that this might be his last chance. For one thing, he no longer had money to burn, although his income had been a large one and Medora's family was also wealthy. But he was getting old and his children needed security, not dreams, to keep them fed and warm. It was time he stopped running, always running before a wind whose source he could not even identify. He had one more chance to prove himself worthy—as in his heart he knew he was not—of Medora's love and faith in him. *This* time, he would persevere. This time, the desert would become an ally, sheltering him from the wrath of his enemies.

Feeling a new surge of strength within him, the Marquis turned back to his letter.

Do not worry for me; the word has been given all over Algeria that an accident to me would be a signal against France. They have every reason to watch over me.

God bless you, Medora. Kiss the children as I kiss you and love you. Remember, I believe in the protection of God and hope in the future. Work and pray and give me time.

Yours ever, Mores

But time was the one gift Medora could not give him.

Mores awoke in the morning to find the shadows gone and the harsh sun beating down on his stifling tent. He was amazed, as always, that the desert could change so easily from engulfing darkness to blinding light—both, it seemed to him, more intense than anywhere else on the earth. As he rose from his cot, he glanced automatically toward the front of the tent where, every morning for the past week, he had been able to see the reassuring shadow of the guard waiting outside.

But this time there was no shadow; there was only the penetrating glare of the morning sun, which pierced the canvas in tiny pinpricks of light. The Marquis hurried across the tent, his breath held back in his throat, and stepped outside, calling, "Henri! Jean!"

He had been wrong. The guard—Jean—was there after all, sprawled unconscious in the dirt, his knife clutched uselessly in his hand. His rifle and ammunition were gone, taken, no doubt, by his attacker. As Mores knelt to check his servant's pulse and assess the damage, Henri came hurrying up.

"What—" he began, but then he saw Jean and the words froze in his throat.

Aware of Henri's sudden inability to act, the Marquis instructed, "If you can get him inside, I'll prepare a cool cloth for his head." When Henri still did not move, Mores added, "He doesn't seem to be hurt too badly. Just a lump on the back of his head. But the damage will be much worse if we leave him out here with his face exposed to the sun."

All at once, Henri knelt beside his friend, muttering, "I knew it. I knew we couldn't trust them."

The Marquis was having a difficult time quelling the panic that had begun to rise the instant he saw Jean's unconscious body, and Henri's distress only made things worse. Turning away abruptly, he tried to marshal his thoughts as he tied open the tent flap and stepped inside. What could have been the purpose of the attack on Jean? he wondered. If they had meant to get to the Marquis himself, why had they not done so? But then, as he glanced about him for a clean cloth, he found the answer.

His largest trunk was missing, the one that had held everything of value on this trip. His money, his papers, his precious maps, and, most important of all, many of his best weapons—gone. They had crept up in the night and unmanned him with an ease that sent a chill racing down his spine.

He realized then, in a blinding flash of clear vision, that he had lost after all. He was dead now, as surely as if they had slit his throat and left him to bleed in the darkness. And it was his own fault. He had been so pre-occupied with the enemies outside his caravan that he had not once looked for the enemies within. But they were there; about that there could no longer be any doubt. Once again, he had been hopelessly blind.

Oddly, now that he knew, his panic subsided and a desperate calm took its place. The doubts and qualms of the past week took on substance and reality as they resolved themselves into the faces of the Touareg men whom he had thought to be his friends. Now he could feel their presence like a pulsing shadow that had hovered over him, unnoticed, for the entire expedition. But somehow he was not afraid. If they thought he would come crawling to them in fear, they would be sadly disappointed. Now that he knew, his course was clear. Quite simply, he had no choice.

When he had settled Jean on the cot and made certain that he was, indeed, unhurt except for the bump on his head, Mores put on a clean white shirt and pants, picked up his broad-brimmed white hat and stepped back into the merciless sunlight. Then, his face creased in lines of grim determination, he buried his hands in his pockets and began his customary morning walk through the camp. It looked much the same as it had the day before at this time; the tents lay in crumpled canvas heaps, while the

Touareg tribesmen, wrapped in their burnooses and flowing robes, busied themselves with packing and folding their few possessions. But there was a subtle difference in the quality of their silence today, almost as if they were holding their collective breath in anticipation.

The Marquis moved slowly down the aisle left by the folded tents, and his boots thudded hollowly against the fine sand that covered the desert floor. The sound echoed the dull pulsing of his own blood in his ears, but he ignored it; at the moment he was more concerned with the response of the men all around him. As he stopped occasionally to greet someone in the few words of their language he had managed to learn, Mores noticed how the men's eyes slid away from his, like the yellow eyes of a reptile. Their answers were polite enough, but their expressions remained veiled and subtly hostile. Why, he wondered, had he never noticed this before? Never once did a single man meet his gaze directly.

When he had reached the end of the camp, the Marquis paused, turning back to look down on the poisonous little kingdom he had built. He stood tall and apparently unconcerned, his broad shoulders unbowed by the weight of his recent knowledge, his hat casting a shadow over the fine, aristocratic lines of his face. With his fingers hooked in his belt, he surveyed his companions in silence, and he knew that he was really seeing them for the first time.

One by one, the Touareg tribesmen stopped their work and turned to stare at Mores; it was as if his gaze was a silken rope that drew them forward against their will, until, at last, every hand was still and every eye was focused on the man who had made himself their master. For a long, tense moment, there was an expectant silence so profound that even the jackal dared not disturb it; even the stifling desert heat was as nothing compared to the power of the Marquis' gaze. Then he bellowed, "Come, you're wasting time, and we have far to go today!" Further, he told himself, than any of them might imagine.

One of the guides translated and the men turned back to their work, relieved to have been so easily released from Mores' spell. Within half an hour, the Marquis was mounted on his camel, surrounded by his servants and ready to go. He was anxious to leave this place behind.

This morning the men were silent as the camels plodded their slow path across the sand, and the sun pelted them from above with punishing intensity. To Mores, the heat was a blessing, because it reminded him that he was still alive, but he could see that Henri and Jean did not feel the same. The latter had recovered from the blow that had knocked him unconscious, but just now, his face, like Henri's, was a study in fear and discontent. Both had donned the native burnoose and haik to protect them from the sun, but still the sweat ran down their sun-browned faces like a straggling muddy river across a parched plain. Clearly, they did not wish to be here, but the Marquis knew he could depend on them, just the same. Their pride would not allow them to sacrifice their loyalty.

Near mid-morning, the caravan came to a ridge, and Mores rode ahead to see what lay beyond. Wiping the sweat from his face with a wrinkled sleeve, he guided his camel upward until he was looking down on what he guessed to be the plain of El Ouatia. It was a desolate stretch of endless sand ringed by bleached cliffs. Only an occasional tamarisk tree or a clump of scrub broke the monotony of stone and sand and quivering summer heat.

The Marquis' brows came together for a moment in intense concentration. Had he been here before? Somehow the landscape was painfully familiar. But perhaps the blazing sunlight had only tricked him into thinking of the past. This was, after all, just one more wilderness. One more sweep of desert whose primitive beauty stung him to the heart as gardens and greenery had never done. It was the very barrenness that so moved him, the absence of life—and his own desire to bring life to a world that others had declared hopeless. Here before him was one more land that refused to be tamed, and this one perhaps his last.

Suddenly aware once again of the forty hostile men behind him, Mores found the path that led to the plain below and started downward. It was not until he reached the valley and the sand glinted like liquid glass beneath his camel's hooves that he first realized he was alone.

The Marquis glanced back to where he had last seen Henri and Jean, but the two Frenchmen had disappeared in a sea of scornful Arab faces. Mores had only a moment to grasp his rifle and check his revolver before two Touaregs were upon him. One came from behind and one from the side, intent on dragging him from his perch, but in seconds he left them both kneeling in the sand, stunned by the impact of his bullets.

The Marquis glanced around wildly, hoping for a sight of Henri or Jean, but he found only a small tamarisk tree that afforded him little protection. Yet there was nowhere else for him to go. The Touaregs were everywhere now, poised like vultures with their long wings flapping in the wind and the deadly gleam in their eyes hidden by the folds of their haiks.

Mores backed himself against the tree, clutching his revolver in one hand and his rifle in the other. The bullets were flying now, the explosion of rifle fire shattering the sky into tiny glittering fragments. The Marquis knew he had been hit more than once, because the pain screamed up his arms, his legs, and zigzagged through his chest with fiery fingers. It was hopeless, he was aware of that, but he swore he would take every one of them with him—every grinning face of the men who had betrayed him.

Time after time he aimed at them and fired, and one after another they fell at his feet. Mores saw that they were inching closer, crawling over the bodies of their dead companions, but his attention was focused on looking for the two Frenchmen. Then, at last, he saw Henri making his slow, painful way forward at the edge of the angry mob. The man came stumbling up to him, clutching his chest with pale, widespread fingers, and groaned, "Jean is dead. They stabbed him. But I had to get to you, sir. I had to—"

Then he pitched forward and fell across the Marquis' shadow, and Mores saw that his body was riddled with bullets. Henri was dead, too, and now he was truly alone.

The Marquis' clothes had long been sodden with blood, which mingled with the rivers of sweat that coursed down his body. The noise was deafening, the Touaregs' surprise that he still stood an almost tangible force between them. The smoke of the rifles rose like a belated sacrament to blot out the blazing sun and, at last, Mores gave in to the dictates of his weakened body and fell to his knees. But even from this position, he continued to fire his revolver, and another man crumpled to the ground not four yards away.

The Touaregs were astonished by the Marquis' perseverance. He had been hit time and again, his clothes were no more than tattered blood-red rags, but still he would not die. He faced them, his head high, and simply refused to fall, until one man crept up behind him and buried a dagger in Mores' back.

But the man had been too careful in his approach; the Touaregs had not seen him until it was too late and their bullets had ripped through his vulnerable flesh. So the Marquis and his murderer fell together in a ghastly tangle of bloody limbs.

Closing his eyes, Mores dragged himself free of the cumbersome weight of his killer and whispered, "Forgive me, Medora." The words were wrenched from him with the force of an explosion, and then, surprisingly, he thought he heard the haunting melody of a distant Indian song.

Above the turmoil of the Touaregs' jubilation, above the sudden cessation of gunfire, above even his own raspingly painful breath, the song came to him like a drink of cool water from a clear mountain stream. Then, as his eyes came open for the last time, he smiled at the sudden piercing memory of an Indian girl long dead.

The Touaregs who were still standing paused for a moment to make certain he was dead, then they shouldered their rifles and turned away. Their job was done, after all, and they had earned their money through the loss of twenty lives. Now, they no longer cared about the man who had led them here, the man who had cut their numbers in half with nothing but his own two guns and the weight of a tamarisk tree to support him.

Shaking their heads at the horror of it all, they gathered their camels and filed out of the valley while the Marquis' body was left behind, its blood soaking slowly into the dry, parched African earth. And the thick red river, full of all that had been one man's futile existence, spread its fingers across the sand, as if in one final attempt to fulfill the Marquis' dream and bring life to a barren waste.

Part I

"For me, danger is everywhere, and much more in France than elsewhere, with the powerful obstinate enemies I have made. I will feel safe only in the desert."
—Marquis de Mores
May, 1897

Chapter 1

"Mama? May I read you a poem?"

Medora de Vallombrosa looked up at her fourteen-year-old daughter, Athenais, who stood beside the desk with a book tucked under her arm. As always, the sight of the girl's dark curly hair and black eyes made the breath lodge painfully in Medora's throat. The other children, Paul and Louis, resembled both parents to some extent, but little Anais was her father all over again. From her olive skin to the fine sculpted lines of her forehead, nose and cheekbones, she was Antoine de Vallombrosa in female form. She even had her handsome father's slight cleft in the chin.

With a stifled sigh, Medora gazed beyond her daughter in an attempt to stop the knife blade of memory from making a rent in the thin veil she had carefully woven across her emotions in the past six months. She had drawn the strength up from the seemingly endless reserve she harbored within and cut herself off from the horror and pain. Now there was only numbness—blessed numbness.

When she turned back to find Anais' eyes fixed questioningly on her, Medora realized that the child was not really like her father at all. She might resemble him physically, but she lacked the vibrancy, the sheer zest for life that had been the Marquis' greatest asset—the quality that had kept him unfailingly cheerful through all the disappointments in his life.

"Not just now," Medora murmured, remembering that the girl had asked her about a poem. "I'm quite busy, as you can see." She indicated the half-finished letter that rested on top of a pile of similar pages. In fact, the desktop was buried in a deluge of papers, pens, and sealing wax.

"You're always busy!" Anais cried fretfully. "You never have time for us anymore. You don't even leave the desk. You might as well bring your pillow down and sleep here so you can be near your precious letters, since they're the only things that matter to you."

Medora reached for her daughter's hand, surprised by the fury of her speech, and by the hurt and frustration shining like a wavering flame in the heart of Anais' black velvet eyes. "Listen to me," she said, drawing the girl closer. "You must understand that I'm doing all this for your father."

"My father is dead." Anais spoke the words in a calm, steady voice, but the strange light in her eyes glowed brighter for a moment; it seemed to echo the pulse of her thoughts.

"Yes," Medora agreed, "but they have not yet discovered his killer. I intend to see that they do. Your father would want that and you should want it too. His murderers shall not go unpunished."

"You don't care what Papa would want. Not really," the girl accused. "You've never even cried for him."

Releasing her daughter's hands, Medora took a deep breath and looked away. She could not look in Anais' eyes in that moment, for she knew their smoldering gaze would pierce her protective veil, leaving her broken and vulnerable. And that she could not allow, because she was afraid of what her emotions, once unleashed, could do to her. It was not so much the pain she feared—she had lived through pain before—but rather the gaping sense of emptiness that hovered just on the other side of the veil. That was the worst—the emptiness. "I can't cry," she whispered, "but it doesn't mean—" She bit her lip, rose from the chair, and placed both hands on Anais' shoulders.

The girl saw the feverish light in her mother's eyes and, all at once, she was afraid. She did not want to know about Medora's pain. Not now, not ever! Anais twisted free of her mother's grasp and backed away. "Listen to me," Medora began, but before she could say any more, a maid entered the room.

"Madame," she said, "Mr. Beaumont and Mr. Van Driesche have returned from Tunisia. They're on their way up."

Medora clasped her hands tightly before her and turned to face the wide doorway that led from the elegant hallway to the austere study. They were back, she told herself, and this time they might have found the answer. Dear God, she hoped so, because, in a way, Anais was right; since the Marquis' death six months ago, Medora had become a woman obsessed with the idea of finding her husband's assassins. She spent the day writing letter after letter to the French government begging for some action; she wrote to the Tunisian government, to the newspapers, to anyone who might be able to give her an answer. And at night her dreams ran with rivers of blood and the vision of her husband's battered body. But no one seemed to know anything.

So she had finally sent William and Phillipe to solve the mystery. Surely in Tunisia itself they could somehow discover the truth, since the French government was so reluctant to help. Quite simply, she refused to give up until she knew what had really happened out there in the stifling, unfriendly desert six months ago. If she owed her husband nothing else, she owed him that.

"Medora!" Phillipe Beaumont, her twenty-seven-year-old stepson, came into the room with his hands outstretched and, crossing the floor in three long strides, he took her hands in his. "How have you been?" he asked, his deep blue eyes full of concern. In less than a moment he had recognized the sharp lines that had deepened between her nose and mouth in the three months since he had been away. She looked older, somehow, and the gray had begun to appear in her long red hair, which was braided and wrapped tightly around her head. And her severe widow's gown of black crepe seemed to bleach the natural color from her skin, leaving her cheeks as pale as the white walls.

"I'm fine," Medora told him, realizing as she said it how much she welcomed the sight of his light brown hair and clear blue eyes, though once his appearance had caused her such pain. When he had first come to them so many years ago, another woman's son, Medora had mistrusted him on sight. In those days he had been a painful reminder of her own failure to give her husband the sons he desired so fervently. But now she had two boys of her own, and over the years she had come to think of Phillipe as a member of the family—and a friend.

Behind Phillipe came William Van Driesche, who had changed very little from the man she had first met fifteen years ago. Only the creases in his forehead were deeper and his sandy brown hair slightly thinner. But his brown eyes still had the same serious, steady expression, even if their light had been somewhat strained of late. He had been the Marquis' companion, valet, secretary, and friend since childhood, and Medora had long ago learned to depend on William absolutely, as she could depend on no other. Because William never changed; he just grew more steadfast as he grew older.

"Welcome home," she said, just managing to keep her voice steady. "Sit down and tell me what you've learned." She waited impatiently as the two men seated themselves on the plain gray sofa. She ought to give them time to rest, she knew, but she had to hear their news now.

Anais stood perfectly still, watching the reunion with dark, stormy eyes. She realized with a sharp pang of envy that to Medora, her daughter had disappeared, become no more than a vaporous shadow hovering in the far corner of the room. Anais sucked in her breath in despair and, throwing Phillipe a look of utter hatred which he did not notice, the young girl left the room.

Medora did not even see her go. The woman's still, green gaze was fixed on William and Phillipe, who shifted uncomfortably under her appraisal. "Well?" she said at last. "Tell me."

With an oblique glance at Phillipe, the older man cleared his throat and murmured, "We were able to find out where the Touaregs who killed Mores were hiding and we tracked them down, though the government was not much help. But, unfortunately, Rebillet, the military attaché, was close behind us, and when we did find the assassins, the government took them into custody."

Medora's heartbeat quickened. So the men had actually been caught. Now it was only a matter of time before they could be made to tell the government who had paid them. Oddly, she did not hate the Touareg murderers as much as she should. She knew they had only been hired gunmen. It was their employer she was after—the man who had paid to have the Marquis killed. He had many enemies, she knew, but surely the Touaregs would break down and name the one that mattered. "Have they been made to talk yet?" she asked.

Phillipe and William exchanged a long, thoughtful look, then the younger man turned back to his stepmother. "No," he told her. "The assassins never had a chance to say a word."

Medora stared at him. "Never had a chance?" she repeated numbly.

Closing his eyes to block out the expression of bleak denial in Medora's eyes, Phillipe said softly, "They were executed. In less than three hours after we brought them in, Rebillet had them slaughtered like dogs before they could speak to anyone."

Medora swayed for a moment as her pulse seemed to cease altogether. Dead. The murderers were dead. She should be glad to see them punished. Except that they had taken with them the answer to the question that had haunted her dreams for so long. When those men died, they had killed her last hope of discovering who had paid them.

As she sat unmoving, staring blankly before her, she realized that a tiny rent had appeared in her protective veil. She had kept herself alive on hope the past few months, and now she felt that hope crumbling into sand.

"I'm sorry," William said. "We did our best, but we couldn't stop it. The government wanted those men dead and there was nothing we could do."

His voice came to her as if through a heavy fog, distorted and unfamiliar, like the call of a distant sea bird, and his face was no more than a blur that wavered before her eyes. "Please," she said softly, "I'd like to be alone for a while. I need time to think." But when they rose and turned to go, she added, "Thank you both for all you've done." But it wasn't enough, her heart cried. It would never be enough.

The day had faded inevitably into evening, and still Medora sat unmoving at her cluttered desk. Even her thoughts had ceased, and in the hush that remained, she seemed to wait, heart throbbing dully, for some momentous event to shake her from her lethargy.

"Excuse me, madame," a strange voice murmured unexpectedly. "I want to speak to you."

Medora stood and whirled to face the intruder, who leaned negligently against the doorjamb, his piercing gray eyes half-covered by bluish lids. A man of about thirty, he was thin and wiry, and his body seemed to radiate a kind of restless energy that kept his long, slender fingers constantly in motion.

"How did you get in here?" Medora demanded.

The stranger smiled smugly. "I told the maid not to bother to announce me, and I gather she was afraid to object. You see, I'm Colonel Rebillet."

Medora stiffened imperceptibly. So this was the man who the Marquis had recognized as an enemy long ago. The man who had thwarted first her husband, then Phillipe and William at every turn, and who, finally, had ordered the executions that had ruined her plans. He was not a man she was likely to forget. Turning her back on her visitor, Medora went to stand before the French doors that led to the wide expanse of lawn and garden beyond. "What do you want?" she asked stiffly.

Rebillet came farther into the room, apparently unmoved by the chill in her voice. "I came to tell you, madame, that your husband's assassins have been apprehended and executed. The case is now officially closed."

"No," Medora said without turning away from the window.

Sucking in his breath to quell his anger, the colonel repeated, "The assassins have been executed as prescribed by law. You asked to have them punished and they were. It's really quite simple."

"I don't think it is."

He let out his breath in a rush and the lines of his face seemed to harden into stone. "We've done what we can for you, and now you must cease this relentless campaign to befuddle the government with your personal problems. Frankly, we don't care about you *or* your dead husband, and I strongly suggest that you drop the whole thing."

Now, finally, she turned, her green eyes blazing. "I can't do that."

Rebillet's eyes narrowed into tiny silver slits. "You'd better. The government is annoyed with you, as are the French people. We would have no way to protect you if the Marquis' enemies decided to make you pay for his mistakes. You'd best keep that in mind when you make your decision."

The pulse began to pound monotonously inside Medora's head as the anger built into a blinding wave. Then, all at once, she really saw the colonel's face for the first time. She saw the taut lines that creased his forehead, the unnatural pallor of his skin, the way his upper lip twitched now and then. Suddenly it occurred to her to wonder what, exactly, this man was so afraid of. Why had he bothered to come all the way to Paris to tell her something she already knew? Was he somehow trying to protect *himself?*

"I don't think you fully realize what your husband started out there," Rebillet continued doggedly. "I've never known a man with so many enemies—a man so hated, feared and despised as the Marquis de Mores. They don't care about him, don't you see that? The entire world is grateful that Antoine de Vallombrosa is dead. . . .

. . . . *July, 1897—Faces streaked with tears and hands full of flowers, the mourners lined the streets, tossing their offerings onto the pavement before the funeral cortège.* From the moment the Marquis' coffin, draped with the French tricolor, had been lowered from the ship at Marseilles, it had been showered with flowers of every kind and color. Not once had the wheels of the funeral wagon touched cold, packed pavement, for the path had been covered from end to end with thousands and thousands of summer blossoms. In Paris it had been the same.

As she stood at the edge of the grave hidden away in the cemetery of Montmartre, watching the coffin being lowered into the gaping earth, Medora remembered the grief-ravaged faces of those people and the crushed and wilted flowers they had grasped so tenaciously. But even the vivid memory of those faces could not pierce the curious numbness that had invaded her body, turning her blood into rivers of ice and her heart into a lifeless piece of lead. She had always known this moment would come someday, from the time when her husband's life had first been threatened in North Dakota fourteen years ago. There had always been too many people who hated him, envied him, wanted him dead, and she had lived in a kind of suspended animation all these years, waiting. But now that the day was here, she felt nothing.

The clods of dirt began to thump with grim finality on the top of the casket, and Medora swept her wide black skirts over her arm and turned away with others. She was moving in a dream, aware of the sympathy and good wishes that swirled around her, but unresponsive to their import. And the liquid eyes of the people in the streets burned across her inner vision—a desperate warning of the debilitating power of sorrow.

"Madame!"

The imperious voice broke through the haze that enveloped her, forcing Medora to glance up into the still-handsome face of Richard, Duc de Vallombrosa, the Marquis' estranged father. His handsome, aristocratic features were unmarred by grief, his black eyes as hollow and empty as Medora's own.

Taking her arm in a firm grip, the Duc drew his daughter-in-law into the shade of a nearby tree. Medora looked up at the man curiously. He had not spoken to her in over three years, and she wondered why he had chosen to do so now.

"I did not want to come to your home," he told her abruptly. "I once swore that I would never step over that threshold so long as it belonged to my son, and you know I always keep my word. But I thought it only fair to warn you, so I came here."

"Warn me?"

"Yes. I wanted to tell you not to feel too comfortable in the villa your husband so thoughtfully provided for you, because I intend to get it back."

Medora flung back her veil and stared at him, stunned. "What do you mean?"

"I'm planning to sue for Mores' entire fortune in order to bring it back to the family, where it belongs. He gave up on us a long time ago; now I owe him nothing. I intend to take everything he's got, and you know very well that I have the power to do it."

Swallowing twice to force the air past the rage that had begun to build in her throat, his daughter-in-law choked, "Your son has just been killed. His body had not even been decently buried, and yet you stand here—"

The Duc held up a restraining hand. "My son, as you call him, made his own choice eleven years ago to become a socialist rabble-rouser. He chose to despise everything I have ever stood for, but, more than that, he chose to attempt to destroy it. He's caused me so much pain by now that I've just stopped caring. I had no choice."

Medora's heartbeat had begun to thunder in her ears, drowning out the voice of common sense that had kept her steady over the past month. "So now you're paying him back, is that it? Making us suffer for what you imagine he did to you?"

There was no answer and, as she gazed up at him, Medora realized that she had been wrong; his eyes were not empty, they were full to the brim with a hatred so cold

*and implacable that it pierced her fragile armor like a
deadly blade of ice. . . .*

. . . . Rebillet's ice-silver gaze was fixed on Medora's
face with an almost desperate intensity and, unaccountably, she shivered.

"Ah," the colonel sighed in triumph, "I see that you
understand my meaning quite well. I'm warning you, madame, your husband was an enemy of the state and that
makes his family worthy of suspicion as well. You would
be wise to remember that you can push us only so far."

Medora stood unmoving and let his threats fly by unheeded. She knew the risk; her awareness of the family's
vulnerability had become her most constant companion
of late. But she would not let Rebillet see her thoughts.

"I'll be going now," the colonel announced abruptly,
"but I want you to think about what I've said. There have
already been too many casualties on the Marquis' account.
Don't make yourself another."

Then, with a low, graceful bow and a mocking smile,
he turned on his heel and left her.

Chapter 2

Medora awoke the next morning with a cold feeling of dread in the pit of her stomach. Since Rebillet had gone yesterday evening, she had moved through the house as if trapped in the unreality of a nightmare. Still, her mind was strangely clouded and empty of thought, except for the hollow echo of her husband's name. But she told herself again and again not to listen to that desperate voice, for she knew that it had the power to break her. Once released, the wash of pain and realization would be too great to bear, and she fought to keep the agony away.

From the moment she left it yesterday, she had avoided the study with blind determination, but this morning the force that drove her was stronger than her will, and she was drawn inexorably to the desk where she had spent so many hours recently. When she stood in silence, facing the evidence of the collapse of her all-consuming campaign in the last six months, she knew at last that those months had been wasted. There was no longer any hope. Yet the piles of letters, pleas, and curt replies lay there like a mute accusation—an unrelenting reminder of the days and weeks of futile energy she had wasted on a battle which had been hopeless from the beginning.

Then, half-hidden among the stacks of correspondence, she recognized the Marquis' handwriting on a single sheet of paper. With fingers that trembled just a little, she withdrew the six-month-old letter and began to read.

Remember the concentration of wills on the same object is a power, and *your* will must push me across the desert and not pull me back. Your confidence gives confidence to others, and their opinions help me, as many people fear to be mixed up in a failure do not pronounce themselves.

Remember, dear Medora, your will must be with me.

But Medora knew it had not been. She had not really had faith in his power to achieve what he desired. She had tried, dear God, how she had tried, but not for a moment had she thought his dream would come true. And, in that way, she knew she had failed him unforgivably.

She had loved the Marquis with every fiber of her being, trusted him, respected him, but she had never really believed in him. Not once had she been able to throw herself heart and soul into his grand plans and dreams. There, at least, Mores had always been alone.

Too late, Medora had tried to make it up to him by finding and punishing his killers. But she had failed at that, too.

He was dead. The word rang hollowly through her head like a bell in an empty stone church. Dead. Dead. There was nothing she could do for him anymore. Nothing.

Forcing herself to read on, she came to the end of the letter.

I feel you will one day be repaid for all this and bless the day I came to Africa.

No! her soul cried in horror. Never! It was only then, when the floodtide of fear and emptiness began to wash over her, that Medora realized her protective veil had fallen in tatters to her feet. And now, dear God, the deep black river of agony that swept through her veins! Closing her eyes to block the sight of the familiar writing which had somehow ripped the pain from where she had it hidden, Medora gave in at last. With a shudder that began at her feet and ended at the top of her head, she gasped and began to weep.

So intense was her grief, so blind her torment, that she did not realize she was not alone until a pair of strong, warm arms closed tightly around her. She tried to look up, but Phillipe pressed her head against his shoulder, whispering, "No, don't think of me. Just cry. You've been waiting six months, Medora. It's time to let it go."

All at once, she found herself clinging to him as the sobs wrenched through her body, and she realized she was grateful for his presence, his understanding silence, and the broad expanse of his chest beneath her wet cheeks. She knew in that moment that if her stepson let her go, she would fall. She had held herself upright through sheer force of will for too long, and now, suddenly, her strength had been swept away on the raging tide of her pain.

William stood in the doorway, his face ravaged with the knowledge of his own helplessness. He wanted to comfort Medora, more than anything on earth he wanted that, but Phillipe had gotten to her first. Besides, it was right that the younger man should be there—he had no gnawing guilt to hold him back and make his muscles turn to rubber at the sight of Medora's grief.

But Van Driesche was not so lucky. He could not help blaming himself for Mores' death. He had wanted to go on the expedition, had pleaded with the Marquis time and again, but Mores had been adamant in his refusal. He had planned to leave his old friend behind to keep the family safe. So, for the first time, William had stayed in France while the Marquis went off to pursue his dreams. Up until that day last February, the secretary had followed Mores everywhere, from the Badlands of North Dakota to Tonkin to China. But Africa was a land he would never see in the Marquis' company.

William could not rid himself of the notion that, had he been there in the desert as he should have been, he could have stopped his friend's horrible death. Common sense told him he was wrong, that no force on earth could have stopped those angry Touareg bullets, but still he hung on to his guilt.

And it had only grown worse as he had watched Medora try to find Mores' murderers. He couldn't help her any more than he could the Marquis. He couldn't even help to lessen the pain. Yet he could not bear to see her suffer.

A flash of agony ran through his blood when Medora raised her head and he saw the look of desperation in her eyes. William was seized with a furious desire to brush his fingers comfortingly across her tear-stained cheeks, but, of course, he did not move; she did not even know he was nearby. He had believed once that this feeling would dull with the passage of the years until it faded into a vague, disquieting memory, but he had been wrong. Instead, it had grown stronger daily, and now Medora's presence was like salt on a ragged wound. Sometimes he wondered if he would ever look at her again without the gnawing, inevitable pain of loss that left him weak and shaking.

Yet Medora remained blind to this side of his emotions. For that, at least, he was grateful. Only Mores had known his friend's secret, and for reasons of his own, he had never revealed it. Aware, all at once, that Medora might turn and see him, surprising the look of longing on his face, William turned away. She was his one weakness, and he prayed daily that she would never know it.

"Well," Medora said softly, "what are we going to do?"

The children had been put to bed, the servants had withdrawn to their own quarters, and now the villa was strangely quiet, so that, even though she spoke softly, Medora's voice sounded unnaturally loud in the cold evening air. She sat in the drawing room with her black skirts spread around her on the elegant brocade couch; by now the only sign of her earlier breakdown was the flush in her usually pale cheeks and the dark circles under her eyes.

William noticed that she had somehow suppressed the pain, and the lines of her face were once again firm and unyielding. "What do you mean?" he asked.

Medora looked searchingly from one man to the other. "I don't believe we can stay here in Paris. My little conversation with Rebillet convinced me that it just isn't safe anymore. Besides, as you know, the Duc de Vallombrosa is trying to obtain the rights to Antoine's fortune. I believe he might even succeed, and then we would *have* to go. There would be no money left to live on."

William considered this in silence for a moment, then suggested, "What about your father? Von Hoffman has money enough to spare."

"I don't want to have to depend on Papa to keep my family alive. I don't want to depend on anyone but ourselves. I've learned that that's the only way to survive." She paused, running her hand absently across the expensive fabric of the sofa. "I've never really felt this was my home anyway. I've always been something of a stranger in Paris."

Phillipe nodded. He understood that feeling well enough. Ever since he was fourteen, from the day his mother had told him he was a bastard, he had begun to feel like a stranger in his own country. His father had managed to ease the ache a little over the years, but it had never disappeared entirely.

"But where can we go?" William asked, interrupting the younger man's painful thoughts.

"As far as I can see, we have only one choice," Medora informed him. "The Badlands of North Dakota." She had been thinking about this question all day, and she knew there was no other alternative, but the sound of the words falling into expectant silence sent an inexplicable shiver down her spine. She wondered, suddenly, if she dared return to the scene of so much pain and desperation. Could she really stand beneath the multicolored cliffs and gaze on the town that bore her name without falling to pieces. Fourteen years ago, the Marquis had taken her there just after their marriage. He had been pursuing the first of his grandiose projects—this time a plan to change forever the meatpacking industry in America by building his plant in the very spot where the cattle were raised.

He had failed, of course; the competition had been too vicious and Mores too trusting. The idea had been a good one, but, once again, the Marquis' enemies had been too powerful for him. He had never really been a businessman, though he had tried, so, eventually, they had come close to destroying him. Drawing a deep, ragged breath, Medora said the name in her mind—Greg Pendleton. He had been the reason for Mores' failure and, quite nearly, the failure of Medora's marriage as well.

As always, in tense moments like this one, Phillipe seemed to read his stepmother's thoughts. He understood in an instant the necessity of their going to the Badlands and Medora's reluctance to do so. "It makes perfect sense," he began slowly, choosing his words with care. "You already own thousands of acres of land there as well as the house and the packing plant. All we'd need is money enough to get started, and then we could begin all over again and make the meatpacking business a success. We'd have the means right there for making our own fortune."

For a full minute, the only sound was the tapping of naked branches on the latticed window, and when he realized no one was going to object, Phillipe leaned forward eagerly. The more he thought about it, the more he liked the idea. "My father did promise he'd be back you know. Perhaps it's time we kept his word. Now we know what we'd be up against, and you can't deny that Mores might have succeeded if the Pendletons hadn't interfered. The house and plant have been kept up for us by Johnny Goodall, and the whole town is just waiting for our return."

Leaning back, he pictured in his mind the Chateau—the elegant nickname the townspeople had created for the large ranch house—and the river that wound past the base of the bluff. Then, unaccountably, a young girl's lovely face rose to blot out the image. Katherine Pendleton. He thought he had forgotten her years ago, but he found that it was not so. The memory of her face was suddenly as clear and piercing as the day he had first seen her. But now, as then, he could not decide whether her smile was the greeting of a friend or a warning from an enemy.

Medora was grateful that Phillipe had taken the weight of making a convincing argument off her shoulders, and she knew that he was right. If Mores had ever had a chance to succeed, it had been in the Badlands. Perhaps she owed it to him to try and prove that it could be done. Turning to Van Driesche, she asked, "William, what do you think?"

"It would be very difficult," he replied thoughtfully. "And I think the risks would be great. Besides," he added, addressing Phillipe, "won't you mind leaving France? It's your home, after all. And what about Nicole?"

Phillipe shrugged a little too casually at the mention of his mother's name. He had not been close to her for a long time now, although he visited her occasionally at her elegant villa in Cannes. Once, he had worshipped her, but now Nicole Beaumont—the Marquis' first lover, abandoned many years ago—had become little more than a beautiful stranger to her son. "Nicole can take care of herself," he said stiffly.

Van Driesche contemplated the silken folds of the drapery which framed Medora's head in pale cream. It seemed that there was no room for discussion, and he certainly had no alternative to suggest. Yet he was uneasy. When he thought of the Badlands, he felt nothing. To him those years were no more than a blank without meaning or direction. He had never really been a part of that land, although he had managed the Marquis' business interests there for so long. But he felt it was too dangerous for Medora and Phillipe to go back where the wind seemed to stir up emotions better left in darkness. "I suppose it's inevitable," he said at last.

"Think of it this way," Phillipe said. "This is our chance to prove that my father had *one* dream that just might have a chance of coming true."

Van Driesche nodded reluctantly, but he could not suppress a shudder of apprehension. Even in death the Marquis had not left them. Even now his grand schemes ruled the direction of the lives of his loved ones. Always before, those thwarted dreams had brought confusion and devastation in their wake, and William found himself wondering who the dream would destroy this time. For there would be victims; he knew it as surely as he knew that he would never possess the woman he had loved for so long.

"No!" Anais cried, slapping the table with the back of her hairbrush. "I don't want to go!"

Medora sighed wearily when she saw how her daughter's eyes glittered with fury. She had waited until evening, when the children were ready for bed, to tell them about her decision to leave Paris, and now she sat with Louis, Paul, and Anais around the small study table in the girl's bedroom. Clothed in their long, white nightgowns with nothing but the soft glow of the evening fire to light their faces, the children looked suddenly soft and so vulnerable that Medora felt an unaccustomed ache in her throat when she thought of their future.

"I know it will be difficult for you," Medora said, "but we've decided the move would be best for all of us just now."

Anais' chin came up and her eyes continued to flash their anger. "You mean *Phillipe* decided."

"No, of course not." Eyeing her daughter curiously, Medora noted how flushed Anais' cheeks had become. "William, Phillipe, and I talked it over and then I made the decision."

"Is he coming, too?" the girl demanded belligerently.

"Yes."

"There, you see!" Anais looked at her two younger brothers in triumph.

"What do you mean?" Louis, who had just turned eleven, regarded his sister in confusion.

"I mean," the girl pointed out, ignoring Medora's attempt to interrupt, "that Phillipe thinks now that our Papa is dead he can walk right in and take his place. He doesn't care if we want him or not. He doesn't even care that he's nothing but a—"

"Stop it!" Medora snapped. "You should never speak of your brother that way."

"He's not my brother. He's only a bastard. And I won't go to North Dakota with him. I won't! I'll stay alone in Paris if I have to."

"Anais!" Medora warned, rising abruptly from her chair. "That's quite enough."

"Mama?" Little Paul, with his seven-year-old pale

pixie face, his dark blond hair and hazel eyes, gazed up at his mother in mute appeal. "I can't go with you, Mama. I have to stay with Anais. She'd be lonely without me."

Medora reached down to lift the boy in her arms. "Don't worry, little one, Anais will be coming with us."

"But she said—" Paul began, face puckered with doubt.

"And I meant it," Anais interjected.

"Then I have to stay, too." Louis rose and went to stand beside his sister, one hand placed protectively on her shoulder. He looked at his mother through wide brown eyes which did not waver, even when he saw how her face was distorted in anger.

Then, before she could stop him, Paul wriggled free of her arms and joined the other two on the far side of the table.

"Listen to me," Medora said, forcing her voice to stay even. "We'll all be going to North Dakota and that's that. I have discussed it with Phillipe and—"

"Don't want Phillipe!" Paul wailed. "Want Anais." Then he bit his lip and crawled into his sister's lap.

Medora felt her patience begin to give way. "I'm sorry," she said, "but you have no choice. We're going. And now it's time for bed."

Neither Louis nor Anais moved, and, as Medora approached, Paul threw his arms around the girl's neck. "Papa!" he sniffled. "I want Papa."

Medora froze at the note of desperate pleading in her son's voice.

"Papa's gone, Paul," Anais explained softly. "You remember I told you that Papa won't be back."

"But why?" The boy squinted up at her through tear-filled eyes.

"Because he's gone. I told you before."

It was, more than anything else, the toneless quality of Anais' voice which shook Medora to the heart. Her three children stood there with the uncertain firelight touching their faces, and she knew that at any moment the fire would flicker and die, leaving them to be engulfed by the waiting shadows. But just now she could not help them; they were united against her in a cause which they could not begin to understand. Not even Anais, with her fathomless black eyes. "We'll talk again in the morning," Medora said calmly. "I'll send Nanny up now to put you to bed."

Before they could protest, she turned and left the room, but she could not leave behind the memory of Louis standing stiffly with his hand on Anais' shoulder and Paul with his tousled blond head resting beside Anais' dark one. Despite the pitiful light from the fire, the image flared for an instant, then burned itself permanently into her mind.

The children would come around, of course. They had always been obedient to her wishes, even Anais; it was just that the Marquis' death had left them strangely unstable for the moment. Perhaps the trip to North Dakota was even wiser than she had thought at first. Surely, once the children were removed from this house, so full of memories of their father, they would settle down again. They were young; they would forget eventually.

Medora reached the foot of the stairs and glided quietly through the long gilt and silver hall, glancing into the many rooms as she passed. All at once, the elegantly papered walls, the crystal chandeliers, the silk and satin draperies looked too still, almost lifeless, in the fingers of wavering light. And, beneath her feet, the marble floor rang cold and hollow as she moved. The swish of her skirts was an unwelcome whisper of longing that disturbed the fragile silence draped like a silken shroud upon the house. These rooms, so carefully decorated and skillfully maintained, had taken on a dull, stagnant sheen, as if they had already been abandoned long ago.

Part II

New York/The Badlands: Winter, 1898

"My expedition has taken a form and importance I did not expect. It is becoming a national affair and it must succeed. Remember, the concentration of wills on the same object is a power, and your will must push me across the desert and not pull me back."

—Marquis de Mores
May, 1897

Chapter 3

"Louis!" Gretta Von Hoffman stumbled as she crossed the threshold into the study, waving the crumpled letter before her like a tattered victory banner. She brushed one hand awkwardly across the iron-gray curls that had escaped from the mass of hairpins that always proved futile, despite their number.

"What is it?" her husband growled without bothering to rise from his comfortable stuffed chair.

Now that she was in his presence, Gretta found that her excitement had drained away. As always, she was intimidated by Louis' penetrating gaze and by the force of will that kept his shoulders straight and his back unbent, despite the creeping fingers of age which had turned his receding hair and still-thick muttonchop sideburns snowy white. At the age of sixty-two, Von Hoffman's florid skin appeared even more flushed and the long beak of his nose more formidable.

"You have some news, I gather," Louis suggested, indicating the wrinkled page in his wife's hand. "Tell me, then leave me to my work." He nodded toward the table covered with ledgers and reports.

"It's Medora," Gretta said at last. "She's written to say she's coming to New York."

"What?" Von Hoffman was out of his chair in an instant, taking the letter from her hand. "Are you sure?"

"Well, yes," Gretta murmured, astonished at the sudden light in her husband's eyes. "They'll be here within the next month."

"I don't believe it," Louis said, more to himself than to his wife. "At last." Then he did something he had not done in many months; he smiled. "She's bringing the children, of course."

"Oh, yes. Everyone's coming." Gretta's excitement had returned. "It will be so wonderful to have children in the house again."

Louis began to pace before the fireplace, his hands clasped behind his back. "One month," he murmured. "That doesn't give us much time. We must look into schools for the children. Or shall we hire a tutor? I wish I knew what they've been learning over there. Probably nothing of any use, if I knew their father."

"Oh, but Louis," Gretta interrupted, "they won't be staying. They're just coming for a visit."

Von Hoffman turned to glare at her. "What are you babbling about?" His eyes, when they met hers, were turbulent circles of winter gray.

Gretta quailed. "Medora and Phillipe and the children are stopping here on the way to North Dakota," she informed him, while attempting, unsuccessfully, to smooth her wrinkled skirt. "They plan to reopen the packing plant."

"North Dakota!" he groaned in disbelief, then he turned his back on his wife. "So I was wrong. And I really thought that this time she was finally free of him."

"Who?" Gretta asked.

"The Marquis de Mores."

Although she could not see his face, Gretta knew that her husband's lip was curled with disdain for his dead son-in-law. She had never understood Louis' aversion to

Mores; she only knew that it had been a part of his nature from the first moment he had heard the Marquis' name. "But, Louis, she doesn't want to be free of him. He made her so happy."

"Happy!" Von Hoffman snorted in disgust. "What a stupid thing to say, after all the pain he caused my daughter." Grasping the mantel with stiff fingers, he stared furiously into the fire, as if the flames could somehow burn away his anger and carry it away up the chimney to blacken the soot-stained snow beneath the window. "What do *you* know about happiness, anyway?"

Gretta Von Hoffman gazed at the unbending line of her husband's back and the harsh lines of his cheek, as rigid and unchanging as the bleak stone city around her, and all at once her trembling ceased. "Nothing," she said simply. She rose, her hands clasped before her, and started toward the door.

Aware of the hostile silence that followed her, Gretta turned for a moment, while her heart pounded hollowly in her ears. She had waited a long time to speak her mind and suddenly she could wait no longer. "But I know this. I know that Mores changed our daughter. He brought excitement to her life. He took her away from the world of figures and profits and losses you had built around her and turned her from a machine into a woman. He's the only man I've ever known who had the power to lift the gloomy pall of this house off her shoulders and lead her into the sunlight. He made her smile, Louis, or have you forgotten?". . . .

. . . . *April, 1878—Medora's laughter rose with the grace of a sparrow released from long exile, and to her father, the sound was an abomination.* Von Hoffman threw open the door of the study and stood motionless on the threshold, the rage building in his chest at the scene before him.

His daughter was sprawled against the far wall, books scattered all around her. Her tightly braided hair had tumbled halfway down her back and her gown was twisted alarmingly around her legs. But, worst of all, she was gazing up at the boy who stood above her and both were convulsed with laughter.

"Medora!" Von Hoffman bellowed. "What is the meaning of this?"

The laughter ceased as abruptly as the flickering flame of a candle in a sudden gust of chill wind, and Medora looked up at her father in surprise. She rose at once from among the fallen books and began to set herself to rights, while the boy, who Von Hoffman recognized as Gary Treadwell from next door, backed away in stunned silence.

"Get out!" Von Hoffman hissed, his rage boiling just beneath the surface.

Gary was quick to comply. With a single backward glance at Medora, he edged past her father's formidable bulk and disappeared down the hall. Medora herself did not move, once she stood upright with her gown smoothed into decorous folds around her.

When her father had closed the door and turned to face her once again, he saw that she was not cowering; her eyes met his without flinching. She had desecrated his office—the only room in the house where he could escape the irreverence and idiocy of others—she had defiled it with her heedless laughter, but she was not afraid.

"I'll see that Gary is not allowed in this house again," he said at last, perplexed by his daughter's unwavering regard.

"We did nothing wrong," Medora told him calmly. "I tripped and fell, and Gary was helping me up."

"Just the same," Von Hoffman insisted, "he won't be coming here again."

Medora shook her head. "You don't have much faith in me, do you?"

Her father's eyebrows came together in annoyance. "It's not a question of faith, my dear. It's a question of time and money. You have work to do, and that doesn't leave you time to waste with the likes of Gary Treadwell." Von Hoffman approached his daughter and indicated the confusion of books all around her. "You might start by picking these up and restoring my office to its usual condition."

Medora did not move. "Am I never to have any fun, then?"

With an audible sigh of irritation, Von Hoffman sat down behind his desk. "I can only warn you against levity, Medora. A sheer waste of time. There's too much serious work to be done in this world. It's a sin to be idle, and, besides, I have great plans for you. They just don't happen to include gambolling on the study floor."

"Yes, Papa," Medora murmured, but her eyes were veiled and he could not read her thoughts. Without another word, she turned and began to pick up the debris.

Von Hoffman shifted in his chair. He had trained her well, despite this minor lapse. He could see that she was everything he had always hoped she would be, even though she was only seventeen. But, all at once, he realized how dull and drab her face looked now that the light of her laughter had been extinguished.

Suddenly, her father wanted nothing more than to see his daughter smile again as she had for that boy a moment ago. Her body was here before him, but it was as if the warm, breathing girl had ceased to exist the moment Von Hoffman entered the room. "Medora," he said abruptly, "do you remember how ridiculous the gardener's boy looked this morning, covered with dirt from head to toe, except for his bright red hat?"

Medora turned to look at him from where she knelt before the bookcase, a heavy volume in her hand. *"I remember,"* she said, *but her lips remained stiff and unsmiling, and her eyes were as still and untouched as highly polished emeralds. . . .*

. . . . The firelight glittered for an instant in Gretta's colorless gray eyes, and suddenly the silence that pervaded the room became bleak and oppressive to Von Hoffman's ears. "I wanted my daughter home," he said finally, "but not like this."

Gretta closed her fingers tightly around the doorknob. She should not have said it; she knew that now. It was her fault, after all, that they were strangers. Everything was her fault. She had tried to make it up to him over the years, but he had ignored her efforts. Yet she could not let him judge Medora so harshly. "I, for one, will welcome our daughter and the others with open arms, however long they choose to stay."

"My dear Gretta," he explained wearily, "it is most improper for Medora to drag along her husband's bastard and expect us to tolerate him."

Gretta straightened her shoulders defiantly. "Phillipe is part of the family now."

"Hah! He wishes he were. I'm warning you, Gretta, he's only after Medora's money, just as her husband was."

"Oh, no! You must be mistaken," she mumbled. "I don't think—"

"No, my dear, I don't believe you do." Von Hoffman saw how she started, how her cheeks flushed with anger and her fingers twisted themselves into the fabric of her skirt. Then she turned away and ran from the room. He watched her go without regret, until he realized that he was truly alone once again, with nothing but the dull, gnawing ache in his chest to keep him company.

* * *

Katherine Pendleton leaned forward, urging her horse to go faster over the old rutted road, covered here and there with thin patches of muddy snow. At the moment, she was so completely caught up in her own pleasure that she was aware of nothing but the feel of the fine horse beneath her, the piercing chill of the late morning air, and the whistling cry of the wind, which captured her laughter and swept it back over her velvet-clad shoulders.

Katherine's fiancé, David St. Clair, was not far behind, and he smiled when the sound of her laughter reached him for an instant, then vanished into the surprisingly blue sky. Unaware that he was allowing his horse to slow down, David watched Katherine as she flew across the still winter landscape. The sunlight struck her emerald green riding habit and dark brown hair with the same luminous fingers which set the snow fields sparkling and her laughter rose in the bright cold air like a song—or an invitation.

God, but she's magnificent, David thought. All other women paled before her. It was not just her beauty that so enchanted him; it was her energy, her constant drive, her apparently inexhaustible ability to enjoy life. She was a woman like no other, and she had enslaved him.

When Katherine turned once to glance over her shoulder, David realized that the distance between them was widening alarmingly. Suddenly intent on the race, he crouched lower in the saddle and, ignoring the icy curtain of wind, forced his horse to increase its speed. For David knew that although Katherine liked to win, she also loved the competition. Those who could not match her were merely tossed aside, and he did not intend to be one of those.

Brown eyes focused on the road ahead, blond hair flying in all directions, David slowly gained on his opponent until the two horses were thundering side by side as they approached the top of the hill where the wind had swept the snow away. Then, at the last moment, just before they reached the tree stump that marked the end of the race, David pulled ahead. He clung to the reins as the horse slowed down to a normal pace, then David slid to the ground, swallowing huge gulps of air as he leaned against the horse's sweating flanks.

"Well," Katherine managed to gasp as she led her horse up beside him, "I must say, I thought for a minute you wouldn't be able to do it this time." Smiling, she shook her head and released the last of her brown curls from their captivity. Then she reached into the untidy confusion of hair and began to pull out the pins so that the strands clung for an instant, then fell away, one at a time.

David took another deep breath in an attempt to steady the rapid beating of his heart against his chest. "Katherine—" he began.

"Wait," she interrupted, grasping his hand, "let's sit on the boulder while the horses rest. We did come to look at the view, didn't we?"

Following as if hypnotized, David found a comfortable spot on the long, low-slung boulder, while Katherine chose to sit just out of reach on the other side. David gazed at her in admiration and wondered how he had ever convinced her to agree to marry him. His fiancée of two months was unquestionably the best catch in the state of North Dakota, despite the fact that she was twenty-eight years old. Not only was she beautiful, which was rare enough in this uncivilized corner of the Badlands, but she was also rich—the only heir to the great Pendleton cattle empire. But it was not her money or even her beauty which attracted him most. It was, quite simply, Katherine herself. Without her, life would be as bleak and barren as the sculptured ice valley at their feet.

But David was no fool; he knew Katherine could live without him as certainly as he knew he could *not* live without *her.* "Why are you going to marry me?" he asked abruptly. All at once, her answer was the most important thing in the world to him.

"Because," Katherine said idly, "you're the only man who can beat me in a horse race." Then she rose gracefully, without a backward glance, and made her way to the highest part of the hill, where she paused to look down at the shrouded landscape. Even the normally bright cliffs were half-coated with white, their colors muted and diffused in the late morning light. And, of course, the cottonwoods were bare of leaves, mere skeletons that stood close guard over the sluggish Little Missouri River that flowed down the center of the valley. The town itself seemed lifeless and abandoned, with the railroad tracks running across it like a jagged scar.

Katherine shook her head and started to turn away when her eye was caught by a movement on the bluff below her. Only then did she see the number of servants clustered on the porch of the Chateau where the Marquis de Mores had once lived with his family. For twelve years, ever since the Vallombrosas had left the Badlands, the Chateau had been inhabited only by three servants left behind by the Marquis. Mores' last words to Katherine's father had been a promise to return someday, and for years Katherine had waited, fear, dread, and excitement mingled in her blood, but they had never come back. And now she had heard the Marquis was dead.

"David," she said, turning to face him once again, "do you know what's going on at the Chateau?"

David came to join her, and she did not resist when he slid his arm loosely around her waist. "I believe I heard the family is coming back in early spring."

"For a visit?" Katherine just managed to force the words through her suddenly cold lips.

"I don't know for sure. But I think Mama said they were planning to stay."

"They?" she asked.

"Bastard and all, as my father says," David replied blithely. But when he saw her face, the laughter died in his throat. "I heard there was trouble between their family and yours when they were last here, but they had already gone by the time the St. Clairs came. Is it true?"

Katherine smiled crookedly. "I'm not afraid of them, if that's what you mean."

"No," David assured her, "that wasn't—" But before he could finish his sentence, Katherine had turned and left him. David watched helplessly as she mounted her horse and rode away; the chill of her parting glance had turned his blood to ice, and he found he could not move. What was it that had changed her so quickly in the past few minutes? He thought he had learned to know her every mood in the past six months, but he found that he had been mistaken. Never before had he seen her eyes so utterly devoid of human emotion. Still, they had been beautiful—as beautiful as the sweeping sea of crystal white that covered the valley, and equally as empty.

Phillipe stepped out onto the sidewalk and, at the sudden gust of chill wind, wrapped his muffler tighter around his neck. As he began to make his way toward the tavern where he was supposed to meet William, the young man glowered up at the blank faces of the buildings that crowded around him. He grimaced in distaste. He had been in New York for two weeks already, but he had not yet accustomed himself to the bleak grayness of the city. Even the snow, which lay scattered in dingy piles at his feet, was stained with the smoke and mud that were so much a part of New York.

Burying his hands in the deep pockets of his overcoat, Phillipe attempted to fight off the feeling of depression which had settled over him since the family's arrival in the city. It was not only Von Hoffman's barely veiled hostility or Anais' intense dislike which disturbed Phillipe so deeply. Even William's continued reluctance was only a minor irritation. This despondency did not come from the feelings of others; it came, instead, from inside Phillipe himself.

He felt all at once that he had been cast adrift, left without direction in a city in which he could never be more than a stranger. As he walked down the crowded New York street with the lowering sky above him, the bitter wind at his back and the endless puddles of grimy snow at his feet, Phillipe felt that he was being propelled forward against his will. He could not stop now even if he wanted to. It was as if some force outside himself was driving him on, until he sensed that he stood on the brink of a dangerous precipice and that one more step forward would send him hurtling into the yawning abyss. There was only one way to go, and that was backwards, to safety and the familiarity of his past.

Stop it, Phillipe told himself firmly. You're being ridiculous. After all, he had had nothing but good luck with the men he had talked to in New York about reopening the plant. Unlike the Marquis, he meant to prepare a careful base here and in Chicago—the center of the meatpacking industry—before he even approached the doors of the abandoned plant. Already he and William had spoken to butchers, retailers, the fractious members of the Beef Trust, and he planned to go to Chicago in a couple of weeks to see Swift and Armour.

Phillipe was going slowly, taking a single step at a time until he reached his goal. He was determined to accomplish his ends, not only for his own sake, but also for Medora's. He had caused her enough trouble over the years; now was his chance to make it up to her, and to the father he still missed. But he knew that Louis Von Hoffman was watching his every move with the impatience of a falcon hungry for its prey. Phillipe hoped he could win the man over. They needed Von Hoffman's help if they were ever going to make this plan a reality.

When he reached the corner, Phillipe paused for a moment to get his bearings. He looked up just as a woman left the building across the street and his eyes followed her, although he tried to look away. She moved lithely, her pale blue wool gown dancing around her ankles in the wind, and it was as if she were unaware of the dreariness of her surroundings. Her fur hat could not quite contain the dark, luxuriant curls that fell across her neck and shoulders, and when the wind swept her hair into her face, the woman threw back her head and smiled a secret little smile.

Phillipe sucked in his breath and looked away. In that instant, the woman reminded him of someone, though he could not say who, and suddenly he was possessed of a physical hunger that invaded every part of his body. The strange woman crossed the street and disappeared from sight, but still Phillipe stood unmoving, struggling against a demon he knew he could never defeat.

This was his mother's one legacy to her son—this deep need to fulfill the dictates of his body even when his mind was unwilling. Nicole had passed on to him her one weakness and it would haunt him all his life, just as it had haunted her. Because of her, he could not separate his body from the urgings of his soul and, in consequence, both would always be only half-fulfilled. For, although his mother had instilled the hunger in him, she had not given him the knowledge of how to appease it. It was for that, more than anything else, that he could never forgive her.

Chapter 4

In the first sharp chill of morning, the world was tinged in subtle shades of blue and the bare winter trees had been touched with magic. The branches rose unmoving against the white-blue sky while the sunlight glistened on the ice which tipped the twigs like fragile blown-glass leaves. Beneath these frail crystal creations, the river traced its familiar path, slowed and muted by the thin layer of ice that had begun to spread slowly inward from the bank. To Mianne Goodall, who sat on her carefully folded cloak with the smooth face of a boulder beneath her, the morning was a gift beyond words.

With the ineffectual touch of the sun on her face and the glitter of the ice-leaves above her, she reached back slowly to release her braids from the crown they made around her head. Then, enjoying the soft, teasing song of the river that seemed to echo her own movements, the woman began to unbraid her long, black hair. Although her delicate features had been influenced as much by her white father as by her Indian mother, the hair was a legacy from her mother alone. It fell across her shoulders, sleek and black, without a hint of curl, and it was her hair, more than anything, which betrayed her Sioux heritage.

When her foot dislodged a stone which went tumbling

into the water, Mianne abandoned her task and bent to listen for a moment. She often came here like this, alone, to hear the voice of the river. It was the only sound that could bring comfort to her soul, the only connection she had with the world of her mother, who had long been dead. But there was something else that drew her here day after day, although she was not certain what it could be. It was almost like a presence that lured her away from the Chateau, beckoning with invisible fingers until Mianne answered. It was there now, when she closed her eyes and leaned back, listening—that presence like the fleeting touch of a human hand. It was almost as if it were waiting for something, but Mianne could not guess what it was. She did not try. She had been bewitched by the spell of the river and she was content that it should be so.

But perhaps it would not be so for long. Her eyes opened wide as she remembered that the Vallombrosas were coming home, and she must see that they were comfortable here. After all, she owed them everything, did she not? They had welcomed her when her father first brought her here many years ago, a ragged and undisciplined child of fourteen. Then, ignoring the fact that she was a half-breed, they had taken her into their home and offered to turn her into a lady. But they had gone away too soon, leaving behind a girl half-wild, half-tame, and completely miserable.

Still, they had allowed her to live with her father in the Chateau, as long as they kept it up for the family's return someday. And, for the past twelve years, Mianne and Johnny Goodall had existed in isolation in the house on the bluff, ignored by the people of the valley. Mianne had come to be grateful for this isolation, for she preferred the company of the river to the sound of human voices, though, over the years, she had learned to live in two worlds. At the Chateau, she was everything a young woman of twenty-six should be—graceful and proper and accomplished at womanly arts—but here she escaped from her self-imposed restrictions and her Indian half came back to life.

Here she was wild again, with her hair tumbled around her shoulders and her spirit singing within her. She came to the river like a woman parched from thirst and let the music of the water slide down her throat like a soothing balm.

But the Vallombrosas were coming back, and she knew very well that their very presence could destroy her ordered world. She was troubled by distant memories of a force that had threatened to break her, even then, but these she refused to recognize. Today she would recognize only the murmuring water at her feet and the world of ice crystals above her head, because it was all that mattered to her. This place, this moment, this magic were everything.

Stretching out on the boulder, Mianne gazed into the icy river, searching for the message it sometimes gave her, but today the babble meant nothing. Unaware that her hair had fallen across her shoulders until it touched the ice beneath her hand, she reached out to dip her fingers in the water. The chill which traveled through her body pierced her to the very bone, and it was then that she felt the first stirrings of a vague foreboding. The river whispered words of warning, but Mianne could not understand, though she reached blindly into the center of her soul. She could only sit and wait, unmoving, for whatever the future held, and in that moment, even the song of the water could not comfort her.

Medora sat curled on the windowseat in her simple but elegant gray gown, resting her cheek against the cold glass that kept her apart from the frosty world outside. She could just make out the sweep of snow-covered lawn with the stark trees rising like thorny sentinels through the grayish powder. But the approaching dusk had already reached out with shadowed fingers to enwrap the scenery in its nightly shroud, and soon all she could see was her own reflection and the pulsating light of the fire. Her father had had new electric lights installed, but Medora thought them cold and harsh, and she preferred the soft firelight.

It was warm inside, and, just at the moment, she felt oddly at peace, although she was concerned about Phillipe, who was still in the city somewhere. In the month they had been in New York, he had spent only two days at home. The rest of the time he was out paving the way for their return to the Badlands.

She knew he was accomplishing a great deal, but she also knew that the business was not the only thing which kept him away. The young man had recognized Von Hoffman's hostility from the moment he entered his house, and Medora guessed that Phillipe was keeping himself busy elsewhere in order to make this visit as comfortable as possible for her.

"You wanted to speak to me?" Louis Von Hoffman asked.

Medora looked up at her father, who stood with his hands clasped behind his back, staring moodily into the fire.

"Yes." She uncurled her legs from beneath her, but did not rise. "I want to discuss a business proposal with you and—" She stopped when she saw that her daughter was hovering in the doorway, as if waiting for someone to notice her. Medora knew that now was not the time to attempt to talk to the girl, yet she did not want to send her away. Anais had begun to seem so fragile of late, despite the hard shell of indifference she gathered around herself.

"Not now, dear," Louis said before Medora could speak. "Your Mama and I have to talk. But I'll come up and see you before you go to bed."

Medora watched the girl nod slightly, then glide away,

but her attention was really focused on Von Hoffman. She had been astonished by the softness in his voice when he spoke to Anais. She was even more astonished when he turned to her accusingly.

"That girl is very unhappy." He said it as if it were entirely his daughter's fault.

"I know, but I can't see how to help her." Medora was angry at her father's presumption, but she did not want to fight with him just now.

"This week she's sulking because you won't let the children ride those bicycles I gave them," Von Hoffman reminded her.

"Oh, but I couldn't. It's much too dangerous. I know the streets are swept free of snow, but there are still patches of ice and slush." She wondered why she was bothering to explain herself to him. "And I've been wondering," she added after a moment's thought, "why you gave them the bicycles anyway."

Von Hoffman shrugged. "Anais wrote about their popularity in Paris and how she regretted having to leave hers behind. I just wanted to make them all feel more at home. But surely you did not call me here to talk about bicycles," Von Hoffman said.

Medora turned slowly to face him. "No," she agreed. "I asked you to come because I need your help."

"So you've finally realized it, have you?" His tone was as cold as it had been since the day she had arrived, and his eyes were still and wary.

"I've known it all along, Papa. I'm not a dolt. We need you to help finance the opening of the packing plant until we can begin making money again," she told him matter-of-factly.

Louis took a step backward, surprised by her bluntness. He had known this was coming, because he knew his daughter's financial situation better than anyone. This was the moment he had been waiting for, the moment when he took the reins in hand once again. Money was the only weapon he had against Medora's obstinacy, but it was a potent one, and he knew how to use it well. "If you're not a dolt, then you know my answer. I will not pay to watch you ruin your life." He paused and began to pace across the room, his rotund figure casting long, wavering shadows on the fine Persian carpet.

"Papa—"

"However, should you choose to remain here in New York—"

"We're going to the Badlands; I've told you that a hundred times," Medora insisted.

"Without money?"

"We'll find the money one way or another. I intend to go through with this, you see; nothing you can say will change my mind."

"Your children don't want to go," he pointed out, just managing to keep his voice steady.

"I believe I know what's best for my children better than they do. And I know what's best for me."

Von Hoffman glared at her, his red cheeks puffing in and out with the pulse of his growing anger. "And what's best for Phillipe, of course," he sneered.

Medora whirled to face him. "What does that mean?"

"Don't be so pitifully blind, my dear. That man is his father's son. You know that as well as I do. Which means he's after only one thing from you."

"Yes?" she prompted from between cold lips.

"Your money, of course. No doubt he's already gotten whatever else you have to offer, or you wouldn't be dragging him along like a tame dog. But you must tell me, we're all so curious, *is* he like his father in every way?"

Blinded by the wave of rage that swept over her, Medora started to turn away.

"Medora," her father called. "Wait!"

She spun around, eyes blazing, and said, "You're

wrong, you know. I'm not surprised that you have no faith in Phillipe; you don't know him after all. But I would have thought you believed in me, at least a little."

"You don't have much faith in me, do you?" she had asked him once. When Von Hoffman tried to speak, the words could not get past the lump in his throat. I must not lose her, he thought wildly, not now, when she finally has a chance to free herself from the past. "Don't go," he pleaded. "I'm sorry for what I said, believe me." He knew that at least she was listening, even though she stood before him as stiff and cold as the icicles that hung outside the window. He did not want to beg her—he deplored weakness in anyone—but he had to keep her here, whatever the cost.

"It's just that I can't bear to watch you making the same mistakes all over again," he explained haltingly. "I can't bear your stubbornness and your disregard for practicality and common sense. You've forgotten how to listen, Medora, and you've become no more than an obstinate fool."

Medora closed her eyes, but even behind the blue-veined lids, she could see the flickering fingers of fire that had turned her father's eyes into two glowing coals. "I'm sorry, Papa," she said at last. "But I'm afraid you can only blame yourself. It was you, after all, who made me what I am."

Katherine rode blindly, forcing her mind to remain a total blank. It seemed to her that she had been wandering like this forever, though it had only been a little over a week. Ever since the day when she had discovered that the Marquis' family was returning to the Chateau, she had begun to feel cut off from those around her—like an unwanted stranger. She had spoken to no one about it; she had only herself to depend on. Only she could understand. Today, as always, she had left the comfort of her home—which threatened to suffocate her—and escaped into the biting winter cold. Trusting the instincts of her surefooted horse, Katherine abandoned herself to the icy caress of the wind as the animal found its own way across the snowbound landscape. She was grateful for the numbness which began, sluggishly, to invade her body, one limb at a time. Her deadened senses were just another form of insurance against the painful pinpricks of memory that grew so easily into knife blades.

It had always been this way for her; her mind simply closed down whenever she thought about—No! The iron door clanged shut before the harm was done and Katherine found, to her dismay, that her horse stood snorting at the edge of the river.

What was worse, he had somehow brought her to the very spot where she least wanted to be. Or had she guided him without realizing it? But that was impossible. She would never have come here of her own free will. Nevertheless, she did not turn away. Instead, she slid from the saddle, then stood there, leaning against the warm, heaving sides of the animal in an effort to stop her own trembling. This was silly, she told herself. She was a grown woman of twenty-eight, not a child of ten, and she had the strength to do anything she wanted. She had within her the power to turn away from the half-frozen pond and never look back, but she did not do it.

Katherine tied her horse to the nearest tree and crossed the marshy, slush-covered ground until she came to the water's edge. Her breath, a burst of white smoke in the cold air, obscured her vision, as did the thin layer of ice which covered the pond. But still she stood there, unmoving, staring downward past the dirty ice to the water that flowed beneath; she could hear it rumbling over the rocks where the pond narrowed and became the river again, but here there was only stillness. Drawing a deep, uneven breath, Katherine leaned out over the ice and closed her eyes, pretending she could see her face reflected there. . . .

. . . . July, 1885—The image of dark hair and deep brown eyes wavered for an instant, disturbed by a single gust of wind that rippled the surface of the pond. Katherine smiled to herself. It was a pleasing reflection, she knew, and the knowledge helped assuage her boredom and restlessness just a little. She looked up when she thought she heard a commotion behind her, and then she was propelled rudely into the icy water by a force she could not immediately identify. Clawing and kicking, she dragged the dripping hair back from her face and confronted her assailant.

"Good afternoon, my dear. Nice day for a swim, don't you agree?" Phillipe Beaumont drawled casually, eyeing her body from head to toe.

"Phillipe!" she gasped in fury. "You—"

He silenced her by drawing her forward until her skin met his, but he was wise enough to hold her hands tightly behind her back. "You should be glad it was me who found you," he suggested. "Or don't you mind if everyone sees you stark naked in the middle of the day?"

"No one comes here but you. You know that," she spat. "And the trees provide plenty of protection. Except from you."

Phillipe smiled. "Exactly. There is no protection from me. Someday you'll learn that."

Katherine started to protest, but Phillipe's lips covered hers in a long, warm kiss. "Let's not fight, Kathy," he murmured. "There are much better things we could be doing."

Clenching her hands together, Katherine focused all her energy on breaking Phillipe's grasp on her wrists and, with one violent pull, she broke free. "My name is Katherine," she hissed.

The boy seemed undisturbed by her hostility. "I know that," he told her. "But Kathy is my special name for you."

"It's undignified," Katherine maintained, slowly making her way to the edge of the pond.

"I know that too. That's exactly why I like it." Phillipe followed her, determined not to let her go, despite the expression in her eyes. "The nickname makes you sound as if maybe you have a heart after all." His voice had a teasing note, but his face was grim when he finally caught hold of her hand again.

Katherine gazed back at him with the implacable, imperious eyes of a falcon he had seen once in France. There was no youth there, no laughter, nothing but disdain. "But you *don't* have a heart, do you?" he asked stiffly.

Then, for the first time, Katherine smiled. "No," she told him, "I was lucky enough to be born without one. So you needn't worry that you will break me. I can't be broken."

Her lopsided smile was a challenge, and Phillipe reached for her blindly, hungry all at once for the feel of her body next to his. "Kathy," he breathed as his arms closed around her and she fell against him, brushing her breasts against his chest. *And this time she did not correct him, but followed him willingly back and back to the heart of the pond where the water caressed them with the all-encompassing grasp of an icy hand. . . .*

. . . . Beneath the dulled and spotted sheet of ice, the water circled darkly, waiting for the touch of sunlight that would free it once again, and Katherine stood there transfixed, consumed by her memories in spite of her resolution to obliterate them. Phillipe was coming back. That could not be. She could not let it happen.

She could never forgive him for what he had done to her. She could never forget the agony, the humiliation he had caused. And the pain—Dear God, the pain he had left behind. Yet she had no power to stop him from returning. All at once, the future loomed before her—a huge, gaping blank. She was helpless.

Katherine folded her arms tightly across her body. She felt it coming—the tautness in her chest, the twisting of her insides and, worst of all, the terrible laughter. It was rising inside her like a tidal wave, and she knew she would drown if she did not stop it. So, with every last ounce of her strength, she fought the hysteria. She stood with her fists clenched and her muscles knotted and struggled to keep the blackness at bay.

"Katherine?"

It was David St. Clair's hesitant voice floating toward her from beyond the sheltering trees that finally brought her back.

"Katherine? Are you there?"

He was coming in her direction and she knew he would find her soon. Lately, he had begun to follow her, watching, as if he sensed the turmoil in her soul. His questioning gaze annoyed her, and she wished futilely that he would leave her alone, especially today. She did not speak or move or give him the slightest indication she was there. She merely waited for him to discover her.

And by the time David had fought his way through the gnarled, barren branches of the cottonwoods to the little clearing where she stood, Katherine was smiling.

Anais fastened the Turkish trousers of her velvet cycling outfit, made certain the jacket was buttoned, and pulled on her brown kid gloves. Then, setting her fur hat at a jaunty angle on her tightly braided hair, she opened the bedroom door and stood listening for a long moment. When she was certain that no one was nearby, she slipped into the hall and began to descend the stairs.

Holding her breath so that she would not make any unnecessary noise, the girl made her way through the strangely silent house until she reached the back door. When the door was closed behind her, she breathed a sigh of relief and went to get her bicycle from among the bushes where she had hidden it.

Today was the day. She could bear staying quiet in that gloomy house no longer. For over a month, she had moved through this strange house, as lost as if she had been left alone in a foreign country. She found that Von Hoffman was her only real friend here. He had taught her a little about how to keep the ledgers which always seemed to cover his desk, and she had spent much of her time with him. But when he was busy, which was often, she had nowhere else to go.

She had tried to keep herself occupied, but the dim halls, where the daylight never seemed to penetrate, had become like a prison. She was a captive in New York and her mother was the warden who held the key. Anais had begun to think she would go mad with frustration and boredom. Then, today, she had realized what she must do. She had to escape, at least for a moment. And the new bicycle her grandfather had bought for her was waiting to be put to use. So, snow or no snow, she was going to fly away.

As she wheeled the bicycle out to the street and turned it away from the house, she was grateful for the comfort of her warm, double-breasted jacket with its fashionably puffed sleeves. And she had learned to love the freedom of wearing the baggy pants, which were gathered tightly together just above her high-button shoes. She was pleased with the unusual outfit because she knew it set her apart.

Anais made certain that the street had been swept free of most of the snow, and when she was far enough away from the many searching eyes of the Von Hoffman house, she mounted the bicycle. After a few false starts, she managed to get it rolling. Then she saw that it would be easy after all; her two years of cycling in Paris would serve her well. So entranced was she with the wonderful feeling of being in motion again that she did not even notice that she was being followed.

Anais wanted to close her eyes and throw back her head, as if to drink in the coolness of the clear afternoon. All at once she was flying free with the cold air touching her cheeks and singing in her eyes. Even the grim, lifeless houses, touched by an indiscriminate gray hand, or the occasional patches of mud-darkened snow did not detract from her enjoyment of this moment. For Anais saw nothing, was aware of nothing but her own racing pulse and the tingling exhilaration of rushing blindly with the wind at her back.

She rode through the puddles of melted snow without once pausing to shake the water away. She had been released from her bondage at last, and she knew that nothing could stop her now. She would ride until the demons that peopled her dreams were no more than memories left to die on the stark winter branches, until she had forgotten her mother and the Badlands and the image of her father's laughing face. He would haunt her no more, because she was free, she cried inwardly, desperate to make herself believe it was true. She would forget everything but the powder blue winter sky and the distant undulating waves of crystal snow. She would lose herself in the landscape where they could never find her.

Anais did not see the thick patch of dirty ice that lay hidden in the shadows until it was too late and her bicycle was wrenched from her control. She had only a moment in which she realized what was happening, then, as she flung her arms upward in a futile attempt to protect herself, she flew over the handlebars. In the instant when her head hit the ground, she saw that the snow had turned to ashes and the blue sky to deep black thunder.

Chapter 5

"Why didn't you tell me?" Katherine demanded, facing her father across his huge oak desk.

The sun had just begun to set, and in the last flash of late afternoon light, Greg Pendleton could just discern the smoldering eyes of his only child. "Tell you what?" he asked, resting his elbows on the cluttered desktop.

"You know very well that I'm talking about the Vallombrosas' coming back to the Badlands. You got a letter three weeks ago. Why didn't you tell me?"

Greg gazed beyond his daughter to the far wall of the room, which had already been swallowed by the hungry shadows. Why *hadn't* he told her? he wondered. Was it just because he could not bring himself to say the words? Certainly it was the name Vallombrosa that had first brought gray to his thick brown hair, until now, at forty-eight, his hair had become an echo of his steel-gray eyes. In fact, everything that was ugly in his life could be traced somehow to the Vallombrosas, even his father's death from a debilitating disease several years before. Greg had convinced himself of that long ago.

"Father, I'm waiting."

"I thought it would be wisest to keep the news to myself for a while until I decided what to do," he explained.

"Safer, you mean. You just didn't want Mama to know. You were afraid of what she might do, weren't you?"

"My reasons are not really your concern, Katherine."

Katherine leaned forward until her eyes were level with her father's. "She'll have to learn the truth sometime. You can't keep it from her forever."

Greg winced at the slight emphasis his daughter put on the word "truth." Katherine had always known far too much for her own good, or his, but there was nothing to be done about it just now. "*I* will decide when to tell her. You mind your own business."

"But, Father," Katherine purred, "I just don't think it's fair, keeping her always in the dark like you do."

When he recognized the gleam in Katherine's eyes, Greg's hand closed heavily over hers. "Don't do it, I'm warning you," he snapped. "Leave your mother alone."

Katherine shrugged and sat back in her chair, pulling her hand away from her father's. "And when did you intend to tell *me?*" she demanded.

"All in good time."

"On the day they arrived, perhaps? After I had stumbled over them in town and made an utter fool of myself?"

"My dear," Greg said, clasping his hands behind his head, "it has never taken my intervention to force you to make a fool of yourself with *that* family. You do quite well all on your own. Which reminds me," he leaned forward, suddenly intense, "you'd better watch yourself this time. Don't make the same mistake with Phillipe as you did before. In fact, you might even pretend, if you can manage it, that you've matured a little over the years."

"If I were you," Katherine cried, rising precipitously from her chair, "I wouldn't dare talk about anyone but you making a fool of himself. You weren't immune to the power of the Vallombrosas any more than I was. And if you think—"

"Oh, dear, you're fighting again. I don't know why you

two must always be fighting with each other," Cory Pendleton sighed in agitation from the doorway.

Katherine looked up at her mother and grimaced. Although the woman was only forty-six, she might have been eighty, so frail were her bones and so transparent her skin. And the patched, worn gown she refused to change did nothing to enhance her faded looks. It was almost as if she had been touched by a hand that drained all the color from her, leaving behind no more than a transparent shell. Her once thick and lovely blond hair was now thin and dulled with age and even her blue eyes had faded to indeterminate gray. Katherine took a deep breath and turned away; she could not bear to look at her mother for more than an instant. To her, Cory Pendleton was the epitome of everything that was weak and useless in a woman—from her adulation of her husband to the blank, sterile expression in her eyes.

"What is it you're fighting about this time?" Cory repeated, determined to get an answer.

"Nothing. We were just talking. You're imagining things again," Greg rose and went around the desk to stand beside his wife. Amazing, he thought, how sensitive she was to conflict. They had not even raised their voices, yet she had known they were disagreeing and had come to set things right. As if she could. As if she could ever set anything right for him again. Dear God, sometimes he hated her so much that his body shook with long-suppressed emotion. She had tried to make it up to him time and again in the past twelve years, but she had failed. She would always fail; she was that kind of woman.

"But I *know* something was wrong," she insisted pettishly. "And if you won't tell me the truth, Greg, then I'm sure Katherine will. Won't you, dear?"

Katherine whirled to find her mother's pale, disturbing gaze resting on her intently. "I don't—"

"Stop!" Cory said. "I'm tired of being lied to. Tell me the truth."

Glancing at her father from beneath half-lowered lids, Katherine said, "Go ahead. Tell her the truth."

The lines of Greg's face seemed to harden into granite, and he slid an arm around his wife's waist. "Let's go back to bed," he suggested, not quite able to banish the fury from his voice.

"What does Katherine mean?" Cory stepped away from her husband and turned to face him accusingly.

"I don't know what she means. No doubt she's playing one of her little games. Only she ought to know that the games get more dangerous all the time."

"Tell her," Katherine repeated stiffly. "Tell her that her worst nightmare is coming true. Go ahead."

Suddenly, Cory knew. "No!" she screamed, sagging back against the doorjamb. "She's coming back, isn't she?" Gazing up at her husband and her daughter, Cory seemed to plead for one of them to deny it, but neither one moved or spoke. "No! No! No!" she wailed, wrapping her bony arms around her shoulders and beginning to rock back and forth. "She can't come back. She's dead," the woman choked. "Dead. Deeaad—" Her voice rose in a piercing wail that died out only when Greg lifted her in his arms and carried her out of the room.

Katherine shuddered briefly, then carefully closed the door and went to light the lamps.

"Mama!" little Louis cried, throwing himself into Medora's arms. "Mama, she's dead and it's all my fault!"

Medora drew in a deep breath as she raised her son's face and looked into his eyes, which were awash with tears. She had never seen him like this before, and, for a moment, her heart paused in its normal rhythm. "Who's dead, Louis? What do you mean?"

"Anais! She fell, and I shouldn't have let her go."

"Where is she?" his mother gasped, gripping his shoulders with trembling hands.

"Out there. I sent Phillipe to get her. But she's dead. I know she is."

Medora rose and started for the door, then glanced back at the hysterical child who stood so forlornly in the center of the room. Gretta saw her daughter's dilemma and said, "Go to Anais, my dear. I'll take care of Louis."

When Medora had gone, Gretta turned to her grandson. "Tell me what happened."

"I saw her sneaking out to ride her bicycle," he gulped, wiping a rush of tears away before another took its place. "I knew she wasn't supposed to, but I thought it would be fun"—he paused and shuddered over the word—"to follow and see what she did. But I didn't know she was going to fall. I wouldn't have let her go if I knew."

"Of course you wouldn't have. But it's not your fault, you know. She would have gone anyway," Gretta assured him soothingly. "You did what you could."

The boy gazed up at her through a shifting curtain of tears. "Do you really think so?"

His grandmother nodded, but inside, her heart was pounding and her stomach had tied itself into queer little knots. Absently, she stroked the child's head, and she was aware, through some sixth sense, that he had begun to regain control. But then Medora walked in, followed by Phillipe with Anais in his arms.

She hung limply, her hands flung outward as if in surrender, and her face and neck were covered with blood.

"Is she—" Gretta began.

"Just unconscious," Phillipe replied. "But we'd better get her to bed and call a doctor."

"I'll call Dr. Richards," Von Hoffman said, appearing suddenly at Phillipe's shoulder. "You take her up to her room."

Until that moment, little Louis had stood facing the window, turning his back resolutely on the sight of his sister, but now he whirled around in time to see Phillipe carry her from the room. "No!" the child wailed. "She's dead! I told you. And I couldn't stop it!"

Medora stood uncertainly, torn between the boy who needed her now and the girl who might not even know her mother was there, but, once again, Gretta came to the rescue. "Go on," she said.

Giving her mother a look of deep gratitude, Medora ran from the room.

"Listen to me, Louis," his grandmother said, pulling the boy toward her with gentle hands. "Phillipe says Anais is not dead; she's only unconscious."

"What's that?" he asked through trembling lips.

"It means that she hit her head and went to sleep, but it's a very deep sleep."

"She'll wake up?" Louis inquired hopefully.

Gretta considered carefully before she answered, "It's quite likely."

The child swallowed twice, then whispered, "She's not dead." Then he buried his face in his grandmother's lap and began to weep from sheer relief.

"The doctor is on his way," Von Hoffman said, stopping on the threshold of the drawing room. As he glowered at the picture of the boy in Gretta's lap, Von Hoffman's eyes took on a strange, glacial sheen.

At that moment, Gretta was more aware of her husband, who stared at her with the eyes of a stranger, than she was of the trembling shoulders and wrenching sobs of the child who clutched her so frantically, begging for comfort. . . .

. . . . *March, 1862—Jordan Davidson knelt at Gretta's feet, his eyes full of tears, one hand on her knee and one clasped pleadingly around her trembling fingers.* He could not take his eyes from her as she sat before him, poised on the edge of the velvet couch in her apricot silk gown with her blond hair piled high on her head. At her back, the window was unshuttered, allowing the afternoon sunlight to touch her with an unnatural radiance. She was everything to him, but he knew that he was going to lose her.

Gretta looked down at the young man with the tousled brown hair who had once been her fiancé, and who, since her marriage to Louis Von Hoffman, had become her friend. Her soul bled for him just now.

"I'm sorry," she murmured, "but—"

"So." The single word, uttered in her husband's bland, precise voice shattered the stillness in the room like the well-timed crack of a whip.

"Louis!" Gretta cried in bewilderment as she removed her hand from Jordan's grasp.

The young man himself was on his feet instantly. With a shuddering breath that shook his body from head to toe, he turned to face Von Hoffman. "You don't understand," Jordan spluttered, waving his hands in the air ineffectually. "It's not at all what you think. It's really quite—"

"Be quiet," Von Hoffman ordered crisply.

"Jordan," Gretta murmured, "Please leave us. I'll explain."

"But—"

"Please."

Bowing slightly, the young man reached for Gretta's hand, saw his mistake and turned away. "Goodbye," he said. But she did not answer.

When he was gone, Louis held up his hand to keep her from speaking. "There's no need to explain, my dear. I have eyes. It's quite clear that you've been carrying on your little affair under my nose. I suspected all along that you hadn't really forgotten the snivelling womanish boy."

Gretta shivered at her husband's utter calm and the level tone of his voice. Somehow this cool detachment was worse than anger would have been. "I married *you,*" she reminded him.

"Why, I wonder? No doubt it was the money, or your parents forced you into it, or both. Or perhaps you disliked me enough to want to make me into a laughingstock by taking lovers every time you got a chance."

"Stop it!" she cried. "Your daughter might hear you. She's only four. She wouldn't understand."

"Is she my daughter?" Now, for the first time, a shadow of pain crossed his face and his eyes, as empty as polished stones, came to blazing life.

"Of course she is. How dare you—"

"Do you know why I married you?" Louis continued as if he had not heard her. "Because I thought you were different from all the other flighty, undependable women who care for nothing but themselves. But I see now that you are just as weak as they." He gazed beyond his wife to the sparkling sunlit window, but the light was not reflected in his eyes.

"I despise weakness, my dear, in anyone. But most especially in my wife. I see now that you were not worth my time and effort after all. A waste of emotion, no more and no less. Evidently you don't care, so I'll oblige by returning the favor." Then he stepped back and scrutinized her one last time, to see if she would even bother to protest, but when his wife did not move as much as an eyelash, Von Hoffman let out his breath in a brief sigh and the shutters in his eyes snapped permanently closed.

Gretta knew that he would never look at her again with anything but this icy regard, but she did not stop him when he turned to go. She did not attempt to explain that he was wrong and that Jordan had never been her lover. She did not tell him that the young man's tears had been the result of Gretta's decision that she should never see him again. She did not tell her husband that he had misjudged her brutally, that she was not flighty or undependable or weak.

She let him go, because in one thing he had been right; she had married him for the money, because her family had insisted. She had come to him unwillingly, caring for him not at all. And she *had* loved Jordan, always, with every fiber of her being. Or at least she had thought so—until the instant when she saw the coldly disappointed look on Louis' face. At the very moment when he shut her out of his heart forever, she had seen the truth about her feelings, and now, suddenly, the pain of loss was suffocating.

"Louis," she cried impulsively, but he was already gone, and, despite the wash of sunlight, the room—and her arms—were bleak and cold and empty. . . .

. . . . Gretta clutched tighter at the boy whose head rested on her knee, but he drew away from her and began to wipe the tears from his cheeks. "Men don't cry," he told her gravely. "I forgot."

The sudden stinging in the back of her eyes made Gretta glance up to the place where her husband had stood a moment before, but he had disappeared, leaving behind nothing but the hollow echo of his footsteps in the empty hall.

After he had held Cory, listened to her ravings, forced her to take her laudanum and watched her cry herself to sleep, Greg went looking for Katherine. He found her sitting comfortably behind his desk in the study, going through his papers with tireless energy. Without making a sound, he crept into the room and came up behind her. Then, when she sensed his presence and turned to face him, he grasped her shoulders in a bruising grip and lifted her forcibly from the chair. "Bitch!" he hissed and, pushing her away from him, he slapped her across the face with all his strength.

Katherine gasped, rubbed her cheek for an instant, then lunged for the letter opener that lay on the desk between them. Raising it threateningly in her father's direction, she cried raggedly, "If you ever touch me again, I swear I'll kill you."

Greg sensed that she meant it; there was no mistaking the murderous light in her eyes. "You aren't afraid of hanging?" he inquired, making an effort to hold his anger in check.

By now Katherine had recovered from her own surprise and sudden rage, but she held the letter opener between them as a warning just the same. "I'd tell them Mama did it," she explained casually. "I can prove that she's mad easily enough. Besides, we both know that murderers don't always pay for their crimes."

Greg realized she was deliberately baiting him and decided he would not play along. "Well," he said, "you'd just better be damned sure I'm dead before you go, because you know as well as I do that it wouldn't be a good idea to make me your enemy."

"Just what does that mean?"

"It means I have the power to destroy you, my dear." Taking a cigar out of the carved silver box on the desktop, he busied himself with lighting it while Katherine stood watching in silence.

"You see," Greg continued, seating himself in the chair and placing his feet on the edge of the desk, "I know things about you that you might not want to become common knowledge. I know you want to get married—you told me so. But I'll tell you a little secret. You may be very rich and very beautiful, but there are just certain things most men can't accept in their wives. You'd best take care with me, Katherine, because if you push me too far, I'll make certain you spend the rest of your life alone."

For a long moment after he had finished speaking, Katherine did not move so much as a muscle, so rigid was her fury. And what angered her the most was that she knew he was right; he *could* ruin her. "I know things, too," she said at last in a surprisingly steady voice. "And I could *make* Mama kill you. All I'd have to do is tell her the truth about you and—"

"Don't say it!" Greg warned. "Just don't. I can understand your desire to get back at me, but I want to know how you can even consider doing something like that to your mother?"

"You don't care what you do to me," his daughter replied. "Perhaps it's a family weakness."

Her tone was light and falsely unconcerned—the tone her father hated most. "You really *don't* care, do you?" His eyebrows came together in concentration as he searched her eyes, looking for a sign of human understanding, but they were blank, just as he had known they would be.

"I follow your example, Papa," she told him. "I care only for myself." Then she dropped the letter opener on the desk with a clatter and left the room, her head high.

She reminded him, in that instant, of the proud and fearless woman who had stepped into his life one day fourteen years ago and torn his world up by the roots. A flash of remembered pain ripped through his chest, but he struggled ruthlessly to suppress the memories that came with it. It was then that he realized how little the agony had receded over the past few years; it was with him now, as vibrant and devastating as the day when she had left him without a backward glance. He had thought he would forget, but he had been wrong. Then, at last, he allowed himself to repeat aloud the name that had haunted him for so long. "Medora," he groaned and buried his head in his hands.

Chapter 6

Medora hovered at Phillipe's shoulder, watching anxiously as **he** lowered Anais on to her bed. Then they worked together to remove the soiled jacket and wash away the blood from the girl's face.

"How is she, really?" Medora asked, when Anais lay still with the blankets tucked around her.

"She may have a concussion, but I don't think anything's broken," Phillipe whispered. Laying a hand on his stepmother's shoulder, he added, "She'll be all right. I know it. And the doctor should be here soon."

When Medora nodded dumbly and did not move, Phillipe pulled a chair up to the bedside and directed her toward it. "Sit down," he advised. "You look a little pale yourself."

Medora did as he told her, but her eyes never left her daughter's face. She was not even aware that her stepson had left the room, nor did she see the look of compassion with which he had regarded her as he slipped quietly away.

Braiding her hands together in her lap, Medora gazed down at Anais' pale, almost transparent skin, colored only by the jagged gash that ran across her forehead and disappeared into her thick black hair. The child's breathing was slow and labored, and Medora felt each struggling heartbeat as if it were her own. It was not until she had seen her daughter lying helpless and unconscious before her that Medora realized how precious the girl had become to her. Anais was all she had left of Antoine and it hurt her too much to sit here helplessly looking into that familiar and vulnerable face. Dear God, if she were to lose this child too—

"Mama?" Anais' eyelids fluttered open and she seemed to focus on her mother's face with difficulty. "Mama, it hurts."

The rush of relief that surged through Medora's body carried with it a terrible welling of anger at the nearness of another catastrophe. "Anais, why did you do such a thing? Surely you must have known—"

The girl's eyes filled with tears as the mist began to clear from her numbed brain. "I'm sorry, Mama, really. I didn't mean to cause you trouble. I just—I had to get away. I'm sorry." The tears trickled over onto her cheeks and she bit her lip and turned away.

Medora's breath caught in her throat as she realized that she had turned her own frustration against her injured child. "It's all right," she murmured. "I'm the one who's sorry. Now, let me see your head."

Anais looked up and, at the expression on her mother's face, she reached up blindly. Medora caught her daughter in her arms and they clung together, unaware, for the moment, of the many sturdy walls of stone that had begun to rise between them.

"I won't ride in the snow again," Anais said as she collapsed once more into the pillows, wincing at the streak of agony that made the bright colors explode in her head.

"No," Medora agreed softly. Then she brushed the hair back from her daughter's face with a hand that had long been a stranger to those dark, dishevelled curls.

"The doctor is here," Von Hoffman announced, opening

the door to usher the man into the bedroom. "We should leave him to do his work alone, I think," Louis added.

Medora nodded, gave Anais one more trembling smile, then rose and left the room. When the door was safely shut behind her, she closed her eyes and leaned against the nearest wall, as if she could no longer stand on her own. *"How* could she have been so stupid?" she demanded, addressing a dark, silent corner of the hallway.

Medora had barely spoken to her father in the past few days; the two seemed to be balanced on a precarious tightrope which had begun to stretch to the breaking point. "Perhaps," Von Hoffman suggested stiffly, "it's because she is so much like her mother."

His daughter gave him a long, searching look, then, remembering her son weeping downstairs, she went to see how the boy was doing.

Von Hoffman waited until the doctor had checked Anais over, proclaimed that nothing was broken, and put a few stitches in the wound on her forehead. But when the man had gone, Louis went to sit beside his granddaughter. He had grown fond of this moody, dark-haired child in the past month, and it disturbed him to see her lying with her hair tumbled in disorder across the pillow, her face the color of bleached ashes. Her smooth skin was marred by a jagged cut which ran from just above her ear to the middle of her forehead. But at least it followed the hairline; if there was a scar, her thick black curls would cover it.

Anais opened her eyes, her long lashes fluttering for a moment against her pale cheeks. Her gaze was steady as she contemplated the man at her bedside, but there was some deep, disquieting emotion glowing in those wide black eyes.

Von Hoffman waited a moment to see if the girl would speak, but when she did not, he asked finally, "What are you thinking?"

"That I don't want to go to North Dakota," she said,

her voice taut with sudden determination. "That I'll hate it there, but no one will listen to me." Her voice rose with every word until she propped herself up on her elbow, wincing at the pain it caused her, and pleaded, "Let me stay here, Grandfather. I won't be any trouble. I promise."

Von Hoffman was touched in spite of himself by the desperation of her plea, and he did not like the flush of color that rushed to her cheeks, then disappeared, leaving her paler than ever before. He would miss her when she went, he realized, more than he had imagined. "I can't my dear," he told her.

Anais clutched the cool white sheet with trembling fingers. She had decided long ago that she had found a kindred spirit in her grandfather. He seemed to be the only one besides herself who understood the madness in Medora's plan. And suddenly the need to stay behind was so great in her that it eclipsed even the shooting pain in her head. She was choking with the strength of her emotion, and what had once been merely disinclination had become dread. Surely her grandfather would not really let her down. "Please," she whispered.

Leaning back in his chair, Von Hoffman pressed his hands together, fingertip to fingertip. "I'm sorry, Anais," he said. "But I've been thinking a great deal lately, and I've decided that it might just be best for you to go to the Badlands. Your mother has made her decision and you should obey her, even though you feel you'll be unhappy there."

Anais lay back among the pillows and regarded him curiously. "Why?"

"It's just better that way, for all of us. And, who knows, you might even make it easier for me. I'll want to know what's going on out there, and I'm afraid your mother is not a very good correspondent. But you could write regularly and give me the news. I'd appreciate that. In fact," he leaned forward, his eyes fixed on the girl's face, "I'd be very grateful."

Anais wrinkled her brow, then reached up to try to wipe away the pain her action had caused. Her mind was beginning to become foggy and her eyes could no longer focus correctly. It must be the drug the doctor had given her to make her sleep. But she had to think about what Von Hoffman had said just now. She sensed, even in her daze, that he was asking her something important. "I don't—" she began.

"I've asked you to write to me," her grandfather prompted. "Just think about it. But right now you should sleep."

Nodding dumbly, too weary to open her mouth and respond, the girl let her eyelids slide closed. She was vaguely aware when her grandfather rose and left her, and she could not reach out to stop him. So now he had abandoned her, too. Just like all the others. Just like her father.

Anais' chest was suddenly heavy with a weight she could not bear and her eyes burned with agonizing dryness. She would not think about her father, she swore to herself. She would not. But when she opened her eyes and struggled to wipe his image from her mind, she found that he would not leave her. Now, when she didn't want him, he refused to go.

Anais gazed around the empty room while her heart thudded hollowly in her ears, and she wondered why, all at once, the lamplight had faded into dimness, and the melancholy shadows had grown so huge and unforgiving.

The hush of late afternoon had descended on the room where David St. Clair stood at the window, staring out at the winter wasteland before him. With his elbows resting on the windowsill, he sat unmoving, hoping for a flash of deep green to shatter the stillness of infinite white beyond the heavy glass. He was waiting for Katherine to come flying across the snowbound landscape on her fine horse, her laughter riding the back of the wind, but David suspected he waited in vain.

He had not seen his fiancée for two weeks, and he had come to the conclusion that she was avoiding him, though he couldn't say why. He only knew that she had changed since that afternoon on the hill. She had become silent and moody and secretive, and he felt that he did not even know her anymore. It was possible, he admitted reluctantly, that he never *had* known her, not really. He had always realized that Katherine treasured her privacy and that there was a side of her that others rarely saw, but somehow he had never expected this.

It was not that she didn't laugh anymore; it was just that her laughter had a harsh, raw sound that lacked any feeling of real enjoyment. When he was with her, he was always conscious of the tension that made her speak sharply to him, and she no longer let him touch her at all, not even to brush a stray hair from her face. Katherine's world had become a fortress and she had slammed the gate, leaving David to face the cold alone.

David's younger brother Stephen sauntered into the room with the usual book of poetry under his arm, but he paused when he noticed that he was not alone. With a long, speculative look at David, Stephen shook his pale blond head and went to stand beside his brother. "Still waiting for Katherine?" he asked, running one hand absently through his curly reddish beard.

David turned in surprise, ashamed that he had been discovered once again. "I suppose so," he muttered.

Stephen moved a stack of books aside and sat down in a nearby chair. He was ten years younger than his brother, just twenty, yet sometimes he felt a great deal older. Obviously, David had never learned how to assert himself. "If I were you, I'd just go after her."

David shook his head. "She has to come to me."

"I don't see why." Stephen focused his pale blue eyes intently on his brother's face. "You're still engaged, aren't you?"

"Yes."

"Well, then, just go over to the ranch and make her listen to you."

"What would you suggest I say?" He knew he should not have asked as soon as he saw the flickering light in Stephen's eyes.

"Ask her to set the wedding date," the younger brother suggested with a smug little smile.

David looked away. He had already done so, many times, but Katherine merely put him off with one excuse after another.

"It's time she decided," Stephen declared. It annoyed him that this woman could make his brother squirm so. Stephen himself had done it often, but that was different. "You can't wait much longer and neither can we," he added slyly.

"I know," David said as he rose impatiently from his seat. He was aware that his brother was referring to the family's financial situation, which had begun to look worse every day. Most of the St. Clair cattle had died last year from some mysterious disease, and now the government was raising property taxes yet again. The St. Clair fortune had dwindled steadily away in the five years since they had come to the Badlands and they were becoming desperate. Under those circumstances, David's engagement to Katherine Pendleton, the wealthiest woman in the valley, had seemed like a blessing sent directly from heaven.

But Katherine was hesitating, and David could feel the anxiety of his parents hovering over him every minute of the day. He was their only chance. But now it seemed that he was losing her, and he feared that loss more deeply than any of them could imagine. It was not that he might never see her money. It was, instead, that he might never see her face again.

"I'll do what I can to force a decision," David assured his brother, "but I'm afraid Katherine has a mind of her own." As he turned toward the window again, he thought he saw a brief flash of doubt cross Stephen's face. But it was always so difficult to read the thoughts that burned behind those strange, pale eyes, which always seemed to be looking for something just out of reach.

"I don't understand why you just don't grab her by the shoulders and ask her straight out," the younger man said.

But David understood. As he gazed out the window at the winged shadows which the fast-moving clouds made on the fields of clean white snow, he knew that he dared not ask Katherine about her intentions because he thought he already knew her answer. And it was an answer he could not bear to hear.

Louis Von Hoffman sat staring glumly at his fine china plate and the elegant silver which framed it. For once he was not pleased with his possessions, not even the expensive crystal glasses which, with the light of the many candles, painted rainbows on the fine lace tablecloth. In deference to Medora's distaste, he had turned off the electric lights for the evening. For six weeks he had sat at this table with Gretta and Medora on his left and Phillipe and William on his right, but never before had the silence hung above them as it did now, draping the table in an invisible pall. Or maybe it was just his own sick fancies that made this dinner seem so interminable.

Von Hoffman divided his time between watching the handsome young Phillipe, who seemed to hold Medora's future in his hands, and Medora herself, whose gaze was always bleak and forbidding. Her father found that for the first time in his life, he was intimidated by his daughter. The strain between them had not lessened in the past weeks, and he had finally begun to realize that he could not bear it anymore. Something, or someone, had to break.

"You're leaving for Chicago in the morning?" Louis asked, turning in Phillipe's direction.

"Yes. We've already arranged several meetings with Swift," William answered. He had become used to fielding Von Hoffman's numerous inquiries into the progress of their plans, since Phillipe had been attempting to remain in the background, at least in Von Hoffman's presence. He was determined not to give Medora's father grounds for his unreasonable anger.

"Why Swift? He's the biggest meatpacker in the country. He certainly doesn't need to talk to small fry like you," Louis observed, watching closely for Phillipe's reaction.

"He doesn't *need* to," the young man replied, speaking up for the first time in the long, tedious meal, "but he wants to."

"We're bringing along several members of the Beef Trust and a couple of wholesalers to help us state our case," William interjected. "We thought it might be more convincing if we presented Swift with a well-organized group effort."

Von Hoffman swirled the wine in his glass and ignored the half-finished meal on his plate. "You trust these, shall we call them 'allies,' implicitly, of course?"

"No, sir," Phillipe assured him. He was aware that Louis was trying to make him slip, to catch him up in some unpardonable error of judgment, but he did not intend to be baited. "At the moment I make it worth their while to stand by me. They can see that beef that need not be transported across the country on the hoof will be cheaper for them, and that is a language they understand. I trust them now because I'm offering them the best possibility for profit, but if a better offer comes along, I don't doubt they would desert me without a qualm. You see, I've been thinking ahead, laying a careful groundwork before I act. It's the only way to succeed."

Von Hoffman took a sip of wine in order to stifle the snort of disbelief that rose in his throat. "Do you really think you're any more likely to do it than your father was?"

Drawing a deep breath, Phillipe looked the older man directly in the eye and said, "Mr. Von Hoffman, I am *not* my father."

Louis did not look at Medora, but he could feel her expressionless gaze fixed on him. "No?" he said. "Are you certain?"

"Yes, sir. I've learned a great deal from the Marquis, it's true, but I've taken my lessons from his failures as well as his successes."

Von Hoffman knew he should stop this exchange here and now, but he simply could not do it. "I wasn't aware he had had any successes."

The expression on Phillipe's face did not alter by so much as the twitch of a muscle. "You're wrong, sir. He married your daughter, didn't he?"

The utter stillness that descended on the group in that moment was so fragile that a single breath might have shattered it. Von Hoffman stared intently into his blood-red wine and a flash of anger rose, then faded into a dull glow. The young man was not afraid, that was certain. And he was no fool either. As Phillipe had said, he was not like his father. It was only then that Louis realized he had begun to conceive a grudging admiration for the man in the past month. He was ashamed to admit it—he was dazed by the realization—but it was, nevertheless, true. "Is no one going to eat?" he asked finally.

Gretta turned back to her food at once, and soon everyone else did likewise. The rest of the meal was accomplished in silence, but Von Hoffman was uncomfortably aware of the dull green gleam of Medora's gaze; he felt it upon him time and again like the probing of a doctor's finger in an open wound.

When at last dessert was served, Louis found that he could not stand another moment of his daughter's eyes upon him. "I have decided," he announced abruptly, "to help finance the reopening of the packing plant. It just might work."

Phillipe and William exchanged triumphant smiles, but when they started to thank him, Von Hoffman interrupted. "We'll draw up the papers in the morning. But just now I want to enjoy my coffee and dessert."

It was not until the others had left the dining room and only Medora remained that Louis spoke again. "Could you stay for a moment?" he asked.

Medora rose and came to stand beside him. "Thank you, Papa."

Von Hoffman looked up at her in the brilliant lamplight, and he saw for the first time that the red hair he had always loved had begun to show traces of gray. The light was unfriendly to his daughter's face and the absence of shadow made her appear unnaturally harsh. The tension in her body was reflected in her deep green eyes, and he realized all at once that she was as fragile as the rainbow crystal which graced his table—her presence was as fascinating, her beauty as easily shattered. This was Medora, who was stronger than any woman he had ever known. Medora, who could not be broken. How frightening, he thought. How dismal and futile everything was. "Will you forgive me now?" he asked simply.

Medora's brows came together in a frown and there was a flash of what might have been pity in her eyes. "Do you really want me to forgive you just because of the money?"

Louis reached out to lay a hand on her arm. "I want your forgiveness, Medora. Whatever the cost."

There was a long, painful silence during which the soft pulse of the lamplight became almost audible. Then Medora whispered, "The 'cost' is your faith in me, Papa, and I'm afraid it just doesn't exist." Her hand closed over his for a moment and then she shook her head in despair. "Perhaps it never did." Her voice shook a little and, for an instant, her face softened enough to reveal a shadow of her pain, but her eyes were as bleak and barren as a winter garden. "Goodnight," she murmured before she released his hand and turned away.

Von Hoffman let her go. He knew now that there was nothing left to say. Because he realized all at once that his daughter had spoken no less than the truth. He watched the softly curved line of her retreating back and his heart twisted inside him. For suddenly Medora was a stranger to him; it was as if he had never known her at all. And reality closed around him like a suffocating shadow in the room of blazing light.

With her breath coming in wrenching gasps, Cory Pendleton ran blindly. She had to get away, she thought, stumbling across the uneven ground, her feet sinking into the powdered snow. She must go while she still could, before they came and put her away. Oblivious to the stinging cold that penetrated her thin dress, Cory clutched her ancient shawl around her and tried ineffectually to keep the limp strands of hair out of her face. She knew she must move quickly or it would be too late. Once Medora arrived—

Cory bit her lip at the torment that name inspired in her.

But Medora was dead, she assured herself, turning back once to make sure that the house was out of sight. Medora was certainly dead. Or was she? Cory could not remember.

She felt the scream rising in her throat, but she choked it down. She had to try to remember, but she knew it was hopeless. When she thought of the world back then, it was nothing but darkness, broken now and then by shooting many-colored lights. There was nothing clear, only insubstantial shadows. Except for Greg's face—that she would never forget.

He would come after her soon, she knew. But why was he so angry? Why did he look at her with such hatred? Cory tripped over a root just then and fell sprawling into a snowdrift at the base of an old weathered tree. Floundering wildly with outflung arms, she tried to grasp the trunk and pull herself upright, but her hands would not obey her mind. It was because she could not remember, she knew. If only she could remember, then everything would be all right, and the blackness would not stalk her anymore. But for now she was powerless to stop it, because her mind had snapped closed against invasion. Finally, she collapsed into the snow and lay there sobbing, the tree trunk less than an inch beyond her outstretched hands.

When Katherine came upon her mother a few minutes later, she had to fight to keep the sickness away. Cory lay there like an animal, huddled in the snow, shivering uncontrollably. She was wet and bedraggled, and her colorless hair was in wild disarray, but it was her hands, spread clawlike at the top of the drift, which held Katherine's attention. "How could you do this to us?" the young woman demanded. "Someone might have seen you."

Still weeping, her cheeks stained deep red from the cold, Cory looked up at her daughter with eyes that were absolutely blank.

Katherine shuddered convulsively without bothering to hide her disgust. "You know you're not supposed to go out alone," she said in a voice that was strangely unlike her own.

Her mother shook her head furiously. "I had to get away," she cried.

"From what?"

Drawing her brows together in concentration, Cory opened her lips several times before she managed to gasp, "I don't remember. I've tried to remember, but I just can't. Won't you help me, Katherine? I don't know what to do."

Katherine clenched her fists and her muscles turned to stone. "I'll take you home," she said firmly.

"NO-O-O-o-o-o!" Cory's wail held a terror that was almost inhuman. "They'll take me away, don't you understand? Don't make me go back. Please!"

Before Katherine realized what her mother intended, Cory had reached up and grasped her daughter's skirt with thin, bony fingers. "Please, please, please," she begged, repeating the single word like a sacred litany.

Katherine wanted to turn and flee. She wanted to remove those skeletal hands and get away where she could retch in the bushes alone. She wanted to escape the horror, the degradation of this whimpering, helpless woman who looked at her with the eyes of a hunted deer. Dear God, she wanted to wipe her mother from her memory so she need never again be sickened by the madness that had turned her into something less than a human being.

"Please, Katherine, help me!" Cory moaned in a voice from the center of her daughter's deepest nightmare.

She wanted to go, but something inside would not let her. Something forced her to drop to her knees and lay her hands on her mother's heaving shoulders.

"No! Don't take me back," the woman whispered. "She's coming and I can't—"

"Hush, Mama," Katherine murmured. "Hush now. No one's going to hurt you." Then she took her mother in her arms like a newborn child, cradling the dishevelled head against her sturdy shoulder. Katherine wanted to run, but she knew she could not do it. She was not quite ready to turn her back entirely. "Hush," she chanted, "everything will be all right. Hush now, Mama. I won't let them take you."

They knelt together, mother and daughter, rocking slowly back and forth, while the snow melted beneath them and the moisture crept into the folds of their gowns. And soon Katherine's crooning became one with her mother's sobs, and both were caught up in the cry of the bitter wind. But still they crouched there, swaying, swaying endlessly, as if to a song of despair that only they could hear.

Part III

The Badlands: Summer, 1898

"Life is but a battle and a passage. Life is worthwhile only through action; too bad if that action is fatal."
—Marquis de Mores
May, 1897

Chapter 7

The sky was a dazzling canopy of blue that stretched from one end of the North Dakota Badlands to the other, unbroken by a single hint of white. Shading his eyes against the blazing April sunlight, Phillipe shifted in his saddle and looked back over the familiar landscape that seemed to have materialized out of his dreams. The small town of Medora spread beneath him with its neatly ordered streets and buildings which faded into insignificance beside the power of the red-brown cliffs that circled it on two sides. The sculpted stone, carved by the ancient onslaught of wind and water, was more magnificent than Phillipe remembered, its bands of dark and light, sandstone, shale and burning lignite as unchanging as the wide expanse of vibrant azure sky. He sucked in his breath, amazed all over again at the beauty that rose like an unexpected blessing from the flat, rolling prairie all around.

"Did your memories do it justice?"

Phillipe turned until he could look into Johnny Goodall's weathered face. "I don't think any memory could be that powerful," the young man said.

"No," Goodall agreed, "nor any man either."

Phillipe had been surprised at how glad he had been to see Johnny waiting on the station platform as the train pulled in half an hour before. Goodall had been the foreman of Mores' ranch ever since the Marquis had first come to the Badlands, and Phillipe knew he was still a strong, dependable man.

Johnny had aged gracefully since the two men had last met, and though his sandy brown hair was now almost completely gray, it was still thick and healthy, and his hazel eyes had not yet lost their brightness. Even his tanned skin spoke of a man who still worked long hours beneath the fiery Dakota sun.

The two men turned toward the bluff in companionable silence, but Phillipe was still intensely aware of the curious glances that had followed the little group from the train station. The townspeople had lined the streets, their eyes full of questions, excitement and a certain degree of wariness. Phillipe hoped to banish those doubts in the next few weeks, though he knew it would be a difficult task. These people had not yet forgotten the dashing Frenchman who had earned their hatred in the two short years he had spent here. Brows furrowed in thought, the young man glanced at Medora who rode a little ahead of him. He would have to plan carefully to avoid the snares that had caught his father, and he knew Medora would be able to help him do so.

His stepmother carried her son Paul in the saddle before her, and her gaze seemed to devour the scene around her. She could not help but be moved by the wild beauty of the waving sea of blue-green buffalo grass, sprinkled here and there with a splash of orange wild lilies or red loco-weeds. And though the branches of the cottonwoods that hugged the riverbank were still stark against the sky, they were touched at every gnarled tip with new leaf buds. Even the majestic bald eagle, circling lazily overhead, brought a lump to her throat. But Medora was even more deeply moved by the memories that lay in wait in every curve and hollow.

She was not alone, she knew. They were riding, every

one of them, into a place where the past swept over them with the force of a Badlands wind in the heat of midsummer. And, like the heat, the images shimmered and wavered, distorting the scene like a thin silk curtain. Medora did not have to see Phillipe's face, or William's, to know they were feeling the same. Now, more than in Paris, the past was with them, holding them all in its unforgiving grip with the tenacity of a lion grasping its prey.

But that, too, was forgotten in the instant when she caught sight of the house the Marquis had built for her so long ago. It rested on the high, carved bluff just ahead, simple and low, with its clean white walls and bright red shutters. No doubt Johnny had seen that it was given a fresh coat of paint before they arrived, for it looked as new as the day she had first seen it. Medora paused, gazing up at the Chateau in silence, and when she felt a presence beside her, she looked up into Phillipe's eyes. She saw at once that he understood what she was feeling, and they exchanged a long, knowing smile. Nothing really mattered, she realized—not her pain or the spectre of the past or the knowledge she had gained through so much torment. They were all unimportant in the face of one simple fact—they were finally home.

The afternoon air was hushed and waiting as the wild dancing flames exploded suddenly into the stillness. The scattered pieces of dried wood blazed into radiant orange light and the grass shriveled beneath the reaching fingers of fire that swept across the flat ground just beyond the water. Ringed by the river and a straggling offshoot that had been created in the early spring floods, the flames spat and crackled and turned the air to smoke and shimmering waves of heat.

Stephen St. Clair pulled tight on the reins so that his restless horse paused at the outer edge of the small, raging

tendrils that twined themselves together, then sprang apart
in red-gold arcs of flame. For an instant the pulsing golden
light was reflected in his pale eyes, then his hands locked
together until the blood had drained from his cool fingers.
There was nothing he could do to stop the rising waves
of flame and he knew it. But at least it was far enough
away from any structures to not threaten more than this
lonely stretch of ground. And, though the spring mud had
finally begun to harden, the ground was still damp from
the deep winter snow that had melted away less than a
month ago. With any luck at all, the flames would continue to burn toward the river, where they would eventually devour themselves and fade into harmless ashes.

Stephen sat motionless, guarding the seething fire that
moved like a live thing at his feet. What a homecoming
for the Vallombrosas, he thought. But, then, maybe it was
no more than they deserved. He had ridden down to the
river today to see the arrival of the family whose unexpected return had rocked the valley from end to end, but
Stephen himself had not been impressed. Because he
knew, although David had been too blind to guess, that it
was the knowledge of today's arrival which had upset
Katherine Pendleton so badly.

For that reason alone, Stephen had been curious to
catch a glimpse of the interlopers. If they threatened
David's marriage, then they were worth his younger
brother's attention. An arm of bright red flame rose suddenly, then collapsed upon itself, and Stephen shifted in
the saddle. He had been pleased to see that there were
children in the family. That might just give him the excuse
he needed—

His thoughts were interrupted when he heard a hint of
movement behind him. Stephen turned in time to see a
woman in gray stop at the edge of the fire and stare in
fascination at the changing colors. She stood still for only
a moment, but it was long enough for St. Clair to note

her misshapen, tattered gray gown and the forlorn, lifeless strands of her colorless hair. Then without looking up, she turned to flee wildly, her ragged shawl flapping behind her, as if all the demons of hell were following at her heels. Stephen saw only a flash of a pale, drawn face and wide, empty eyes, but he had not needed to see more.

There had been nothing in those hollow eyes but fear— a fear so all-consuming that it verged on utter madness.

The woman moved on feet that were unnaturally silent, and once she had disappeared into the trees, Stephen could not tell which direction she had taken. When he knew she was gone, he sat running his fingers thoughtfully through his beard. Surely that pitiful woman had been Cory Pendleton. But what was she doing hovering near the river like a silent wraith and dressed like a beggar? And what was she so afraid of?

Glancing back at the fire, Stephen listened for the whisper of retreating footsteps, and his eyes narrowed in speculation at the vivid memory of that ravaged face, touched by the raging light of these colored flames. So, he mused silently, that was how things were, and his eyes flicked back and forth, back and forth between the place where Cory Pendleton had disappeared and the brilliant fire that burned at his feet.

The Chateau, which had appeared silent and deserted, as if it slumbered in the warmth of late afternoon, came suddenly to life as Cassie, the cook, came running around the side of the house with several of the maids following behind.

Phillipe leapt from his horse, but before he could open his mouth to greet her, he was enveloped by a pair of fleshy arms that threatened to squeeze the breath out of him. Then Cassie released him and stood back, contemplating the young man who stood before her, laughing.

"Well," she muttered, "I guess you figured if you waited long enough to come back I wouldn't recognize you anymore. But you was wrong, as always." She busied herself with wiping her hands on her huge apron, which betrayed the amount of activity that had been going on in the kitchen that afternoon.

"Cassie," Phillipe said, "I didn't realize how much I'd missed you until I saw you standing there, just exactly the same as on the day we left."

The cook grunted in disbelief and shook her wiry gray head at the young man's foolishness. "I'm fifty-one years old, boy. And you can't tell me that it don't show on my face. Or here." She pointed to her ever-expanding belly.

It was true that her seamed, leathery face was crisscrossed with a few more lines than he remembered, and her body was certainly more rotund, but her lopsided smile was the same, and she wore the same kind of tattered men's walking boots which showed beneath her old-fashioned checkered skirt. Linking his arm with hers, Phillipe drew her toward the others.

Medora took a long, fond look at the woman who, nearly fifteen years before, had delivered Anais in the midst of a hail of bullets, then she threw her arms around Cassie's neck. "It's good to be back," Medora said fervently.

"And good to have you, too," the cook muttered. "Thought I'd die of boredom a thousand times while you was away, but I knew I'd better pull myself through or you'd starve plumb to death when you *did* come back."

Anais stood apart and listened to these warm greetings in silence. She did not remember Cassie, or the house, or this bleak stone valley; she had been too young when they left here. And now she was, as always, a stranger, forgotten in the excitement of the moment. But as she guided her horse around the long, covered porch that surrounded the house on two sides, a slight tinge of distant memory tugged at the back of her mind. There *had* been a face that meant something to her then, but she didn't know whose. Anais closed her eyes and tried to bring the distorted features into focus, but they hovered just beyond her vision, dark and shadowed with the things that had happened to the girl since she had last lived here.

Shaking her head to clear it of confusion, Anais opened her eyes and glanced once down at the river that curled past at the foot of the bluff. It was then that she saw the smoke twining its soft gray fingers among the branches of the cottonwoods. Her heart contracted painfully at the knowledge that a fire burned somewhere just out of sight. Their first day here and already the land was rejecting them. But the house blocked the distant billows of smoke from the sight of the others, and they were too blind to know what it meant anyway. With a brief look over her shoulder, the girl urged her horse down the hill. She did not know what instinct pulled her; she only knew she had to go.

Long before the trees parted to reveal the dance of the flames, Anais smelled the acrid smoke and her heart beat faster. Then, all at once, she was there, and her horse whinnied nervously as the blaze came into view. It was beautiful in a way, she thought. Almost magic as the colors melded and separated into red-gold and orange in shifting patterns of burning light. The warped emotions of others could put no restraints on this living, changing thing that consumed the ground beneath her feet, and the fire was pure, untainted, unrestrained.

Drawing a deep breath, she smiled a strange half-smile, then Anais looked up and her eyes met the searching gaze of a tall, blond stranger. From across the blaze, through the moving, shivering air, they stared at one another and neither felt the slightest inclination to move. It was as if some invisible force had brought them here, to this precise moment, to give them both a message whose import they could not even guess. Anais did not know what that message might be; she only knew that those pale blue eyes held her, in that instant, with the force of steel hands.

She had just opened her mouth to speak when a soft, musical voice said, "Is that you, Athenais?"

For a moment, she was certain it was the man who had spoken, but then she felt a presence beside her and realized she had been mistaken. The woman who stood with her hand resting on the horse's flank looked up at Anais with troubled eyes, and her lips slightly parted, as if the words had barely slipped away. She was half-covered with shadow, but the girl recognized her beauty just the same. Her delicately carved features and soft brown skin were framed by thick black braids that circled her head, and her eyes were dark brown and full of mystery. "They call me Anais now," the girl replied.

Mianne Goodall nodded gravely. "I wonder if you remember that we were friends a long time ago." She kept her voice steady with great difficulty, for she did not want to frighten this fragile spirit away. But Mianne was deeply disturbed by the fire that seemed to have sprung up out of nowhere. She had been even more troubled to find Anais staring, enthralled, as if the fire had already made her its slave. She had known that this day would bring change to her sheltered life, but she had never expected this. She had come to the river for comfort and found instead a blazing reminder of her premonition of trouble to come.

Anais chewed her lip thoughtfully as she considered the woman's lilting voice. Could this be the face she had known once before? "I think I do remember." Wrinkling her forehead in concentration, she sought to catch the memory and hold it fast, but the past was still too far away. "It must have been difficult then," she said at last.

Mianne thought of the girl she had been long ago, and her eyes clouded briefly with remembered pain. When

Anais saw that pain, she felt a sudden tightness in her throat. Only once before in her life had she seen the expression of helpless despair that gave this woman's eyes such a disturbing radiance, and that had been just after the Marquis' death, when Anais had looked long and carefully into her own mirror.

"We must go now," Mianne prompted, shattering the girl's moment of recognition. "It's too dangerous here, and I think the others are coming to try to put the fire out."

When Anais heard the thundering of hooves echoing through the ground, she realized that the men from the Chateau must have seen the smoke at last, and now they were coming down the path to the river toward the flames.

"Come," Mianne urged again.

Only then did Anais turn back to the fire, and she saw with a flicker of disappointment that the blue-eyed stranger had vanished. Reluctantly, she turned her horse and followed Mianne away from the pulsing golden center of the flames that had held her captive in a world beyond her own, if only for a brief glittering moment.

Chapter 8

Medora leaned down to whisper reassurance to her horse as it flew across the rolling fields and left the sleeping house behind. She had awakened this morning cold and restless after her first night in the Badlands, and decided to take a long ride over the land she and her husband had abandoned long ago. Medora wanted to see it all, to reassure herself that it had not changed—that all the hills and hollows were the same ones she had known before. So she had crept down to the stables while the morning mist still clung tenaciously to the budding treetops, saddled her horse, and ridden away.

The brisk air felt invigorating as the wind carried it across her cheeks, and Medora felt a rush of excitement at the promise of success she sensed in the cool breeze. Everywhere she looked, she could see the evidence of Goodall's careful stewardship. The grass was long and thick, the cattle scattered across the range healthy and contented. She understood that the packing plant had been kept up as carefully as the ranch, and Medora knew that her plans were well on the way to becoming reality.

On an impulse, she turned her horse toward the river, where the water rumbled by, as unchanging as the wide sky above. It was peaceful here, she noticed as the horse paused on the muddy bank. Closing her eyes, Medora let the sounds of the morning flutter past, and she found that she was content for the first time in many months. But then a jingle of reins and bit that did not belong to the morning roused her, and she looked up to find herself facing Greg Pendleton across the narrow river.

Medora's fingers tightened convulsively on the reins, and even the river seemed to cease as she stared into the angular face of the man who had ridden out of her nightmare to meet her here on the bank. She was frozen for an instant, as if bound by the weight of hard winter ice, and she saw that he was no more able to move than she. A profound silence fell upon them, linking them across the water like an invisible bridge that held them apart, then Greg's horse snorted—a simple sound that nevertheless destroyed the waiting stillness in an instant. . . .

. . . . June, 1884—The distant bleating of the lost calf broke through the numbing haze of afternoon heat, and Medora urged her horse toward the pitiful cry that seemed to rise from the center of the still green leaves. The calf had wandered away from the rest of the herd the night before, and Medora had been searching for the animal since late morning. She recognized the fear in those faraway bleats of distress, and she leaned forward in the saddle, as if her determination to find the calf would somehow speed her progress.

Just when her horse seemed to join with the racing wind in its course toward the group of box elder that hid the calf from sight, the animal exploded from among the low bushes and stumbled blindly toward the river. Medora held her breath back in her throat as she pulled sharply on the reins. She had to get to the river before the calf, in its headlong flight, stumbled blindly into the rushing water. She had to stop it before it destroyed itself.

Then, all at once, the tiny animal veered away from its path and began to run toward its pursuer. Medora let her breath escape in surprise, then she saw the reason for the sudden change. Greg Pendleton was bearing down on the animal from the far left, and he took a moment to look up and motion for Medora to approach from the other side. She was angry that he should presume to instruct her and angry that he had intruded on the chase which, she realized, she had been enjoying until a moment ago. Still, she could see that the calf could not outrun both riders, so she followed Greg's directions, swerving her animal from side to side until the calf cowered helplessly with the formidable wall of bushes and trees at its back.

Greg paused to catch his breath, then leaned toward Medora. "You see that two is better than one, my dear. Just remember, together we can do anything."

In that moment, his triumphant smile reminded her of her father, but Medora suppressed the thought before it could become fully formed. This man was no knight who had come to her aid—unasked, she reminded herself—but her enemy. She had nothing to say to him. Sliding from her saddle, she took a step toward the cornered calf, but before she could take another, Greg had joined her on the ground. He closed his warm fingers around her arm and shook his head warningly. "Let him get over his fright. If you try to take him now, he'll only find a way to run again. And while you're waiting, I'm sure we can find something to occupy us."

His head came down and his seeking lips met hers, but Medora pushed him away. "Don't touch me again," she hissed.

This time, Greg's smile was slightly strained. "There was a time when your body begged for me to touch it. That night changed things between us, Medora. You know that as well as I do."

Shaking her head in denial, Medora stood facing him

with icy green fire in her eyes. She did not like to be reminded of that night on the riverbank with Greg, but she knew the memory would follow her for the rest of her days. It had been insane, and she knew she could not let this man fuel her madness any further. "I made a mistake," she said, each word clear and distinct. "It won't ever happen again."

With hands that were suddenly brutal, Greg dragged her toward him. "Don't be a fool," he snarled. "The cost of your petty morality is far too high."

"*You* are the fool. I don't want you. Can't you understand that?"

Greg closed his eyes for a moment, to hide the flash of pain that he knew she must never see, then he whispered raggedly, "No, I can't."

His hands slackened their grip a little, and Medora pulled herself free of his grasp. "Leave me alone, Greg," she warned. "I won't stand by calmly and allow you to ruin my life and my husband's. And I'll tell you this only once more; I made my *one* mistake and it's the last you'll ever know." *Then she turned away, but as she approached the trembling calf, determined at last to put Greg Pendleton out of her mind, she could feel his steel gray eyes burning into her back like molten fire. . . .*

. . . . Greg's eyes were as still as frozen silver—not a glimmer of emotion marred their placid surface, but his gaze seemed to burn through Medora as if she were made of the vaporous mist that had disappeared with the growing heat of the sun. He saw her tense briefly, but then her eyes grew as blank as his, and Greg knew that Medora could no more read his thoughts than he could read hers. The years had made them into strangers after all, though they had not altered the clean, firm lines of her face or the calm directness of her gaze. The woman who sat before him now was still Medora, and she still had the power to shake him. It seemed to him that she had come back for no other reason than to torment him.

"Medora," he greeted her stiffly.

"Good morning, Greg." Medora was not yet ready to say more than that to the man who had nearly put an end to her marriage many years ago. She could not look him in the face without remembering her weakness, for which she had never been able to forgive herself. Antoine had forgiven her long ago, and he had never mentioned Greg's name again, but Medora wondered if she had been worthy of that kind of faith.

She was shocked at the sudden rush of grief for her dead husband that swept through her, raw and painful and frighteningly real. She had almost forgotten the bitter emptiness of her loss in the past few months, but this man, this place had brought it all back. And she could not bear to face it now, with Greg looking on, so, nodding slightly in a gesture of dismissal, Medora guided her horse up over the bank and away from Pendleton's empty gaze.

She was not aware that the man sat immobile, watching until long after she had disappeared. He could not rid himself of the image of that last imperious nod. How regal she appeared in her disdain, even after all these years. She was still unbowed by the weight of her recent grief and all the tragedies that had beset her—Medora was, without question, the strongest woman he had ever known. And, having seen her again, he now knew that, were he to continue to survive in the Badlands, he had no choice but to find a way to bring her permanently to her knees.

The light that filtered through the glass seemed to wrap Mianne in a tenuous net of woven radiance, and Phillipe paused on the threshold, contemplating the woman in front of him as if he had never seen her before. She was dressed simply in a plain shirtwaist and skirt, and her hair was tightly confined in the inevitable crown of braids. This elegant lady with her hands clasped loosely before her was not the same Mianne he had known years ago. It seemed she had grown up. He had been here three days already, and not once had Mianne spoken to him of her own accord, although she was unfailingly polite whenever *he* spoke to her. He sensed that something had changed in her—something so fundamental that she no longer even resembled the free wild spirit he had so admired once. Phillipe found that he was vaguely disappointed.

Sensing a presence behind her, Mianne moved slowly out of the pattern of light and turned to face Phillipe.

"I'm sorry to disturb you," he said. "I didn't realize anyone else would be up so early."

"You didn't disturb me," she replied placidly. But it was a lie. Since the moment of his family's arrival, Mianne had been plagued by some indefinable tension in the air which only she seemed to recognize. She could not forget the fire, so small that no one else had been troubled by it. But Mianne knew that the ground was still too damp from the winter for the fire to have begun on its own. Which left only one possibility, as far as she could see—it had been set on purpose.

Mianne felt strongly that those dancing flames had been merely a warning, a hint of what was to come if the Vallombrosas stayed in the Badlands. Yet the members of the family itself seemed unaware of the hidden danger—everyone except Anais.

But Mianne realized as she looked into Phillipe's clear blue eyes that the threat he had brought with him was more than just a danger to his family, for it threatened Mianne herself, though she could not say why. She only knew that suddenly the clear morning air had become thick and clouded with vague, disturbing images of the future, and she had to escape from their grasping spell. "I have chores," she said quietly. "If you'll excuse me."

"Mianne—" Phillipe called out in an attempt to stop her, but she had already gone. He stood for a moment where she had left him, remembering her eyes. They had been cold and empty; the flame that had once made them lovely had flickered and died long ago. And if Mianne had so easily become a stranger, what had happened to the others he had known here? Surprising himself with his sudden determination, he left the house and moved as if by instinct around the hilltop and down the path that led to the river.

Soon the vegetation beneath his booted feet became more lush, the blossoms of false lupine and the white pasqueflower more frequent, but Phillipe's attention was caught by the soft breath of spring wind that played in the sculptured branches of the cottonwoods overhead. At least these had not changed; the bare, graceful arms touched here and there with new buds moved languidly in the breeze, and their slow dance seemed to temper the wild pulse of rushing water below.

Phillipe found his way easily to the little clearing which he used to visit often in order to swim in the still icy pond at its center. The morning sun penetrated the tangle of branches overhead to touch the water with rippling fingers of light, and Phillipe realized how good it was to be back. But there was something missing, some spark that had made this place magic. "Katherine," he said aloud, as if speaking her name would conjure her out of the sparkling water.

And then, before his voice had quite died out, she was there, stepping out gracefully from under the trees, her dark hair spilling over her shoulders, her eyes glowing with her private thoughts. Her lips were turned up in the soft secret smile he remembered so well, and her beige cashmere gown clung to her body, emphasizing the swell of her hips. As always, she had chosen her moment with care, and the very sight of her caused the blood to race in his veins.

Katherine stopped a few feet away from him and stood with her hands resting on her hips, surveying him with idle curiosity. Phillipe was intrigued all over again at her ability to turn the most dramatic meeting into a casual occurrence. He had not seen her for thirteen years, but he could see she had not changed. She did not even have to speak for him to know that Katherine was still Katherine.

"Aren't you even going to say hello?" she asked, shattering the mood of subtle invitation that her very presence had created. Katherine saw Phillipe's answering smile, and she hoped he would never know how much those few words had cost her. To speak at all had been an effort that had required every ounce of her strength, because, in spite of everything, the sight of him had hit her like an unexpected torrent of icy rain.

She had waited and watched for the past three days, wondering if she could face Phillipe at all after the way he had twisted her past into a nightmare. But then, slowly, she had come to realize that she *must* face him if both were to continue living in the Badlands. There would come a time when she could no longer escape him. And, if that were true, then she had no choice; she must meet him again on her own terms. She would take the power into her own capable hands and eventually she would bend him to her will. Katherine was fully aware that there was only one way to do that—she had recognized Phillipe's one weakness a long time ago, and she knew it would not have changed. So she would draw him into her orbit, tempt him unmercifully, then, slowly and inexorably, she would make him pay.

As if released all at once from the spell that had held him immobile, Phillipe closed the space between them and took Katherine's hands. "Do you know," he said, oblivious of the effort of will that kept her hands steady, "I believe I missed you."

Katherine's left eyebrow rose a fraction of an inch. "Really? Do you mean there was no one else willing to climb into your bed?"

He looked away for an instant, unwilling to let her see that her sharp tongue was as effective as ever, but then Phillipe's eyes met hers and he smiled. "There was no one like *you*." He could feel the feather touch of her breath on his cheek, and he longed to smooth the untidy curls that strayed across her face with every breath of wind.

She was aware of his desire, which burned from his blood into her own, and her lips curved into a half-smile. "No," she admitted, "there is only one like me."

"Katherine—" Phillipe began, but she stopped him by pressing her hand to his lips.

"We were never very successful at talking, Phillipe. And today I don't want to argue, so don't bother to court me."

Her eyes glittered with the same message that her parted lips gave him, and as she swayed forward, his arms closed easily around her. He had been gone for a long time, but it was as if he had left her only yesterday, and the remembered feel of her willing body made the breath lodge painfully in his throat. There was something wrong, his mind cried into the void left by his growing desire; there had been no struggle. It was almost as if Katherine had come here for no other purpose than to throw herself into his willing arms. But why? he wondered. After all the bitterness that had raged between them, was she likely to toss the past aside so carelessly?

No, he told himself. Not Katherine. But his doubts were drowning in the scent of her hair, which was like wine to his starved senses. And the warm mouth that opened under his lit a fire in his veins that consumed his reason in a single rush of orange flame. "Does this mean you have forgiven me?" he whispered, trailing his lips along her chin. He could not remember what he had done, but he knew that she had been angry with him when he left the Badlands.

Katherine did not answer; she merely cupped his face in her hands and drew him even closer. She knew her own desire was fuelled only by her anger, but still she was frightened by the answer her body gave him. She knew that her eyes were as radiant as Phillipe's just then, and that her pounding heart echoed the ragged beat of his, but this time she would not lose control as she had before. This time she knew all about him and the knowledge would keep her safe.

When they dropped to their knees on the soft, marshy ground, Phillipe raised his head to protest. "Not here. There are no leaves to protect us. It's too dangerous. Let's meet—"

"Hush!" Katherine demanded. "I like danger, or have you forgotten?"

Phillipe smiled, because he had not forgotten. "You're mad," he told her, winding his hands into her hair as he lowered his lips to hers.

Stiffening in spite of her resolve, Katherine tried to back away, but he held her immobile.

"Did you know you're still as beautiful as always?" he murmured. He released her hair with a sigh, and his hands slid over her shoulders, tracing the line of her back through the soft, clinging gown.

Katherine nodded and did not stop him, even when his fingers cupped her breasts and he buried his mouth in the hollow of her throat. But when he reached for the buttons of her dress, she turned her head away and said, "I have to go."

"Now?" Phillipe sat up abruptly at the note of cold command in Katherine's voice.

"Yes, now. My fiancé is waiting."

He blinked, swallowed once, and stared at her in dawning realization. "You're engaged?"

"Oh, yes." She smiled. "You didn't really think I would wait for *you,* did you?" Her tone was steady and the glow had disappeared from her eyes, though her breathing was still slightly ragged.

"No," Phillipe replied stiffly, "I don't suppose I did. But it also had not occurred to me that you might come and ask me to make love to you while your fiancé was waiting."

"Well then," Katherine said, rising in one smooth motion and turning away from him, "perhaps you don't know me as well as you thought you did."

She left the clearing without looking back. Phillipe watched her go while the slow anger built in his chest. It was a long time before the sound of her voice died away, but the echo of her words clung to him still, firing the frustration that left him breathless. She had done it again, just as she had so many times before; she had offered him the sun, then hidden it away just when he reached out to touch it. And he had been fool enough to let it happen.

He knew then that the game had begun again, but this time, he realized, the stakes were much higher. Because in one thing, at least, he had been right—despite the passage of time and the agony and grief that had come between them over the years, Katherine Pendleton had not changed at all.

David St. Clair left his horse standing docilely at the edge of the field and went to inspect the several head of cattle that were grazing on the thick prairie grass. So far this year the animals were healthy, and David meant to see that they remained so. He knew the St. Clair stock was strong, and he had heard rumors which hinted that the Vallombrosas would be buying up a large number of head this year to keep their packing plant operating to capacity. David fully intended for St. Clair cattle to be among those sold. He had heard that Phillipe Beaumont would pay a good price for the beef, and, for the first time in many months, David began to see a flicker of hope for his family's crumbling fortunes.

But thoughts of his own future brought no such hope. The cattle might be well, but that was little consolation when he still had not seen Katherine in six weeks. Finally, in desperation, he had taken Stephen's advice and gone to confront his fiancée, but somehow she always eluded him. Like a deer intent on protecting her freedom, Katherine disappeared lithely into the trees whenever he came looking for her. She was always just out of reach, hovering maddeningly on the periphery of his vision. But then, he reminded himself with a deep sigh, that was Katherine.

"David!"

When her voice came floating to him from across the open field, he thought at first that he had imagined it. But then he looked up, shading his eyes against the sun which had bleached the afternoon sky nearly white, and saw her riding toward him. As she approached, David saw that she was smiling, and that this time she had not even pretended to contain the flying tendrils of her deep brown hair.

"Come on!" Katherine called as she reined in her horse a few feet away from him. The animal snorted and pawed the ground, echoing the impatience on Katherine's face. "I want to race," she informed him, and motioned toward his waiting horse. "Follow me."

With a dazzling smile, she started away. David did not hesitate for an instant. Abandoning the cattle without a second thought, he mounted his horse and did as she had bid him. It was a miracle, he told himself. Katherine had come back.

They galloped over the still soft ground at a furious pace, while the sun touched their heads with warmth and brought the raging color into their cheeks. David rode a little behind Katherine, and he saw that there was something unusual about her today—a recklessness which removed the last of her inhibitions and imbued her with the wild grace of a sleek mountain lion running before the wind. Just now her beauty and her spirit were overpowering, a force which obliterated all that stood in its way, and David was afraid, even as he exulted. No one woman could be so much and not explode eventually with the intensity of her own passionate spirit.

Bending forward so that he felt the rhythm of the horse beneath him as if it were his own, David concentrated on the challenge of the race. It was good to feel the wind that ran through his hair and the panting breath of the strong animal that did not falter, though Katherine set a killing pace. When at last she dragged back the reins and brought her horse to an abrupt halt, with David just a little behind her, it was good to hear her delighted laughter once again.

"I knew I'd beat you someday," she said, tossing her hair back over her shoulder as she dismounted.

David nodded and slid from the saddle, too winded to speak. Besides, he was afraid to risk shattering this moment with mundane words.

"I think," Katherine said, "that you'd better give me a victory kiss to prove you're glad I won. I wouldn't want you to hold a grudge."

This time David did not hesitate either, although the smiling challenge in her voice took him by surprise. Drawing her forward, he leaned down to touch her lips with his own, but Katherine pulled him closer and opened her mouth hungrily, inviting him to give in to his passion.

When she pulled away at last, David thought that he would never again be able to catch his breath, for Katherine had sucked it from him with the intensity of her kiss.

"I think it's time we talked about the wedding," she suggested while he attempted to regain his equilibrium. "How do you feel about August?"

For a long moment, David could only stare at her, stunned by her unexpected eagerness. He had wanted her to say it, had waited a long time to hear it, yet he had never really believed in the possibility. But here she was, smiling up at him, her hair tumbled around her shoulders, her cheeks flushed with pleasure, waiting for his answer. "August would be lovely." He did not know how he forced the words from between his lips; he only knew that saying them had somehow released him from a long and terrible bondage.

Katherine nodded, and, just for an instant, her eyes wandered away from her fiancé. She was not thinking of David's flushed and ecstatic face; instead, she was remembering the dazed expression she had seen that morning in Phillipe's hypnotic blue eyes.

Chapter 9

"The problem, as I see it," William said, "will be the power that the railroads have in North Dakota. The rates are already too high, and there's no one to stop them from getting higher."

Phillipe nodded in agreement and shifted his chair so he had a better view of the hillside that curved down to the river. He and Van Driesche and Medora had taken their chairs out onto the porch in order to enjoy the clear May morning, but they had not left their business problems behind. In the past month, since their arrival in the Badlands, all three had been kept busy preparing the ground for the reopening of the packing plant, but their efforts had extended far beyond the plant itself. By now, Phillipe had finalized his agreement with the Beef Trust in New York, and the members had begun to set up a retail network which would handle the new supply of beef when it came in. And Swift was still interested in making a deal to purchase the cut beef, although he had not yet made an official commitment.

"Is there some way we can break their power?" Medora asked. She had abandoned her chair to stand at the rail, where she could watch the dance of the new leaves of the cottonwoods in the morning breeze.

"I think we can accomplish a great deal by allying ourselves with Alexander Mackensie," Phillipe said. "He's their political agent in North Dakota. People are already unhappy with the railroad monopolies, and with Mackensie's help, we should be able to make some changes. He *is* the political boss in this state, after all."

William looked skeptical. "Why would he want to ally himself with us?"

"Because he realizes that someday we'll have a lot of power in the Badlands. Mackensie knows as well as we do that if we succeed, we'll bring in a lot more than a few local jobs for bankrupt ranchers." Phillipe rose as he spoke and began to pace before the railing. He had worked hard in the last month to insure that the packing plant would bring benefits to everyone in the Badlands. The small ranchers and farmers who had come here, lured by the free land promised by the Homestead Act, had found themselves in financial trouble, and the jobs the new plant offered would be a welcome relief. At the same time, big ranchers like the St. Clairs would be able to sell their cattle at a higher price, and the reduced rates that William wanted from the railroads would help these families, too.

"We'll manage," Phillipe said firmly.

Medora noticed that his usual trace of arrogance was missing, and she could not help but smile at her stepson's determination. The plant was nearly ready for its opening celebration in two weeks. She sensed that they would succeed this time, and she knew without a doubt that Phillipe was the reason. He had handled the local people with tact and kindness, and never once had he resorted to the wild promises his father had often made without thinking. He had offered only what he knew he could deliver, but Medora suspected that even Phillipe himself would be surprised with the results.

As she watched him leaning out with his forearms resting on the railing, her face glowed with pride in the man who had once been such a troublesome boy. He had changed so much over the years, more than even she had realized, and she knew suddenly that he was everything his father might have been, had fate dealt with him a little differently.

William started when he saw the look on Medora's face, rose abruptly and strode to the end of the porch, his jaw stiff and his hands clenched roughly at his sides. He had never seen that expression in her eyes before, not even when she looked at the Marquis. Van Driesche suspected that she had always thought her husband something of a foolish dreamer, although she had loved the man wildly just the same. But Phillipe was not a fool, not in any way but one, and that was his stubborn blindness. Heaven forbid that he should ever open his eyes and see the truth.

But, for the moment, William alone seemed to be aware of the inquisitive glances that passed between the townspeople whenever Phillipe and Medora were mentioned in the same breath. He alone recognized the gnawing curiosity that lit the people's eyes with questions they dared not ask. *Why* had this widow left her home so soon after her husband's death, and why on earth had she brought the Marquis' bastard with her? Van Driesche knew that it was only a matter of time before Medora answered those questions for herself. What would he do, he wondered, when she finally saw what he had always known? He must think carefully and then, perhaps, he could help her avoid the disaster which he feared was inevitable.

William was relieved to see a young man approaching from the bottom of the hill with a heavy book under his arm. A distraction from his own uneasy thoughts would be welcome just now.

"Good morning," the young man said as he mounted the steps and started upward. "I'm Stephen St. Clair." He nodded politely at William and Phillipe as he passed them, but his intention was clearly to speak to Medora. "You must be the Marquise," he guessed.

"Yes?" Medora's voice was the slightest bit chilly toward this stranger whose name she had heard only once.

Stephen recognized her reservations and smiled with studied charm. "I'm sorry to appear without a proper introduction, but I was reading down by the river," he indicated the book under his arm, "and I saw you sitting on the porch, so I thought I'd come up right away. There's no time like the present, don't you agree?"

The speech sounded a little too practiced to Phillipe's ears, and he waited curiously to see how St. Clair would explain himself.

"I understand you might be looking for a tutor for the children," the young man said, brushing a stray blond hair back from his face. "I'd like to apply for the job." He did not add that he intended to have it regardless of her wishes. Nor did he explain why. How could he tell her, or anyone, that in the instant when he had seen her young daughter across the leaping tongues of flame that first day by the river, he had made a sacred vow? Since then he had learned only that the girl's name was Anais, and, although his gaze had locked with hers for only a moment, he had recognized the dark, bitter secrets in her eyes. He had been intrigued by that glimpse of another shadowed soul, and his questioning mind had brought him here to discover Anais' secret.

Phillipe moved closer to his stepmother and considered the intruder in silence, St. Clair was attractive enough in his own way, with his pale blue eyes, flyaway hair, and curly red beard. But his smile was strangely stiff and there was something disturbing about his intent gaze. "I thought you were a rancher," Phillipe said.

Stephen shrugged. "My father and brother are, certainly, but I've always liked to think of myself as a scholar." He turned his attention back to Medora. "I attended the University of North Dakota in Bismarck for three years, and I tutored others to pay my tuition."

Medora sensed Phillipe's disquiet, although she did not understand it. "Why did you quit?"

He had anticipated the question, and Stephen knew that his answer must not betray a single flicker of the truth. With a little half-smile, he told them, "My family decided they needed me here. I tried for a while to educate *them,* but, as Mr. Beaumont pointed out, they're cattlemen. And cattlemen have little appreciation for books. But I thought surely children raised in Paris would be more civilized, so I came to you in desperation. You're my last hope for culture in this godforsaken valley." Stephen looked at her pleadingly, grasping his book before him like a protective shield.

"You have references?" Medora asked.

"I can get them. Whatever you need," he replied slyly.

"Then we'll see. Bring them with you tomorrow and I'll let you know."

Stephen leaned down unexpectedly and took her hand. "Bless you," he murmured with mock gravity as he brushed a kiss across the end of her fingers. That was easy, he thought, despite Beaumont's searching looks. Things were beginning to go his way at last.

But just as St. Clair took a few steps backwards and started to turn away, the morning stillness was decimated by a sudden eruption of rifle fire.

A bullet flew past Phillipe's head and, without thinking, he lunged toward Medora and pushed her down against the rough boards of the porch. Before he had even taken a breath, he had his revolver in his hand, and he raised his head a fraction of an inch, just in time to see a second bullet slamming into the wall in front of which he and his stepmother had been standing a moment before. He saw with relief that William and Stephen had also dropped to the ground, and when the whine of the third bullet was followed by a long, strained silence, he whispered, "Medora? Are you all right?"

When she looked up and nodded, still too stunned to speak, Phillipe turned to the two men. "If we want to catch whoever it is, we have to go now. He won't wait around for us to recover our equilibrium. I'm certain the shots came from the vicinity of the river, so, William, you head in that direction from the far end of the porch, but stay out of the line of fire, just in case our intruder hasn't given up. I'll go down the hill from the other end."

"I'm coming with you," St. Clair called as he rose and hurriedly brushed his pants free of dust.

"You don't have a gun," Phillipe pointed out.

"I'm coming anyway."

There was no time for further protests, and when he saw that Medora had slipped inside the house, Phillipe moved quickly to the end of the porch and slid between the rails. Stephen followed close behind, but Phillipe was too preoccupied with listening for more rifle fire to pay much attention. Eyes narrowed against the bright sun, he crept quietly toward the river. The attacker must have hidden himself among the cottonwoods where he could fire a long-range rifle without being seen, Phillipe thought. He could only hope that the gunman had not yet escaped to the rough terrain on the far side of the water. But, as he approached the trees, listening intently for the whine of a bullet which never came, he heard the cracking of several branches, then the violent pounding of hooves on the soft earth of the riverbank.

"Damn!" he cursed under his breath as he plunged headlong into the wall of protective leaves. He saw only the tail of the horse as it disappeared downstream, and he followed doggedly, though he knew he could never catch up.

Only Stephen noticed the rustling of leaves and the snapping of twigs that came from the opposite direction. Leaving Phillipe to pursue his hopeless course, St. Clair

fell to his knees and crawled through the underbrush that
crowded the soggy bank until the bushes thinned, then
left a wide gap which allowed the sunlight to enter.
Stephen was rewarded with the distant sight of a flash of
color just before the gunman vanished into a far grove of
trees. Just a glimpse, he told himself with a satisfied
smile, but it had been enough.

He did not even attempt to follow. It was the knowledge
he wanted, not the attacker, and he returned to the place
where Phillipe had left him as unobtrusively as he had
slipped away. He found William waiting there, his revolver clutched in rigid fingers, staring helplessly into the confusion of leaves and shadows before him.

"Did you see anything?" Van Driesche asked.

"Nothing." Shrugging casually, the man turned his
shuttered gaze on Phillipe, who had come back empty-
handed.

"The horse had no rider," he explained in disgust. "He
was probably sent this way to distract us from the gunman.
I didn't find a trace of anyone. How about you, William?
St. Clair?"

Both men shook their heads, then Stephen leaned forward and said in a confidential whisper, "I'll tell you one
thing I learned, though. Someone sure doesn't like the job
you're doing here, Mr. Beaumont. And whoever it is,
they're awfully clever."

Phillipe gazed beyond the young man as if he had not
heard him. So it was beginning again—the unexpected
danger, the deceit, and the bullets which, as he had
learned through painful experience, always found the
way to their target eventually. He had thought that this
time they might actually escape all this, but he realized
now that he had been a fool, and—quite nearly—a dead
man.

* * *

A sleek, dark head broke the surface of the pond, scattering fragments of glistening water into the still waiting air. Anais shivered and rubbed her forearms in sympathy as Mianne rose to her feet gracefully, the water making tiny glittering streams in her straight black hair and across her brown shoulders. Dark and fluid and completely naked, the woman stepped barefoot onto the muddy shore and made her way to a large, flat boulder, where she slipped her buckskin dress over her head, then sat with her face tilted toward the warm sun.

Anais, who had sat drawing nearby while Mianne took her swim, leaned forward and shuddered, "How can you bear it? It looks so cold."

Mianne shook her head, causing her hair to sway behind her. "I like the cold, and I can never resist the river. You know that."

With her head thrown back, her arms extended to support her from behind, and her long, dark legs stretched out before her, Mianne resembled some wild and beautiful priestess who found herself stranded somehow in the wrong century. Her eyes seemed to look beyond the shaded green leaves overhead to a vision which only she could see.

"You're different when you come here," Anais observed. It was the first time she had dared to say those words to the woman who had become her friend so easily, though the girl had been struck often by the change that came over Mianne when she reached the river.

"Yes," Mianne agreed. "Here there's no need to pretend." And, she added silently, here by the water the troubles at the Chateau seem far away, almost unreal. Here she could forget warnings of fire, the attempt on Phillipe's life, and the danger that she believed stalked every one of them.

Anais considered Mianne's statement for a long moment. "Are you hiding from them?" she asked at last, nodding toward the house which the trees hid from their sight.

Mianne looked away, shaken by the wave of rebellion that surged through her at those certain words. "No, of course not," she said, but even to her own ears, her voice sounded hollow and unnatural above the music of the river that rumbled by at her feet. . . .

. . . . June, 1885—The wind cried out in protest as Mianne fled wildly over the marshy ground, the throbbing of her own blood echoing like the pulsing chant of an ancient Indian song. She did not really know why she was running with her hair flowing behind her like a ragged banner of her suffering; she only knew she had to get away. As far as possible from the stifling walls of the Chateau which threatened daily to close around her forever and hold her captive in a prison which was not of her own making.

With her wrinkled skirt gathered in her arms, she flew unerringly toward the only solace she had found in these unfriendly Badlands. Just when she thought she was finally free, when the sheltering leaves opened before her and beckoned her to come to the side of the river, a voice called her name and she stopped as still as the fox who knows the hunter is nearby. Maybe if she did not move, he would think he had lost her and give up the chase. But, of course, it was only a fleeting wish.

"Mianne," Phillipe said softly as he came up beside her, "why are you always hiding from me?"

She stiffened and turned to face him defiantly. "I'm *not* hiding."

"Yes, you are. You're always escaping to the river, as if you're afraid to face me." He saw the light of fury that flickered in the depths of her eyes, and he knew that this time the battle would be easy. "You *are* afraid, aren't you?"

"No!" Mianne hissed. They had had this argument before and she knew where it would lead, but just now she didn't care. She would not let anyone call her a coward.

"Then why don't you let me kiss you?" Phillipe wheedled. He often wondered why he was so intent on breaking down this girl's thick armor, and, although he could not explain it even to himself, he was aware that he could not abandon the game.

The boy had put his hand on Mianne's shoulder, and she flung it away, crying, "I have better things to do."

"You're afraid."

His fingers closed around her upper arms as she looked up at him, her eyes blazing. Damn him! She could not fight him this way and he knew it. "Let me go!"

Drawing her closer, Phillipe whispered, "One kiss, and then I'll set you free."

Mianne gritted her teeth while the battle raged within her. Perhaps she should give in and then he would leave her in peace. Besides, she would do anything to show him she was not a coward. "All right," she said and, closing her eyes, she waited coldly for the inevitable. But his lips, when they met hers at last, were unexpectedly warm, and, despite the anger and the fear that made him always her enemy, she felt a flicker of response from somewhere deep in the center of her body. His mouth seemed to draw her soul up from the dark corner where she had it hidden, and, before she realized what she was doing, she had slipped her arms around his neck.

Phillipe raised his head and smiled gently down at her. "You see, little one, you've proven you're not afraid, and I've proven that you may be human and not a savage after all."

Mianne shuddered and backed away. She did not want to be human. When you were human it meant that others could understand you, and once they understood, they had the power to hurt you until you lay broken at their feet. She would never let that happen. Never! "No!" she spat the word in his face, and before Phillipe could stop her, Mianne reached up and dragged her nails across his cheek until the blood swelled beneath her fingers. Then she whirled away from him while he stood paralyzed with surprise.

Mianne flew on bare feet toward the comfort she knew she would find in the river, but she knew in her heart that this was a coward's escape after all. *When she knelt at last on the muddy shore, the water laughed and gurgled at her weakness, mocking her as surely as did the noisy squawk of the magpie overhead. . . .*

. . . . The sound of Anais' voice rode the undulating back of the rushing river and made itself one with the soft babble of the water. Mianne shook Phillipe from her mind with difficulty and turned instead to her friend, whose fingers were busy with the charcoal and paper she carried with her everywhere. Anais' head was bent over her work in intense concentration and Mianne smiled, pleased that the girl had found something that interested her.

It had not taken Mianne long to discover Anais' talent for drawing and painting, but she seemed to be the only one who appreciated the sensitive portraits and brooding landscapes this girl created with a few well-placed strokes. Anais drew with charcoal because she had nothing better, though Mianne had mentioned her lack of proper tools to both Medora and Phillipe. But they hadn't listened. They were too busy waging a war against an enemy they could not even see.

Anais looked up from her drawing and found her friend's eyes upon her. "If you're not hiding," she persisted, "then why do you always slip away when no one's looking?"

"Because," Mianne murmured, "this is the part of me they don't want to know. And I don't want to tell them." She rose to her feet and turned to face the water, then stood perfectly still with the river glimmering before her, barefoot in her soft gown that reached a little below her knee, her thick black hair falling across her shoulders and down to her waist. And the look in her eyes when she moved at last was distant and unreadable. She was no longer the prim and proper Mianne who moved like a wraith through the Chateau seeing that everyone's needs were met. Instead, she was a wild bird with the body of a woman.

"Don't you want to go back to the Indians?" Anais asked through the sudden tightness in her throat. "You don't seem to belong here. You must have been happier there, with your own people."

"No." Mianne's eyes were touched with fleeting memories which went beyond the comfort of the river.

Anais looked away. "I was."

"What?" The woman seemed to bring her thoughts back to Anais with difficulty.

"I was happier in Paris."

Mianne's eyes focused slowly on the girl's troubled face. "Were you?" she asked. "Are you certain of that?"

For a moment, Anais was confused by the searching look which Mianne gave her—a look that threatened to pierce her suddenly brittle defenses with its keen perception. "Yes," the girl declared obstinately. "I was much happier then." She did not even notice that her fingers were gripping the edge of her drawing pad until the blood had drained from them completely.

The horse snorted, tossing its head from side to side with impatience while Phillipe sat contemplating the patterned cliffs that rose before him. He knew Katherine was waiting for him somewhere in the midst of the sculpted spires, but he lingered along the way, savoring the anticipation of their encounter as he savored the fine brandy he drank every night after dinner.

He had fallen into the habit of meeting her often in the past month, despite the bitterness of their first reunion. For he knew Katherine well enough to realize that she had only wanted to prove a point that morning by the pond—to show him that she had not forgotten their past battles and that she was still determined as ever to be the ultimate winner. He knew it was a game to her, but he intended to play it out to the end.

At night he hated himself for his weakness and cursed his mother time and again, but when he was with Katherine, he forgot everything but the fire in his blood. He could not resist her, because she was the only one who shared his desire, and the anger that flared between them was as much a part of their mutual attraction as was their insatiable hunger. Besides, in her arms he could forget the worries that plagued him now. He remembered with painful clarity the hiss of that bullet going by his head, and he wondered often if Stephen St. Clair was right. Was it true that someone was determined to see that he did not succeed? It was a question he dared not ask himself too often.

Phillipe stopped and dismounted when he came to the opening in the stone that would lead him to Katherine. He had thought it odd at first when she had insisted that they no longer meet by the pond, but he had agreed readily enough, since it seemed so important to her. Shading his eyes with one hand, Phillipe looked up the path that led through the ravine to the maze of colored rock beyond and, for an instant, only the distant babble of the river disturbed the deep stillness all around him. But then the hush was shattered by the crackling ascent of a couple of magpies from the heart of the maze, and Phillipe realized that Katherine was there, waiting for him to find her.

He began to climb upward, walking carefully on the rocky path that twisted and curved at alarming angles, and now and then he had to put out a hand to brace himself against the sheer walls that rose on either side. Once, as he rounded a corner and paused to listen for an instant, he caught sight of a flash of deep blue which disappeared over a low barrier of stone, followed by a hint of teasing laughter.

"Katherine!" he called in exasperation, but she did not answer. It was then that he saw the pair of riding boots left standing in a cleft in the rock. Phillipe smiled and set out after her once again.

When he came to the low barrier, he paused to run his hand over the silk stockings that had been tossed carelessly aside; up ahead, he could see a long, violet scarf that graced the top of a carved spire. Now he was getting closer, and he could hear the tiny rocks that scattered in her wake, so he did not stop when he discovered the leather gloves she had left behind in the middle of the path. By now her laughter had become an open invitation that the wind carried back to taunt him, and he followed, mesmerized by the promise of her musical voice.

"Katherine!" he called again, anxious now to bring the pursuit to an end. His answer was a pale blue blouse which floated downward with the grace of winter snowflakes and came to rest at his feet. He glanced up quickly and saw her smiling down at him, then she turned and disappeared once more.

Phillipe had had enough. Taking a deep breath, he leapt up onto the ledge that blocked the path and moved swiftly across the small flat area where Katherine had crouched above him. Then, noting a break in the rock, he slipped through in time to stop her as she came up the regular path. Catching her in his arms, he leaned down to kiss her before she could speak, and her lips were warm with the breath of her laughter.

Katherine's arms closed around him, and when he raised his head, she said, "I thought you'd never catch up!" She had discarded every piece of clothing but her petticoat, and her hair was braided loosely, so that it fell across her shoulder in one long coil.

Phillipe glanced down appreciatively at the swell of her breasts which rose and fell as she tried to catch her breath, and his smile was slow and lazy. "You're the only woman I know who would dare to do this."

Reaching for her petticoat, she pulled it over her head and tossed it aside. "I would dare a great many things," she told him, her voice husky.

Phillipe drew her toward him, his hands tracing intimate patterns on her skin, and whispered into her hair, "You're evil, Kathy, did you know?"

Her answering smile was dazzling. "That's precisely what binds you to me," she murmured as her fingers worked their way inside his shirt to curl themselves into the hairs on his chest.

Phillipe knew that it was true, but he did not care. Her hands on his body and the touch of her lips made him forget everything but the pulse of their mutual hunger. For he knew that, at this moment, she needed him as much as he needed her, and it was enough for now.

As Katherine unbuttoned Phillipe's shirt, the blood began to race in her veins, and she had to remind herself, as always, that he was the enemy. But when his fingers brushed her naked breast and his lips found their way to the throbbing hollow in her throat, she closed her eyes and let the waves of pleasure run over her. His expert hands moved like magic across her skin, drawing the heat up from the very center of her being until her face was flushed with the splendid agony of anticipation.

She must remember, she thought wildly; not for a moment could she forget her purpose in being here. Nothing must drive that knowledge from her mind, not even the desire that urged her to draw him closer until his body had become one with her own. He had brought her to the brink of destruction once, and it must never happen again, not even if she had to set her passion aflame until it burned away to still, gray ashes.

But, God! the warmth of his tongue as it probed her willing mouth, the wonder of his gentle, searching hands, the urgency in his blood which commanded her surrender. How could she remember to hate him when she could not even see his face through the desire that raged between them, leaving her completely blind? "Why did you come back?" she moaned.

Phillipe raised his head and his hands tightened where they rested on her shoulders. "Now, Kathy?"

"I want to know why."

He sensed the note of desperation in her voice and reached up to brush a stray hair from her cheek. "For my father's sake," he said.

"Liar! You came for your own sake, because you're the same as the Marquis," she accused him. "You only want to prove that you can achieve the impossible. You're a hopeless dreamer, just as he was."

Phillipe was surprised by the bitterness she no longer bothered to hide. A moment ago they had been lovers and now, all at once, they were adversaries once again. He could not understand her, no matter how he tried. "It's not impossible, Katherine. We're going to succeed this time. And, besides, the meatpacking business was not the only thing that brought me back here. There were pleasant memories as well." He trailed a finger down her cheekbone, then pressed it lightly against her lips.

"Liar," she repeated. But she could not help but wonder if he were telling the truth.

Chapter 10

The wind raced across the field, turning the grass into a raging sea of green, dappled here and there with the shadows of the whirling box elder leaves. Johnny Goodall smiled in contentment, pushing his hat back on his head so the last of the afternoon sun could bathe his face with fleeting warmth. "Beautiful, isn't it?" he said, shifting in the saddle so he could see William's expression.

Van Driesche nodded in silent agreement, because he knew that Johnny expected it, but in *his* eyes even this peaceful scene was bleak. How could it be otherwise, with the brooding stone cliffs that circled the edge of the valley, sheathing the landscape around them with their grim, ghostly shadows?

"We'd best try the west pasture," Johnny suggested. "We don't want to wander too far from home with darkness coming."

"Lead the way," William said. It was absurd that he should let these fancies disturb him so, he told himself firmly. He had chosen to come with the foreman to inspect the cattle in order to get away from the house for a while. He thought if he looked at another paper covered with figures, he would go blind with boredom and enforced inactivity. He had thought a ride would be a welcome relief. But he found that he liked this land no more now than when he had first seen it with the Marquis many years ago. The painted stones, split and scarred by jagged ravines and deep chasms, was too charged with savage loneliness for his taste; he found the Badlands unsettling in their vast magnificence. And no matter how long he stayed, he knew that would never change.

"We should be seeing some cattle grazing in the far field," Johnny said, his forehead creased with sudden concern. "They can't all have wandered away. Do you see any animals, Mr. Van Driesche? Your eyes are younger than mine."

William stared into the lengthening shadows, turning in the saddle to look both to right and left, but he saw no bulky red-brown shapes rising out of the tall, waving buffalo grass. "None," he asserted. He could feel Goodall's disquiet, and it only increased his own misgivings.

"Come on!" Johnny dug his heels into the horse's sides and rode ahead while the wind whipped his thick gray hair around his head and his hands gripped the reins more tightly.

William followed close behind, searching as he went for the cattle which should be all around him now, but there was nothing. Only the cry of the wind and the hollow pounding of the horses' hooves on the soft dirt. Then Johnny reined in abruptly, and his shocked exclamation came back to Van Driesche with the raging force of the wind behind it.

"GODDAMN!"

The foreman sat stiffly on the back of his horse, staring at the ground below with a black scowl twisting his features, and as Van Driesche rode up beside him, he felt as if the breath had been knocked from his body. At Johnny's feet lay the first of many carcasses that were scattered with abandon across the entire field, and every one of them bloated and ugly and quite obviously dead. William saw how this animal's head was twisted back in agony, and he looked away. "What is it?" His strangled question came out no more than a whisper.

Goodall looked out over the corpse-strewn field and shook his head. "I'll tell you this," he said grimly, "I've never seen a disease that could do this to this many animals in less than three days."

"Then how—?"

Johnny's expression was bleak when he replied, "My guess is poison. What do you think?"

William shrugged, stunned into silence by Goodall's observation. The foreman must be right; Van Driesche, at least, could not contradict him. What did the secretary know of cattle and disease, after all? And if Goodall *was* right—he did not even want to think what that might mean.

"Let's look around some," Johnny said heavily. "Maybe we can find something. If it *was* poison, it had to come from somewhere."

At Johnny's request, William set out to circle the field on the opposite side from the foreman, but he knew he would not find anything. All he could see was corpse after bloated corpse being devoured by the fast-moving evening shadows, and all he could hear was the moaning of the wind. When at last he rejoined Goodall, William was no closer to an explanation.

"I can't find any signs," Johnny informed him as they paused by a natural waterhole. "But it must be here in the water. That's the easiest to tamper with."

Van Driesche said nothing. He could not have spoken even if he had wanted to, because the disquiet that had followed him since he left France had lodged itself in his throat and he could not make it go away.

"Well," Johnny muttered, "I guess we'd better go tell the Marquise."

Medora. William could only nod dumbly, his knuckles

bleached white where he clutched the reins, his eyes fixed on the clear, deadly water at his feet.

Stephen St. Clair glanced at Anais where she lay stretched out on the drawing room floor toying with a piece of charcoal, then he turned to Medora. "We're finished for today," he informed his new employer. "The boys have already escaped to the kitchen, where I'm sure Cassie is plying them with cake and cookies." But his thoughts were clearly not concerned with Paul and Louis; he was thinking of Anais.

He had met her officially only yesterday, the first day of his new job, but already he could see that he had been right about the girl. She had a wonderfully sharp mind, once you managed to penetrate the barrier that glowed in her eyes. Stephen shook his head, reminded himself that he had important things to do, and gave Medora a little bow. "I'll see you tomorrow," he said.

Medora nodded, but she was too preoccupied with her own thoughts to notice the brief, intense look that passed between her daughter and the tutor before he left the room. Medora was more concerned than ever about Anais, who was not recovering as her mother had expected her to, once Paris was behind her. In fact, she seemed to be slipping inexorably away from Medora and everyone else. Everyone, that is, except Mianne.

Medora hoped that hiring a tutor would help bring the girl back to the real world, but she wondered now if even that would have any effect. Suddenly, she was possessed by a desperate desire to bridge the chasm that was slowly widening between mother and daughter. "Anais," she murmured, "may I see your drawing?"

Without looking up, the girl pulled her knees in under her body until she huddled protectively over the picture. "No. It's mine."

"I don't want to take it away from you. I just want to see it." When Anais did not move, Medora looked away. "Why aren't you off to the kitchen with the boys?" she asked, determined to somehow break through the shell of indifference that surrounded the girl like a thick velvet curtain.

"I don't like them. They're too young and silly," Anais replied primly.

"But surely you miss their company. In Paris you always—"

"I don't want to talk about Paris."

"Anais," Medora said softly, "it doesn't do any good to ignore your problems. I know you're unhappy, but I don't know why. You have to talk to me if you want me to understand."

The girl's eyebrows came together in a frown, but she did not answer.

In the face of her daughter's stubborn silence, Medora reached for the only reason she could imagine. "Is it because you still miss your father?"

"I don't miss him!" Anais declared, forced at last out of her detachment. "I never did."

Her mother saw the hard glitter in the girl's eyes and was appalled. "Surely—" she began feebly.

"Why *should* I miss him? He was never at home anyway. He was too busy conquering the world to think about me. He didn't even write very often, but that's because I wasn't a boy. Paul and Louis got letters all the time." By now she had forgotten her drawing and was sitting up glaring at the woman who sat unmoving across the room. "But I don't care about that, because he wasn't really *my* father anyway. He belonged to Phillipe and to you and no one else. And I don't even care!"

Her brilliant black eyes were fixed on her mother as if challenging her to deny it, but Medora found that her lips simply would not move. She was staggered by the bitterness the girl must have been hiding for years, and she knew for herself how such bitterness could eat away at a person's faith, leaving nothing but naked bones behind. What could she say to her daughter now that would not sound trite and empty in the face of her pain? For no matter how many times Anais repeated that she did not care, her mother did not believe it. Those deep black eyes were full to the brim with suffering, and Medora knew that she could not even begin to assuage it. "Anais," she murmured, leaning forward with her hands outstretched in a silent plea.

"We've got to talk to you, ma'am," Johnny Goodall said as he stepped into the room, his hat held awkwardly in his hands.

Medora looked up at him in distress. "Not just now," she said. She could feel her daughter's gaze upon her, and she wished the shadows would swallow up Johnny and William, who hovered at the foreman's shoulder.

"I don't think this can wait," Goodall insisted.

It was not until then that Medora saw how haggard Johnny's face looked, and, behind him, William was even paler.

"It's important," Van Driesche added when Medora continued to hesitate.

"All right," she sighed in defeat. Then she turned back to Anais. "I'm sorry," she explained, "but I have to go now. We can talk later, after dinner."

"About what?" the girl asked as she gathered her charcoal and paper together and prepared to leave the room. "I don't remember what we were saying anyway." Then, without a backward glance, she turned and walked away.

Medora watched her go and suddenly she wanted to run after Anais and take her in her arms, but she knew her daughter would only back away. "What is it?" she said, whirling to face the two men.

Johnny cleared his throat and told her without preamble,

"Someone poisoned the waterhole in the west pasture. At least thirty cattle are dead."

Medora had not yet recovered from her confrontation with Anais, and she found that, at Goodall's news, her legs would no longer support her. Collapsing onto the couch, she managed to ask, "What shall we do?" Her mind was numb with shock; she could not think.

"I've already sent the men around to test the other holes, and we'll have to do something to stop the animals from drinking at the west one," Johnny explained. "But the most important thing we have to do is find out who's responsible, if we don't know already," he finished ominously.

Medora knew what he was thinking—the Pendletons. They had tried to destroy the Vallombrosas once, and there was no reason to doubt that they would do so again. Up until now, she had avoided facing the grim facts, even after the attempt on Phillipe's life. But now Medora sensed that she could hide no longer. The game had become deadly, and she did not know if she had the strength to bear it this time. Not again. Turning to William, she asked, "How can we stop it?"

Van Driesche could see by her colorless cheeks that she was deeply distressed, and he wanted nothing more than to offer his comfort. He wanted to keep her safe from the wrath of the Pendletons, from the stray bullets that might take her life next time, if Phillipe's were not enough. And he wanted to protect her from herself and her stubborn belief that she could overcome any hardship. She was only a woman, after all. But even as the thought formed itself in his mind, he knew he was wrong. Medora did not need his protection. She had lived through tragedy time and again, and she would continue to do so. She did not need him.

At the moment, he was so overcome by his own feeling of helplessness that he could not even give her the answer she wanted. "I don't know if we have the *power* to stop it," he said.

"But we can sure as hell try!" Johnny cried, his jaw set in a stubborn line.

"Yes," Medora agreed. It seemed that the sound of Goodall's voice had brought her to her senses. "We'll talk to Phillipe tonight and decide what we should do."

William took a deep breath in an attempt to dislodge the weight that had settled like lead in his stomach. Of course Phillipe would think of a way. How could he fail to do so? He was their savior, was he not? He was the one with the magic touch and so he would succeed, as always, where anyone else could only fail.

Phillipe stared blindly into the heavy darkness and, despite the warmth of the blankets, he shivered. He had lain awake for an hour, the thoughts whirling in his tired brain, then, finally, the pieces of the puzzle had fallen into place. Only now did he begin to understand the pattern of disaster which had formed itself around them since their return to the Badlands. First, a harmless blaze, too small to do any damage, then the scattered rifle fire, and now the poisoned cattle. The message was getting through at last.

These little incidents had been warnings, one after the other, and no one had really been in danger—yet. But what would happen when the Pendletons realized that Phillipe did not intend to back away and that the plant would open in one week, just as scheduled? He could not afford to listen to the warnings now, but he knew that if he ignored them, the next bullet might very well find its target. The knowledge only made him more determined to go ahead with his plans.

But, at the moment, though his mind rejected the idea of sleep, his body craved it. He was weary to the center of his being, and he thought that he would gladly trade the next three nights for just an hour or two of rest right now. He must think, he told himself, but his heavy eyelids would not listen and they fluttered closed at last, blocking the night with a colored darkness of their own.

In his dream it was bright, warm summer, and the heat shimmered off the roof like the water from a sudden summer shower. Phillipe wandered up the hill, contented with the world and himself and anxious to see what Cassie had prepared for lunch. He was sixteen and hungry.

Phillipe opened the kitchen door, calling for Cassie, but she was not there. In fact, the house was strangely silent for such a fine summer morning. Had everyone disappeared in the trembling heat waves that had already crept up the hill from the river? Moving carefully, afraid to disturb the stillness, Phillipe opened the door and went through to the dining room, which was also empty, and then to the parlor. He had just decided that everyone had left the house when he heard his father's voice raised in anger.

"Did you know?"

"No!" Medora's voice cried. "I didn't know, damn you! I didn't!"

Phillipe stood frozen, afraid to stay and listen and afraid to turn away. There was a long moment of silence and then he heard Medora cry, "Where are you going?"

The boy heard footsteps coming his way, and he realized in sudden panic that he might be discovered. Searching for the nearest cover, he crouched down behind the sofa and, for an instant, the rushing of his own blood drowned out the voices. But then, as the Marquis came into the room, the boy heard him call back over his shoulder, "She died because of her loyalty to me. The very least I can do is risk my life for her."

Phillipe was bewildered by the bitterness in his father's voice and, all at once, being discovered did not seem as important as finding the cause of that bitterness. Phillipe took a deep breath and raised his head, just as the Marquis pushed open the door, strode out onto the porch and disappeared; but not before the boy saw clearly the blood-covered body of the Indian girl his father held in his arms.

Phillipe sat up sharply, unaware that he had let the covers slip from around his shoulders, but this time the nightmare did not disappear as it usually did the moment he awoke. How could he have forgotten the scene which had burned itself permanently into his memory just before they left the Badlands the last time? How could he have forgotten the nightmares which had haunted him for so long afterwards? Somehow his father's death had pushed those memories from his mind, and he had not seen the dead girl with the dripping black hair for nearly a year.

But she was with him now, along with the questions which he had never dared ask the Marquis. Phillipe had seen the body for only an instant, but he could not forget it, because he sensed that somehow her death had been responsible for their sudden departure from North Dakota. Yet he had never heard her mentioned; he did not even know her name. All at once his curiosity was too great to bear. He had to know. He would ask Medora in the morning. Surely she would answer the question that had disturbed his dreams one night too many.

Once the decision was made, he found that he could breathe evenly again and that his heart had ceased its erratic pounding, but he realized that he was wide awake and would not be able to sleep again for some time. It had always been like this after the nightmare, and so, as he had in Paris, he got out of bed, groping for his robe, and slipped out into the hallway. He did not know where he would go, only that he had to be in motion.

With the deep night silence ringing in his ears, he found his way to the staircase and started downward. Perhaps Cassie would still be awake and puttering around the kitchen, he thought, heading in that direction. He would like someone to talk to.

But it was not Cassie that he discovered seated in a stiff-backed chair in the warm center of a circle of yellow lamplight; it was Mianne. She was dressed in a simple rust-colored robe, and her long, slender fingers were busy with one of Anais' gowns and a needle and thread. She glanced up in distress when she heard him open the door, and the expression lingered in her eyes long after it had disappeared from her face.

"I'm sorry," Phillipe apologized. "I couldn't sleep. I didn't mean to frighten you."

Mianne looked back down at her work and murmured, "You forget. I'm not afraid of anything."

"That used to be true," he mused as he found a chair and drew it into the lamplight, "but I wonder if it still is."

"People don't change so very much." Mianne's voice was low and she did not raise her head.

Phillipe noticed how her long, dark eyelashes made feathery shadows on her cheeks and how her lips were pursed in concentration. "*You* did," he observed.

Mianne did not answer, and her hand did not pause once in its pricking and pulling. With his own hands resting on his knees, Phillipe watched her in fascination. He was intrigued not only by her beauty, which he recognized as rare among the women he had known, but also by the force of will that kept her face always calm and her voice always level. Whenever he was with her, his curiosity drove him to observe her every movement, seeking a single clue as to what had changed her. Had she really destroyed the magic in her soul which had drawn him to her long ago? Somehow he could not quite believe it.

Mianne drew back and closed her eyes for an instant, as if to hide her thoughts from him. She had seen Phillipe watching her lately. She knew that he was searching for some hidden spring inside her; there were questions in his eyes whenever he looked at her. He was seeking the wild Indian girl she had been once, and Mianne knew that he must never find her, because then she would be lost.

Phillipe saw that she had retreated from him, and he could not let it happen. "Tell me about your name," he said. "I've always wondered. It's not Sioux, is it?"

Picking up her needle and sliding it into the fabric across her lap, Mianne shook her head. "My mother wanted to give me an Indian name, but my father had his own ideas. He had decided to name his first daughter after his two favorite aunts, Miriam and Anne, but since he didn't like Miriam Anne, he combined them into Mianne." Her eyes followed her own fingers as they flew at their task, and she knew that her voice had not betrayed her. She had learned to pretend so well that it had become an instinct.

"You speak of Johnny fondly now," Phillipe said, determined to keep the conversation going. "I remember you hated your father once."

"So did you," she countered. "People grow up, that's all. I began to see as I got older that my father was a good, gentle man, and I came to realize that he had acted as he had out of necessity." Mianne dropped the cloth from her hands and gazed before her, beyond the circle of lamplight to the leaden darkness. "But that doesn't mean I have forgotten that he left me behind for all those years. I care about him, but I don't forget."

Her years with the Indians had made her strong, taught her that she could depend on no one but herself, and forced her to realize that love and warmth were only fantasies created by those more fortunate than she. That was why she had learned long ago to hide her emotions within herself, and why, although his presence was to her like the promise of a strange and lovely song, she had to make certain that Phillipe Beaumont never became more than a stranger and a distant dream.

Phillipe was disturbed by the deep, ragged pain he had heard, for an instant, in her voice, and he realized that once you hurt a woman like Mianne as much as her father had long ago, there was nothing in heaven or earth that could ever make it up to her. "Goodnight," he murmured, and then, before she could answer, he rose and left her with the lamplight caressing her shoulders like the soft, warm hand of a stranger.

Chapter 11

The sudden rattling of his window awakened David St. Clair from a light slumber. For a full minute, he lay in bed listening, certain that he had imagined the sound, but then it came again—the irregular tap-tap-tapping, almost as if someone were tossing pebbles against the glass. David opened his eyes wide and sat up in bed. Surely it couldn't be—but there it was again. Throwing the covers aside, he swung his feet to the floor, wincing as the cold engulfed him, and made his way to the window through the gloom.

David raised the glass to peer out, and a breath of cold came rushing inward, damp with heavy mist. For a moment he could see nothing by the uneven light of early morning. It could be no more than just after dawn, he judged—and the swathes of mist draped the world in soft, white folds, but then he heard laughter directly beneath him. There she stood, covered from head to toe in a deep purple hooded cloak, with her flushed face tilted upward and the morning mist clinging to her shoulders and circling her feet.

"Come out," Katherine called. "I want to talk to you."

David shook his head in disbelief. "It's barely dawn," he said.

"I want to talk to you."

"Katherine," he sighed, "you must be mad."

There was a moment of deep silence during which David was certain he could hear the mist creeping forward, then Katherine turned away, her face shielded by the hood of her cloak.

"Wait!" David called after her, but she glided away until the mist curled around her, wrapping her in a gossamer veil of white that took her from his sight. "Katherine!" he repeated. There was no response.

David felt the panic begin to rise in his throat. He did not want to make her angry, and he knew how easy that was to do. Searching wildly around the room for something to wear, he found the shirt and pants from yesterday and threw them on, then left the room and made his way quickly and silently through the sleeping house. He had to find Katherine before she got away altogether.

The mist closed around him as he stepped outside, and he shivered once as he tried to think which way she might have gone. In the end, he had to follow his instincts, and, as he moved away from the house, the haze began to dissipate a little, so that the landscape was touched here and there with softness. At last he found Katherine's footprints in the wet grass. Breathing a sigh of profound relief, he followed this tenuous trail until he saw her sitting beneath a box elder tree, her cloak wrapped tightly around her, her head resting on her knees.

"Katherine," he panted as he came up beside her. "I'm sorry." He was not certain exactly what he was apologizing for, but he knew that she was waiting for an apology just the same.

Katherine turned her head and considered him coldly, her expression barely visible beneath the purple hood. "Are you?" she asked. "I wonder."

"Of course I am." He sat beside her, but did not move to take her hand.

Shrugging in apparent indifference, she said, "I thought you didn't want to see me after all, so I decided to leave."

"But you didn't go very far," he suggested hopefully.

Katherine allowed a tiny smile to touch her lips. "I wanted you to be able to find me."

David's heart began to pound, as it always did when Katherine smiled that way. "What was it you wanted to talk about?"

Running her tongue over her lips, she seemed to consider the question carefully before she answered, "I want you to kiss me, but not like the other times. Now I want you to *really* kiss me. Do you know what I mean?"

"You came to my window at dawn to get a kiss?" he asked, incredulous.

"A *real* kiss, David. I need to see—" her voice trailed off, but she sat there looking at him expectantly, her lips slightly parted in invitation.

David leaned forward and grasped her chin in one trembling hand, then slowly lowered his mouth to hers. He was completely unprepared, however, when she unfastened her cloak and flung it off her shoulders, then threw her arms around his neck. Her tongue entered his mouth and circled there, seeking something which he could not name, and he drew her closer, until her warm body was pressed so close to his that he could hear the beating of her heart. Only then did he realize that she wore nothing more than a thin shift, through which her pale skin was maddeningly invisible. "Katherine!" he gasped, "my God!" Then her hands began to move across his back, tracing slow, sensuous patterns through the softness of his shirt.

David's kiss grew more demanding, and his own tongue probed her mouth as his hands explored the yielding curves of her waist and hips, wondering how different they would feel without the hindrance of clothes to make a barrier against his searching fingers. But she would be magnificent, of course; he had known that all along. She was that kind of exciting, sensual woman.

When Katherine sensed that David was about to lose control, she backed away, attempting to hide her own disappointment. His lips had been warm, but there had been no fire in her blood, no deep, gnawing hunger that made her senses reel. "Ah!" she said, raising a hand in warning between them, "you mustn't, you know. We're not married yet." But her smile was bright with teasing.

"Katherine," David groaned, "don't do this to me."

"I told you, we're not married. Surely you don't expect—"

"I may be in love with you," he interrupted, "but I'm not a complete fool. And I know this, Katherine Pendleton. A woman like you, at the age of twenty-eight, is not likely—" David paused when he realized what he was saying.

"To still be a virgin?" Katherine suggested. Her smile did not dim for an instant.

"I didn't—I don't mean—" he stammered, confused by her attitude.

"You did and you do," she contradicted him. "But I'll tell you something, David. You can wonder and you can guess and you can think all you like, but you'll never know the truth until *I* choose to tell you. A 'woman like me' has to have her secrets, after all." With that, she picked up her cloak and started away. She had not gone more than three steps when she turned back. "You'll never know," she repeated, and her smile was so all-knowing, so infinitely enticing, that it turned David's blood to raging fire.

Stephen St. Clair watched from behind a concealing curtain as his brother made his weary way back to the house. The mist had burned away by now, and Stephen could see quite clearly the expression of bemused frustration on David's face.

"Damn!" the younger brother cursed under his breath. Why did David have to be such a fool for his fiancée? Stephen hated the way his brother let Katherine rule him—like a tame dog or a dancing monkey. It was disgusting that any man should bow to any woman, and especially *this* woman. Unfortunately, this marriage was necessary, but if it weren't for that—Stephen's lips twisted into a half-sneer and his eyes glistened with thoughts he knew he dared not even complete. There would be time, he told himself. Time enough to see that justice was done.

"I want to talk to you," Phillipe said as he closed the study door behind him.

Medora looked up questioningly at her stepson, and she was distressed by the dark circles under his eyes and the lines of weariness that creased his forehead. He must not have slept well last night. "About the poisoned cattle?" she asked, motioning him to a chair.

Phillipe shifted uneasily under Medora's gaze, but remained standing. Actually, he realized, he had forgotten all about the cattle the moment the nightmare came back. He was uncomfortably aware that he had let a bad dream overshadow their pressing problems. Besides, now that she stood before him, he had begun to wonder at the wisdom of this meeting. Suddenly he was remembering all too vividly the despair in her voice when she had asked his father, *Where are you going?* Running his hand absently through his untidy brown hair, he cleared his throat and said, "No, not the cattle. There's something else I've been wondering about."

The more she watched him, the more concerned Medora became. This haggard young man was not the Phillipe she knew at all. "Well, then, what is it?"

"It was a long time ago," Phillipe began, "before we left the Chateau to go back to Paris."

Medora nodded and waited, perching uncomfortably on the edge of the desk.

"One afternoon I overheard a disagreement between you and my father, and I saw him leave. He was obviously angry and"—he had been looking beyond her at the map of North Dakota on the wall, but now his eyes met hers directly—"and he was carrying a woman's body."

Closing her eyes, Medora took a deep breath and said nothing.

"I want you to tell me about that Indian girl," Phillipe finished. "Tell me what happened that day."

When Medora opened her eyes, they were empty of expression. "No," she murmured. "As you say, it was a long time ago, and it's no longer important. We have far more critical problems to consider at the moment."

Phillipe did not like the way she brushed the question aside so casually. "It's important to *me*," he said quietly.

"It's in the past. Forget it, Phillipe." By now some of her agitation had begun to betray itself in her trembling voice.

"I can't forget it. I have dreams about it all the time. I need to know what happened."

Medora shook her head and looked away, unable to hide the pain in her eyes any longer.

"Medora," Phillipe took a step forward, his hand outstretched, "I thought we were friends."

"We *are* friends," she replied stiffly, "and partners and allies. But it's *my* past, and you have no right to intrude on my memories."

Phillipe was hurt by her indifference, but it only made him all the more determined to learn the truth. "You won't talk about it at all?"

"No."

There was a pause—a moment taut with the battle between their opposing emotions—during which Phillipe closed his eyes and saw again the Indian girl's body with her long black hair hanging over the Marquis' arm. He shuddered. "Did you kill her?"

"Get out of here," Medora hissed. "Leave me alone. I don't have time to listen to your childish fascination with people long dead. I have important work to do, even if you don't, and I intend to do it now."

Medora would not look at him, and Phillipe stood frozen, stunned by the harsh, unforgiving tone of her voice. Never before had she spoken to him that way. Never before had he seen the kind of fear that seemed to hold her in its grasp at this moment. And never had her eyes glittered at him like the eyes of a stranger, cold and green and empty, as they did now.

Phillipe looked away. She would not answer his question, so he would have to answer it himself, and it seemed to him that there could only be one explanation for the fury in her that had raised a wall of lead between them. She must have killed the Indian girl herself.

All at once he felt abandoned, outcast, betrayed by the one woman he had trusted above all others. And it was then, as the pain of loss began to rage through his body with cold, stinging fingers, that he realized for the first time how much he had changed in the past year. And, worst of all, he realized that he had come to think of Medora not as a partner, ally, stepmother, or even friend, but as something much, much more.

Horrified by the shock of his discovery, he turned away, groping blindly for the door. Then, at last he pushed it open and stumbled outside to the porch railing where he stopped, swallowing huge, ragged gulps of air. With his fingers gripping the railing so tightly that he thought it might shatter beneath his hand, he shook his head and closed his eyes against the morning sun, which was, to him, a violation.

Katherine slipped silently into the drawing room, grateful for the heavy brocade curtains that kept out the sun. Just now she wanted nothing more than the comfort of soothing darkness, where she could ponder the things she had discovered. Dropping her still damp cloak on an empty chair, she sank down on the sofa and rested her head against the high back.

"Where have you been?" Cory's querulous voice demanded.

Katherine looked up in annoyance to find her mother standing in the doorway, looking like a ghost in her floor-length nightgown. "Out," the young woman said, noting with disgust that Cory had not even taken the time to brush her hair.

"Out where?"

"Just out," Katherine sighed in exasperation. "Why don't you go back to bed, Mama? I want to be alone right now."

"Why?" Cory came farther into the room, eyeing her daughter with suspicion.

"I want to think, that's all."

"But maybe I can help you."

Katherine shivered when her mother's hand came to rest on her shoulder. "You can't, Mama. You wouldn't understand."

Cory jerked her hand away at Katherine's disparaging tone. "You think I'm stupid," her mother whined, "but I'm not."

"No one said you were stupid."

"But you think it!" Cory accused. "You think I'm stupid and blind and that I don't know anything. You think

I just lie in my bed all day and stare blankly at the ceiling—"

"Stop!" Katherine cried, covering her ears with her hands. "Just leave me alone."

Cory ignored her. "Well, you're wrong," she said. "I *do* know things. You think that I don't know that you go to meet Phillipe Beaumont, but I do."

"Stop it!" Katherine warned.

"And you thought I didn't know what happened before when he was here. But I saw things. I saw a lot of things." Cory sat next to her daughter and leaned over to whisper in her ear, "I knew all about your trouble, and I watched while you—"

"No!" Katherine stood up sharply, her fists clenched at her sides. "Shut up, Mama," she hissed: "Just shut up and leave me alone. If you want to worry about someone this morning, worry about Father." Her eyes were glistening with fury; this time Cory had gone too far. "Where do you suppose *he* is at this hour?"

Cory shrank back against the sofa and drew her feet defensively toward her body. "I don't know," she whispered. "He said he had business—"

Katherine threw back her head and laughed, but her laughter had no warmth or kindness. *"Now?* At six in the morning? And you believed him?"

With blank, searching eyes, Cory looked up at her daughter. "He doesn't lie to me anymore," she declared. "He told me—"

"Did he tell you he was going up to the Chateau?" Katherine inquired. At her mother's silence, she continued, "No, I don't suppose he did. He probably didn't realize that I would be up this early, too. He didn't know I would see him, so he thought it would be safe not to mention that he was on his way to visit Medora."

"No!" Cory shrieked, rising awkwardly to her feet. "You're the one who's lying, Katherine."

"Would you like me to show you?" her daughter asked calmly. "Father would be angry, of course, but then he's been angry before. Shall we go find out if they're together?"

"No! Because they're not." Cory's rage was suddenly a palpable force which filled the empty room to bursting. "He told me the truth and you lied. You always lie to me. You think I'm too stupid to know it, but I do." Cory backed away until she felt the edge of the table against her spine.

"You're blind, Mama," Katherine purred. "Father loves Medora, and he always will. You're so pitifully blind."

"And you're nothing but a filthy liar, not to mention a filthy whore."

Katherine stiffened and exhaled slowly, then she began to move toward her mother. "Let's prove that I'm a liar. Let's go see."

But when she reached out to take Cory's arm, the older woman cried, "No! Don't touch me! I'll hurt you, Katherine. You know I will!"

It was then that Katherine saw the letter opener in her mother's hand. She held it perfectly steady, despite her rage, and Katherine shivered. She had seen that look in her mother's eyes before, and she knew what Cory was capable of. "Now, wait," she began soothingly, "you don't want to do this."

"Don't touch me!" Cory repeated, and when Katherine tried to wrench the opener out of her grasp, she twisted away. "I mean it. Don't."

Then, unexpectedly, Cory lunged for her daughter, aiming the weapon toward her heart. "You won't lie to me anymore," the woman shrieked.

Katherine caught her arm in an iron grip, and they stood there, weaving from side to side, neither one able to break away from the other. "Don't," Katherine pleaded. "Remember what happened before—" Her voice trailed off suggestively.

As the words penetrated her haze of anger, Cory tensed, then her fingers relaxed their grip on the letter opener. *Remember what happened before*— But she didn't remember, and she didn't want to. Not now, not ever! The past was too dangerous; she dared not bring it rushing back. When Katherine's pale face came into focus, Cory sagged against her daughter and murmured, "Take me to bed."

Katherine closed her eyes with a fervent sigh of relief. The emptiness was back in her mother's tone, and that meant she was safe again. It had always been this way—one moment of uncontrolled rage, the urge toward violence, then the lost docility once again. Thank God she had so easily found the words to break the spell that had held Cory in its grasp. *This* time she found them, but what about next time? Even Katherine recognized that she could not always be so lucky. And what would happen when the luck finally ran out?

Chapter 12

Phillipe and Medora sat in the study watching the evening approach on silent feet, while all around them the Chateau hummed with activity as the servants scurried about, preparing for the celebration that would take place later. Early that morning, Phillipe had thrown open the doors of the packing plant for the first time in thirteen years, while the curious townspeople looked on. Then, accompanied by a roar of approval from the crowd, Phillipe had rolled up his sleeves and gone inside to butcher the first steer himself. By the time the sun began to sink beyond the patterned cliffs, fifty head of beef had been processed; they were ready to be transported to Chicago and New York in the refrigerated railroad cars that lined the tracks beside the plant.

"The opening went beautifully, Phillipe," Medora said as she smiled with pure relief. This was the first time all day when she had had a moment to sit down and relax, but even this interval would not last long. She would have to be up soon attending to the last details for the party.

Her stepson returned Medora's smile a little stiffly. It had been an exhausting day. It was also the first time he had been alone with Medora since he had made the discovery about his feelings for her, and he was uneasy. His stepmother had apologized for her behavior that day, but she still refused to discuss the subject any further. Although he still did not understand, Phillipe had ceased to blame her; he was too busy berating himself for his own betrayal of his father's memory. He had been grateful for the work which had kept him busy for the last week, but even the constant activity had not kept his thoughts from tormenting him.

When Medora saw that Phillipe did not intend to respond, she leaned forward and put her hand on his arm. She was not aware of the steely control which kept him from drawing away. "You were a great success with the townspeople, too. I think they've actually come to trust you," she told him. And it was true. It seemed that Phillipe had a knack with crowds; by the end of the day he had won over the entire town. She had never been more proud of him, or any man, than when he stepped outside the plant, his arms covered in blood to the elbows, and held up the first cut of beef as a symbol of the new beginning that he alone had engineered. Her heart had swollen with admiration, and she had finally seen for herself that, bullets or no bullets, Phillipe would make this business work, even if he had no more than his own two hands to do it with.

"Medora! Phillipe!" William's excited voice dragged Medora back from her moment of triumph and into the present. She looked up curiously as he entered the room, waving a yellow telegram form in the air.

"What is it?" Phillipe asked when he saw the look of triumph on Van Driesche's face.

"Swift has signed the contract making us one of his major suppliers if the first carloads of beef are satisfactory."

Phillipe was out of his chair in an instant, and he read the telegram several times, as if to reassure himself that it was really true.

"Congratulations," Medora cried as she clasped Phillipe's hands in both of hers. "You did it!"

"*We* did it," her stepson corrected her with a broad smile. His blood raced through his veins as the realization of the import of this victory hit him full force, but he was not prepared when Medora threw her arms around his neck and kissed him on the cheek.

"We've waited a long time for this," she said, "and it never would have happened without you."

In that instant, Phillipe forgot everything but the thrill of triumph that had taken possession of him and the feel of Medora's arms around his neck. He forgot his self-disgust and his doubts and his wisdom, and when at last she drew away from him, their gazes met and held.

To Medora there was suddenly nothing in the world beyond the look in Phillipe's deep blue eyes, because it told her, more clearly than words, that for him there was nothing in the world beyond her. And, in the moment when Phillipe's soul was bared before her, she looked into her own and saw, for the first time, the depth and magnitude of the feelings for this man that she had always refused to recognize. What a fool she had been, she thought in wonder, not to have seen it before. And what would she do now that she had?

Neither Phillipe nor Medora was aware of William, frozen and still beside them. He saw the look that passed between the green eyes and the blue, and he understood, with a chest full of sinking despair, what message that look carried. Not now! he cried silently. Not tonight when the whole of the Badlands was coming to celebrate their victory. But, as he closed his eyes and struggled to gain control of his emotions, he realized that, for him, this moment would have been as ill-timed whenever it happened. Because, to him, it meant, quite simply, that all he valued in this world had moved beyond his reach.

He thought at first that he would never be able to force himself to move again, but then he heard the rustle of Mianne's skirts approaching, and he cleared his throat loudly and prayed it would break the spell. But when Medora and Phillipe turned to look at him, he realized with a shiver of apprehension that to them he was no more than one of the shadows that clung to the walls and hovered darkly in the empty corners.

Medora slipped among the brightly colored silks and satins of her guests, smiling and nodding as each stopped to congratulate her. The faces were no more than a blur of eyes and chattering mouths, and, although she was gracious to those who spoke to her, Medora's thoughts were elsewhere. Everyone in the Badlands seemed to be here tonight, whirling in the false light of the lanterns, their faces flushed with exhilaration, but to Medora their laughter was as distant a music as the song of the river far below. She moved in and out of the glittering, fragmented lamplight, from radiance to soft shadow and back again, but her eyes remained untouched by the dancing light.

When Medora saw her two sons huddled in the doorway of the dining room, their faces glowing with delight as they watched the party swirl around them, she smiled and knelt beside them. She was glad she had decided to let them watch for a little while; she suspected their dreams would be peopled with laughing dancers and the pleasing clink of crystal for some time to come. For them, there was not much in the Badlands that could compare with this brilliant collection of color and excitement. "Are you having a good time?" she asked.

"Oh, yes!" Paul said eagerly, while Louis attempted to cover his delight with a thin veneer of maturity. "It's very interesting," the older boy declared.

Medora nodded gravely. "Where is Anais?"

"She didn't want to come," Louis explained. "She said it was silly."

"Did she? Well, I think I'll go and ask if she's changed her mind," his mother said.

"She hasn't," Louis informed her. "Anais never changes her mind."

As she rose and found her way to the bottom of the staircase, Medora hoped her son was wrong. She had been deeply concerned about Anais since the day when the girl had revealed so much about her feelings for her father, but Anais had refused to discuss the subject further. She had become a shadow in the past week; she came and went quietly, usually without speaking, and the rest of the time she cut herself off from people and sat alone. Only Mianne was allowed to intrude on Anais' solitude.

Medora fully expected to find the two together, but when she knocked on Anais' door and pushed it open, she saw that the girl was alone. She was huddled over her desk writing furiously, and when she saw her mother, she leaned further forward, so that her shadow covered the page before her. Her expression, Medora mused, was almost furtive.

"Why don't you come down to the party for a while, dear. You could even have a dance or two if you'd like."

Anais shook her head. "I don't want to. I'm busy writing to Grandfather."

"It's nice of you to do that, but don't you think you could finish it tomorrow? The party is only for tonight." Medora closed the door behind her and glided toward her daughter, one hand stretched out in invitation. "Won't you come, just for a little bit?"

"No. I told you, I'm busy." As her mother came closer, Anais picked up the paper she had been working on and crushed it to her chest with the blank side outward. "And you don't have to bother to try and read my letter over my shoulder. It's *my* letter, and you can't see it!" She was fifteen years old, after all, she told herself, certainly old enough to deserve some privacy from her mother's prying eyes.

Medora's hand fell back among the folds of her skirt, and she just managed to stifle a deep sigh. No matter how often she approached the girl, her response was always the same, and Medora had begun to wonder if she would ever be able to reach her daughter again. Keeping her eyes on the belligerent twist of Anais' mouth, Medora sat on the edge of the bed, her hands resting in her lap. "Listen to me—" she began.

Anais turned back to her desk. "If you want someone to talk to, go find Phillipe. He's sure to listen, but *I* have other things to do."

Medora was startled by the intense bitterness in the girl's tone. Anais' voice was transformed by her anger into that of a stranger, and the attack had been so sudden that for an instant Medora could think of nothing to say. Then she asked in bewilderment, "You hate Phillipe, don't you?"

Anais shrugged without raising her head. "I told you, Mama, I'm busy right now and I don't—"

"Look at me." Medora's voice was perfectly steady, but there was a note of command in her tone which even Anais dared not disobey.

Reluctantly, the girl turned to meet her mother's questioning gaze.

"What did Phillipe do to make you so angry?"

Pursing her lips thoughtfully, Anais replied, "He brought me here, didn't he?"

"*I* brought you here," Medora reminded her. "But I don't think that's the reason anyway. There's something else and I want to know what it is."

"There's nothing," Anais insisted, but she could not hide the agitation which made her hands tremble and sent a rush of color into her cheeks.

"Tell me the truth," Medora demanded, rising until she stood above her daughter, looking downward with piercing green eyes. "You *do* hate him, don't you?"

"Yes," Anais spluttered, "I do! Now will you leave me alone?" Her voice quavered with rising panic as her mother's shadow fell across her like a threat from out of the deep black night beyond her window.

"Not until you tell me why," Medora persisted.

"Go away!" Anais cried. "I don't want to talk to you."

Medora reached out and took her daughter's shoulders in her hands. Lifting the girl from her chair, she looked down into Anais' fathomless black eyes and asked, "Why do you hate Phillipe so much?"

Wrenching wildly in an effort to escape, Anais hissed, "Because *you* love him!"

Suddenly, she was free. Unaccountably the hands that had held her prisoner had fallen away, and Medora's anger had transformed itself to disbelief. She stood unmoving, as if the life had been drained from her, and her deep green eyes seemed suddenly out of place in her pale, colorless face. Medora stared blankly at the child before her and wondered how much Anais knew. How much had she seen with those eyes that seemed to fall with equal indifference on everyone around her? The girl was obviously more aware than Medora had realized, and far, far too perceptive. But just now Anais was staring at her curiously, her body still taut with rage, and her mother knew she had to tell the girl something.

"I love *you*, too," she managed to breathe. "It's just that I don't know how to talk to you."

Anais crossed her arms and tilted her chin defiantly. "That's funny," she snapped. "You always seem to know what to say to Phillipe."

Closing her eyes to block out the image of Anais' spiteful accusation, Medora shook her head sadly. "Not always," she said. But she was not talking to her daughter. "Listen, Anais," she continued, opening her eyes once more, "you can't blame Phillipe for all your personal pain; it isn't fair. It isn't his fault that your father died."

"How do you know?" Anais demanded. "You never found out who paid the assassins, did you? It might have been anyone. It might even have been Phillipe and you together. Maybe the two of you had my father killed so you could—"

Her voice died out abruptly when Medora's hand hit the girl's cheek with bruising force. "I never want to hear you say that again," her mother warned.

Anais did not move; she simply stood and stared at Medora's face, her eyes blazing with an intensity of emotion which turned them into glowing coals. Medora hovered for an instant, held by the look in those eyes, but then she took a deep breath and turned away. When she reached the door and the smooth, cool knob was in her hand, Anais called after her one last warning.

"I'm not the only one who's thought of that, Mama. You're crazy if you think no one's watching you. You and Phillipe are all they see."

Medora opened the door, then closed it at her back, her hand still clasped around the knob as if to steady her. Anais was wrong, of course; she was exaggerating out of her own rage and pain. But as Medora started down the stairs, she could not banish the burning memory of her daughter's implacable expression and the deep black eyes that had threatened to swallow Medora in their luminous, searching gaze.

The owls were calling throatily overhead, their voices blending with the pulse of the river, and Katherine leaned back, excitement beating in her veins. Phillipe would come to her tonight, she knew, because she had willed it so, and she would be waiting, her exquisite blue satin gown spread like morning mist on the boulder behind her. This was hardly the ideal setting for the beaded gown trimmed with dark fur, but she did not care about that. Phillipe did not need to see her in daylight, or even soft lamplight, to know how desirable she was.

Tossing her hair back over her shoulders, Katherine enjoyed the feel of the thick, cool tendrils on her back, and she was glad she had chosen a low-cut gown. Tonight she wanted to be completely aware of her body and all that it could do for her, and the soft murmur of the river promised she would not be disappointed. He would come, she thought, even though he had seemed reluctant when she asked him earlier in the evening. He would come because he could not help himself any more than she could.

Still, she was surprised when he appeared with the stealth of a phantom. He seemed to rise out of the darkness to stand at her feet, the moonlight touching his face with an uncertain radiance. Katherine smiled her secret smile and waited.

"You're very beautiful," Phillipe said as he extended his hands to her. "Come here; I want you."

Katherine rose slowly, aware, even as she glided into his arms, that his voice was taut with a strange new desperation. The knowledge only made her heart beat faster, for she sensed that tonight his need was even more intense than it had been so many times in the past. His lips, when they touched hers, were warm and fiercely demanding, and Katherine leaned into him, twining her arms around his neck as his kiss raced through her waiting blood.

She could feel his body trembling with desire for her, and before he had even released her lips, she reached back to open her gown. "A moment," she whispered, stepping away from him. When she slid the blue satin off her shoulders and let it fall, unheeded, to the ground, Phillipe saw that she wore nothing underneath. She stood before him, tall, naked and achingly lovely, and her lips were curved in a smile that froze his heart in his chest. If anyone could make him forget the weight of despair that lay curled in his belly, it was Katherine, and he drew her to him without regret, praying that he could lose himself in the dark, fragrant strands of her hair. "Dear God, Kathy," he gasped as she began to unfasten his trousers, "I don't believe there is another woman like you in all the world."

"No," she murmured, trailing her tongue down the line of his throat, "not even one."

Phillipe drew her down beside him until they lay stretched out on the riverbank, and he could feel the cool presence of the water rustling past just as he could feel Katherine's breath on his body as she removed his clothing, piece by piece. Her hands traced magic patterns on his skin which made him forget that she had no heart. He could not let her go, he thought, when she knew his body as no woman had ever known it before. To lose her would be to live without water in a desert wilderness.

As their bodies met and clung in the cool darkness, Katherine read the hunger in Phillipe's eyes and she knew that he shared her desperate need. She had been slow to recognize how deeply he had penetrated her consciousness, but now she realized that he had become necessary to her, like a drug that kept her satisfied and sane. For a long time Katherine had denied the truth. She had stared it arrogantly in the face and simply refused to recognize it, but now, at last, her eyes were open. And foolish David had been the one to make her see.

Despite the hatred, the fear, the pain and anger she had nurtured inside herself for twelve long years, despite the constant battle that made them enemies, despite the knowledge that he alone had the power to destroy her, Phillipe was in her blood. He was as much a part of her as her own beating heart, and had been, long before he left her twelve years ago.

When their bodies were finally still, Phillipe pulled Katherine against him and murmured into her hair, "I need you, Kathy."

She smiled to herself. She had won the first battle. His need for her was enough for now, because she was aware of the magnitude of her power. His hunger would bring him back time and again, and that was all she asked—for the moment.

But soon, very soon, things would change for him as they had for her. It must be so, because Katherine had finally realized that it did not matter if she had vowed to get revenge against him and that the victory she had sought so long hovered now within her grasp. Nothing mattered anymore but this one appalling fact: Of all the men she had ever known, Phillipe alone had the power to make her happy.

Her heart raced as his hand came up to cup her breast and her arms closed around him without hesitation. "I will have you, Phillipe," she whispered, "whatever the cost!" But her words were drowned in the heedless rush of the singing river.

Noiselessly, Medora slipped out the back door and wound her way down the path across the bluff until she came to the river. She wanted the sound of the water to carry away the image of Anais' hate-filled eyes and the memory of her accusing words. Just now Medora could not face the guests and their sparkling laughter. She sought instead the comfort of the moon-softened darkness.

But thoughts of her daughter's inexplicable anger would not leave her, and finally she paused beneath a cottonwood and closed her eyes. Maybe the colored darkness behind her lids would wipe away her memory of the past several minutes.

Then, slowly, a new sound intruded on her thoughts—the crackling of twigs and the whisper of words because of their very softness rose above the rumble of the river nearby. Medora turned her head for a moment, seeking the source of this disturbance. At first she could see nothing, for the shifting shadows clouded her vision. But then the leaves overhead began to sway and in the sudden glow of moonlight, she saw clearly the two naked bodies locked together, their heated breath rising rhythmically, the sheen of their skin almost golden.

The earth began to rock beneath her and with a will of iron, Medora forced her breath to come slowly so that the lovers would not hear her. To be discovered now would be more than she could bear. Turning away as silently as she had come, she left the riverbank and started back toward the house, amazed that her legs continued to function.

She had seen the couple for only an instant, but she had needed no more than that to recognize the dark tumble of Katherine's hair and the curve of Phillipe's naked shoulders in the moonlight. At first, shock kept the image frozen in her mind, but as the evening air struck her face again and again, her thoughts began to thaw and move.

He is young, she told herself in an attempt to explain that moment away. And she had known all along that he had needs she could not even begin to understand. But Katherine Pendleton! she cried out silently. Your enemy and his. It wasn't fair. Worse, it was utter madness.

And yet—Medora, after all, was a mature adult, not a selfish child who wanted everything she could not have. It was better by far that those golden hands never touch her body. Katherine was young and willing. It was right that those two should be there together. Where else could Phillipe find what Medora could never give him?

But the explanation, rational though it was, did nothing to ease the ache inside her. She was a fool, and she knew it, but that could not change the truth of what she felt in that moment.

When she was far enough away that she was certain they could not hear her, Medora began to run. Suddenly, the moonlight had become an enemy she could not escape quickly enough. But no matter how fast she ran, her thoughts—and the pain—would not leave her.

Chapter 13

A rush of dry, cold air escaped into the room from the open window, and William breathed it in with a sigh of relief. Despite the coolness of the evening, inside the air was warm and thick with the motion of rotating bodies, the soft swell of violin music, and the gusts and eddies of animated conversation. Apparently the celebrating dancers were oblivious to the strange tension that tainted the air; bent on enjoying themselves, they felt nothing but the exciting pulse of the music.

William took a sip from the goblet he held in his hand, noting, as he did so, that the lamplight caught the ruby color of the glass and scattered it across the floor in dancing red patterns. But his thoughts were not really concerned with the ever-changing patterns of light. He was thinking, instead, about Medora. Now that she had finally recognized her weakness, Van Driesche knew that he had to act. Somehow he must save her from herself—and whoever else might threaten her. But what could he do? The answer came to him, as it had many times before, so quietly that he was not certain he had heard the thought at all.

There was a sudden increase in the volume of chatter around him, and William looked up to see Medora standing in the doorway across the room. There was something different about her tonight, and as he watched her move lithely among the guests, he realized that, for the first time, she had discarded the black and gray gowns she had worn in mourning for her husband for the past year. She wore a long, graceful caftan of beige cloth, draped skillfully over a fitted gown of light green velvet with a raised design of darker green. Both gown and caftan were simple and flowing, with only a touch of lace at the throat and wrists, and together they made Medora's petite body seem taller and more commanding. She had even abandoned the severe braids she usually wore, and her hair was piled in curls on her head, except where one thick strand waved softly across her shoulder, a streak of sunset red against the forest green of her gown.

Turning away in order to steady his labored breathing, Van Driesche shut his eyes and hoped she would disappear, but all at once she was beside him, her hand on his arm and her voice whispering urgently in his ear, "I need to talk to you, William. Will you come to the study with me?"

He could not resist the plea he saw reflected in her eyes, and, though it cost him a great effort, he smiled reassuringly at her and nodded.

When the study door was safely shut, Medora turned to face Van Driesche with a dangerous brilliance in her eyes. "I want to know the truth," she began. "What are people saying?"

William blinked at her in astonishment; her voice was so taut with suppressed fury. "Saying?" he repeated.

"About Phillipe and me."

Shifting uncomfortably, William searched for words with which to answer her, but none came. "I don't—"

"Please," Medora interrupted. "The truth. You saw what passed between us this evening?"

William nodded and looked away.

"Does anyone else know?" She could not bring herself

to ask him the question that had been eating away at her since the little scene with Anais. Did others think as her daughter apparently did?

"They don't *know*," Van Driesche told her, "but they wonder. I've heard rumors."

"The rumors must be stopped," Medora declared in a voice of steel. "Even the hint of scandal could make them doubt Phillipe, and that could ruin all our plans." How could she speak so calmly, she wondered, when the mere pressure of her rising breath was almost too much to bear?

William knew Medora was right. He had known it from the beginning. "Yes, it could," he said simply.

Medora moved closer and her eyes searched his face as if seeking a solution to her problem. "What shall I do? Should I go away?" And if I did, she added silently, could I ever go far enough to escape the things I have seen tonight?

It was the only answer that had never occurred to William. "I think that would only make them more suspicious. It might even convince them that you're guilty. 'Why else would she run?' they'll ask themselves." He spoke in a perfectly steady voice, but inside his body was in turmoil. He had not known it would be so painful.

"What other choice is there?" Medora asked.

With a single deep breath, William said, "You must force their attention away from the two of you. Give them a diversion."

Medora almost laughed aloud, but she caught herself in time. Phillipe was doing quite a good job of creating his own diversion. "How?"

He had thought his answer out long ago, in case she ever asked him that question, but now that the moment had come, he found it difficult to form the words. "If you were to marry someone else, it might make them forget."

Medora shook her head vaguely, unable, for the moment, to understand what he was suggesting. But then his meaning struck her like a blow somewhere near the base of her spine. Could she do something like that, even to save Phillipe? "Isn't there some other way?"

"You tell *me*."

But she knew as well as he did that she had no alternatives to offer. Medora grasped blindly for any excuse to free herself. "No one would agree to enter into a loveless marriage with me in order to save a business that has already failed once."

"I would." William was surprised he had had the courage to speak those words aloud.

Medora's eyes widened in astonishment. She had always known the man was loyal, but she had never realized before how deep that loyalty went. "You would do that for me?" she asked.

"I would do anything," Van Driesche paused, swallowed once and continued, "to make this business project a success."

Medora nodded and went to stand before the glass doors that led onto the porch. When she was so close that she could feel the cold radiating inward, she raised one hand and pressed it against a single pane. She realized that if she were to decide to marry, William was the only man she would consider. She had known him for years, and never once in that time had he disappointed her. He had always been there, patient, silent, and wholly trustworthy, to take the burdens from her shoulders whenever they became too heavy. What was more, he cared about the business as much as she did, and she knew that he would do anything to keep it alive. "Do you really think my marriage would make a difference?" she inquired, her hand still pressed against the glass.

"Single women excite interest, Medora, especially you, if for no other reason than that you are the Marquis' widow. I believe marriage would deprive you of some of your glitter in the people's eyes, make you a little more ordinary."

Medora nodded for the second time, but she had not really heard what he said, because, as she stared at her face in the window, her eyes had transformed themselves into Phillipe's as they had looked at her this evening. She knew that there was only one man who could fill the emptiness left by Antoine's death, and he was the one man she could not have. Whether she chose to marry William or not, she had no choice but to turn Phillipe away. And apparently, he knew it too. He had already begun to leave her behind. Yet this man—who was really little more than a boy—had made himself the center and focus of her life, and now she had to deny him—and herself—everything which she most wanted to give.

She was just about to tell William she could not do it when Anais' bitter accusation began to echo inside her head. *Maybe the two of you had my father killed so you could—* Dear God. *I'm not the only one who's thought of that, Mama. You're crazy if you think no one's watching you. You and Phillipe are all they see.* Dear God in heaven!

"All right," she said, turning to William with stately calm. "I will marry you. Perhaps you can find Johnny Goodall and ask him to announce our engagement now. I assume we should do this as quickly as possible." *Before I have a chance to change my mind,* she added silently.

Van Driesche tried desperately to catch his breath, but it had somehow escaped him with the first words Medora had spoken. He had not expected this sudden acquiescence. In fact, he realized, he had not expected her to agree at all. "Don't you want to think about it?" he asked.

From out of the half-darkness beyond the window, the image of the lovely Katherine clasped tightly in Phillipe's strong arms rose before Medora. "No," she murmured softly. "I've made my decision. And I think now is the time to let everyone know, while they're all together."

Now, she pleaded with her eyes, because I know I'll never have the courage again.

She began to move toward the door, but William stopped her. "Don't you think you should tell Phillipe in private?"

Medora shook her head. That was one thing she could not bring herself to do. "Johnny will make a general announcement," she repeated firmly. "I really believe that would be best for everyone." But then she opened the door and stood on the threshold of all the gaiety and light and music, and she found herself wondering, in that instant, if it was really Phillipe she sought to protect—or was it herself?

Mianne stood at the edge of the drawing room, inconspicuous in her simple linen gown of soft brown. Several young men had asked her to dance in the course of the evening, but she had politely refused every one. Instead, her eyes had followed Phillipe since he returned from whatever secret meeting had drawn him outside earlier in the evening. Mianne had never noticed before how tall Phillipe was, but tonight she found it easy to pick him out in the crowd; his light brown hair was always visible above the heads of those around him. And he moved with such grace, his eyes always sparkling, despite the unease that she sensed in him, even from across the room. His energy and enthusiasm were manufactured to conceal whatever thoughts were troubling him inside.

When the study door opened and William and Medora stepped into the room, calling for Johnny Goodall, Mianne saw how Phillipe's eyes flashed to his stepmother, but Medora would not look at him. And when at last Johnny was found, and William engaged him in a minute of animated conversation, Mianne felt a tremor of curiosity run through the room. But not until the foreman approached the piano, his face split in a grin from ear to ear, did the merrymakers begin to turn toward him.

"I have an announcement!" Johnny bellowed, his deep, gravelly voice carrying easily across the crowded room. And while Medora and William stood silently, their eyes on Goodall, an expectant stillness fell upon the uplifted faces.

"Well, get on with it!" someone coaxed.

Johnny smiled, cleared his throat dramatically, and said, "It's my pleasure to inform you that we'll be having a wedding soon at the Chateau. The Marquise de Mores has agreed to marry William Van Driesche sometime within the next two weeks. And that makes this a double celebration." Raising his glass toward the couple, he shouted, "A toast to your future happiness!" The crowd roared out its approbation.

Mianne's eyes left her father and sought out Phillipe, where he stood unmoving, his hands clenched at his sides. No one else was looking at him, so no one but her saw the pain that ravaged his face for an instant, before he managed to regain control. Mianne looked away, wondering at the pang of regret that shot through her own chest. She felt his struggle to hide his feelings as if it were her own, and she pitied him, in that instant, as she had never pitied another human being.

Compassion turned to bitter admiration as he began to move toward the end of the room where Medora and William stood, accepting the good wishes of their many guests. The very force of Phillipe's personality seemed to clear a path before him, although he did not speak or turn his head. But the people fell back one by one to let him pass, and by the time he reached the couple, a second hush had taken away the voices of everyone around him.

Mianne took a deep breath as Phillipe took William's hand and shook it warmly. "Congratulations," the young man said in apparent sincerity. Only Mianne heard the slight quaver in his tone. And then Phillipe turned to Medora and reached for her hand, which he carried gracefully to his lips. "I hope you'll be happy," he said. Still Medora could not bear to meet his eyes.

Then, suddenly, the stillness exploded as the window behind the couple shattered inward, striking the little group by the piano with hundreds of tiny fragments of glittering glass. For the briefest of seconds, everyone stood silent, stunned into immobility, then they heard the rapid fire of a repeater rifle and another pane of glass burst into dangerous slivers of rainbow light.

With a strength born of near panic, Phillipe forced Medora and William to the floor as he roared, "Everyone get down!" He could only hope they had followed his order; for now, his major concern was to get to the gunman before the sporadic rifle fire ceased.

"Are you all right, Medora, William?" he hissed. When he heard their muffled assurances, Phillipe heaved a single heartfelt sigh of relief before he ordered, "Stay here. I'm going out."

Slowly, every muscle in his body taut with fear and cold anger, he disentangled himself from the others and began to slither across the glistening debris that littered the floor. Above his head, he could still hear the hiss of bullets flying past at irregular intervals, then he became aware of a presence behind him.

"You're not going to do it alone, you fool," Johnny Goodall whispered. "Like it or not, I'm coming too. But I'll go around to the south side and you take the other. Maybe we can catch the gunman in the middle."

Phillipe took an instant to nod before he continued his painful progress toward the door. By now his hands were cut and bleeding from the broken glass, but he had no time to worry about that. As he reached the doorway, the shadows of the darkened room closed around him and he realized the rifle had fallen silent at last. With a fresh

burst of determination, he rose to his feet and, opening
the outside door as quietly as possible, he slipped outside.

He could see little, though the moon had touched the
night with soft, uncertain light. Like a wildcat intent on
stalking his prey, Phillipe crept forward, praying that this
time the assailant had not had a chance to get away into
the protective blanket of darkness. Then he saw it—the
distant shadow that paused like an insubstantial spirit at
the edge of the bluff, as if waiting for some dark and
secret lover. Phillipe swung himself over the porch railing
and started to run on silent feet, but the shadow seemed
to sense his presence and it wavered for a moment before
turning to flee into the night.

Doggedly, he pursued the mysterious figure that was always just beyond his reach, every nerve alert with the driving need to outrun the person who darted lithely in and out
of the bushes up ahead. Phillipe's heart had begun to pound
furiously in his chest with the unaccustomed exertion when
the shadow found it necessary to come into the open for
an instant. But Phillipe needed no more than the hint of
the wide swirl of dark skirts to tell him that the figure was
a woman. But who?

He ran faster and ever faster, swerving in and out as
he followed the woman's wild flight. She carried no rifle,
he realized, so she must have thrown it over the cliff or
merely left it behind. But it didn't matter. It was the assailant he sought, not her weapon. However, he had begun
to think she would defeat him after all; his body was crying out in tormented denial at the seemingly endless
chase. The breath seared his chest with burning fingers
and muscles screamed with each step, but he refused to
listen. He had failed once to catch the gunman who had
threatened his life, and he swore he would not fail again.

Then, all at once, the hissing of the woman's ragged
breath came to him on the back of a whisper of wind and
he realized she was tiring, too. When she tripped and

stumbled, he forced his legs to propel him forward in one final rush of energy. Unable to stop himself in time, he crashed into her, and the two struggling bodies fell to the ground. For a full minute, they tumbled over the grass while the woman groaned and spat and clawed in an effort to gain her freedom. But then, at last, Phillipe caught her beneath him and pinned her arms to the ground with his bloodstained hands.

Still she tried to fight him, but he was bigger and stronger, and the outcome of the battle was inevitable. With a deep, wrenching breath, Phillipe held both her hands in one of his, then brushed the concealing hair from her face. In that instant, his heart ceased its labored beating and the air seemed to rush from his protesting lungs in a single jagged exclamation. "Christ!"

For the glittering dark eyes that looked up at him with such bitter hatred belonged to his half-sister, Anais.

Chapter 14

"Tell me about it," Stephen coaxed.

Anais looked up at the tutor with a bleak smile. "What? The wedding? There's not much to tell. A justice of the peace came and married them, that's all." She did not bother to suppress a snort of disgust at the memory of her mother's hurried marriage to William Van Driesche. They had been engaged for exactly a week, and this morning a brief ceremony had made them man and wife. There had been no flowers, no music, not even a cake, and to Anais it had seemed more like a funeral than a celebration.

"I didn't mean the wedding," Stephen said with a sigh of irritation. "I want you to tell me what happened the night of the party." This was the first time he had been allowed to see Anais in a week, and Stephen was determined to discover the truth, no matter how reluctant she was to reveal it.

Anais braided her fingers together and stared intently at the pattern they made against her deep green skirt. She did not want to talk about that night. To say the words aloud would only make her remember everything—the tears, the shouting, the horrible accusations that had assaulted her like a swarm of locusts all through the night and into the morning. Shivering with fear and anger, she had sat without speaking after her first attempt to deny that she had fired a rifle from the safety of the darkness. They had not heard her, had not wanted to hear her, and she had sunk into a chair and faced them defiantly through all the rest of those nightmare hours, refusing to defend herself.

Then, finally, when Medora's fury had drained her of the power to hurt her daughter anymore, Anais had told her stiffly, "I went for a walk outside, that's all. The house was too hot. I heard the rifle fire and the breaking glass, then whoever it was ran down the hill to the river. I don't know where they went, and I don't know who it was."

Medora and Phillipe and William and Johnny had not been satisfied with her explanation, and Anais winced at the memory of their obstinate questions. "Why were you walking so late?" "Why did you run from Phillipe?" "What did you hope to accomplish?" "What did you do with the rifle?" It was the rifle that had saved her in the end. They had combed the area all the next day, but had found no trace of the gun. And surely if Anais had thrown it over the cliff, they would have been able to locate it eventually. Besides, there had been no betraying carbon on her hands.

It had been late the next day before they had really begun to listen to her, but by then the damage had been done. And even after they said they believed her, they had watched her every movement warily, kept her away from her lessons with the boys—as if they were waiting for her to make another mistake. The week had been the worst hell she had ever lived through, worse even than the day she had learned that her father was dead. She could only hate them now, in silence, and pray that she would never have to live through torment like that again.

She did not realize she had been speaking her thoughts aloud until Stephen touched her arm with long, cool fingers. "But they trust you now?" he asked softly.

Anais shuddered at the force of her memories and tried to make the tutor's face come into focus. "I don't know. I suppose they believe I didn't do it, but it's almost as if just suspecting me has changed the way they look at me."

Stephen gazed beyond Anais to the swell of waving grass outside the window, and the afternoon light seemed to drain his pale blue eyes of color altogether. "They're fools," he murmured. "You mustn't worry about what they think. *You* are the one who knows what's important."

Anais was not exactly certain what he meant, but she nodded her head in agreement just the same. After all, this man seemed to be her only ally, the only one who believed in her implicitly.

"But tell me the truth," Stephen said, bringing his eyes back to rest on her face. "You *do* hate Phillipe, don't you? I've heard it in your voice when you speak his name."

Biting her lip nervously, Anais tried to look away, but his eyes held her immobile.

"You can tell *me*," he declared. "I'm your friend, remember?"

There was something in his tone which disturbed her, but Anais was not sure what it was. And, at the moment, his hand on her arm was comforting, and she did not want to turn him away. "Yes," she muttered. "I hate him."

A spark flared briefly in Stephen's eyes at the intensity of her tone. "Enough to kill him?" he asked.

Anais opened her mouth to lie, but her tongue seemed to have a life of its own. "Sometimes," she whispered.

"Ah," Stephen murmured with a knowing smile. "Just as I thought."

"But I didn't try to kill him the other night!" the girl asserted, frightened by the look in the tutor's eyes.

"No, of course you didn't. But, just the same, I thought I'd mention that you'd be wise to take care in the future. Don't ever let them see inside you, Athenais. It's a sight they're not strong enough to bear. And once they've seen it, they'd have no choice but to try to destroy you."

The clouds, which earlier that morning had been no more than tufts of white in a clear blue sky, had begun to swell and darken as the afternoon progressed. David St. Clair cocked his head at the low-pitched whistle of the wind, which seemed to ricochet off the distant cliffs with the whine of a bullet gone astray. There was a storm coming, he thought, no doubt about it, and he'd better start back to the house before it broke, or he might be caught in the far north field until the rain let up. He had seen enough Badlands storms to know that the man who tried to ride through the slashing rain was a fool; this was one time when it paid to admit that the screeching wind was your master—to struggle was hopeless, to give in wise.

The cattle would find their own shelter, he knew, and in the morning they would discover the animals huddled against the cliffs and lost in the chasms where they had wandered seeking protection from the impervious storm. Pushing his hat further down on his head, David surveyed the field once more, assured himself that everything was as it should be, and turned his horse toward home. It was nearly June already, he realized. Maybe this would be the first summer cloudburst.

He had not gone far when he heard the distant thrumming of hooves across the grassy range and turned to find Katherine riding toward him from the direction of the house. David smiled and urged his horse forward; he had not seen her in too long, and the motion of her body against the threatening sky reminded him of that morning when she had come to him out of the mist.

"Where have you been?" she called as the two horses approached each other and stood prancing impatiently. They, too, could smell the coming rain and were anxious for the warmth of their stable. "I've come to see you three times in the past two weeks, but you've never been at home."

"I've been busy with the ranch," David apologized. "Dad hasn't been feeling well, and Stephen's gone every day to tutor the children at the Chateau, so there's only me to take care of the animals. But now that you're here, we can find a place to hide from the rain and keep each other warm for the rest of the afternoon." He maneuvered his horse so that he could reach out to press a hand on Katherine's knee.

"No, David," she said, pulling away from him.

"Do you mean we still have to play your little courtship game?" His voice was angry but his eyes were smiling. He thought he had discovered how his fiancée's mind worked at last, and he knew if he were only patient long enough, she would come to him willingly. But it had to be her choice.

"It's not a game anymore," Katherine told him stiffly. "In fact, it's nothing anymore."

David considered the closed expression on her face and his heartbeat quickened just a little. There was something different about her today, an indefinable quality of taut expectancy. "What does that mean?" he asked.

"I'm sorry," Katherine said, "but I can't marry you."

The sky rumbled with impatience and the wind swept across the open field, sending a chill down David's neck. He had finally convinced himself that he would never hear those words, but here they were, hovering in the air before him like a bitter reflection of all the fears he had cast away. "Why?" It was the only word his lips could form.

"I just can't."

Katherine met his gaze without shrinking, but he could read nothing in her eyes. He realized then that she did not even intend to explain. She meant to leave him without a backward glance, tearing his world up by the roots when she went, and she would not even tell him why. "I want to know," he said, his voice strangely hollow in his own ears.

Katherine hesitated, then told him matter-of-factly, "Because I don't love you. I thought for awhile that it would work between us, but I was wrong, that's all."

That's all. As if it were that simple to dismiss a relationship which had become a burden. "You won't change your mind again?" David knew what her answer would be, but he had to ask the question, just the same.

"No."

Nodding dumbly, he looked away to stare off into the gray, threatening sky. He could not look at her now that he had lost her; she was too beautiful, and her beauty was a cruel reminder of all that he would never have.

"I'm sorry," Katherine repeated.

This time David thought he heard a note of real sympathy in her voice, but when she reached out to touch his arm, he backed away. He wanted all from her or nothing, and as far as he was concerned, his horse could batter her offer of sympathy into the ground beneath its hooves until it became indistinguishable from the mud-stained grass. "Goodbye," he said, still refusing to look at her. "I want to get back before the rain comes." Then he wheeled his horse and rode away, without having spoken a single word that might have convinced her to stay. He could not fight for her, for with Katherine he would always be the loser. He had known it from the beginning, and it had only been his own hunger which had made him forget.

Katherine watched him go, her eyes narrowed in speculation. She was surprised at how easy it had been after all. But it didn't really matter, anyway, because now she was ready. As the wind came up beside her, moaning out its promise of rain, she turned her horse toward home, oblivious to the lowering clouds overhead. Digging her heels into the animal's sides, she let the mask of indifference fall from her face, and her mouth broke into a smile that climbed as high as her sparkling eyes. Katherine leaned forward in the saddle, her heart pounding wildly in her ears, and she laughed with uncontrolled delight. She had done it at last. She was finally free!

With one last look at Medora's face, soft and unlined now that she had finally fallen asleep, William drew the covers up over her shoulders and slipped out of bed. He found his robe easily and put it on, painfully aware at every moment of the stillness in the air, which was disturbed only by Medora's regular breathing. He did not look at her again as he unlatched the door and stepped out onto the porch; it stretched before him into the darkness, shadowed and empty in the silent heart of the night, and the blackness seemed to beckon to the lone intruder.

What had he done? William asked himself as the cool, damp air touched his face and lingered there. What wild and unthinkable motive had urged him to take Medora as his wife? Perhaps he had been wrong after all; perhaps this marriage was not the best thing for either of them. Certainly not for him.

Why *had* he married her? he asked the unforgiving night. The only answer was the cry of the wind in the cool dampness that had lingered long after the storm—a cry that came to him out of the darkness like the mad shriek of bullets gone wild in the still, heavy air. . . .

. . . . *August, 1890—The screaming of deadly bullets overhead was the only sound piercing enough to penetrate the humid heat that had draped itself around them, despite the heavy darkness just beyond the window.* William crouched next to the Marquis, his revolver in his hand, and fired blindly into the seething blackness, but he knew that he and his friend made better targets than the men who crept silently through the trees outside.

"I should not have brought you here to face the bullets meant for me," Mores whispered.

William crouched lower and shook his head. He had *chosen* to come with the Marquis to Tonkin where they planned to start a railroad that would carry them all the way to China when it was finished. But Mores had not realized that the local hostility would be so great. The men had come from their nearby villages in the deep night and sent sporadic rounds of rifle fire into the long, low building that the two men had made their own. Van Driesche ducked as a bullet whistled by his head and paused to reload his gun. "I've faced bullets with you before," he told his friend. "And I don't imagine this will be the last time, either. I've become accustomed to it over the years. Besides, the French soldiers should be here soon."

Sinking to the floor with his back against the wall, Mores wiped the sweat from his forehead with the back of his hand. "William," he said, "I have a favor to ask you. You've never turned me down before, but—" He paused as he tried to see Van Driesche's expression through the almost liquid darkness.

William eyed the Marquis curiously, and the blood slowed to a snail's pace in his veins. Rarely had he heard such desperation in his friend's voice. "What is it?"

"If anything happens to me, I want you to take care of Medora."

Thank God for the darkness that hid the spasm of pain which twisted William's face. "Medora won't need me," he objected. "She's always taken care of herself."

"She's not as strong as you think," Mores said. "I know it looks as if she's made of iron, but her heart is very vulnerable."

William did not think so, but this was hardly the time to argue. The floor on which he knelt was already littered with broken glass, and the night seemed to spit an endless supply of hot lead toward the two men who were helpless against the enemies they could not even see.

Suddenly the Marquis closed one hand tightly around Van Driesche's arm. "Promise me," he insisted, "that you'll keep my wife safe, whatever happens."

"I promise." The words were nearly drowned by the shattering of another pane of glass, but Mores heard them, just the same, and his fingers tightened on William's arm in a gesture of gratitude.

"Then I won't worry about dying," he said. "I know a man like you would never break a promise."

Closing his eyes against the haunting image of Medora's face, William turned back to the relative safety of the window and the bullets and the suffocating heat of the black, starless night. . . .

. . . . The scattered stars glimmered in the night sky behind trailing wisps of cloud that formed themselves out of the chill mist as William watched. He had not thought of the Marquis since he suggested this marriage to Medora a week ago, but Van Driesche knew now that Mores had been with him always. The man's shadow was so large that not even death had destroyed it; it hovered now above his friend's head like a painful reminder of all the promises that William knew in his heart he could never fulfill. Even this choice had not really been his own. The Marquis had made it for him long ago. Mores had led him to this night of unsatisfied hunger in Medora's bed as surely as he had led him to the wilds of Tonkin.

Van Driesche realized as the whispers of night settled around him that he was helpless. He could not protect Medora from her enemies any more than he could make love to her in the heart of the night. Groaning at the memory of his own inadequacy, he ran his hands along the railing as if it were a woman's body, soft and yielding to his touch.

Dear God, how he loved Medora, how long he had waited to have her. Yet, now that she was within his grasp, he found he could not take her. He knew, deep inside, that she was not really his, and that she never would be, despite the plain gold band she wore. Even lying naked in his bed, she would always be a dream to him and nothing more. He had realized tonight, too late, that having nothing at all was a great deal less painful than having only a little and never quite enough.

With a sigh of resignation, he turned back to the door and stood with the blackness behind him, looking into the soft light of his wife's room. Just then, Medora flung her arm outward, as if seeking the comfort of human warmth. William started toward her in answer to her silent plea when, drugged with sleep, she curled her fingers into the empty pillow beside her and moaned her stepson's name.

Van Driesche stopped still in the center of the room as the pain of loss throbbed wildly from his chest to the tips of his fingers. Only then did he see that he had been mistaken. It was not the Marquis' shadow that hovered like a leaden sky above him; it was Phillipe's.

Phillipe leaned back in his chair, uncomfortably aware of the dark circles under Medora's eyes and the air of weariness that clung to her this morning. He supposed it was the uncertainty of their situation that had begun to drain her of her usual spirit. The two attacks on the Chateau, along with the poisoned cattle, had left everyone feeling unsettled, perhaps even afraid of what the future would bring. And, despite hours of combing the riverbank and questioning men, Phillipe had been unable to discover who had fired that rifle or killed those cattle.

Yet he sensed that Medora had something else on her

mind today. And he was very much afraid that he knew what it was. They had not yet mentioned to each other that moment just before the party when the walls had crumbled to dust between them, but he knew that the subject could be avoided no longer. "What do you want me to do?" he asked.

"William and I have been talking a great deal, and we think it would be a good idea for you to marry also."

Phillipe stiffened and said foolishly, "Your marriage has made you so happy in just one night that you can't wait to recommend it to others?"

"Please don't, Phillipe. This is difficult enough without letting your anger make it worse."

"Oh, yes, I forgot. We've all decided to be civilized and ignore our emotions, haven't we?"

"Please," Medora murmured, her eyes full of pleading.

With a long sigh, Phillipe nodded and whispered, "I'm sorry." For the moment, his compassion for Medora had overcome his frustration.

"The thing is," his stepmother continued as if there had been no interruption, "you're twenty-seven years old and the head of a large business enterprise. It's time you found a wife anyway. People expect it."

"I know," Phillipe conceded. "I've thought of that myself. But somehow the time just never seemed right."

"It's right now." For a moment her eyes met his, and then she rose and went to stand at the window where, a week ago, she had accepted William's proposal. Now the daylight streamed through the glass, and where she had seen only her own features, she now saw the entire sweep of the Badlands. "Besides," she added, "I think it will be safer."

Phillipe did not move. He knew she was right, as she always was. Medora could be depended upon to choose the proper path in all things, and she did not allow emotion to cloud her clear vision. But, dear God, if only she could force a little human warmth into her voice! Her tone was so steady that she might have been making the kind of decision she made every day, only this time it was his future she was planning. "Who are you thinking of?" he asked finally. "Katherine?"

"Good heavens, no!" Medora replied, whirling to face him. She hoped he could not read in her eyes the memory of that moonlit night. "Katherine is too great a risk," she said carefully. "Remember, we still don't know who poisoned those cattle."

"Katherine certainly didn't," Phillipe said. "Besides, she's different from her father. In fact, she's a law unto herself."

"Believe that as long as you can, Phillipe," Medora told him grimly, "but you're wrong. That woman is more Pendleton than anything else, and I, for one, would not feel comfortable knowing she was a member of our family." Medora leaned against the desk top, tapping her lips thoughtfully with one finger. "You're not in love with her, are you?"

"You know I'm not."

Medora found Phillipe's steady blue gaze disturbing; she could not mistake the message she read there. How could he be in love with Katherine when Medora knew very well that he was in love with her?

When the silence stretched between them like a fragile glass thread that might shatter at any moment, Phillipe stood up and took Medora's place at the window. "If not Katherine, then who?"

"Have you ever thought of Mianne Goodall?"

"I think of her a great deal," the young man answered, "but not as a wife."

"She's just a year younger than you," Medora reminded him. "She runs this house with exemplary skill, and she's very fond of the children. You know as well as I do that she has a good heart and—"

"And?" he prompted.

"And she's very beautiful. I don't see how you could ask for more."

Phillipe stared out at the cluster of cottonwood leaves that hid the river from his sight, and in their place he saw Mianne, surrounded with lamplight, her face soft and her eyes full of secrets.

"You like her, don't you?" Medora persisted. "I see you talking with her often. I thought the two of you were friends."

"I doubt if anyone is Mianne's friend," Phillipe mused. "Not really. But you're right; I'm very fond of her."

"And she is fond of you."

There was something in Medora's voice that made him turn to look at her with a question gathered across his brow. "How can you know that?"

"I know." She did not tell him why or how, for someday Phillipe would discover the truth for himself. Nor did she tell him how very much this decision had cost her; *that* she prayed he would never know.

"Well?" she asked, when Phillipe turned back to the window as if seeking the comfort of an old friend. "Will you think about it?"

"I'll think," he answered softly, but his eyes were fixed on the multicolored cliffs—the carved, magnificent cliffs which dwarfed the twisted valley below, making it appear insignificant by cruel comparison. He could not make a decision now, he told himself. Not while everything was so unstable. Daily he sought answers and found only more questions. And everywhere he looked another threat arose—to the land, his life—even love had not escaped. Nothing in his world was safe and secure anymore, nor had it been since the day when the Marquis had given up the last of his deep red blood to the windswept, barren desert.

Chapter 15

Bands of clouds in pale gray and white had woven themselves across the sky, shrouding the blazing sun and touching the landscape below with welcome coolness. The morning air was clear and piercing with the scent of sagebrush and wild roses, and the only sound to disturb the waiting stillness was the chattering of birds hidden among the thick summer leaves. Katherine pulled her rifle in closer to her body and urged her horse forward silently, hoping that the thick grass underfoot, still wet with dew, would muffle the sound of the hoofbeats.

At the edge of the copse of box elder and wild plum trees, the white-tailed deer stood grazing, oblivious, as yet, to the woman who had been watching it so closely for so long. Katherine checked to see that her small-brimmed hat was secure and her belt tightly fastened. She was glad she had decided to wear her hunting costume this morning; its tightly fitting brown jacket, short skirt and matching bloomers left her freer to move as she chose, and she enjoyed the feel of the knee-length leather boots against her legs. With her rifle resting across the saddle horn, she moved slowly, letting her horse find its own way across the field.

But then, before she had time to raise her gun and aim,

the deer raised its head for an instant and bolted into the protective shadows of the trees.

"Damn!" Katherine cursed, digging her heels into her horse's sides. She had to have that deer, she had decided, and now it seemed that the animal would escape her.

She caught sight of the deer again as the shadows of the leaves fell on her face. The animal was leaping gracefully across a rotted log that blocked the path, its legs folded lithely beneath its pale brown body, its head high, seeking the path to escape. Katherine crouched lower in the saddle to avoid the confusion of branches overhead, and she clutched her rifle against her body as the horse galloped wildly after the fleeing deer.

As horse and rider erupted from among the trees, Katherine glanced around, her eyes dark with grim determination. But already she could see that the pursuit was hopeless. The deer had headed blindly for the only shelter—the twisting gullies and ravines that permeated the stone cliffs, and she knew she would never be able to follow it there. The paths were too narrow, their course too erratic, and her horse could not even begin to make its way through the wandering maze.

"Damn!" she cursed again, but she did not release her rifle, and, as her eyes moved over the still landscape, she sought other game. She had come out to hunt this morning, and hunt she would. While the clouds overhead shifted time and again, weaving and unweaving their dappled patterns, Katherine waited with the barrel of the rifle cool in her hands. Her horse snorted occasionally, curious about the delay, but Katherine did not move to reassure the animal. The smell of sagebrush was strong in her nostrils when she finally saw what she had been seeking—a fat, gray rabbit gambolling in the tall buffalo grass half a field away.

Sliding quickly from the saddle, Katherine cradled her rifle in the curve of her arm and started forward, moving with the stealth and grace of a golden bobcat. She had wanted a deer, but a rabbit would satisfy at least some of her hunger for the excitement of the hunt. She crouched lower as she went, making herself as inconspicuous as possible, and soon the animal was so close that she could hear it scrabbling about in the soft earth. Katherine knelt and raised the rifle to her chest, gripping the barrel firmly with one hand and the stock with the other. Then, bracing the gun against her shoulder, she took a deep breath, cocked and fired.

The rabbit stopped its playing as if frozen by a sudden fall of ice, and then its tiny body seemed to explode with the force of its own blood. In less than an instant, it lay perfectly still in a spreading pool of red at Katherine's feet.

"Should I applaud? It hardly seems worthwhile for such a pitiful trophy."

Katherine looked up to find her father watching her from the back of his horse and his lips were twisted in an ironic grin. "Go away," she snapped.

"Don't you want me to help gut the animal? I doubt if you can handle it all by yourself."

His mocking tone only fuelled her anger, and she turned away and started back toward her horse.

"Don't go, Katherine!" her father called after her. "I need to talk to you."

Katherine did not stop. "About what?"

"Phillipe Beaumont."

This time she paused and revolved slowly. "Yes?" Her left eyebrow was quirked in mild curiosity, but there was no other sign of the sudden quickening of her pulse.

"Do you know what he's been doing these past two weeks?" Greg demanded.

Katherine shrugged. "How should I know?"

"You would if you were making the slightest effort to protect the interests of this family," he accused. "Beaumont has spent his time recently in St. Paul with Alexander Mackensie. He's intent on winning the man over, and he's even gone so far as to agitate for legislation regulating the railroad rates."

"How is that a threat to us?"

"Beaumont's continued presence alone is threat enough, and you know it. Besides, we have certain agreements with the railroad officials. Phillipe's campaign is threatening those." His jaw set in a harsh line, he leaned forward and looked his daughter in the eyes. "It's time we started fighting back."

"You could always poison more cattle, I suppose," Katherine suggested.

A muscle in Greg's jaw twitched ominously. "That was just a little warning, to let them know we haven't forgotten."

"I think they know that by now, but it was the long-distance rifle, not the cattle, that gave it away."

Greg stiffened. "Don't!" he warned.

"But, Father, if these attacks continue, and the family is killed off one by one, it would solve your problem quite effectively, don't you think?"

"Drop it, Katherine!"

His voice held a note of command which she dared not disobey. Katherine sensed that she had gone too far, and her common sense took over at last. She must take care, for there was a constant awareness between them of things that must never be said and thoughts that must never be revealed. And *she* must not be the one to break the unspoken rules. "All right," she sighed. "What do you want me to do?"

"I'm planning to start some politicking myself with the railroad officials and the men who oppose limitation of rates. But I'll need your help. We all know how much more carefully a man listens to a beautiful woman. And, then, after your wedding with David St. Clair—"

"There isn't going to be a wedding," Katherine interrupted.

Greg sat up straighter in the saddle. "What do you mean?"

"I broke the engagement."

"Why?" The word came out a strangled whisper.

"Because I have other plans," she told him matter-of-factly.

Closing his eyes, Greg drew a deep breath. "With Phillipe?" he asked, his forehead creased in anger.

Katherine smiled her secret smile. "Perhaps."

"You're in love with him?" He could barely force himself to form the words, but he had to know the answer.

"Of course not," Katherine said, praying that her father would not see beyond her careless tone of voice to the turmoil of pain and joy inside. "But I mean to have him, if only to teach him a lesson."

"You don't love him, but you want to marry him?" Greg waited expectantly for her response as the clouds shifted behind him and released the sun from its bondage for a moment. The sudden shadow which the light created moved out across the grassy field, shading the pitiful dead rabbit from the sun and just touching the toes of Katherine's leather boots. "Answer me!" he snapped.

"I don't just *want* to marry Phillipe," Katherine announced calmly. "I *will* marry him!" Then she turned and walked toward her waiting horse, moving confidently out of the reach of her father's shadow.

Phillipe pushed his hat back on his head and wiped a hand across his damp forehead. By now the sun had consumed the morning clouds and the blue in the sky, so that everything was bathed in radiant yellow. The heat only added to Phillipe's weariness—he had been cramped in the train for most of the night and now he was on his way back to the Chateau on horseback—but he did not slow his pace. He was anxious to get home after two long weeks in St. Paul.

Phillipe had discovered that campaigning for support among the politicians and others was far more exhausting than physical labor. He would rather spend his days in the plant, covered with blood to the elbows, than sit with Mackensie for an entire afternoon. Still, Phillipe knew how important it was to win the politician over, so he had given it his best effort. But Mackensie was careful; he listened and nodded and smiled and refused to give a firm commitment.

As he neared the Chateau, the young man pushed Mackensie to the back of his mind. He was tired to the very center of his bones, and even the thought of seeing Medora again did not cause him the usual pain. He had learned in the past two weeks that he would survive, and he found that constant activity kept his mind away from thoughts better left in darkness. He had just guided his horse around the hill toward the stables below when he saw the flames.

The stable roof was alight from end to end with a riot of heat and color that seemed to swallow the sky in its hungry grasp, and Phillipe sat perfectly still, mesmerized by the grim magnificence of the fire. Then, as the message from those leaping flames penetrated his paralyzed thoughts, he shook the spell away and tried to think what he should do. He realized with a groan of dismay that no one else was in sight. No doubt they were all occupied in the far fields or in town. The smoke would bring them running eventually, but for now he was alone.

The stables would probably be lost, but he must keep the fire from spreading. Thank God the house was high above the burning buildings; if he raced back to town and sent the fire engine at once, the Chateau could be saved. His decision made, he had just begun to turn his horse around when he saw a flash of movement down below. He thought someone had entered the flaming building, but surely he had been mistaken. Phillipe wasted precious seconds staring blindly into the fire that had found its way to the wide open doors, then he froze in astonishment.

The terrified whinny of a horse exploded from within the burning doorway, and then the animal appeared, tossing its head, its eyes rolling back in fear. But what held Phillipe's attention was the slender woman who paused for an instant to draw the horse out after her as the frenzied flames encircled her in blazing light. Mianne. Then, before he could open his mouth to call to her, she had led the animal to freedom and turned back to penetrate the raging fire once again.

Phillipe dug his heels viciously into his horse's sides. He had to get to her and drag her out before the heat and smoke engulfed her. But as he approached the stable, he saw that the front wall was a solid sheet of flame, except for a tiny opening where the door swung inward, propelled by the wind created by the fire. He slid from the saddle and came as close as he dared, but he could see that there was nothing he could do. He had waited too long.

But then the neighing of another horse brought his head back sharply, and Mianne appeared again, choking and gasping, her fingers clenched tightly on the animal's bridle. With a strength Phillipe had never known another human being to possess, she dragged the frightened horse from among the flames, and even above the roar of the fire Phillipe could hear the soothing chant she whispered in the animal's ear in an effort to calm it. When the horse had bolted across the sloping field nearby, Phillipe realized that Mianne had collapsed just beyond the reach of the white, hot blaze.

By now he could hear the shouts of the other men who

had seen the smoke at last, and he could even discern the distant clamor of the fire engine bell. Closing his eyes in a brief prayer of thanks, Phillipe called to the woman who had performed no less than a miracle while he stood watching. He ran to where she lay with her arms clasped tightly across her chest, as if to protect her from the flames, and lifted her in his arms. While the men shouted and scurried around behind him, he carried Mianne gently away from the stable and its suffocating smoke to the cool, flowing river below.

"Are you hurt?" he demanded when she lay on the bank staring up at him in confusion.

Mianne shook her head, and only then did Phillipe see that, although her body was blackened with soot and her breath was coming in stifled gasps, she did not appear to be burned. But how could that be? Had she not walked through a wall of fire that would have scorched to dust any mortal man? He held her loosely, his eyes searching her face for some sign of the magic that had kept her safe. "Are you mad?" he hissed at last.

Mianne swallowed with difficulty, and her answer was no more than a choked whisper. "I had to save the horses. I couldn't bear to let them burn."

Phillipe shuddered uncontrollably at the wild risk she had taken. "The horses are not worth your life, Mianne. You shouldn't even have attempted it."

Smiling slightly, she met his eyes directly for the first time. "I had to prove to myself that I could."

Her gaze said even more as a wordless communication passed between them, and suddenly Phillipe understood. Had he not stalked a wounded mountain lion once and nearly lost his own life in the process? Had he not felt and understood that all-consuming need to prove himself? In that instant, as he looked into Mianne's dark eyes, he knew that she had struck a chord within him that he hadn't known existed. And all at once Medora's words flashed through his mind. *Have you thought of Mianne Goodall?* He knew then what he had to do, and before he could stop to think, Phillipe blurted, "Mianne, will you marry me?"

Mianne stiffened and, although she did not move, he could have sworn she retreated from him, and the shutters fell across her eyes. "Don't."

But Phillipe was in the grip of some instinct beyond his control and he told her, "I mean it. I want you to be my wife."

When she saw that he was serious, Mianne's heart contracted painfully and she wanted, more than anything in the world, to escape from his compelling presence. "No!" she cried.

Phillipe tightened his hold and drew her nearer; he knew there was nothing else he could do. "Please," he whispered. "I want you." Then he lowered his head and brushed her lips with his.

Shuddering as if he had struck her, Mianne groaned, "No," and closed her eyes. But she could not shut out the image of the red-orange flames that leapt and twisted beyond Phillipe's back. . . .

. . . . *April, 1876—The flickering light from the cedar fire burned in the center of the tipi, casting mysterious shadows on Mianne's young face.* Johnny Goodall tried to read her expression in the uncertain glow, but he could not guess what she was thinking, and his own sorrow hung heavy in the back of his throat. But he tried to hide it from the Indians seated around the fire in rigid silence. "Listen to me, little one," he whispered, holding her firmly by the shoulders. "It's time for me to go."

Mianne had been gazing curiously at the brightly decorated quill-work that adorned the plain brown walls, but when her father spoke, she fixed her eyes on his haggard face. "I will go with you," she told him simply.

Goodall closed his eyes and shook his head. It was a long moment before he could find the strength to speak again. "No, Mianne. You must stay here and I must go. That was Kiwani's wish."

At the mention of her mother's name, a bleak shadow touched the child's eyes. "My mother is gone," she said, and Johnny nodded. But Mianne did not understand. She knew only that she had awakened one morning to find that Kiwani had left without a word. The girl had asked her father time and again where her mother was, but there had been no answer. Then, one day, Johnny had taken Mianne onto his lap and explained brokenly, "Your mother is gone, little one. She'll not be coming back." "But why?" the child asked, and her father had shaken his head, answering, "There was something she felt she had to do. You wouldn't understand."

Mianne had not understood. She had moved in a daze for a week, unable to comprehend the creeping blackness that had consumed her until it blocked all else from her sight. "She is gone," the girl had repeated over and over. "Gone." But she did not really understand. And now her father had said that he was going, too.

"No!" the child cried, flinging her arms around Johnny's neck. "I will come with you." But when she heard the Indian boys snickering from the dark recesses of the tipi, she stiffened and tried to choke back the tears that blinded her.

Her father's arms closed around her and he murmured, "You don't understand, little one. It must be like this. Here you will have your aunts to care for you, and I can't do that by myself. It's better that you stay. Please, Mianne, be a good girl and let me go now."

Because her own vision was blurred with tears barely held in check, Mianne did not see that Johnny's eyes were also damp and that his face was twisted with misery. He had said he wanted to leave her; that was all she could comprehend at the moment. She did not protest when he removed her arms from around his neck, nor did she respond when he kissed her one last time.

The child stood framed in the triangular doorway, watching him go, while the shadows from the flames wavered across her shoulders. It was then that she heard the taunting whisper, "Half-breed!" from somewhere at her back. She had heard it before, but the word was just another thing that she could not understand. However, she knew instinctively that it was an insult and that it had something to do with her father. As long as he had been beside her, it had not mattered, but now the boys' laughter made her shiver. Somehow Mianne could not make herself believe that Johnny was really gone.

She had loved her father, blindly, wildly, for all her young life. He had been the center of her world—her only god. But in the instant when he turned and left her behind, he had become her greatest enemy. Twice she had been abandoned, twice broken, twice forgotten, but she swore it would not happen a third time. She would simply have to be stronger than the others—stronger than her father and mother, who had disappeared from her life, stronger than the boys who were laughing now behind her back—as strong as the slow-burning cliffs in the distance. *And as Johnny vanished in the cool evening air, Mianne made a promise in the dark center of her secret heart that no one would ever have the power to make her love them again. . . .*

. . . . Phillipe pressed closer, his hands sliding softly across her back until his heart was beating against hers. "Don't make me a stranger again," he pleaded. "Marry me."

Mianne was becoming desperate to get away from him, and she struggled to break free of his arms. "Why me?" she asked.

"Because we—*I* think you're the one."

All at once, Mianne understood. This had been Medora's idea. She wanted her stepson married, and anyone would do. Wincing at the sudden flash of pain that touched her heart, Mianne shook her head and turned away. "No," she repeated, remembering his pleading eyes. But she had seen those eyes when they looked at Medora with all their secrets revealed, and she knew, as certainly as if the river had told her so, that whether he gave her his hand or his name or his body, Phillipe would never be hers.

Chapter 16

"You're not going to do it, are you?" Anais demanded as she burst into Mianne's bedroom.

The woman turned away from the image of the smoke-hazed sunset through the window glass and looked at her friend in surprise. "Do what?" It did not take more than a glance to tell her that Anais was deeply distressed, but then, ever since the night of the party, the girl had changed, become moody and secretive.

"I heard Phillipe tell Mama that he asked you to marry him," Anais said accusingly.

Mianne's eyes grew dark and distant as she murmured, "I told him no."

"Did you mean it?" the girl asked. "You really aren't going to marry him?" Her face was shadowed with a kind of pleading that made Mianne want to comfort Anais as if she were a small, lost child. "No, I'm not."

"Because I couldn't bear it if you did. I just couldn't."

How fragile this girl seemed suddenly, as if a rush of warm breath might shatter her beyond repair. "It's not your choice," Mianne said softly, "but it doesn't matter. I have no intention of becoming Phillipe's wife."

"Do you promise?" Anais persisted.

With a long, searching look into the girl's troubled eyes, Mianne whispered, "I promise."

Before Anais could respond, Johnny knocked on the door. "I'd like to talk to you, Mianne," he said.

The girl saw the significant glance that passed between father and daughter, and she sensed that they wanted to be alone. "I have reading to do," she said as she started for the door. But when she reached the threshold, she turned back to meet Mianne's eyes for a moment, as if to remind her of her promise. Then she whirled and vanished into the hall.

When Anais was gone, Johnny closed the door and faced his daughter. "Is it true that Phillipe proposed?"

Mianne looked down at her hands in order to hide her expression from her father's probing gaze. Was she to hear of nothing but Phillipe for the rest of her life, just because, in a moment of madness, he had forgotten his common sense? "Yes," she muttered.

"Well, what did you say?"

Drawing a deep breath, his daughter said calmly, "I turned him down."

Johnny gaped at her, incredulous. "Why, in God's name?"

Mianne felt a flash of deep anger which she quickly suppressed. "He's not for me, that's all."

"I don't see why not. He's handsome, rich, and a hell of a businessman. And, besides that, he's a better man than most. You know that as well as I do. If you married him, he'd see that you were taken care of for the rest of your life."

"I don't *want* to marry him!"

Johnny rubbed one hand across the back of his neck, and his face was suddenly full of misery. "Then what does that leave for you? Are you planning to stay here as a housekeeper for the rest of your life?"

For a moment, Mianne could not bring herself to answer him. The one thing she had avoided in the past twelve years was wondering about the future. It had always been too painful to even contemplate. "I hadn't thought—"

"Well, you'd better think now," Johnny interrupted. "Phillipe has just given you your one chance to escape the drudgery that is all this house can promise you. You'll always have a home here, you know that, but you can never expect anything more. You're only twenty-six, my dear, and that's too young to hide yourself away on this bluff forever. Is that really what you want to do?"

Mianne stared blindly at the floor, waiting for the waves of grim realization to stop their ceaseless assault. "No, it isn't," she whispered.

"Then think carefully before you throw this chance away. And tell me what you're going to do."

Suddenly, Mianne felt that the walls were closing in on her. It seemed that nothing was sacred anymore—not her will or her thoughts or even her life. Every day brought danger of one kind or another, and Phillipe was the greatest danger of all. Mianne knew that if she stayed, he would eventually destroy her—she had known it from the moment when he first stepped back into her life.

And her father was right; there was nothing for her here but people who wanted more than anything else to take control of her destiny and bend it in their own willing hands. She had always chosen her own path before, but now it seemed the choice had been taken from her. "I don't need to think," she said, raising her head to meet Johnny's questioning gaze. Her voice was heavy with a brief pang of sorrow, but she shook it away. "It's obvious that I have only one choice. There are certain things I must do first, but I promise you that, within the month, I will leave the Badlands forever."

* * *

Stephen St. Clair entered the drawing room to find his brother gazing wistfully out the wide windows at the first purple flush of coming night. No doubt David found consolation in the darkness, which reflected his own mood so well, Stephen thought in irritation. Ever since Katherine had broken their engagement, David had moved through this house like a ghost without the energy or stamina to drag himself back from the edge of the blackness that haunted him. Usually the younger brother tried to avoid his morbid sibling, but tonight he had had enough. "David," he said, "whatever are you thinking about that makes you look as if death were one day away?"

"You know what," David replied without turning away from the window.

"Katherine again, I suppose."

The older brother actually flinched at the mention of that forbidden name, and Stephen barely stifled a snort of disgust. "If she hurt you so much, why don't you do something about it?"

"There's nothing to be done. She made her choice and I have nothing to say about it."

"*I* would if I were you," his brother muttered. "But you don't even blame her, do you?"

David revolved to face the younger man. "Blame her? For what?"

Clenching his fists to keep his temper under control, Stephen snapped, "For treating you like dirt. For leading you on, then dropping you without a second thought." He was not aware of the spasm of anguish that crossed his brother's face; Stephen was angry, and all he could see at the moment was the magnitude of Katherine's sin.

"I'm sure she had her reasons," David murmured. "Her feelings changed, that's all. She couldn't help that."

"For Christ's sake, David, you're so damned naive!" Stephen rolled his eyes in disbelief. "She had a reason all right, and its name is Phillipe Beaumont."

Take 4 FREE Books!

We created our convenient Home Subscription Service so you'll be sure to have the hottest new romances delivered each month right to your doorstep — usually before they are available in book stores. Just to show you how convenient Zebra Home Subscription Service is, we would like to send you 4 Kensington Choice Historical Romances as a FREE gift. You receive a gift worth up to $24.96 — absolutely FREE. There's no extra charge for shipping and handling. There's no obligation to buy anything - ever!

Save Up To 32% On Home Delivery!

Accept your FREE gift and each month we'll deliver 4 brand new titles as soon as they are published. They'll be yours to examine FREE for 10 days. Then if you decide to keep the books, you'll pay the preferred subscriber's price of just $4.20 per title. That's $16.80 for all 4 books for a savings of up to 32% off the cover price! Just add $1.50 to offset the cost of shipping and handling. Remember, you are under no obligation to buy any of these books at any time! If you are not delighted with them, simply return them and owe nothing. But if you enjoy Kensington Choice Historical Romances as much as we think you will, pay the special preferred subscriber rate of only $16.80 each month and save over $8.00 off the bookstore price!

We have 4 FREE BOOKS for you as your introduction to
KENSINGTON CHOICE!

To get your FREE BOOKS, worth up to $24.96, mail the card below or call TOLL-FREE 1-888-345-BOOK Visit our website at www.kensingtonbooks.com.

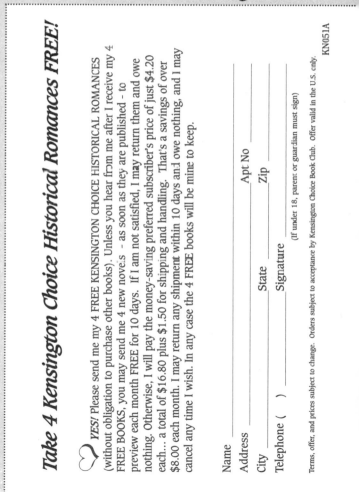

Take 4 Kensington Choice Historical Romances FREE!

YES! Please send me my 4 FREE KENSINGTON CHOICE HISTORICAL ROMANCES (without obligation to purchase other books). Unless you hear from me after I receive my 4 FREE BOOKS, you may send me 4 new novels - as soon as they are published - to preview each month FREE for 10 days. If I am not satisfied, I may return them and owe nothing. Otherwise, I will pay the money-saving preferred subscriber's price of just $4.20 each... a total of $16.80 plus $1.50 for shipping and handling. That's a savings of over $8.00 each month. I may return any shipment within 10 days and I owe nothing, and I may cancel any time I wish. In any case the 4 FREE books will be mine to keep.

Name _____

Address _____ Apt No _____

City _____ State _____ Zip _____

Telephone ( ) _____ Signature _____

(If under 18, parent or guardian must sign)

Terms, offer, and prices subject to change. Orders subject to acceptance by Kensington Choice Book Club. Offer valid in the U.S. only.

KN051A

4 FREE
Kensington
Choice
Historical
Romances
are waiting
for you to
claim them!

(worth up
to $24.96)

See details
inside....

David regarded his brother in silence, brow furrowed in thought. "What does that mean?"

Turning away before he exploded, Stephen buried his hands in his pockets and hissed, "Guess, big brother. I know you're not as stupid as you look. See if you can tax your brain far enough to figure out why both Katherine and Phillipe disappeared from that party for over an hour at the same time. And wasn't it just after that night that your fiancée decided to break your engagement?"

"Stephen—" David said no more than that one word, but it expressed a warning that was deep and dangerous.

Stephen whirled to face his brother. *"Don't* be a fool anymore! Just stop for a minute and listen to me. Katherine used you, from the very beginning, and you know it. She never meant to marry you at all. You were just a temporary diversion—a means of making Phillipe recognize that Katherine did not belong to him alone. Wake *up,* David, and begin to fight back. Start playing her game and see if you can't make her squirm a little."

David's hazel eyes glittered with cold anger, and only by clenching his hands into brutal fists did he manage to keep them at his sides. "You're mad!" he cried. "And I don't want to hear any more." With that, he swung on his heel and left the room.

Stephen glared after him in helpless fury, but then an idea began to form in his head and he could not help but smile. If David wouldn't fight back, Stephen would have to do it for him. Katherine had made a dreadful mistake in treating David as she had, but then she would pay. Because, if there was only one thing in this world that Stephen St. Clair believed in, it was making people pay for their mistakes. And he would do this, even if he had to do it alone. David or no David, he would think of a way.

* * *

Mianne threw her shawl across her shoulders and closed the kitchen door behind her. Glancing up as she hurried away from the house, she saw that the sky was scattered with stars and that the moon touched her path with a soft, blue wash of color. The night was welcoming her, as always, enfolding her in the cool half-darkness with the effortless grace of a light summer breeze. She had been right to come here tonight, seeking the voice of the river, for there lay her only comfort.

As the murmur of the water came to her from out of the darkness, she began to run, desiring nothing more than to submerge herself in the night songs of the river. She had to get away this time. She had to flee beyond the reach of the voices at the Chateau and drown the memory of their rigid tones. She would put them behind her as easily as she put the house behind her, and with the soothing rumble of the water, she would forget.

Stumbling as she reached the riverbank, Mianne found her way to the abandoned hut where she kept her secret nature hidden. Tonight she would reach out to her Indian past and lose herself in the magic of a life long dead. She discarded her shawl, blouse, skirt and petticoat quickly, unfastened her chemise and dropped it in a darkened corner of the hut. Then, groping through the blackness where the moonlight could not penetrate, she found the buckskin dress and paused for an instant to caress the soft hide with her fingertips. Finally, when she had pulled the gown over her head, she reached up to uncoil her long, black hair. She was alone now, completely herself, and they would not ever find her here.

Mianne stepped out into the night, smiling, and turned to raise her hands toward the softly pulsing river. Then, shaking her head, she revelled in the feel of moonlight on her upraised face and the whisper of her hair against her beaded dress. Slowly she rotated on one foot with her arms raised before her, then she let her hands fall to her sides and began to run, drawn forward by the power of the singing river. Then it was there with her again, that tentative brush of a bird's wing against her cheek, that presence which touched her without speaking and seemed to promise everything in a single breath of wind.

Mianne was not sure exactly when she became aware that she was not alone; she only knew that she must keep running, ever faster, if she were to escape. But the presence would guide her to safety; she was certain of it.

Behind her, Phillipe followed slowly, confused by the ceiling of leaves that sometimes blocked the moonlight from his sight. He did not know what instinct had made him follow Mianne when she left the Chateau; perhaps he had sensed the depth of her distress. Or perhaps it had been Johnny's warning that she was planning to leave the Badlands. The moment he had heard those words, Phillipe had realized that he could not let her go. He had known since he had seen her strength and courage this afternoon that he had to have her, and now it was not just Medora's wish that urged him onward; it was his own.

He had known he wanted her then, but the knowledge could not compare with the compulsion that gripped him tonight. Because now he had seen her exulting when she believed no one was near; he had seen her need, her vision, and her magic all in the instant when she had reached out to worship the river at her feet. This was a spirit from another world, who wove her webs and cast them out over the water, forming a bond that could not be broken. And Phillipe knew that, regardless of her wishes, he could not set her free. He had to have her, to study her, to understand her secret. Mianne had become an obsession to him. *Someday,* he had told her once, *I will make you my slave.*

When the river narrowed until its song was nothing more than a whisper and Mianne found that she could no longer draw her breath from the cool night breeze, she fell to her knees on the spongy bank and closed her eyes in silent supplication. She could not run forever; her body could not match the willingness of her spirit. She was aware that Phillipe dropped down beside her, but she did not raise her head to look at him.

For a minute, both sat silent, catching their breath, then Phillipe said quietly, "You're going away?"

"Yes," Mianne told him. "I've decided."

He could see the profile of her face in the moonlight, and he recognized the instant of uncertainty that lightened her dark brown eyes before she turned away. What was more, he had seen her commune with the river, and he knew that she loved it, possibly beyond anything else in this life. She did not really want to go; he knew it as certainly as if she had shouted it to the glittering stars. And she was weakening. For a moment she had let him see her regret. "Where will you go?" he asked.

Mianne hesitated, then murmured, "Back to the Sioux."

"But you'll be a stranger there, Mianne. Are you so certain you can go back and begin again?"

She could not and she knew it. Mianne leaned forward to trail a hand through the water. Phillipe was right—she would fit in with the Indians from her past no better than she did with the people in her present. In reality, she belonged nowhere, and now, at last, she saw what she had most feared all her life—the vision of her own future stretching empty and black before her. Suddenly the moonlight, the stars, and even the rustle of the wind were no more than a cruel joke, because she saw that in the end she must lose everything that she had come to love. She would leave behind the Chateau which had become home to her, her father, who had made himself into her only friend, and the singing, rushing river, which held within its banks every dream she had ever dreamt and every moment of joy she had ever known. "I must do this," she said grimly, as if in an effort to convince herself.

"Why?" Phillipe's question was so soft that it was almost lost in the sounds of the night.

"Because." Mianne looked up at him for the first time as the thought of leaving tore at her insides with the precision of a well-aimed arrow. And now her eyes were wide open, full of some desperate message which he thought he understood.

"Don't go," he said, as he reached for her hand.

"I must—"

"I don't want you to go."

His eyes held her gaze for a full minute, and even Mianne, blind as she was, could read the sincerity there.

"Please stay," he murmured. Then he leaned closer and ran his fingers down the side of her face. "Please."

Cupping her chin in his hand, he drew her toward him until his lips brushed gently across hers. Mianne shivered, but she did not back away, not even when he circled her shoulders with his other arm and pulled her firmly against him, so that she could feel his breath on her face.

"Mianne," he breathed into her hair, "I want you."

Closing her eyes, she realized that his face was before her even then and that she could not block it from her sight. Mianne realized in that instant that she was afraid of Phillipe, desperately afraid. And it was a depth of fear that she had never known before. Yet she did not have the power to resist him just now. He had come to her when she was not ready, when her mind was lost somewhere in the magic of the river, and her spirit had revealed itself to him against her will.

Phillipe left a trail of warm, light kisses across Mianne's forehead and down her cheek before he found her mouth again. But now, when he kissed her, she opened her lips to him, tentatively, and her hands came up to cup his face. As her fingers crept back into his hair, he drew a deep breath, surprised by the wave of desire that swept through him. Her lips seemed to send out rivers of warmth that crept through his skin and into his blood as he pulled her body close and guided her down to the grass beside him.

With infinite care, he slipped the buckskin dress over her shoulders, dropping it into the moonstruck darkness. Then, when he had removed his own clothes, he bent over her, aware of the waiting glow of her eyes, and began to kiss her bare neck and the sloping curve of her shoulder. As he explored her body gently, slowly, with his willing fingertips, he found that she was even more beautiful than he had imagined. Her long, slender legs wrapped themselves around him, and her full, round breasts rose and fell with her ragged breathing. And, despite the chill in the night air, the heat of her skin seemed to fill his senses, even down to the center of his bones.

Mianne held him against her, skin to skin and breath to breath, and prayed that he would never let her go. To her, the tender touch of his hands was as gentle as the pulsing of the river, and the passion that rose in her chest was no more than an echo of the water, swollen by spring rain. What magic was it that this man possessed that could make her blood sing like this—softly, with the cry of the wind in her ears? Even when he entered her, and the pain shot through her thighs like a brand, she did not shrink away from him, for the slow rhythm of his body against hers drugged her with its rocking. Her arms wound around him and her lips clung to his, and the response that swept through her left her blind with its wonder.

When it was over, Phillipe found that he could not let her go. Instead, he drew her into the circle of his arm with her head resting in the curved hollow of his shoulder. With her body pressed to his, he lay unmoving, letting the warmth of her invade his senses and linger there, like an unspoken promise. He had never known a woman like her before—with Katherine, the hunger of their bodies had driven them into the heart of a pitched battle, and it was always a struggle, even to the end when they lay panting side by side. With Mianne, the coming together had been a gift—almost a benediction. Phillipe bent down to kiss her face, looking for tears of regret or shame, but Mianne's cheeks were dry.

It was then that she rolled away from him and sat up in order to hide her expression from the many eyes of the night. "I must go back," she said to the deaf, trembling leaves of the cottonwoods overhead.

Phillipe did not argue; he knew there was nothing more to say just now. Nothing, at least, that Mianne would care to listen to. He dressed quickly while she found her gown and pulled it over her head, then they turned and started for home. They walked in silence, but as they came closer to the Chateau, Phillipe sensed that Mianne was slipping further and further back behind the wall she had built between herself and the world. He felt that she was leaving him, but he did not know how to stop her.

"I must change," she said, speaking for the first time when they reached the hut. "But you needn't wait for me."

"Mianne—" He reached out to touch her cheek, but she shook her head.

"Please leave me," she pleaded. "I must be alone."

But he was there, just the same, when she stepped out in her everyday blouse and shirtwaist, her hair braided tightly around her head. And although he did not speak or try to touch her, Phillipe stayed by her side until they came to the empty porch of the Chateau. Then, just as she reached out to open the door, he said, "Mianne?"

She kept her eyes on the promise of light and warmth inside the kitchen, though his presence burned through her mind like an accusation. "What is it?" she murmured.

"Will you marry me now?"

She had known it was coming and, from the instant when his hands had claimed her body, she had known what her answer would be. "Yes," she breathed, then quickly opened the door and stepped inside, before he could read the torment in her fathomless brown eyes.

"Katherine!" Greg called. "Could you come here for a minute?"

Katherine left her book and went to the doorway of the study where her father stood talking to Stephen St. Clair.

"What is it?" she asked impatiently.

Stephen sat on the edge of the desk, one leg swinging slowly back and forth, and eyed the woman intently, his lips curved in the tiniest of smiles. "I just came by to ask if you'd heard the news," he said idly.

"What news?" Katherine had only seen Stephen twice since she had broken her engagement to his brother, but both times she had sensed an undercurrent of hostility in his voice. No doubt he was angry for David's sake, but, after all, that was hardly her concern.

"I thought you'd be the first to know," Stephen continued.

He seemed to be enjoying prolonging the suspense, and his casual attitude annoyed Katherine. "I'm not interested in your little game, Stephen," she snapped, "so just tell me what you've come to say."

Greg shook his head. "Katherine, I swear you will ruin yourself with your impatience someday," he warned, but his daughter was not listening.

"I thought you'd be interested to hear," Stephen said, "that Phillipe Beaumont is engaged to Mianne Goodall. The wedding is planned for early August."

His eyes were bright with interest as he watched her face, but Katherine did not move a muscle. He was lying. He must be. It was just a cruel joke. But she knew in her heart that it wasn't.

"I told him you would want to know," Greg said, "since you and Phillipe are such old friends."

Katherine struggled to keep her hands steady and her head high. They were waiting for her to break down, she could see it in their eyes, but she would not give them the satisfaction. She wondered how much Stephen had seen of her and Phillipe. Or had he only guessed? Either way, she had clearly underestimated his hostility for her. And what about Greg? He had called her here on purpose to humiliate her.

There they stood, the two of them, smiling at their little joke, while inside Katherine's heart was pounding furiously. She had lost Phillipe after all, lost him without even knowing that she had. And to a woman like Mianne Goodall—a shadow in the background, a nothing, a half-breed. The pain rose in her body like an ice-cold flame, obliterating all the warmth that had once touched the blood that flowed through her veins. And when her father spoke to her again, she turned to him, her face a mask of lovely marble.

"What are you going to do, my dear?" he asked, with a trace of a smile in his eyes.

"I don't know," Katherine responded blandly, but beneath the calm in face and voice, there was a thread of rage so cold that even Greg could not suppress a shiver of apprehension.

Chapter 17

"Well, I see that the coming wedding hasn't kept you from your work," Louis Von Hoffman observed without enthusiasm.

Phillipe and Medora exchanged glances before Phillipe replied, "No, sir."

The three of them sat on their horses at the top of a hill, looking out over the fields, where the greens and browns ran together from the force of the liquid August heat. Von Hoffman had come to the Badlands the day before Phillipe and Mianne's wedding, ostensibly to join in the celebration tomorrow, but while he was here, he was taking a thorough look at the operation of the ranch and business which he had helped support.

Medora and her stepson had already shown the old man around the plant in town, which was slaughtering one hundred head of cattle a day, and he had been forced to admit that the three trainloads of beef already delivered to Swift in Chicago had turned a tidy profit. And now, as he wiped the beads of sweat from his flushed forehead, Louis could see that the scattered cattle grazing across the field or lying in the shade were fat and healthy. He had to recognize that Phillipe was a good manager, but the admission was not a pleasant one. "No more attempts on your life, Phillipe?"

Medora stiffened and glanced questioningly at her stepson out of the corner of her eye. "How did you know about those?"

"Anais mentioned them in one of her letters. And I must tell you, I don't like the sound of these repeated attacks."

"There hasn't been any further trouble," Phillipe assured him.

"No?" Von Hoffman eyed the young man warily. "What about the fires? I see you've had the stable rebuilt, but that doesn't mean this firebug, whoever he is, will give up."

"We don't know that the fire was set on purpose," Medora interjected.

"Maybe not, but when you think about the other problems you've had, it makes the possibility look pretty strong. Did you even check to see what caused the blaze?"

"We looked, but we didn't find anything," Phillipe said.

"Well, just maybe you didn't look far enough."

The younger man shook his head. It seemed to him that Von Hoffman was determined to find fault with the way Phillipe was running the business, and since the packing plant itself was doing so well, the old man was looking elsewhere for his ammunition. "We've done everything possible to ensure that nothing of the kind happens again, Mr. Von Hoffman."

"Humph," the old man snorted. "We'll see about that. But just now I wonder if you'd allow me to speak to my daughter alone?"

Phillipe nodded, relieved to be free of Von Hoffman's endless questions. "I'll see you both at dinner," he called as he guided his horse down the hill and left them with a final wave of his hand.

"Let's ride," Medora suggested.

"You have been wise," Von Hoffman said after a long, uncomfortable silence. "It's good that Phillipe is finally marrying." It was true that Louis had been surprised at the young man's choice, but, then, no doubt a bastard had to take what he could get, even if it was only a half-breed.

"I don't see how Phillipe's marriage makes me wise," Medora responded suspiciously. How much did her father know, anyway?

Von Hoffman smiled slightly. "Combined with your own recent marriage, I just think it's the best thing, that's all." Not that he was entirely pleased with William as a son-in-law. He was still a Frenchman, after all, but Van Driesche was at least inoffensive in his manner. And, unlike Phillipe, he was safe for Medora. "You've probably managed to suppress the rumors quite nicely," he added, but his tone was heavy with unanswered questions.

Medora pulled her horse up short and twisted in the saddle to face her father. "What rumors?" she demanded.

"About you and Phillipe, of course."

"Where did you hear that? In another of Anais' letters? My daughter appears to have been quite busy over the last few months." Medora did not like the expression of curious detachment that crossed her father's face.

"Someone had to tell me what was going on here," Von Hoffman reminded her. "You never do. Anais knew I would be concerned about you, so she kindly wrote to give me the news."

"And that's why you're here, isn't it? To see if Phillipe and I are endangering your investment?" Medora was angry at her daughter's impertinence, but, more than that, she was angry at the memory of her father's accusation about Phillipe long ago in New York. He had been right after all, and she was furious that he should have guessed her weakness when she herself had still been unaware of it. "Well, you needn't worry, Papa. I have no intention of ruining our chances here. I came for the sake of my dead husband, and no one is going to stop me from succeeding—not Phillipe or any other man."

Wincing at the reference to the Marquis, whom Von Hoffman struggled daily to forget, Louis put his hand on his daughter's horse's bridle. "Tell me," he asked quietly, "are you happy now?"

Medora looked away, "Yes, I am."

Her father knew she was lying; he could see it in the stiff line of her jaw and the blank expression in her hooded eyes. "What is it?" he persisted. "Isn't your new husband good to you?"

"My relationship with my husband is no business of yours, and never has been," Medora told him. But inside she trembled because her father was right again. It was true that William was kind and patient and as considerate as always, but now he seemed to prefer his own company to anyone else's and his face was often creased with grooves of worry. She suspected that his discontent had something to do with his continued inability to make love to her.

"But are you satisfied?" her father said, bringing her back to the reality of his flushed face and brown eyes, narrowed now in speculation.

"I'll survive, Papa," she answered, "and the business will continue to prosper, and that's all that's important to you, isn't it?"

"No," her father said. He was disturbed by the suppressed anger in his daughter's tone.

"But I thought that all you cared about was money," Medora accused him.

"I know it's difficult for you to believe," Von Hoffman said, sitting straighter in the saddle, "but the possibility does exist, just the same, that maybe, for the first time in your utterly blameless life, you are absolutely wrong." He did not wait to hear her response, but turned his horse

and started away from her, heading in the direction where
Phillipe had disappeared a few minutes earlier.

The woman in the mirror stared out at the world, an
elegant stranger. Her chemise of the finest cream silk,
edged with delicate French lace, contrasted sharply with
the coil of black hair that fell across her shoulders, and
the soft, flowing petticoat clung to her hips and swept
around her feet in a froth of lace and ribbon. Mianne
looked into her own face and did not recognize it, so pale
was the skin and so still and hollow the deep brown eyes.

"Smile, honey, it's your wedding day," Cassie admonished. The cook was concerned about Mianne, who had
spent the last week gliding in and out of the room like an
obedient shadow, doing what she was told and nothing
else, her face veiled with a look of calm detachment. She
was so quiet that Cassie had begun to wonder if Mianne's
fear had somehow drained the life out of her, leaving behind nothing but this lovely shell. "Don't you *want* to get
married?" the cook asked. Then her eyes narrowed. "Phillipe didn't force you into this, did he?"

"No, he didn't," Mianne replied in a hollow voice, but
she wondered if she had spoken the truth.

"The guests are arriving already," Cassie observed.
Sensing Mianne's reluctance to discuss the subject further,
she went to kneel on the window seat and stuck her head
out the window, oblivious to the fact that her petticoat
and drawers were clearly visible. "Well, I'll be!" she cried,
twisting her head to look at Mianne. "Greg and Katherine
Pendleton are here. Imagine, the nerve of them! As if any-
body here wanted to see them any more than they would
a plague of grasshoppers."

Turning back to her observations, she craned her neck
to get a better view. "Well, if that don't beat all!" she exclaimed without bothering, this time, to pull her head back

inside. "Alexander Mackensie, as I live and breathe. Phillipe'll be surprised to see him, I'll bet. He must've come all the way from St. Paul just for your wedding. He's talkin' to Mr. Von Hoffman now, and it seems to me they're gettin' along just fine. They look alike, you know; they've both got faces the color of beets and bellies as big as a grizzly's. No wonder they have so much to talk about."

Mianne listened absently to the cook's narrative. She knew Cassie was only trying to distract her from her own problems, but she could not seem to focus her attention outside her own numb body. For six weeks she had wandered through a dream that transformed itself often into a nightmare, and she felt as if her soul had left her that night at the riverbank when she had surrender so much more than her virginity to the man who was to become her husband. Since then, she had walked and moved and spoken as if in a trance, her emotions shrouded in a deep, protective haze.

Suddenly the door burst open and Medora rushed into the room. "I'm sorry to disturb you, Mianne, but Anais is gone, and I'm afraid you're the only one who might know where to find her."

Turning away from the reflection which had held her fascinated for so long, Mianne said softly, "Let her go for now. She'll come back when she's ready." The thought of Anais still had the power to bring Mianne's stifled feelings back to life for an instant. The girl had not spoken to her since the day of Phillipe's proposal, and Mianne knew that it was because Anais felt that her only friend had betrayed her. Mianne had made a promise and broken it in less than a day, and she doubted if the girl would ever forgive her.

"But she'll miss the wedding," Cassie said, abandoning her post by the window.

"That's her choice," Mianne murmured, then her eyes

met Medora's and she pleaded, "Let her be today. She wants to be alone with her unhappiness."

Medora nodded reluctantly. She knew that Mianne understood Anais best, and her mother would not have known what to say to the girl even if she had been found. With an effort, Medora turned her attention to the bride. "You'll be lovely today, Mianne, and you know I wish you only the best."

"I—know," Mianne said awkwardly, for she was not certain it was true. "I only hope you won't be disappointed in me."

"Phillipe will be your husband," Medora reminded her. "It's him you have to please."

"Is it?" the younger woman asked softly, and her eyes, when they met Medora's, were full of a knowledge that shook the older woman to the very heart.

Yesterday's heat had dissipated somewhat, and the deep blue sky was relieved by occasional fluffs of white that cast their moving shadows on the land beneath. As she moved slowly through the crowd, Katherine noticed that everything was ready for the ceremony she had dreaded for so long. The chairs had been set in rows on the lawn, and the tiny altar draped with flowers stood waiting at the edge of the bluff, shaded by the huge box elder tree. Katherine forced herself to look away.

She had sworn that she would not speak to Phillipe today, but she had come to watch him, just the same. She wanted to remind herself of what he had done to her, how he had made a fool of her for the second time. She wanted to look at his handsome face and remember the feel of his hands on her body, so that her rage would not die from neglect. Her one desire now was to fuel that rage until it consumed her, and he who had betrayed her. So she had come today, to look at him, and hate him, and make her plans to destroy him. For only then would she be able to tear the constant, gnawing pain from the center of her body and trample it beneath her feet.

Katherine smiled when she recognized David St. Clair talking to his brother in the shade of the porch, near the musicians. She had seen the desire that still burned in his eyes when he glanced at her as she arrived, and she meant to make use of that desire. "David," she murmured, as she approached and slipped her arm through his. "How nice to see you again." She was aware of Stephen's hostile gaze, but she did not care about him just now. It was David she was interested in. "Do you know," she said, tilting her head to look at him with slightly parted lips, "I've missed you."

David clenched his fists but did not draw away from her; she seemed to have drained his will from him with the touch of her hand. "You sound surprised," he said.

"Perhaps I was. I didn't realize how much you meant to me until you were gone."

Katherine's brown eyes, fringed by thick lashes, were gazing up at him with some kind of plea in their hollow depths, and David shivered at the answer his body gave her. He knew he should hate her, that he should turn away right now and never look at her again, but he could not do it. "It was you who told me to go," he reminded her.

"Maybe I was wrong." Twining her fingers more tightly around his arm, Katherine smiled when she felt the jolt that ran through his body.

David did not even look up when he heard his brother snort in disgust and walk away; just now there was only Katherine and her magic touch to move him, and he knew, as his hand closed over hers, that he was lost again. Even if she had toyed with him, then discarded him heartlessly, even if Stephen were right about her feelings for Phillipe Beaumont, even if she only meant to break him all over again, he could not send her away. He needed her as much as he wanted her, for he had discovered in the last two months that life without her was nothing but a desert.

"Will you sit with me, David?" she asked.

"You know I will." He was a fool, and he knew it, but there was nothing he could do.

It was then that the violinists on the porch began to play, and just a moment after everyone had found their seats, Mianne came around the back of the house on her father's arm. As one, the crowd turned to stare in awe at the bride who stood so tall and regal in her white satin gown with the wide lace collar and high puffed sleeves which narrowed to fit her slender wrists tightly. The lace jabot, that curved diagonally from her right shoulder to her waist, only emphasized the fine lines of her body, and the long, lace-edged train swept out behind her, losing itself in the folds of her long tulle veil. But it was her face that caught their attention, holding them in a tenuous web that would not let them look away. Even covered with the thin netting of her veil, Mianne's eyes glowed with a strangely compelling radiance that was not joy, and her lips were open, as if in a silent plea which no one there could understand. They only knew that she was beautiful and that her lovely eyes held secrets they would never know.

Aware of the sudden stillness their appearance had caused, Johnny squeezed his daughter's arm and whispered, "I've never been so proud of you, Mianne. And I know you're doing the right thing. God bless you, little one."

His daughter touched his hand briefly with hers, but she did not look at him. She could not, for she had just seen Phillipe dressed in his fashionable pin-striped suit, waiting for her at the improvised altar, and the fear had suddenly risen in her throat, stealing her voice away. She knew that she must not look into her father's smiling face or she would turn and flee.

There were no bridesmaids, for Mianne had wanted none, so she and her father began to move down the aisle with the music swelling over them in a wave of empty promises. Mianne walked slowly, her veil like a whisper against her face, her gown swirling gracefully around her feet. Then her father released her and she glided up to join Phillipe, whose face was no more than a blur and a flash of blue, seeking eyes.

He watched his bride float toward him with a strange numbness in his chest. Phillipe still was not certain what compulsion it was that had brought him to this moment; he only knew that some inner force had bade him to make Mianne his wife, and he had been powerless to refuse.

When he finally took her cool hand in his, the music rose for an instant, then faded into stillness, as did Mianne's awareness of the burning eyes of those who watched her. Johnny became merely a memory, and Medora and Anais and the moments of her past were as nothing while she stood on the bluff overlooking the river, with Phillipe at her side and the song of the water at her feet, and quietly but clearly promised her life away.

Chapter 18

Phillipe was oddly silent during the toasts and back-slapping and good-humored jokes that followed him at the reception. He was aware of Mianne standing beside him, smiling whenever someone came to congratulate her, and he sensed her disquiet, though he could not explain it. It was true that she had not let him touch her since that night by the river, but he had been certain that she would accustom herself to the idea of marriage soon. It would just take time.

"Congratulations, my boy!" Von Hoffman cried, raising his glass of champagne in tribute to Phillipe and his bride. "You did it!"

Phillipe understood, when Louis glanced at Mackensie, who was laughing nearby, that the old man was not referring to the marriage, but to the political triumph which Mackensie's presence represented. "I'll bet you think nothing can stop you now."

Until that moment, the young man had not even realized the significance of Mackensie's arrival, but now he felt exultant. Perhaps all the hard work had paid off after all. With a whispered apology to Mianne, he left her to join the broad-shouldered politician.

Mianne let him go without protest, and turned away to

look for Anais. Although she had sensed that the girl would not attend the reception, she had hoped to see her anyway. Somehow, she could not quite believe that Anais would desert her entirely. It seemed that everyone else had. They were all so wrapped up in the unexpected pleasure of drinking French champagne and eating gourmet delicacies that they had quite nearly forgotten the woman who had so recently become a bride.

But Medora had not forgotten. She watched Mianne weave her way through the noisy crowd and wondered at the expression of tense expectation on the young woman's face. Medora refused to think about Phillipe, for his name alone caused a painful tightening in her chest today. And even her awareness of Greg Pendleton's watchful eyes upon her could not completely obliterate the knowledge of Phillipe's presence somewhere nearby.

Standing beside his wife with her hand resting on his arm, William read her thoughts as if they were written across her eyes, and a pang of bitter jealousy ripped through his chest. He should have learned by now how to stop the pain from coming, but it only grew worse daily. To him, Medora had become a constant reminder of his own inadequacy, and her very presence was a kind of agony that had worked its way into his blood, and which he knew would never leave him.

He was tempted to turn away and leave her in order to seek solace in the heat outside, but William sensed that today Medora needed him to lean upon. His presence seemed to calm her, the touch of his hand to reassure her, and he did not have the strength to abandon her now. For he knew that his loyalty was all he could ever give her and that her gratitude was all he would ever receive in return. But it wasn't enough, his soul cried out in anguish. It would never be enough!

* * *

When the swell of the music and the cackle of voices had begun to beat against Mianne's ears like the monotonous thump of a distant drum, she slipped up the stairs, hoping to find peace in her own room. This was Phillipe's party, after all; it was he who belonged among the well-dressed guests, who knew how to court them and smile at them and make them believe. But Mianne was an outsider. This was not her world, and she knew it never would be.

When she finally closed her bedroom door behind her, shutting out some of the noise from below, Mianne leaned back and closed her eyes. Perhaps this was all just a bad dream and the feel of Phillipe's cool lips on hers a creation of her own troubled mind. For that kiss, which had sealed the bargain between them, might have been the casual meeting of two strangers. The wonder of that night by the river had ceased to exist. It had become instead the babble of unfamiliar voices and the ebb and flow of unfamiliar feelings which left her bewildered. If only she could escape.

Then Mianne opened her eyes and saw the tiny folded sheet of paper, wrapped in red ribbon, that someone had left in the center of her bed. She knew at once that it was from Anais, and she hurried to untie the ribbon and unfold the heavy parchment. She knew which drawing it would be, even before she looked at it, but she held it in trembling fingers and gazed at Anais' work as if she had never seen it before.

The subject of the drawing was Mianne herself, dressed in her buckskin gown, her feet bare, her face raised in joy toward the sun. It was the Mianne she had lost six weeks ago, the moment she told Phillipe she would be his wife. The Mianne who had run free by the river, creating a separate world for herself and the girl who had loved her. She had surrendered at last to the pull of that other world that existed inside the Chateau, and she knew, as she stared blindly at the beautiful portrait in her hand, that it was not really a gift, but rather an accusation.

Phillipe stood at the foot of the stairs, looking upward expectantly. He had seen Mianne come this way some time ago, and he had been waiting for her to return ever since. He had sensed her need to be alone for a few moments, so he had let her go, but now the guests were beginning to ask for her. He would have to go and bring her down, although he was reluctant to do so.

"Mianne," he called softly as he reached the top of the stairs. But her door was closed tight and he heard no response from within. Phillipe knocked lightly, then called again, "Mianne." When she still did not answer, he turned the knob and pushed the door inward, then paused on the threshold, his breath held back in his throat.

His wife stood before the window with her back to him, dressed only in her thin chemise. She had uncoiled her hair, letting it fall down her back in gleaming black waves, and her arms were raised, as if in benediction to the sun, which struck the glass with the last fury of late afternoon. Legs spread and fingers reaching outward, she stood like a primitive sculpture of an Indian priestess, and even her silk chemise could not destroy the aura of rare, savage abandon that clung about her.

It was as if she had left this world and taken wing, and Phillipe was enthralled by the power of her presence. She was the spirit of a lost world, the last surviving remnant of a race that had been decimated at the massacre of Wounded Knee eight years before. Phillipe moved forward to speak to her, feeling incredibly tender toward this wild and passionate woman who was his wife, and it was then that she sensed his presence and whirled to face him.

Mianne stood before him with a face made unutterably lovely by the magic of centuries, and, as he watched, the light drained from her, and her eyes became cold and dark and empty. But not before he caught a glimpse of an instant of ineffable sorrow that turned her eyes to a flaming yellow that burned his breath to ashes. The image of her suffering was a palpable force between them, and it stopped the labored beating of his heart in his chest.

For a full minute, they stood frozen, facing each other across a wasteland of words without meaning, and then Mianne said softly, "Please."

Phillipe understood that she wanted to be alone, and he did not have the power to resist the plea in her eyes. Forcing his frozen muscles into action, he revolved slowly and left the room, but the memory of her burning eyes stayed with him, even when he descended the stairs and the raucous laughter closed around him like the warmth of a familiar room after a long and painful absence.

Katherine saw William standing alone on the porch as the guests began to trickle away, and she went to lean on the railing next to him. The sun was setting at last, and the blue sky was tinged purple and wine in the last moments of early evening. The heat had finally faded into a promise of coolness, and Katherine was relieved to find that her silken petticoat no longer clung to her legs.

"Mr. Van Driesche?" she said, when the secretary did not look her way. "I want to talk to you."

"I don't think we have much to say to each other," William told her. He was annoyed that she had disturbed his one moment of peace in a long and hectic day.

"All you have to do is listen." Katherine sat on the railing, her hands curled around the wood on either side. "The thing is, I've been watching you, and I must say I admire your work."

William shook his head imperceptibly. He could not imagine what the woman was leading up to.

"But, to tell you the truth, I suspect the Vallombrosas don't really appreciate your talents. I wonder if they have any idea of your real worth?" She glanced up at him, but he did not respond. Katherine shrugged and continued, "You're no more than a shadow to them, aren't you? And that must be why you're so unhappy here."

William winced as if she had struck him, for he could not deny that she had probed a raw and painful wound. But, most of all, he was angry at himself for letting others see. He had always kept his feelings hidden in the past, so why couldn't he do so now? "You're wrong, Miss Pendleton. Besides which, my relationship with the Vallombrosas is none of your business."

Katherine was not deterred by his abrupt tone, for she had seen him flinch at the truth she had hit upon. "I just wanted to let you know that if you worked for the Pendletons, you'd be much more appreciated. We know the value of good men, Mr. Van Driesche. I don't mean that we would want you to leave your present employer. No, we'd rather you stay here. And, now and then, if you happened to come across something we might be interested in knowing, we'd be willing to pay you quite well for the information."

Now, at last, William turned to face her. "Get out of my house!" he said stiffly. "And don't bother to come back."

Katherine raised one eyebrow and smiled. "It's not your house; it's theirs, and always will be. And *you'll* always be nothing more than a convenience for the Vallombrosas, a servant who works without pay. That's not much for a husband to expect from his wife."

William looked away so she would not see the flash of pain in his eyes, but he found that he could not force himself to speak.

"When you decide you want more, come to me," Katherine offered. "I'll be waiting." Then she smiled a crooked smile and walked away.

Stunned by the self-assurance that had made those words flow off her tongue so blithely, William watched her go with a rush of horror. But underneath he knew that most of the anger came from the realization that she had recognized his weakness and put a name to his discontent. He knew he would never degrade himself by going to work for the Pendletons, but as he watched the sun sink behind the red-stained cliffs in the distance, he also knew that he would never tell his wife about Katherine's offer. If he did, he would have to tell her why, and that was something he was not prepared to do—not now, not ever.

The lamps had been turned down long ago, and the night silence had fallen upon the sleeping house like a shroud, but still Mianne was alone. She lay waiting in the strange double bed which had become her own, her mind a tangle of dread and expectation, but her new husband did not come to her. Only the shadows which hovered in the corners of the room were familiar, and the feel of the cool sheets against her skin; everything else was strange and unsettling.

Finally, when the strain of the heavy silence became too great for her to bear, she rose from the bed, slipped on her nightgown, and set out to find Phillipe. As she moved slowly, stumbling in the darkness, the walls seemed to close around her like the bars of a cage, and she found that her heart was pounding wildly. She walked through room after room, her hands guiding her along the walls, but her husband seemed to have disappeared. Then she came to the study and pushed open the door.

Phillipe sat in the wing-backed chair, a glass of brandy on the table beside him and his head resting in his hands, as if he no longer had the strength to hold it upright. He had turned the lamp down to a dull glow, so that his body was covered with flickering shadows and the rest of the room was lost in darkness. He had come here to escape his disturbing thoughts, but they had followed him, and as he emptied the brandy bottle one glass at a time, he found that his guilt only grew more intense.

He had slept for a moment, but the nightmare of the dead Indian girl had come back to haunt him, and when he opened his eyes, the image of the dead girl's face had become Mianne's as he had seen it for an instant this afternoon. That single look, lasting no more than a second, had shaken him as nothing had ever shaken him before, except perhaps the moment when he had learned he was a bastard. He had seen in that flash of wild brown eyes that this woman had a soul the beauty of which he could not even begin to comprehend, yet he had chosen to crush that spirit in the palm of his hand.

What had he done by forcing Mianne to marry him? For he knew, as surely as if she had shouted the words at him, that he had followed her that night by the river in order to force her hand. She had welcomed his advances, it was true, but it had only been because she was hurt and vulnerable and needed the touch of a human hand. And he, Phillipe, the strong and wise, had taken advantage of her weakness. She would never have married him if he had not made love to her on the riverbank; he had known that even then.

"Phillipe?" His wife's voice came to him like an echo from a distant valley, and for a moment he thought he had imagined it. But then he looked up and saw her poised in the doorway, dressed in her long, white nightgown with her beautiful black hair cascading over her shoulders. In that instant, she looked like a child to him, and he drew in his breath sharply and looked away.

"Come in, Mianne," he said. "Sit down."

Mianne did as he had bid her, seating herself in a stiff-backed chair so that she could see his face. She did not like the hunted look in his eyes or the way he kept his gaze fixed on the glass in his hand. As he watched the swirling golden liquid, the silence stretched between them and Mianne waited, her eyes full of questions, her long, slender fingers braided together in her lap.

"I'm afraid I've made a terrible mistake," Phillipe whispered at last.

Stiffening her shoulders, his wife remained silent.

"I didn't realize what it meant to marry you, Mianne," he continued, his eyes still on the brandy, "and I know now that I can't go through with it. So I'm setting you free."

Like a wild bird, like an animal he had caged and then grown tired of. Mianne stood up, gathering her dignity around her like a tattered cloak. "No," she said.

Phillipe looked up in surprise at her tone. "I want to make it right," he explained feebly. "I want you to understand—"

"No." She was finding it difficult to breathe through the weight that had settled in her chest, but her voice was steady. "You will not humiliate me like this. We were married before many people, everyone of importance in the Badlands, and I won't have them laughing at me behind my back. It's done now; we are tied together, and that's how we will remain."

"I'm doing this for you!" he cried in despair.

"I don't think so. But it's not important why. I am your wife." She did not understand why her voice did not quaver. So soon, so soon. He could not even bear it for a single day.

Phillipe shook his head, wondering at the strength that had transformed that broken spirit this afternoon into the woman who faced him now. But it did not matter. He had to make it up to her; he had to set things right. "Listen to me!" he pleaded.

This time it was Mianne who shook her head. She could see that he was determined, and she knew she had to change his mind. She could not allow him to abandon her like this, whatever his reasons. But she could see only one alternative.

Mianne closed her eyes in concentration, for she knew she was about to make the most difficult decision of her life. She was afraid of what would happen if she surrendered to her husband now, but she knew that if she didn't, she would look like a fool for all the world to pity. And there were two things Mianne had sworn never to be—a coward and a fool. As she watched Phillipe's fingers clench and unclench around the stem of his glass, she realized what she must do.

"Phillipe," she murmured, kneeling before him, "it's your turn to listen." She took the glass from his hand and set it on the table, then kissed his fingers and pressed them against her cool cheek.

Her husband drew back, aware that the hunger in his body could not withstand this kind of attack, but Mianne moved with him until her head was resting on his shoulder and her breath whispered in the hollow of his throat.

"I want you," she murmured, sliding her arms around his neck. "Don't send me away."

Phillipe rose and pushed her from him in one last attempt to save her from herself, but Mianne saw that the glow of righteousness had faded from his eyes, to be replaced with wavering desire. He wanted her, she could feel it, and she went to him and put her arms around his waist, raising her face until their eyes met and held. And when he lowered his lips to hers, he drew her to him as a man lost in the desert reaches for his first drink of water in many days.

They clung together, mouth to mouth and hand to hand, as the flicker of warmth grew to a dancing flame between them, and Mianne knew that she had won. But it had not really been her battle at all. Phillipe had made the choice for both of them that night long ago when the song of the water had taken away her strength, and she knew that now they would both have to live with that choice, whatever the consequences.

Part IV

The Badlands:
Summer, 1899

"In moments of difficulty you must never give up—remember that. Remember in seeking, toward and against everything, justice and truth, you bring yourself nearer to God."

—Marquis de Mores
May, 1897

Chapter 19

"FIRE!"

Phillipe turned in the direction from which the distant shout had reached him and saw the rising billows of deep gray smoke that had begun to stain the sky toward the far southeast corner of the ranch. Kicking his horse into action, he headed by instinct toward the fire which the rolling hills now hid from his view. His first thought was a profound gratitude that he had stayed home from the plant today, his second a burst of fury at his own foolish complacency. He pushed the brown hair back from his forehead and leaned closer to the horse's neck while the distant sky grew choked with heavy smoke and the smell of charred wood drifted into his nostrils and clung there, bitter and acrid.

He had been a fool, Phillipe chided himself as he rode. He had convinced himself so easily that things were all going his way. The family's winter in New York had been calm and productive, and Phillipe himself had made an important contact with Theodore Roosevelt, whom he had known as a boy. Then they had returned to the Badlands to find that the winter had been mild and they had lost few cattle to the cold, while the plant continued production at the rate of 125 head a day. Even the Pendletons had been quiet.

Everything had been going so well, and now this! Let the fire be a small one, he prayed, and as easily contained as the one last year in the stable. But then the final hills faded behind him, and he came face-to-face with the blazing wall of flame that blocked all else from his sight. In the unreality of the snapping, hissing blaze, he was encased in a cloak of cloying smoke and raging color—a devouring heat that melted the world into shimmering liquid fire.

"Mr. Beaumont! Thank God!" Johnny Goodall appeared, his weathered face streaked with gray and his forehead covered with sweat. Grasping Phillipe's bridle in a firm grip, he cried, "Send the horse away and let's get to work."

Phillipe forced his body into motion and swung himself to the ground. "There's no point in going for the fire pump, is there?"

"None at all. The fire's already covered too much ground."

"So soon?" The younger man looked up at the smoke-gray sky and dragged the back of his hand across his already damp forehead. "There's not even any wind today. How could it have spread so quickly?"

Johnny's lips were set in a grim line as he replied, "There's only one way *I* know of. It must have started in several places at once, and that means someone set it on purpose."

Staring into the raging furnace that was sucking the landscape into itself, Phillipe suppressed a shudder. "We'll deal with that later. Right now, we have to stop this before it destroys the whole ranch. Thank God the house is so far away."

"I only hope it's far enough," Johnny muttered.

Phillipe ignored his pessimism. "Send some men to make certain all the animals are out of the path of the fire," he instructed. "Another group should begin to dig a trench there, to the east of the flames and far enough away to give them time to work. You see to that, Johnny, and I'll work on a backfire. It should be safe enough, since there's no wind."

"The fire's moving so fast there's not much chance of making a good firebreak," Goodall reminded him.

"It's the only chance we have. We'll have to hope we can stop it on this side and just let it burn itself into the cliffs on the other."

"The Pendletons are gathering their men down south," Johnny said. "The fire's right on the border between their ranch and ours. It's burning toward us now, but if the wind comes up, it could spread onto their property."

"Then make use of them, too," Phillipe told the foreman as he began to move gingerly around the edge of the scarlet and orange conflagration. By now, the heat was so intense that it seemed to wrap his muscles in cotton wool, and he had to force himself to walk forward. "Send someone back for shovels and anything else they can find that might help us clear the land," he ordered through dry lips, "and get the Pendletons to do the same. They might hate us, but I doubt if they'll risk their own ranch even for the pleasure of watching ours destroyed."

Fighting his way through the smoke and heat that attempted to hold him back, Phillipe found one after another of the men and directed them to their tasks. He knew they were fighting against time, and that they had little chance of success—the flames were hungry and seemed intent on swallowing the Badlands in one hungry gulp—but they had to try. Peering up at the pall of black that made a false ceiling beneath the sky, Phillipe prayed for rain, or a fair wind, or a miracle, but he knew that all he could depend upon were his own two hands and those of his men. If there were to be a miracle, they would have to make it themselves. For the roaring, leaping fury of hungry flame that rose in terrible magnificence all around him had a power the likes of which he had never seen, and before which he knew himself to be utterly helpless.

Anais bent over the handlebars of her bicycle, riding as if every nightmare she had ever dreamt were at her back. With her eyes fixed on the path ahead, she pumped her legs up and down until the muscles screamed in protest, but even then she did not stop. She had to get away, as far away as possible from the riot of orange flames that were melting the world at her back. Away from the thick black smoke that wrapped itself around her like a heavy cloak, bringing tears to her eyes and dry, wrenching gasps to her throat.

She had come to her secret place today, as she always did, to escape the people who surrounded her at the Chateau—strangers, every one of them. Long ago she had discovered a path fairly free from rocks which followed the gentle rise and fall of nearby hills, and she had brought her bicycle here often. Usually she found that, when she mounted it and rode away, all her thoughts and troubles disappeared as if by magic into the clear blue sky. But not today. Today the flames had blocked her path, and they roared behind her now, sending the fear like poison through her veins. Today the nightmare was with her, licking at her heels, more real, more threatening than ever before. The fire itself was a reflection of her inner terror, and even when she turned away, the image of the gold and scarlet flames would not leave her.

Standing at the top of the hill above the Chateau, where she could see the distant fury of smoke and dancing heat, Mianne watched Anais approach. The girl was hunched awkwardly over the handlebars, and her hands gripped the metal until the blood had drained from every finger. Her eyes were wild with fear, and her face, though flushed with the exertion, was deathly pale beneath.

"Wait, Anais!" Mianne called, moving her now bulky body so that it nearly blocked the path. "Where are you going?"

Anais gave a gasp of surprise, astonished to find the other woman in the heart of her nightmare, then she brought the bicycle to an abrupt stop. "Get out of my way!" she cried.

"I just want to know where you're going in such a hurry. You could easily hurt yourself riding over this terrain like that." Mianne put her hand on the girl's arm but Anais flung it away.

"Let me go," she said, the desperation creeping into her voice. "I have to get away."

Mianne saw that the girl did not really know her, so caught up was she in her private fear, but then that had been true ever since the wedding. Yet now there was something new in Anais' face, and it forced Mianne to take the chance she had not dared to take before. "Tell me what you're afraid of," she murmured, covering the girl's hand with her own.

Anais hesitated and started to move away, but Mianne had recognized the girl's need and could not let her go. "Talk to me, Anais, just as you used to. Tell me what's troubling you."

For a moment longer, the girl kept her lips pressed firmly closed, but then the vision of the flames rose before her, and she shuddered uncontrollably. "It's horrible!" she wailed. "I didn't know it would be like that. Everyone is there, trying to stop the fire, but they won't. It will swallow them whole and turn them to ashes. Even Stephen." Closing her eyes, she tried to control the trembling in her body, but, by now, even her teeth were chattering together. "I didn't know!" she repeated. "I can't look anymore."

Mianne stood uncertainly before the shivering girl and wondered what to do. She was deeply disturbed by Anais' overwhelming terror and the glaze of desperation that turned her eyes into polished stones. The woman had watched the girl slipping further and further into herself in the past year. Anais had begun to build herself an impregnable world that existed for no one but her, and she had pushed her family away one by one, until now there was no one left.

Mianne felt that she had to reach Anais somehow, and maybe, now that she was shaken and afraid, the girl would relax the barrier between them, if only for an instant. Mianne slid one arm around Anais' shoulders and pulled the girl to her. "The fire is too far away to hurt you," she whispered. "Why are you still afraid?"

Anais let her body go limp for a moment, but when she felt the hard roundness of Mianne's belly, she gasped and backed away. She had nearly forgotten her friend's betrayal in her weakness, but now it came back to her in a rush. The woman was seven months pregnant with Phillipe's child, and her swollen body was a constant reminder of the promise she had broken. Mianne had abandoned Anais long ago; it was too late now to make amends. Pulling away, the girl hissed, "Let me go!"

Astonished by the hostility in Anais' voice, Mianne stepped back and let her arm fall to her side. She could feel the anger that radiated from the girl's smoldering eyes—a kind of rage that made her body quiver from head to toe. Anais hated so many people with the same hurt fury, and she refused so adamantly to acknowledge the pain that lay beneath the surface. Mianne wondered just how far this girl would go to get back at the people who had earned her rage. As she watched Anais ride away, framed by the billowing smoke-filled sky and the distant leaping flames, Mianne found herself remembering with dread the entranced look in the girl's black eyes as she stared blindly at that other fire on the very day of her arrival in the Badlands.

No, Mianne told herself, intense as it was, even Anais' hatred was not strong enough to make her destroy everyone she had ever loved. But with the flames dancing before her eyes, a pulsing threat to land and people alike, Mianne found that she was not so certain.

Phillipe stood at the edge of the band of blazing grass and shrubs and shaded his eyes with his blackened hand. He could only hope that the wide path of his own fire would leave a charred waste that even that blazing inferno could not cross. Glancing down the line of anxious men, he watched their frenzied digging and felt a brief pang of despair. Surely they were too few, even with the help of the Pendletons, and surely the fire would find a way to thwart them.

By now the heat had become unbearable, and Phillipe's mouth was parched with aching thirst—a thirst that would not be assuaged by the occasional trickle of water that he swallowed as he passed the canteen on to the next man. It clung to him like a leech that would not be shaken away, and he began to wonder if he would ever cool the rasping dryness in his throat.

Then, as he moved among the men, he caught a flash of bright red skirt and worn black boots, and he began to run. "Cassie! What the hell are you doing here?"

The cook glanced over her shoulder for an instant, then went back to the shovelful of earth she had just dug up. "Fighting the fire, what else?" she muttered, tucking her long, wiry hair behind her ear. "And don't tell me to go sit and watch with the other women, 'cause I don't mean to sit idle. Besides, you know you need all the help you can get."

Phillipe began to protest, but at that instant he heard a bellow and a hail of sparks came flying at him. His shirt was aflame before he had time to breathe, then Cassie was shouting and pushing him down to the ground on the far side of the ditch where the grass had not yet burned.

"Roll!" she cried. "Make the fire choke for air!" While he concentrated on smothering the flames against the ground, the cook beat at them with her ragged skirt.

Phillipe gasped as he inhaled a mouthful of gray, dusty air, then he realized that, although his shirt hung in charred tatters from his chest, he was still whole and alive, and the fire had been smothered into lifelessness. His skin was burnt—he could feel the shooting fingers of pain that ran all up and down his chest—but he knew he would survive.

"You'd best go back to the house and have those burns seen to," Cassie advised as she bent over, eying him carefully.

"Not yet." Phillipe winced as he shifted his weight and the remains of his shirt brushed the raw skin. "We still have a fire to fight," he said through rigid lips. "I'll stay."

"Well, then, so will I, I reckon," Cassie told him smugly.

It was then that Stephen St. Clair came running toward them, calling at the top of his lungs, "The wind has come up and Johnny says, the way the air is moving, the fire will probably be burning toward the Pendleton place now." The young man was flushed with the heat of the fire, but even the blackened rivers of dirt and sweat that covered his cheeks could not hide the light of triumph in his pale blue eyes.

Phillipe rose gingerly, closing his eyes for an instant as the pain washed over him. Then, moving with unusual care, he brushed the dirt and charred cloth from his body and grunted an acknowledgment. "That just means we have to shift the thrust of our efforts to the south," he said.

Shaking his head in disbelief, Stephen cried, "Why not let it burn? It might teach the bastards a lesson."

With a sidelong glance at Cassie, Phillipe shook his head.

"You forget that your brother's over there," he pointed out. "Besides, if you ask me, bastards just don't learn, no matter how hard you try to teach them."

"Ha! Ain't that the God's truth!" Cassie hooted.

"This is not a joke," Stephen said.

"No, it isn't." Phillipe considered the other man thoughtfully, and he found that, even after a year of steady service and the incredible strength and will Stephen had put into fighting the fire today, Phillipe still could not quite bring himself to trust the tutor. "And the longer we stand here wasting time, the more likely the wind is to change direction and bury us in flame." With a last warning look, Phillipe turned back to the half-finished ditch.

Shrugging, Stephen went his own way, but the set of his mouth was grim with his discontent.

Cassie followed more slowly. She was painfully aware of her brittle, aging bones, and her leathery skin burnt red by the heat, but she did not intend to give in to her exhaustion. The cook bent to her task with fresh determination, and, although she tried to focus on the ever-widening trench at her feet, she knew her dreams would be haunted for some time to come with the feel and sight and sound of the seething, changing mass of gold and red that flared at her back, melting, devouring, destroying every living thing in its path.

For hours Phillipe worked steadily, racing an enemy as unpredictable and violent as the devastating summer storms, but far more destructive in its awesome strength. For hours he waited, watching for the unexpected sheet of flame that would swallow him where he stood and leave him indistinguishable from the charred and barren landscape. For hours he circled the periphery of the blaze, trying to block its path with a ring of empty earth and scorched grass. Then a shout went up. Phillipe looked up from the trench where he stood, covered with dirt to the knees, and saw Johnny's grimly triumphant face above him. "I've had a few men watching from above"—he indicated the hills that rose where the flames had not yet gone—"and they tell me it seems to be contained. With the Pendletons and their men working from the other side, we've managed to pretty well block the advance, and now it seems the wind has shifted so the fire is moving toward the cliffs like we hoped it would."

Phillipe released a deep sigh of relief and dropped his shovel in the dirt. "Still, we can't be sure it's over," he said. "We'd better leave some men to keep watch. And there must be something I can do—"

"There's nothing for you to do now but watch it die slowly, and I've a suspicion you should go have those burns taken care of. You've left them too long as it is. The danger's over now. Go back and relax in case we need you again."

Reluctantly, Phillipe agreed, but as he turned to go, he paused and took one last, long look at the fire which had obliterated the broad expanse of sky for a full day. Never before had he seen a force with the power to do that, but, at the moment, the magnificence had no more strength to move him. Just now, he could think of only one thing—the long, cool drink that would slide down his raw throat and soothe away, once and for all, the thirst that had drained his body of the last of its strength many hours before.

Chapter 20

Greg leaned back in his chair and closed his eyes, letting the cool evening breeze touch his raw skin with soothing fingers. It had been a long and trying day, but the struggle was finally over. The fire had blackened acre upon acre, but he and his men had proven themselves stronger than the flames, and now he knew that he was invincible. That was why he had called Katherine into the study so soon after his return. He wanted to talk to her while the feeling of power was still upon him.

"Well?" his daughter prompted, annoyed that he had apparently forgotten her. "If you called me here to watch you sleep, I must tell you that I have more important things to do—"

Greg opened his eyes and leaned forward. "There is nothing more important than our plans for the Vallombrosas, and that's what I want to talk to you about. We've already let it go too long."

Considering her father in the last rays of daylight, Katherine noted his filthy clothing and reddened skin and the cracked, dry surface of his hands. "Wasn't the fire enough?" she asked.

"I've told you time and again, I'm not a fool, my dear. I would never set a fire so close to my own land, not even to avert suspicion. And that's just the point. Whoever did do it is clumsy and didn't care if they hurt others besides the Vallombrosas." He reached for a cigar and twirled it absently in his fingers. "I want that family out of the Badlands before we're all ruined. Fire is never a good means of exacting vengeance. It gets out of control too easily."

"This one didn't," Katherine pointed out. "Maybe Phillipe has a mandate from heaven to protect him from mad arsonists."

Greg ignored his daughter's ironic tone and continued, "I don't know about a mandate from heaven, but he certainly has one from Alexander Mackensie, which, in this state, amounts to the same thing. We've got to change that, you and I, and soon, before the vote comes up on limiting railroad rates. I understand your friend has even made contact with the Vice President, Theodore Roosevelt, and he's not only an old friend, but a man too willing to listen to reformers. We've got to stop Phillipe before he wins this victory, or we've lost altogether."

"If he has everyone's support, how do you plan to do that?"

Greg smiled knowingly and leaned back, tapping his cigar on the chair arm. "*We* also have friends in high places and, given enough incentive, they might be convinced to help Mackensie change his mind."

"What am I to do, then?"

"While I work on my contacts, I want you to go to St. Paul before the vote in June. Remind Mackensie that he's still a vigorous man, and when you've done that, you might just hint that he doesn't *really* want to lose the support of the railroads. All you have to do is be more charming than Phillipe. I know you can do it if you work hard enough."

"If you mean what I think you do, you can go to hell," Katherine said.

"Come now, my dear, you've often said you'd do anything to get back at Phillipe. Well, here's your chance."

With her head high and her eyes gleaming, Katherine rose and moved toward the door. "I'll think about it," she murmured.

"There's one more thing," Greg called. "I noticed that Cory was out roaming around again this morning. You've got to be more careful to keep her inside. You know very well she can't be trusted."

"Mama is hardly my responsibility." Katherine whirled to face him. "I have better things to do than spend my time being her jailer."

"You'd better *make* her your responsibility. I've told you before, one more incident and I'll have her put away."

His daughter flinched as if he had struck her. "Don't worry," she said, "I'll see that she doesn't cause any trouble."

"How can you do that," Greg inquired, "when you can't even control your own husband?"

Stiffening visibly, Katherine kept her temper only through sheer force of will. She had finally married David St. Clair that winter, and he had come to live on the ranch with her. Ever since the wedding, Greg had been insisting that she force David to stop selling St. Clair cattle to Phillipe. Katherine had tried to oblige. Usually David did exactly what she bid him, but this time he had refused to give in. It was not a subject she liked to remember. "You let me worry about David," Katherine snapped. "Right now we're talking about Mama."

"The point is that you and I have important things to accomplish just now. We can't risk letting Cory ruin our plans," Greg warned.

Brown eyes blazing a warning of her own, Katherine took one step forward and whispered, "You won't put her away. You're too afraid she'll tell everyone the truth about you."

"Don't push me, Katherine," her father snarled. "I mean it this time. That woman has become a weight around my neck, and I intend to rid myself of her before she drags us all down with her. You know better than anyone that I won't let that happen. I'd do anything to stop it—anything at all."

Phillipe twisted and turned in the darkness, his dreams full of raging fire. Somehow the vibrant, all-consuming flames had moved outside his control, and the world was a single shimmering explosion of gold and orange that swallowed all else in its white-hot fury. Phillipe wanted to turn and run from the incandescent surge of heat that changed the night to morning, but then he saw a figure through the flames and his feet refused to answer his will.

Shading his eyes with his hand, Phillipe gazed into the center of the fire, trying to force the distant figure into focus, but he could see no more than a dark, wavering shadow. Still, he knew that someone was there, and that he had to get them out, although the flames might easily devour them both. Phillipe put his arms in front of his face as a shield and began to fight his way past the fierce heat which tempted him again and again to retreat. But always the shadow was before him, beckoning from the heart of the flames, and he knew he could not leave it here. He had to get to it somehow, though his clothing had turned to blackened dust and his eyes were burned blind.

Then, just when he thought to put out his hand and grasp the illusive figure, the fire exploded in upon itself in a roar of frenzied, writhing flames that sent Phillipe reeling backwards. Struggling to make himself stand upright, he raised his head and saw the figure coming toward him from the very center of the blaze. In that instant, he recognized his father, the Marquis, carrying the mysterious Indian girl's dead body.

Phillipe shuddered and tossed the covers away as his eyes opened and the dream faded into the darkness. Even the whisper of the sheets across his chest was agony, and he realized that the pain of his burns must have caused the unsettling nightmare. But even in the safety of his own bedroom, where the only fire was contained in the pot-bellied stove in the corner, the Indian girl's face rose to haunt him. Who was she, he wondered, wincing at a raw spark of pain, and why did she continue to appear in his dreams?

"Phillipe?" Mianne rose awkwardly on one arm, placing the other protectively before her swollen belly. "The pain is troubling you, isn't it?"

"I'll be all right as soon as I relax a little," he replied.

"Hmmm," his wife murmured skeptically. "Cassie has already put her special cream on the burns. I think now it would be best to leave them alone. The air will heal them eventually."

"I told you, I'm fine." Phillipe was surprised by the concern in her voice. It was almost as if she regretted her inability to ease his discomfort. He smiled in bemusement, wondering if he would ever understand this woman who was his wife. She was seven months pregnant with his child, yet he did not really know her at all. She was always kind to him and she never rejected his advances in bed, but he knew she was still a stranger to him. Mianne kept a careful distance between them, and sometimes he felt she was further away from him now than before she had become his wife.

"Tell me about your dream," Mianne said unexpectedly.

"Dream?" Phillipe eyed her warily, wondering, as he did so often, if she could somehow read his mind.

"The one that has come four times since we've shared a bed. The one which leaves you hollow-eyed and silent in the morning, as if it had drained your spirit during the night. I've watched you suffer through it long enough. Now I want to know."

Astonished that she had been watching him so closely, her husband hesitated for only a moment before he told her everything, from the moment when he had seen the Marquis with the dead woman in his arms to the confrontation with Medora the summer before. "I don't know why it is," he mused, "but I feel that I can't rest easy until I've discovered who she was and why she died. It's almost as if she were leading me somewhere, but I can't find the way."

Mianne looked down at her hands. She knew that feeling so well. "I saw her sometimes many years ago," she said "She used to appear by the river, but I never dared speak to her. Then one day she disappeared entirely. I suppose that was when she died."

Phillipe could tell by the muted reverence in Mianne's voice that, in her own way, she had been as struck by the Indian girl as he had been. Only her image of the woman was not stained with violence as his was. "But do you know who she was?" he demanded.

"No, but my father does, I think. He would never talk to me about it, but I knew there was a secret about your sudden departure from the Badlands. And wait!" Mianne put her hand on her husband's arm in her excitement. "I think I know her name. It must have been Ileya. I remember my father came in to breakfast one morning and said something about Ileya."

"Ileya," Phillipe repeated thoughtfully. "Is it a Sioux name?"

"Yes. It means 'The Shining One,' " Mianne told him. "But I know no more than that. You must ask my father for the rest of the story. And promise to tell me what you learn. I wonder about her sometimes, too."

"I promise," Phillipe said, laying his hand gently on top of hers.

Suddenly, Mianne sat bolt upright with a gasp of surprise, then she cradled her belly with both hands. "The baby kicked," she said in a whisper. "He must be angry tonight."

Then, taking her husband's hand in hers, she pressed it against her warm abdomen and he felt a jolt against his palm. "You see," she said. "He's complaining." Her eyes held her husband's for a long moment, and a shadow of a smile crossed her face. For this instant, at least, they were sharing a feeling of awe which brought them close, and the fragile thread that had been forged between them long ago gained another strand. Then Mianne closed her eyes and turned away.

Phillipe sensed her withdrawal from him, and some instinct made him take her hand and whisper, "Have you forgiven me yet?"

His wife shook her head. "There's nothing to forgive." But she knew she was lying. She could never forgive him for being what he was—the only man on earth with the ability to pierce her outer shell and see the true, tormented spirit underneath. Her only consolation was that Phillipe himself did not know it. She hoped fervently that he never would.

The door inched open, and Katherine's dark head emerged from the shadows of the hall into the warm lamplight of the bedroom. David watched as she went to her dressing table without glancing in his direction and began to remove the pins from her hair. As always, she seemed to enjoy the ritual; her eyes were fixed on her own reflection in the mirror with peculiar fascination, and her fingers trailed languidly through her brown curls as they tumbled over her shoulders. Her new husband looked away. "It's quite late," he said, a hint of accusation in his voice.

Katherine smiled at herself and shrugged. "I had plans to make."

"Plans for the family at the Chateau?" David asked.

Glancing at her husband's reflection in the mirror, Katherine saw that he was not looking at her. "Maybe," she said.

David sat up abruptly, his forehead furrowed with concern. "Why do you hate them so much, Katherine?"

"They're a threat to us," his wife replied stiffly. Shifting so she could look at him over her shoulder, she asked, "How do you know about my plans, David? *I've* certainly never told you."

David met her gaze squarely, unintimidated by the cool expression in her eyes. "I overheard you talking to your father this evening."

Katherine turned back to her mirror. "Haven't you got anything better to do than listen at doorways?"

"I want to know what's going on, and *you* won't ever tell me. But that's not the point right now. Tell me why you dislike the Vallombrosas and Phillipe. They helped save your land, after all. They could have just stood by and let it burn when the wind shifted," David pointed out.

Katherine pursed her lips in annoyance. "That was *their* choice," she said. "And, if you ask me, it makes them look a little like fools." She saw her husband shake his head in disbelief, and Katherine had to stifle a sigh of irritation. She wondered, for the hundredth time, why she had even married him. He had no backbone, no spirit of adventure. In fact, David St. Clair was not really her kind of man at all.

Unaware of her building anger, David continued, "I want to know how far you would go to hurt them." He could not help thinking of those other fires last year, the poisoned cattle, even the attempts on Phillipe's life. "Tell me the truth, Katherine," he pleaded, asking her to salvage his own peace of mind. "Would you actually kill to make them leave the Badlands?"

His wife dropped her hairbrush among the many delicate crystal bottles of perfume that cluttered the tabletop. David might be a fool, but obviously his curiosity was dangerous. If there was one thing she did not need just now, it was another conscience to torment her at night. She would have to distract him, make him forget his fears and doubts, and she knew how to do it. David was a simple man and easily pleased, when one knew the secret. "I don't want to talk anymore," she said, rising to stand before the window where her image wavered in the glass behind her.

Then Katherine reached up and spread her hair across her shoulders, shaking the long tendrils so the lamplight danced across the glimmering curls. She smiled and began to untie her robe, slowly, so that David could not help but watch her fingers as they moved rhythmically, first tossing the robe aside, then drawing her unbuttoned nightgown up over her long, fine legs, her hips, her breasts.

David sat unmoving, hypnotized by the play of the lamplight on his wife's gleaming skin. He was always surprised by the beauty of her naked body, no matter how many times he had seen it before, because he could not bring himself to believe it was really his. He remembered how stunned he had been, how frozen with awe on their wedding night, when she had stood before this very window in her silver beaded gown with the snow, touched by moonlight, stretching endlessly at her back. How slowly and sensuously she had moved, her body a glittering flame of silver light, her secrets hidden by the fine, undulating silver chain of her veil. And, as she had lifted the veil with widespread fingers, so that the chain caught the lamplight and sent it shivering across the room, he had found that the breath had caught in his throat. The dancing lights of her gown and veil set off an answering flame in his chest, and he knew he was forever enthralled by the ice princess who swayed before him with the promise of flames in her eyes.

Katherine, too, was thinking of their wedding night, for she could see the reflection of David's thoughts in his eyes. The event had been everything she had wanted it to be; she had taken the icy coldness of winter and twisted it to her advantage. She knew the locals still called that grand celebration the "snow wedding." Everything there had been white and silver, winter and ice, crisp and coolly beautiful—from David's white suit and her silver gown to the white roses brought from California on refrigerated railroad cars. Even the cake had been decorated with tiny silver candles.

The wedding had been magnificent; it had outdone even Phillipe and Mianne's last August. It had been a spectacle the locals would never forget, but for Katherine it had been cold and empty. Empty because Phillipe had not been there to see it, to envy it, to wish it had been his. She knew in her heart that all the splendor had been for him, and the knowledge only fuelled her outraged anger that he did not care. She had put her soul into that wedding, for Phillipe's sake, but she wondered daily if it had been worth the effort. What had she gained from it after all? Nothing but a bitter memory and a husband who was a fool.

"Katherine," David breathed, as her nightgown slid to the floor and her naked body was revealed, "please come here."

She moved toward him slowly, regally, aware of the blatant adoration in his eyes but strangely unmoved by his reverence. His hands, as they drew her down beside him, were like the memory of cool water on her heated skin—soothing but unexciting.

"God, but you're beautiful," he murmured, his body taut with hunger. Then he buried his face in her hair, trailing his tongue along the contours of her white neck while his hands found their own paths across her breasts and belly. As always, her very presence had the power to rob him of his senses, and he knew he could wait no longer to have her.

Katherine wrapped her arms around her husband as he entered her, and she clung to him, rocking, rocking with the sway of his passion. Though her lips whispered her delight into his waiting ears, her body was cool and silent beneath his assault. The hunger still raged within her, as vivid and frenzied as the fire that had blackened her land this afternoon, and she wanted David to appease it. Nightly, she begged him silently to appease it before it consumed her from within, but he simply could not do it. His breath on her face, his skin pressed to hers, the movement of his body in the moment of fulfillment, meant nothing to her. Although she wished with all her heart that it was different, she had known from the night of their wedding that it never would be. While her body set David on fire, he left her cold and empty, like the frozen touch of an icy winter hand. This was the fate she had chosen, and, because of her pride, and the biting memory of Phillipe, this was the fate she would suffer for all her barren life. But she would not be the only one to suffer, for she had sworn that the man who had forced her into this hopeless marriage would pay, somehow, twice over, for her unhappiness.

Chapter 21

"Cory!" Greg gasped as he stumbled in the first light of dawn. "Where are you? CORY!" He pushed his way under the trees that lined the river and called his wife's name again and again. "Cory! Come back, please! I want to talk to you."

He had discovered his wife was missing when he awakened this morning, and he was still painfully aware of the fight they had had the night before. As always, Medora's name had figured prominently in his wife's attack, and the futility of the entire argument had struck him as ridiculous, until he had seen that Cory was gone. Greg paused for a moment to rest his weight against the trunk of a cottonwood while his breath came in wrenching gasps, but he knew he had to go on. He had to find Cory before anyone else did, before she did something foolish.

"Cory!" he cried as the still morning air crawled down the open neck of his shirt. "Cory, please!"

It was then that he saw the neatly folded shawl and the unfinished confusion of yarn and knitting needles that Cory took with her everywhere. She had left them beneath a tree, just out of reach of the rushing river, as if she intended to return and take up her task at any moment, but of Cory herself there was no sign. But at least he knew now that she had come this way. He would find her, Greg told himself. He had to.

"I know you're there!" he called hoarsely. "Come back to me, Cory."

Greg paused when he heard the distant trilling of a high, sweet voice, and he stopped, paralyzed by the sound. Surely that could not be Cory singing as if the world lay like a sparkling jewel at her feet? He had heard her sing like this, so sweet and pure and contented, only once before, and it was a memory he suppressed with brutal determination. There were very few things that made Cory happy. Unfortunately, he knew quite well what her happiness meant for others.

"Cory!" he bellowed.

The singing stopped, and, in the sudden silence, the hush of morning lay upon the landscape like a fragile glass shroud. Greg brushed the hanging leaves aside and stepped into a tiny clearing where his wife stood waiting expectantly, her eyebrows quirked in curiosity to see who had come to disturb her.

"Greg," she laughed when she recognized her husband. "How lovely of you to come visit. I hope you don't mind, but I had the urge to take an early walk before the rest of the world was stirring."

Greg breathed a single sigh of relief. At least she was not still angry about last night. Yet there was something vaguely disturbing about his wife just the same. She wore her usual faded gown, but it seemed less baggy this morning, as if she had taken some care to make it hang properly. And her hair was combed neatly down over her ears, the wispy silver strands just touching her white collar. She had obviously taken the trouble to try and make herself attractive today. Greg shivered again as the gently swaying leaves made their dappled shadows on the grass. "Let's go home," he said softly.

"Oh, but I can't just yet," Cory told him. "I haven't fin-

ished. Do you notice how early the fall has come this year?
I've been spending the morning gathering colored leaves
for the table. I've always loved autumn leaves, haven't you?
They're so crisp and bright and fragile."

Turning away from her for an instant, Greg drew a deep,
ragged breath.

"Look at my leaves," Cory said, unsatisfied by his response. "I've taken such care in collecting them that it
would break my heart if you didn't like them." She came
within three steps of her husband and raised her full basket before him, as if asking for his approval.

Greg glanced down at the pile of spring flowers in
Cory's hand, and his breath twisted inside him. Cory
smiled and reached for the wild lily that lay on top. "This
is my favorite," she said. "I love the golden cottonwood
leaves."

"Let's go home," her husband repeated. "I'll carry your
basket for you."

He reached out to take the basket, but Cory pulled it
away from him. "No!" she cried. "They're mine. You
can't have them."

"Cory, I don't want—" he began.

"No!" she wailed, stumbling backwards. Then she lost
her footing and sprawled on the still damp grass. The
flowers scattered over the ground, and Greg saw with a
shudder what lay beneath.

With trembling fingers he picked up the carefully tied
stack of matches that had lain hidden in the bottom of the
basket. If he closed his eyes, he could still smell the cloying acrid odor of charred wood that had clung to his nostrils yesterday as he fought the fire. "Someone must have
set it on purpose," David had said, and Greg had nodded
in grim agreement. He remembered, too, that Cory had
escaped him yesterday morning as well, and that he had
found her dishevelled and filthy, wandering at the far

southern edge of their land. "What are you doing with these?" he demanded, waving the matches before her face.

Cory gnawed her lip, her forehead puckered in concentration, but she could not remember why she had brought the matches. "Maybe I meant to use them to burn the leaves. You know how annoyingly they crunch beneath your feet, and I must have— "

"Stop it!" Greg snarled. "This has gone far enough." Dropping the matches, he reached out to drag Cory to her feet. His fingers bit into her arm with punishing intensity. "I've warned you, Cory, but you wouldn't listen, and now it's too late. I can't wait any longer or you'll destroy us all."

His wife gaped at him, confused by his taut, steely anger. She closed her eyes and tried to pull free of his painful grip, but his hands were locked around her arms and he would not let her go. Why was he so furious? she wondered desperately, her heart pounding in her ears. And why did he suddenly hate her so much? Cory opened her eyes and shuddered at the force of her husband's anger. She did not understand it; she only knew she had felt it before. He had stood above her then as he did now, his mouth twisted in rage, his gray eyes swirling wildly like the heart of a silver whirlpool. . . .

. . . . *April, 1886—The water circled and eddied beneath her hand, and Cory imagined how her blood would look, curving into the whirlpool she had created, dyeing the tiny puddle red.* First there would be the blood, she knew, then the searing pain, and, finally, the release she had sought for so long. The knife blade gleamed in her other hand, and, for a moment, it blinded her with its promise of escape. Clutching it tightly, she dipped both hands in the water and closed her eyes, swaying with the rhythm of her inner voices.

"Cory! What are you doing?"

Greg's voice shook her awake, and she turned to see him bearing down upon her. But Cory only smiled and raised the knife so he could see it. Surely he would understand her intention now. Surely he would realize that the blade was calling to her.

Greg ran his hands roughly through his hair and tried to fight back the exasperation he felt at finding his wife crouched in the courtyard, her skirt covered with mud, crooning to her own reflection in a rain puddle. But when he saw the knife, he stopped abruptly. "What are you doing?" he repeated. "Answer me!"

Cory shook her head in wonder at the tone of his voice. "I want to die," she said simply.

"You do," he groaned. "You, who has everything to live for? A beautiful daughter, a comfortable home, wealth beyond your wildest dreams, and a husband who will never stray again?" His voice was ragged with bitterness.

"I have nothing but nightmares," Cory cried. "My marriage is ruined—"

"That's not my fault," he interrupted.

His wife closed her eyes at the unforgiving accusation in his voice. "I didn't meant to do it! Can't you understand that? I didn't realize—I just didn't know." The knife lay forgotten in her hand as she stared up into Greg's implacable gaze. "But you don't care that I didn't mean it. You won't forgive me, will you?"

"No." That single word fell between them with indisputable finality.

"Never?" Cory whimpered.

Her answer was silence.

"Please, Greg."

Silence.

"I'll do anything you say, I swear it. I'll go to Medora and beg her to come back to you, if only you'll forgive me."

Greg stifled his disgust with a supreme effort. "You're mad," he said. "Hopelessly mad. And maybe it's time you were put in an institution where you could never hurt yourself or anyone else again."

"No!" his wife wailed. "Don't do that to me, Greg. Please." She came to him, crawling through the mud, and knelt before him. "Please don't do it. Please."

Suddenly Greg could not bear to look at her anymore. He turned away, staring blindly at the house which had become little more than a sickroom in the past two years since the Marquis' departure. The madwoman behind him ruled it with her constant needs, her weeping, and her fears. She had made his home into a prison with bars even stronger than iron. So caught up was he in his personal torment that he was not aware that she had crept away from him.

It was only when he heard her unexpected cry of pain that he turned back to her in time to see the flush of a silver blade and the welling stream of red that stained her outstretched wrist. . . .

. . . . The blood trickled slowly from Cory's lip where she had bitten it. She felt the warmth making an uneven path across her chin, but she did not reach up to brush it away.

Greg bowed his head for a moment, overcome with pity for the broken woman before him. Perhaps, he thought, he should have let her die after all, long ago, while it was still her own choice. Because now she had none. "I'm sorry," he murmured, "but I can't leave you free to threaten everything I hold dear."

Burying her fingers like claws in the fabric of his shirt, Cory tried to gasp out a question, but her mind was full of swirling black and red, and her lips simply could not frame the words she needed so desperately to utter.

Recognizing her confusion, Greg resolutely closed his eyes to it. Leaving the flowers she had gathered scattered like forgotten tender words on the cold, wet grass, he lifted his wife in his arms and carried her, for what he thought was the last time, toward the bleak, sterile prison that was their home.

Cory sat in the rocking chair, her knees pulled tight against her body, moaning softly in time with the rhythmical creaking of the old rocker. Above her head, the harsh voices droned, but she did not like the sound, so the words drifted by and faded into the shadows at her back. There was trouble out there, but she did not want to recognize it. Instead, she drew her legs in closer to her shivering body and stared blankly at the floor.

"What do you think you're doing?" Katherine demanded with a last look at her mother, huddled like a lost child in the corner of the room.

Greg, seated behind his desk with a pen in his hand, looked up in annoyance at his daughter's angry question. "I'm writing a letter to the mental hospital explaining Cory's condition, so they'll know how to treat her when she gets there."

"She won't get there," Katherine said. "I've told you, I won't let you—"

"I've made the decision," Greg reminded her. "There will be no more discussion on the subject. Cory has become a threat to everyone around her. If we kept her here, we'd have to watch her like a criminal, because she simply can't be trusted anymore."

"You don't know for certain that she set that fire."

Closing his eyes, Greg shook his head. "I know enough."

"But what if she didn't?" Katherine insisted.

"What if she *did?* Do *you* want to continue living in the same house with a fire-mad lunatic?"

"I don't care!" his daughter cried. "I won't let you take her away."

Greg drew a deep breath. "Don't push me right now, Katherine. I'm not in the mood to deal with your tantrums. Just leave me to finish my letter so we can get this over with as soon as possible."

Horrified by her father's heartlessness, and aware that he really meant to do it this time, Katherine felt herself begin to lose control. "You can't!" When Greg ignored her and continued with his writing, she reached for the half-covered page and tore it from his grasp. "I won't let you!" she repeated as she ripped the paper into several pieces and tossed them over her shoulder.

"Katherine!" Greg hissed. "I'm warning you!"

Cory's eye was caught by the flutter of the paper as it fell to the floor, and she was distressed by the untidy jumble of white on the bare wood. Could they never keep the house neat anymore? She had to follow her daughter and husband like a constable to clean up after them. Abandoning her chair, she knelt on the floor, shaking her head in irritation, and began to reassemble the torn fragments with painstaking care.

Katherine, who stood facing her father, her hands clenched at her sides, was not aware that her mother had moved. At the moment, as Greg rose from behind the desk, she was aware only of the flashing silver of his eyes and the intransigence of his hard jaw. "I swear I'll stop you," Katherine breathed. "Whatever it takes."

Pausing a few feet away from her, her father shook his head in warning. "Don't threaten me, my dear. Remember, the cost just might be too high. Try, if you can, to be reasonable for a moment. I'm doing this for Cory's sake, too."

"You're doing it for your own! You just can't stand to look at her anymore. Well, that's too bad. You can't escape your past, you know, by hiding it away in some dark corner where you won't have to face it." She paused, took a deep breath, and added, *"You* made her what she is. Now *you* have to live with it!"

Greg could feel the rage building inside him, but he knew that this time he had to keep it in check. Once he lost his temper, he would lose control, and that was the one thing he had sworn not to do. "Your mother was mad from the day I married her," he said in a voice that was dangerously low. "She's always blamed me for everything, just as you have, but you're wrong, both of you. Believe me, I have paid and paid for my mistakes, but now the cost has become too high." Brushing past her, he started for the door. "I'll start getting her things together."

"No!" Katherine pushed him out of the way and stood on the threshold, her arms stretched from side to side, so that she blocked his path. "I want her here, and here she will stay." Panic had begun to poison her blood, and the hard knot of anger in her stomach had grown and spread until she thought she could no longer make her limbs obey her. All Katherine knew was that she must stand firm. She must not give in, no matter what he did to her.

"This house has been ruled by your desires and needs for long enough. It's *my* choice now!" her father declared.

Shaking her head to clear it of the bitter voices that kept intruding on her thoughts, Cory stared in dismay at the fragments which the hem of Katherine's skirt had swept back into disorder as she passed. Just when Cory nearly finished. Why must they be so inconsiderate? she wondered. And why couldn't they go argue somewhere else? Didn't they see that she had important things to do?

Behind Greg's back, Katherine could see her mother biting her lips in concentration as she shuffled the torn paper again and again, searching for a pattern. The sight only stiffened her daughter's resolve. "I'm not going to let you by," she said.

The bright flame of fury in her eyes burned into Greg's mind, and he felt something snap within him. "Damn you!" he snarled. Then he flung himself in her direction and, grasping her by the shoulders, threw her back into the room.

Katherine gasped and struggled to keep her balance, then she lunged forward and wrapped her arms around her father's waist. "You leave Mama alone!"

With a tremendous effort, Greg pried her hands from his body, but when he swung her to face him, he felt her long, hard nails dig into his arm, forging a path of burning fire across his skin.

"I'll stop you!" she cried, raising her hand to strike again, but this time Greg was ready for her. With one hand, he deflected her outstretched fingers, stained now with his blood, and with the other he hit her across the face so hard that she lost her balance and fell sprawling against the desk.

As Cory backed away, suddenly all too aware of the rage that threatened to suck her into its depths, Greg turned to Katherine one last time. "Stop fighting me," he warned, "or I'll begin to fight back in earnest. I can hurt you more than you can hurt me, Katherine. Don't forget that I can tell David the truth."

Katherine touched a claw-like hand to her cheek and forced herself to stand upright. "You wouldn't do that," she said, her voice tinged with desperation.

"Watch me. In fact, the more I think about it, the more I feel it's only fair that your husband know why he'll never have children."

"You won't!" Katherine flung herself at him blindly and struck out with her fists at the hard wall of his chest.

"You're both mad," Greg snorted as he pushed her away from him. "The two of you should be locked away together."

Katherine stood quivering with rage, her body stiff and

unnatural with the force of her passion. "Don't ever say that again," she whispered. "And don't ever lay a hand on me *or* my mother, or I'll kill you where you stand."

Stunned by the emotion which had shaped his daughter into a tower of icy fury, Greg took a single step backward. "You hate her, Katherine. You've told me so a hundred times. I've seen how her spells sicken you. You can't bear to look at her any more than I can. So why are you doing this?"

"I want her here."

"Then it must be for your own purposes. Maybe you have a use for her. Because I'll tell you this: you don't care about Cory and you never did. There's only one thing in this whole goddamned world that you *do* care about, and that's Phillipe Beaumont. And the fact that you can't have him is eating you alive."

"Stop it!"

David's voice came between them like a splash of icy water. Both Katherine and Greg turned to stare at him in disbelief.

"Look at you!" he snapped. "Arguing over Cory while she stands here cowering in terror. You behave as if she didn't even exist. And you might as well stop wondering who cares for her the most, because, quite frankly, I don't think either of you gives a damn one way or the other." As he spoke, he crossed the room to Cory's side and put one arm gently around her trembling shoulders. Then he turned to Greg.

"I saw one of those institutions once," he said. "And I tell you I wouldn't send a sick animal there, let alone a human being. Cory can stay here, with me. I'll see that she gets in no further trouble."

"She needs a full-time keeper," Greg said.

"I'll be it."

"But you have other things to do."

David shrugged. "What things? You run your ranch

quite well without me, and when I married Katherine, my father hired a foreman to replace me. My wife doesn't need me, my father doesn't, and you certainly don't. But Cory does. I'll take care of her, and maybe then I can feel that I'm doing some good for someone."

Clutching her head with both hands, Cory prayed that the incessant ringing would cease. She did not understand the voices, but they would not leave her alone; they beat at the edge of her mind like the flapping of a falcon's heavy wings, and she knew their hollow echoes meant her harm, but she could not escape them. God! If only she could make them go away—the voices and the echoes and the approaching shadows that held her in their grip. If only she could run and hide in the soft, inviting darkness. If only there were somewhere she could go where the terror would not follow her. Then something David had said finally penetrated the heavy curtain that lay across her mind: "I saw one of those institutions—"

"NO!" Cory screamed, breaking free of the arm that tried to hold her. "No, no, no!" She began to run.

Katherine caught her mother in her arms before she reached the doorway.

"It's all right, Mama," she murmured as she drew her mother's quivering body close.

"No! He's going to put me away. He wants to punish me because Medora's dead. He hates me and he means to send me away! But I didn't mean to do it! I told him and he didn't believe me!"

"Hush," Katherine crooned. "No one's going to put you in an institution. You're staying here, where you'll be safe. Greg won't hurt you, Mama, I promise. No one will hurt you."

Greg fought back the rush of nausea that rose in him at the sight of the two women clinging together as if their very lives depended upon that single tenuous connection. Then, with a snort of disgust, he headed for the door.

"Where are you going?" David demanded.

"Away from here!" Greg exploded. "I've had enough of this madhouse for one day." He had not realized how angry he was until the moment when he knew he had lost. But now, suddenly, the rage of frustration was more than he could bear. "And if you had any brains, David, you'd get out, too, before you lose your own sanity." Grabbing his hat from the hat rack, he turned to go.

"But what about Cory?"

"That's your problem now. You made my choice for me, so take her; she's yours." Greg paused with one foot over the threshold and looked back once more at Katherine and Cory huddled together. "Besides," he added, more to himself than to David, "I've just realized that there's something I must do. Something I've been putting off for far too long. If today has taught me anything, it's that waiting too long is a fatal mistake. And one I never intend to make again."

Chapter 22

The mid-morning sun touched the land with unrelenting brightness, and the charred, uneven ground stretched like a barren black ocean at Phillipe's feet. He had come with Johnny Goodall the morning after the fire to see if he could find any sign of what had started the blaze, but just now he could only stand and stare at the wasteland which had been covered with tall, thick buffalo grass the day before. He did not think anything could have survived this devastation, even if the arsonist had been careless, but he bent to his task just the same.

Walking carefully through the ashes which the sun had dried to brittle flakes, Phillipe stooped and sifted and peered until his head was spinning with the smell of charcoal and his hands were stained black, but he found nothing unusual. And there were so many acres to cover. He had just risen to wipe his hands on his already filthy pants when he heard a shout from Goodall, who was working across the field.

"Over here!" Johnny called.

Phillipe joined him quickly, excited by the prospect of some important discovery.

"I don't think we'll find anything," Goodall said. "Someone's been here before us." He pointed to the ground where several footprints were clearly discernible among the ashes. "Whoever it was must've had wet feet. Probably came out before the dew dried," the foreman observed. "That means that even if the fire left traces, they'll be gone now."

"But at least we know it was a man," Phillipe said.

"It was a man who cleaned up, but that doesn't mean it was a man who set the fire. We might as well start back. I was pretty sure this was a hopeless expedition from the beginning anyway."

As the two men made their way toward the box elder where they had tied their horses, Phillipe asked abruptly, "Johnny, did you ever know an Indian girl named Ileya?"

Goodall paused, surprised by the question and uncertain what his answer should be. How much did the young man know, anyway? "I knew her."

"Who was she?" Phillipe persisted.

Burying one hand deep in his pants pocket, Johnny cleared his throat and replied, "She was a friend of your father's."

The realization that Goodall was reluctant to discuss the subject only made Phillipe's curiosity more intense. "Tell me about her," he said. "Especially how she died."

By now they had reached the horses. Johnny patted his mare's neck absently while he thought over Phillipe's request. It couldn't do any harm to tell the truth, Goodall mused. After all, they were both dead now anyway. "The Marquis helped her once when she was in trouble and she never forgot it. They became friends after a while, then she found a way to repay him for his kindness. Ileya helped prove that the Pendletons were heading a cattle rustling ring here in the Badlands. They ended up killing her for her trouble."

So that was it, Phillipe thought. But that still didn't tell him what he wanted to know most. "Was she my father's mistress?" he asked.

Johnny looked away, having discovered a sudden consuming interest in the blackened landscape. "Well," he said, pursing his lips thoughtfully, "to tell you the truth, I don't know." He turned back to look at Phillipe, his eyes dark with some secret knowledge. "But I do know that I saw them together once, and whatever was between them was rare on this earth. It was as if they could talk without words, if you know what I mean."

Phillipe thought of his own rigidly silent wife, and his mouth stretched into a frown. "No, I don't think I do. But, Johnny, can you tell me one more thing? Was Medora involved in Ileya's death in any way?"

"Hell, no!" Goodall hooted. "Where did you get an idea like that? It was the Pendletons all the way, no question about it."

Then why had Medora responded as she had? Phillipe wondered. It just didn't make sense.

"Besides, it doesn't matter now," Johnny said. "It's been over for a long, long time."

But somehow Phillipe could not believe that was true. Something about Ileya's death still troubled him, though he couldn't say exactly what it was. He only knew that he would not forget the Indian girl who had died to help his father; he was not satisfied, although he had heard her story. Something was missing. But what?

"Hey!" Johnny hissed, breaking into his son-in-law's troubled thoughts. "Something moved over there, and I'm guessing it wasn't a prairie chicken."

Phillipe looked up where Goodall was pointing and saw a flash of red moving through a distant stand of trees. "It's a man!" he said as he grasped the pommel with one hand and swung himself into the saddle. "Maybe our arsonist waited around too long this time."

He did not even have to look to know that Johnny was mounted beside him as his horse shot away from the box elder in pursuit of the momentary image of red where only green and brown belonged. Even Ileya was forgotten as Phillipe leaned forward, his legs pressed close to the horse's sides, his eyes fixed on the cottonwoods which sheltered his prey. Now there was nothing but the sound of thundering hooves on the unyielding ground, the pounding of his own heart, and his determination to catch this madman.

"We'll get him," Johnny called, but his words were swallowed in the wind that whipped about their ears and set the ashes dancing at their backs. Still, when they reached the green coolness of the cottonwoods, the man had gone.

"Damn!" Goodall cursed as he ran his hands across his damp forehead.

Phillipe was already passing his father-in-law, and he called back over his shoulder, "There he is, farther down by the river. I saw his red shirt again!"

By now, the heat of the sun had begun to burn its way into his still tender skin, and the fingers of pain were working their way across his blistered chest, but Phillipe did not pause. As long as he could see that swatch of red before him, beckoning like a far flickering lamp, he would ride on, even if the wind should turn against him. "We'll get him!" he repeated Johnny's words over and over, as if to turn them into a magic charm that would bring the man to his feet.

But, thirty minutes later, with the horse sweating beneath him and his own breath harsh and ragged, Phillipe was not so certain. It seemed the man was always before them, clearly in sight but just out of reach. He was taunting them, as if to lead them farther and farther from home.

"I'll tell you what I think," Johnny panted as he came up beside Phillipe's horse. "It looks to me like the bastard is playing a game of hide-and-seek with us. He could have gotten away among the trees lots of times, but he seems to be enjoying the chase. And I doubt seriously that he intends to let us catch him."

"Then what's he hanging around for?"

Johnny scatched his chin thoughtfully and pushed his hat back on his head. "Well, if you ask me, the man's only trying to keep us busy." Drawing his eyebrows together in a frown, he pondered the question for a moment, then snapped his fingers. "I've got it. William is working at the plant this morning, right?"

"Yes."

"Then I guess you see what us being out here chasing a red shirt means?"

Phillipe stared at him in dismay. "That there are no men back at the Chateau?"

"Exactly," Johnny agreed. "And if you and me had half the brains we were born with, we'd have turned our horses toward home long ago. Come on!" he cried, putting spurs to his already exhausted animal. "Let's go find out what the hell is going on back there!"

Medora sat staring blankly at the letter in her hand. It had arrived only that morning from Paris, and, though she had read it several times since then, the import of the words had not yet penetrated. The French government had written to inform her that the Duc de Vallombrosa had been successful in his suit to bring the Marquis' fortune back into his father's family, so the villa in Cannes, the house in Paris, and the last of Mores' money had now been lost to Medora and her children. The letter was signed "Colonel Rebillet." The sight of that name caused Medora to crumple the page in her fist. He must have known that without the Marquis' inheritance she and her family would never return to Paris. No doubt the colonel was merely protecting his own interests, for Medora was certain that he had been involved in Mores' assassination—he had probably ordered it himself—but she knew she could never prove it now.

So France was lost to her. Now she had nothing but the Badlands, nothing but this house on the bluff and the land that surrounded it for thousands of acres. As she sat lost in thought, her forehead wrinkled in concentration, a shadow fell across her desk, darkening the crumpled letter so that the words upon it became indistinguishable. Medora looked up, perplexed, to find Greg Pendleton standing behind her, a strange and dangerous expression in his gray eyes.

Glancing toward the next room as if seeking reassurance, Medora rose abruptly and stood face-to-face with her old enemy.

Greg smiled a broad, false smile that left his eyes like cold quicksilver and then he went to pull the door closed. "Don't worry that we'll be interrupted," he said. "I know William is at the plant this morning, and I've made certain that Phillipe and Goodall are occupied with my men. You see," he said, as he seated himself casually on the edge of the desk, "I wanted to talk to you alone."

"What is it?" Medora asked stiffly.

With surprising patience, Greg appraised her from head to toe, looking for a sign that the pressure had begun to weaken her, but he could find none. She was strong, he remembered with a flash of pain. She was, in fact, everything he had ever admired in a woman. Greg shook the thought away in irritation. This was not what he had come for. "I came to tell you it's time to leave the Badlands," he said.

Medora fixed her clear green gaze on his harsh, sunbrowned face and said firmly, "I can't leave. We have work to do here."

"It's time you faced the truth," Greg insisted. He had known it would not be easy, because he knew what kind of woman Medora was, but he also knew that he had to convince her somehow. "There's only *danger* for you here, not success or glory or wealth." His voice rose with each word he spoke, and his hands shook with a kind of barely controlled anger.

Medora was puzzled by the intensity of his emotion. He had always managed to hide it so well in the past. But just now he reminded her of Rebillet, who had threatened her to make her leave France, and the comparison gave rise to her own boiling anger. "I won't be frightened away by hollow threats, Greg. You know me better than that."

"Yes, to my cost," he groaned. He had seen the obstinate set of her chin before, and he knew very well what it meant. "But it's time you began to look at the facts," he declared with sudden urgency. "The cattle that have died, the fires, the gun shots last year that came so close to hitting someone."

"The facts, as you call them, are these," Medora interrupted. "We came here to make the business a success, and we're staying until that is accomplished."

"Please," Greg urged, "get out while you can!"

It was then that Medora realized what was different about this man today—quite simply, he was desperate, though she could not guess why. "We've survived this far," she reminded him. "The dead cattle have been replaced, the buildings the fires destroyed rebuilt, and Phillipe is still alive, despite the two attempts on his life last summer."

Greg looked away, struggling to find the right words. "Did it never occur to you that Phillipe wasn't the target?"

"What?"

"Both times you were with him, weren't you? Perhaps it was you they meant to kill."

Medora stared at him in shocked silence for a full minute, then she murmured, "It doesn't matter. We're staying just the same."

Closing his eyes, Greg said, "If you ever want to leave

North Dakota alive, Medora, you'd better go now or it will be too late."

"Don't threaten me! Your family is as vulnerable as mine."

"Oh, God!" Greg rose, choking on the strength of his emotions, and paced before the window like a restless wildcat. "Don't make me destroy you, Medora. I made a vow once, and I'll keep it if I have to. Don't, please, force me into a corner, or we'll both have to pay for the rest of our lives."

Before Medora could answer, the door to the porch burst open, and Phillipe stood on the threshold, his revolver in his hand. At the same moment, Johnny nearly wrenched the door to the next room from its hinges, then he paused to raise his rifle until it pointed at the center of Greg's back. "We decided to default on your little game out there," Goodall said. "But I suspect that makes us the winners anyway."

"I suggest you get out, Mr. Pendleton," Phillipe added threateningly, motioning toward the open door with his gun, "and don't come back until you're invited."

Greg took a deep breath, shrugged, and followed the younger man's suggestion, but when he reached the threshold, he turned to look at Medora one last time. "I meant everything," he told her. "Remember what I said." His eyes held hers in a long, penetrating glare, then he turned and disappeared.

Medora watched him go without relief. She would have to forget his warning, for she knew with absolute certainty that now she could no longer afford to remember.

The late afternoon sun gleamed on the latticed window, but somehow the light did not quite reach Anais, who sat huddled on the window seat with her books and her drawings spread before her. Stephen paused as he approached, enchanted with the play of light and shadow that touched the girl's face with mystery. He had come to realize that she was very beautiful indeed, and the blackness of her eyes and hair only emphasized the radiance of the sunlight which could not quite touch her.

Anais sat with her knees pulled up to her chin. Stephen could see from her position that she had retreated into her private world once again, but he did not mind; the more she slipped away from the others, the more she needed him. She was sixteen now, and ever since she had returned to the Badlands this spring, he had found himself more and more fascinated with her strange, moody loveliness. He had sworn to himself, as the days began to stretch into harsh summer, that he would possess her before the fall came again.

Stephen came to stand beside Anais, who did not look up, even when he knelt to examine the picture she had been working on. He smiled to himself at the image of a young woman languishing in a cold stone tower, her eyes turned inward upon herself, her face touched with the pain of ineffable sorrow. It was Anais' interpretation of the Lady of Shallot, of course; the Tennyson poem was her favorite, and Stephen was pleased to have been the one who introduced her to it. "This is you," he said softly, "locked away in a tower with a world of strangers at your feet."

Anais glanced up, pleased by the comparison. "They don't know me at all," she told him. "They watch me and wonder, but they'll never know."

"They don't *want* to know. They're afraid."

Biting her lip at the disturbing thoughts that Stephen's assertion had brought to mind, Anais shook her head to free it of the clinging shadows. "Stephen," she whispered urgently, "there's always someone watching me. They think I'm mad. I know Mianne believes I'm the one setting those fires, and Mama looks at me as if I were a murderer ever since the night when Phillipe was shot at last year. I can feel her eyes on me all the time, waiting and watching, as if she were hoping I would make a mistake so she could catch me."

Stephen wrapped a consoling arm around the trembling girl, his pale blue eyes darkening as he listened. "They don't understand you," he murmured. "They're nothing but a pack of fools."

"Mama won't even talk to me anymore," Anais continued. "She's always too busy with Phillipe and the business. She doesn't care about me at all, except that she's afraid of me. Stephen, even at night I see her watching, green eyes on me—they come in my nightmares to haunt me!"

Swallowing the lump that rose in his throat, Stephen ran his hand gently through the girl's thick, dark hair. She had become precious to him over the last few months, and he could not bear it when the others hurt her this way. She was his creation; he had learned to shape her mind and her passions, and he had vowed that he would protect her from the indifference and hostility of her family. He was the only one who really cared for her, after all, so he and he alone had the power to save her from herself. "Listen, Anais," he whispered, so close to her ear that only she could hear. "You must read and learn and concentrate in the next few months in order to get ready."

"Ready?" She turned to look at him and the light brushed her cheek for an instant. "Ready for what?"

"To leave here, of course," he told her, drawing her back into the friendly shadows. "It's nearly time to prove you're free of them. You don't need them any more than they need you. All you need is me." His eyes glowed with the intensity of his pleasure at the thought.

"You'll take me away?" Anais asked incredulously.

"I'll do anything you want," Stephen answered over the pounding of his own heart. As long, he added silently, as you do exactly as *I* want.

* * *

With the heavy blinds drawn to keep out the glare of the afternoon sun, Medora sat before a desk in the spacious office in town. She had tried working at the Chateau in the past three days, but she found that she could not concentrate with the others coming and going all around her. Restless and dissatisfied with herself, she had finally brought her work to town, where she hoped to catch up on the bookwork in a single afternoon. But even here she found that her mind wandered, seeking answers to questions she could not even verbalize. It was almost as if she were waiting for something to happen—as if Greg's warning had shaken her more than she cared to admit, even to herself.

"Mama!"

Medora looked up in surprise as the door swung shut with a loud bang. Her youngest son Paul stood gaping at her, his hands clasped tightly before him and his hair in wild disarray. "What is it?" she asked as she rose abruptly.

For a moment the child did not move or speak; instead, he concentrated on catching his breath. He must have ridden madly to get here in this condition, Medora thought. And beneath the thin coat of dust, his skin was so dreadfully pale. "Paul," she pleaded, "tell me what's happened."

"It's Mianne," Paul panted. "She said her time has come too soon and she's afraid there'll be trouble. She looked awful ill, Mama, and she sent me to ask you to come."

At the moment, Medora was more alarmed by the child's pallor than by his news. Obviously he had been badly frightened. His mother had not even realized that he cared about Mianne. "Listen to me, Paul," she instructed briskly. "I want to go back to the house right away. Do you think you can find the doctor and ask him to follow?"

Paul stood unmoving, his eyes wide with fear, and tried

to form a rational answer, but the best he could do was nod.

"Good! Then I'll count on you to do that. But take care and ride back slowly. It won't help Mianne if you get hurt, too."

"Yes, Mama," the child gulped.

His mother paused to squeeze his shoulder reassuringly as she passed, then she nodded to him one last time and went to find her horse. Within minutes, she was on her way out of town, but even as she rode as fast as she dared, the image of Paul's stricken face would not leave her. Why had Mianne been so anxious to see Medora, anyway? The two women had never been close. In fact, they spoke to one another rarely, and Medora had always felt that Phillipe's wife resented the older woman. But, then, no doubt fear did strange things to people.

As the buildings disappeared at her back, Medora felt herself possessed by a profound sense of urgency. There had been so much trouble already, and now they might lose the child as well as Mianne. Don't let it happen, she prayed silently, but the deep blue sky was silent above her, and her sense of unease increased with every step the horse took. Dear God, Greg was right—their world was falling apart around them, and there was nothing she could do to stop it. But that was absurd, she told herself. She must not panic. Mianne would need a steady hand to help her through this.

Still, she could not shake the premonition of disaster that had come to her in the instant when she first saw Paul's face. For three days, she had lived with Greg's warning ringing in her ears, and she could not rid herself of the feeling that at last it was coming true.

As the hills rose from out of the heart of the valley to surround her, Medora could not suppress a shiver of apprehension. She must get home, she thought over and over, she must get home before it was too late, but the shadows of the bluff that fell across her face seemed to mock her determination, and the silence of the still afternoon was like an impalpable threat that hovered just above her.

It was not until she reached the turning in the path where the house disappeared from view for a moment that she heard the rattle of falling rocks behind her. Even then she did not pause. She had to get home, she had to—

But the thought froze in her mind, too late, as the roar of the rifle shot shattered the stillness into a thousand glittering fragments. Medora sat bolt upright, aware for the briefest of instants of the deep searing pain that ripped across her chest, and then, with the lights reeling like fireworks in her head, she slumped forward in the saddle as a deep gray silence enveloped her—a hush so profound that it blotted out the endless azure sky.

Chapter 23

Mianne closed her eyes, but the tension in the drawing room beat against her eyelids like the echo of a distant Indian drum. They were here waiting, every one of them, for news of Medora's condition. The doctor was with her now, but they had heard only silence from the room where he had taken her when he found her unconscious on her wandering horse, a bullet hole in her chest. The children sat silent, hands folded and eyes downcast, poised on the couch like lifeless dolls, while Cassie and Johnny paced before the empty fireplace, grunting in discontent each time they met. William stood unmoving in the corner, and, as far as Mianne could tell, his eyes had never once left the firmly shut door that separated him from his wife.

But Mianne's thoughts were really with Phillipe, who seemed to be unable to stand still and unable to keep himself in motion. His face had long ago been drained of all color, perhaps from the very instant when he had heard that Medora had been shot, and his hands beat out a restless tattoo against his legs as he waited. His stepmother had been alive when she was brought here, but Phillipe had seen the wound, and he knew it was deep and dangerous. A hundred times, he had begun to wrench open the door and demand news, but he had held himself back, aware that he must leave the doctor to do his job without interruption.

Mianne sat with one hand resting on her swollen belly and watched her husband as he attempted to hide the depth of his despair, but she was too wise to be fooled. Phillipe was dying a little inside every minute that he waited as surely as Medora's lifeblood was seeping out a little at a time to stain the sheets beneath her. The gray, drawn pallor of Phillipe's skin and the expression that made his face into that of a stranger forced Mianne to look away. She realized then that she could not bear for Medora to die, not for her own sake, but for Phillipe's. His personal agony was tearing her apart, but Mianne prayed fervently that it would not destroy him as well.

The time had come at last when she could no longer hide the truth from herself. She must finally admit that Phillipe had somehow become the center of her little world, and she knew that to lose him would bring pain the like of which she had never suffered before in her life. She had broken her most sacred vow and cast her final support into the river that raced by far below; she realized now that she had come to love Phillipe with the kind of love that ate into her very bones and left her shaking.

Suddenly, the door between the two rooms opened and the doctor stepped out to face the family. "I'm afraid there's nothing more I can do," he said, shaking his head sadly. "I found the bullet, but I just can't stop the bleeding, and she's lost so much blood already."

For a moment, everyone in the room was stunned into silence, but then Cassie folded her arms before her and cried, "Nonsense! You may not know it, Doctor, but we ain't the kind to give up that easy. William!" she barked. "Stop moaning like a lost puppy and go get me a big bowl of kerosene—you know where we keep it—and some clean rags." Turning back to the doctor, she added, "You may not hold with my methods, but I'm willing to bet I've plugged up more bullet holes than you ever will, so get out of my way. I only hope I haven't lost my touch."

Without another word, she swept past the startled man, but he did not try to stop her. "It's too late anyway," he explained. "She can't do any harm, and I've seen a case or two where a woman like her did some good."

So, while William went to do the cook's bidding, the others settled back down to wait. Phillipe tried to force his way into the bedroom to help Cassie, but she shooed him out, her mouth set in a grim line. "It's hope she needs now," the cook admonished him, "not the kind of grief that's turned your face hollow. Stay back and let me do my best."

After William had returned with the kerosene and rags, the door was closed once again and silence fell in the drawing room. Mianne became aware that Paul, who sat beside her, was shaking uncontrollably. When she saw the huge tears that covered his cheeks, she reached over to try to comfort him, but he slid out of her arms and ran from the room. Mianne watched him go, her brow furrowed in curiosity. Paul was so much more emotional than Anais and Louis, who sat as still and silent as if they had been carved from stone. But, then, he was the youngest, and probably the most afraid.

It was a long time before the door opened a second time. Mianne rose with the others, searching anxiously for some sign of hope in Cassie's stern expression. The cook glanced first at Phillipe, then the children, and her wrinkled, leathery face seemed to have aged five years in the hour that she had been away. But her eyes were as bright as ever as she murmured, "It was a hell of a fight, but we got the bleeding stopped. If she can make it with the amount of blood she's lost already, I think the Marquise will be okay after all." She held up a hand to silence the rush of gratitude that threatened to knock her backwards, "I said 'if,' " she reminded them, but her lips cracked into a tiny smile of relief. With hands covered in blood to the elbow, she reached out to slap Phillipe reassuringly on the shoulder.

Mianne sighed, as if she had been holding her breath back in her throat forever, and her gaze flew to Phillipe's face. The look of pure joy that touched his features cut through her heart like the blade of a newly sharpened knife, and she turned away to leave him alone with his happiness. Moving awkwardly under the weight of the heavy child she carried, Mianne left the room without speaking. She knew her husband would not miss her now anyway, but, most of all, she did not want him to look into her eyes and recognize her weakness—the discovery she had made today was one she must never share with anyone, let alone Phillipe. It would be just another of her secrets which she would whisper only to the deep, rushing river that carried all her songs in its clear, crystal heart and swept them away to lands she had never seen and people she would never know.

Medora opened her eyes slowly, and through the haze that clouded her vision, Phillipe's beloved face came into view. Wincing as she reached out to grasp his hand, she drew a deep breath and tried to clear her mind of the clinging mists of confusion. "Shot?" she whispered when her free hand encountered the thick bandage under her nightgown.

"Yes, but you'll be all right now," William assured her from the other side of the bed. His voice was ragged with relief and he saw nothing beyond his wife's pallid face. For two weeks he had sat here waiting, watching for any signs of recovery, but, under the influence of a high fever, Medora had slipped in and out of consciousness without ever really being aware of her surroundings. Surprisingly, in her delirium she had asked for neither William nor

Phillipe, but she had called Paul's name repeatedly and, once or twice, Mianne's.

"Medora?" William murmured.

Medora recognized her husband's voice, but some nagging memory made her hold more tightly to Phillipe's hand. What was it that had brought her to the spot where the day had turned to black night? She knew she had been afraid, but she couldn't remember why. Then it came to her, and she gathered her strength to say a single word. "Mianne?"

Confused by the question in her tone, Phillipe leaned closer. "I don't understand."

"Is—Mianne—all right?" Medora managed to ask.

"She's fine," Phillipe assured her.

"And the baby?"

The pressure of his stepmother's fingers against his was growing tighter with each question, and he did not understand the urgency that turned her green eyes dark. "The baby isn't due for a month and a half," he explained patiently.

Medora closed her eyes for a moment, as if the pain had suddenly become too great for her. "Labor not early?" she said hollowly.

Phillipe's gaze met William's across the bed and neither bothered to hide his concern. "No," Phillipe assured Medora at last. "Nothing has gone wrong. Mianne is fine."

Medora sucked in a painful breath as another memory tugged at the back of her mind. Then, all at once, she tried to raise herself up on her arm. "Bring Paul," she gasped. "At once!"

With hands that were more than gentle, William pushed his wife back down against the pillows. "You need to rest now," he said. "You can see your children later."

If she had had the strength to shake her head, Medora would have done so, but she found that she could not even raise her hand to stop the horrible throbbing that spread outward from her chest and stopped the breath in her throat. "Now!" she insisted, but the word came out little more than a whisper.

"Maybe I'd better get him," Phillipe murmured to William. "She might hurt herself if she keeps fighting us."

The older man nodded dumbly. Medora's strength had been increasing daily, Cassie said, so maybe she could handle a brief interview with Paul. Besides, William himself was curious to know why the child had been so much on his wife's mind in the last two weeks.

When Phillipe returned with the boy, Medora seemed to breathe a deep sigh of relief, but Paul himself was clearly uncomfortable. He shifted from one foot to the other and looked as if he might have turned and bolted if Phillipe had not been standing close behind him.

"Paul," Medora said, speaking slowly, "you told me Mianne was ill. Was it true?" The effort of forming so many words together seemed to drain her for a moment, but she was clearly waiting anxiously for the child's response.

Phillipe saw the anxiety in his stepmother's eyes and suddenly he thought he understood what it was she wanted from her son. He and William had been surprised to learn that Medora had been shot while riding headlong toward the Chateau in the middle of the day. No one could tell them why she had needed to get home so urgently, but several of the townspeople had seen her riding, they said, "as if the devil were at her heels." Then, again, Paul had ridden into town that day, and it had been he who had returned with the doctor. Could it be that Paul had gone to the office to tell Medora that Mianne was ill? Aware that his stepmother did not have the strength to press her son just now, Phillipe pressed a hand down on the boy's shoulder. "Answer your mother," he said firmly. "Was it true?"

Paul stared at his hands, his feet, the patterned carpet,

everywhere but at Medora. Finally he managed a soft, "No."

"Then why did you go all the way to town to tell her my wife was ill?" Phillipe could feel the boy trembling beneath his hand, and the longer the child stood silent, the more uneasy the man became.

"It was a joke," Paul stammered. "I didn't know she'd get hurt."

His voice was strained with misery, and Phillipe found that he believed the boy. But that still didn't explain what had really happened on that day two weeks ago. "Who told you to do it?"

Paul swallowed with difficulty and his body stiffened; he still could not bring himself to meet his mother's eyes. "No one," he muttered. "It was my idea. It was just a joke. I didn't know—"

"A joke?" William interrupted. "Medora was almost killed."

Shivering uncontrollably, Paul tried to fight off threatening tears. "I didn't mean for that to happen. I didn't know. I swear!" The tears began to fall at last, and Paul looked up at his half brother with a desperate plea in his eyes. "Please believe me. Tell Mama I didn't mean it."

Phillipe could see that the boy was about to break down completely, and he sensed that Medora's presence was the reason. Reaching out to lay his hand on his stepmother's, he murmured, "I'll talk to Paul in the other room when he's calmer. You should rest now anyway." Then he brushed her cheek with one finger and turned to lead Paul from the room.

"Would you like to go back to your lessons for a while?" Phillipe asked as the door swung shut behind them.

"No!" Paul wailed, clinging tightly to his half brother's hand. "Please don't send me back! Please!"

"Then why don't you sit here next to me until you feel

more like talking." Phillipe made certain that Paul was comfortable, then he sat back to consider the situation. It was not bad enough that Medora had almost lost her life, but now it seemed that her own son was somehow involved. The boy was clearly frightened half out of his mind, and Phillipe could not understand why.

He waited until the tears had stopped and Paul had made liberal use of his handkerchief, then Phillipe said gently, careful to mask his growing apprehension, "Paul, no one is going to hurt you, you know. I won't let them. You know that I have a lot of power, don't you?"

Paul nodded reluctantly.

"Then you should also know that I'm capable of protecting you from any harm."

The child bit his lip and did not reply.

"I believe you didn't know your mother would be hurt, but the fact remains that she was."

Paul shrank away as if Phillipe had struck him. "I didn't—"

"I know," his half brother interrupted. "I don't blame you, whatever your reason for delivering that message, but you must see how important it is that we find out who wanted to kill Medora."

"It was a joke," the child repeated stubbornly.

"That's what you said before, but now that we're alone, I want you to tell me what really happened. Who told you to go to town that day?"

Stiffening perceptibly, Paul muttered, "No one. It was my idea."

Phillipe sighed in frustration. "I know you're protecting someone, Paul. Who is it?"

The boy shook his head wildly, stood up, and cried, "I *told* you—"

A terrible thought flashed through Phillipe's mind when he saw Paul's determination to keep up the lie. Surely the boy would not be so willing to destroy his mother's trust in him for people he knew as little as the Pendletons. Then who would he defend so fiercely, despite the danger to himself? Phillipe could think of only one answer—Anais.

He buried his face in his hands with a groan as he remembered that long-ago night when a spray of bullets had nearly hit Medora and him as they stood silhouetted against the window. Then, later, he had found Anais wandering by the river with no explanation for her presence there in the middle of the night. Phillipe struggled to disbelieve the obvious implications of his thoughts, but with the image of Paul's wide, desperate eyes before him, he could not quite rid himself of the fear that had taken root in his mind in the last few minutes.

Chapter 24

William stared blindly out the window at the blue sky, which was half-covered with soft clouds like the undulating waves of a woman's white hair. Behind him, he could hear Medora running a brush lightly through her own glorious curls, and he bent his head in gratitude for her recovery. There had been a time, that first day that she lay bleeding, when he had felt his own life draining away as if it had never been. But she had survived. Now, a month after the attack, she was sitting up in bed, and the color had returned at last to her cheeks. The very sight of her was a source of joy which he found it difficult to hide, but tangled in with the happiness there was a strand of growing fear that next time she might not be so lucky.

"William? What are you thinking?" Medora asked.

Her husband turned to face her, wondering if he dared tell her the truth. He had waited a long time as he watched her grow stronger day by day; now he thought he could wait no longer. The fear lay with him nightly as he watched the shadows waver in the corners of his room, and it had begun to eat away at his sanity like an insidious disease. "When will you be strong enough to leave?" he asked abruptly.

Medora shook her head. "I don't intend to leave."

"But surely *now* you can see how great the risk is. You must realize that we can't fight them any longer. We never found a trace of whoever it was that shot you. Not even a bullet casing. We can't even prove they were responsible, let alone stop them from trying it again."

Medora wondered at the intensity of William's response, but his arguments did not impress her. "We'll prove it," she said, "as soon as we convince Paul to tell the truth."

Shaking his head in despair, William growled, "If he hasn't told us yet, he's not going to. For two weeks we've done our best to convince him, but he simply won't cooperate."

"He's a Vallombrosa," Medora murmured with a trace of a smile.

Her husband clenched his hands at his sides in an attempt to control the anger that swept over him. She was actually proud that Paul was so obstinate—proud of the son who had nearly cost her her life. "The Vallombrosas are not always wise," he reminded her. "In fact, I remember a time when you begged the Marquis to leave here before the family was ruined by his wild schemes."

Medora shook her head and looked away. "It's different now, William. He failed so often, and I just can't bear to let his last dream die. We're too close to winning this time. I have to go through with it, don't you understand?"

"I understand one thing," William cried in his frustration. "I know that you won't make up for all the failures in your marriage to a dead husband by getting *yourself* killed as well."

There was a long, taut silence, during which William realized that he had just cut the ground from under his feet, and then his wife looked up and said softly, "And you, my dear William, will not make up for letting your best friend die alone by saving *my* life two years later."

They stared at each other across the crumpled bed, the

air hanging heavy between them with the weight of their private torments. Then, when he could bear the stillness no longer, William whispered, "Forgive me, please. I should never have said that."

"Nor I." Medora braided her fingers together and gazed at them as if they no longer belonged to her. "Besides," she murmured finally, "there's something I should have told you a month ago, but somehow I never got the chance."

She looked up then, her green eyes full of an appeal that caused William's heart to stop beating in his chest for an instant.

"It won't do us any good to argue," his wife continued, "because We couldn't leave the Badlands even if we wanted to. The Duc de Vallombrosa won his suit in France, William, and I'm very much afraid that now we have nowhere else to go."

In that moment, the phantom of fear and premonition which had stalked William since they had first come here became a grim reality, and he knew that the choice had been taken from them. It was as if the Marquis had removed the reassuring presence of his guiding hand at last, leaving his family to stand without protection at the edge of a desolate, black ravine that had no end and held no consolation.

With the hot June wind running across her flushed face, Katherine rode to escape the worries that beset her at home. Lately, her father had begun to hint that the family's financial troubles might be worse than his daughter had imagined, and Katherine could tell by the gleam in his eyes that he was becoming desperate to force the Vallombrosas and Phillipe out of the Badlands. She knew quite well that Greg was capable of just about anything when he felt truly threatened, and she had decided that she'd better make her move before her father did. It would be safer that way.

When Katherine saw the stiffly erect figure of William Van Driesche riding along a distant path, it was as if he had come in answer to her prayers. She had not spoken to him since the wedding last August, but she had been watching him. She knew that, especially since the attack on Medora, his discontent had been growing. She had realized he was afraid, and a man who was afraid was vulnerable. Kicking her horse with sudden determination, she smiled to herself and concentrated on catching up with William.

"Good morning, Mr. Van Driesche," she called as her horse came up beside his.

William nodded, barely glancing in her direction. He did not trust Katherine.

"I'd like to talk to you," she said apparently undismayed by his silence.

"We have nothing to say to each other."

"You're wrong about that. Why don't you start by telling me why you look so grim on such a glorious morning? Are you worried about your wife by any chance?" She kept her voice carefully neutral, but she saw by the way he flinched that she had hit a raw nerve.

"My problems are hardly your concern," William muttered.

"That's not always true," Katherine responded with a slight smile. "Suppose, for example, I could guarantee your wife's safety, or the whole family's, for that matter?"

This time William looked up at her before he could hide his interest, but then he realized that he was speaking to a Pendleton, and he shook his head.

"I can do it. We don't particularly want anyone dead, you see. We just want you gone for good."

They rode in silence for a while as William digested this information, then Katherine began again. "I told you once, we pay our men well, Mr. Van Driesche. Don't you think we could work out some kind of deal?"

Despite his doubts, William could not suppress a tiny flicker of hope at the possibility that somehow he could make it necessary for Medora and her family to leave the Badlands. It was what he prayed for every night, wasn't it? And if the Pendletons only wanted the Badlands to themselves, surely they would be glad to let the Vallombrosas go unharmed. But still the doubts would not be silenced. "What would you want me to do?" he asked.

"We've got to make it impossible for Phillipe to continue making a profit," Katherine replied quickly. "All we'd need from you is information on the weakest points in the business and the best times to prod them. You needn't tell us any family secrets," she added.

William grasped the reins more tightly at the thoughts which raced through his head. It would be a betrayal; he knew that. It would mean destroying the one thing Medora had always admired him for—his unfailing loyalty. But wasn't his concern for her life loyalty of a different kind? It was not himself he was trying to save but his wife and her family. If he could manage somehow to get them safely out of the Badlands, wouldn't it be worth any risk? He had often said he would do anything for Medora. Now he had to stop and ask himself if it were really true.

William drew back the reins. "No one else would be hurt?"

"No one, I promise. I also promise to pay you well for your trouble."

William shook his head. "I don't want money from you. All I want is to wake up one morning and find that my wife is finally free of the spell of these godforsaken cliffs forever."

Intrigued by the note of desperation in his voice, Katherine said, "You'd do anything to get out, wouldn't you?"

"Anything!"

"And it's only to keep your wife safe? You don't have any personal resentment against her success?"

William stiffened and looked away. "It's for Medora's sake," he told her stubbornly.

"Well," Katherine murmured, apparently satisfied, "you'll find you've made the right decision. You might even find that the job will bring you certain other pleasures." Leaning forward, she pressed her leg against his and shook her hair out temptingly.

With a quiver of distaste, Van Driesche backed away. "I want nothing but your promise."

Katherine was annoyed at his blatant rejection. She was beautiful, after all, and she knew that most men would have begged her for the offer William had just turned away. "For you there is no woman in the world but Medora, is there?" she asked, incredulous.

"None," he answered without hesitation.

"And yet you would betray her?"

Wincing at the sudden pain of recognition that flared in his chest, William said softly, "We all do it to those who hold our destinies in their hands. Perhaps it's to pay them back for their indifference. But you know that as well as I do."

Katherine's nostrils flared with the anger she could not disguise as she shook her head in flat denial. Grasping the reins in stiff fingers, she turned the horse away from Van Driesche and called back over her shoulder, "I don't have the faintest idea what you mean." But as she pressed her knees into the warm, trembling sides of her animal, Phillipe's beloved face rose before her like a promise, and she knew that the words she had just spoken were no less than blasphemy.

Far below the Chateau, where Mianne could see an occasional glimpse of the river among the cottonwood leaves, the sun struck the swells of water sharply, turning them to liquid diamonds. She leaned her elbows on the windowsill, cupping her chin in her hands as she gazed longingly at the river, which beckoned her this morning. But today she could not answer. Pressing her lips together, she fought against the urge to cry out at the spasm that set her insides trembling; instead, she turned to her husband.

"Well?" Phillipe demanded impatiently. "You said you wanted to speak to me."

She knew that he had a great deal on his mind of late, but his tone hurt her just the same. Would she never learn to protect herself from the pain this man brought her? she wondered. "I'm worried about Anais," Mianne said, her voice floating out on the cool breath of a sudden breeze. "I've seen how differently you've been treating her lately."

"I *feel* differently. I can't quite bring myself to trust her, and until I can—"

"But you're making her so unhappy," his wife interrupted. "Can't you try to talk to her?"

"I did try. She just wouldn't cooperate. She hates me, you know."

Mianne looked away. "Perhaps you remind her too much of your father."

"I doubt it. She didn't seem to care about the Marquis either. *I* never saw her grieving for him."

"You did," Mianne countered. "You just didn't recognize it. You could make an effort to understand Anais. You just don't *know* her."

"I don't think anyone does. Do you?" Phillipe's eyes were lit with sudden interest. "Do you have any idea what that girl is capable of?"

Mianne winced at the fresh surge of pain and prayed that Phillipe had not seen it reflected in her eyes. She hesitated for a long moment before she answered his question. "I know her well enough to realize that if her family continues to treat her like a leper, she's capable of a great many unpleasant things. She's eaten up by anger inside, and you're all pushing her to desperation with your doubts."

Phillipe leaned forward to put a hand on his wife's shoulder. "Then *you* talk to her. You're her friend."

Mianne swallowed and turned to stare fixedly out the window. "Not any more," she murmured. "Not since I married you."

At last Phillipe recognized the hollow echo of buried pain in her tone and his grip on her shoulder tightened. She did not turn to look at him, but he could still see the accusation that had flared so briefly in her eyes. "Why *did* you marry me?" he demanded.

Her voice was cold and distant when she answered, "I don't know."

Her husband took her chin in his hand and forced her to meet his searching gaze. "But you know it was a mistake?"

"I didn't say that."

"You say it every time you look away from me as if you can't even bear to see my face. You say it when you shrink from the touch of my hand. If you dislike me so much, why didn't you run when I gave you the chance?"

Mianne wrenched free of his hand and turned her back to him. She felt that she was choking, and she knew that if she tried to utter a single word she would weep. Make him go away, she prayed silently. Don't let him see how much I want to take that hand in mine and press my lips against it.

"Mianne," Phillipe's voice was suddenly soft with desperation. "Please look at me."

His wife did not move, for she knew that her eyes would give her away.

For a minute longer, he stood waiting, but when he

realized she was not going to turn away from the window, Phillipe cursed softly under his breath, spun on his heel and left the room. Let her suffer in silence if that was what she wanted. It was her choice, after all.

Mianne sat perfectly still, listening as the sound of her husband's boots against the bare wood floor died away. Then, when she saw him leave the house and stride toward the stable, she held her breath and waited until he had saddled his horse and ridden away. When she was certain at last, she rose awkwardly from the window seat and made her way to the head of the stairs, where, with both hands resting on her belly, she paused to catch her breath. "Cassie!" she called, when she had gathered enough strength to make her voice be heard.

The cook appeared almost instantly at the foot of the stairs. "Anything wrong?" she asked when she saw that the color had drained from Mianne's face.

"I think," the younger woman managed to whisper hoarsely, "that the child has chosen its time. Now!"

Chapter 25

Katherine clutched the reins in hands that were strangely cold, despite the late June heat. For once she was unaware of the dance of the wind in her hair. Her mind was full of the message she had received last night: "I must see you. Meet me tomorrow, 9 AM, you know where. Phillipe."

At first she had been appalled by his arrogance. After nearly a year, how dare he write to her without explanation, like whistling to a wayward dog? Her initial instinct had been to ignore the note. Then she had remembered the feel of his skin beneath her hand, and she had decided to meet him after all. But not because she wanted to see him. No, it was only prudent to wait and see what he was planning, to give herself the chance to rebuild the power she had once wielded over him. Here was her chance to bring him close enough to be within the confines of her carefully woven web. Underneath, she knew her need for him was still overpowering, but she hoped that his hunger, too, would be too great to deny. And even as she rode toward him with the breath held back in her throat in expectation, she could feel the rage that ran like a river of fire beneath the desire.

When Katherine turned the last corner which brought her to the heart of the stone maze where they had met so often, Phillipe stood frozen with the impact of her flushed beauty. He had forgotten how vibrantly lovely she was—how the energy seemed to radiate from her body in a pulse that was inviting and threatening all at once. Katherine was magnificent, it was true, but even her dark, sensual presence could not eradicate this morning's confrontation with Mianne. He did not understand why her reluctance to be his friend disturbed him so deeply. She was a mystery to him, now more than ever, and he had begun to despair of ever breaking through the barrier she had raised between them. But Mianne was not the only problem troubling him. Paul, now pale and haggard, still refused to talk about the day when Medora had been shot, and neither Phillipe nor William nor Johnny had come any closer to discovering who the gunman had been. Phillipe wondered if he would ever know the truth.

"Well?" Katherine snapped as she planted her hand firmly on her silk-clad hips. "What do you want?"

Phillipe dragged his mind back to the woman who stood before him. "I wanted to say that it's time you and your father came to your senses and stopped all this violence—the fires, the attempts on Medora's life, everything. You can see that you haven't achieved a thing. And we won't be frightened away. You should know that by now. We might even begin to fight by your rules, if that's what you force us to do."

Narrowing her eyes into tiny dark slits, Katherine breathed deeply to force down the anger that threatened to freeze the words in her throat. So Phillipe had called her here to discuss business practices. She had thought, for an instant, that he wanted her again, but it seemed he had only come to threaten her. "I can't be frightened with hollow threats either, Phillipe. I belong to the most powerful family in the valley, or have you forgotten?"

Then she smiled and leaned back against a rock, so that the clinging folds of her gown outlined the curve of her leg. "I don't think it would be wise to talk business with you," she murmured. "I'd be a fool to tell you all my secrets. But I suspect we could find *something* to say." She trailed her hand down her hip provocatively, and her eyes skimmed his body with a question in their dark brown depths.

Phillipe looked away. He wanted the truth desperately enough to wrest it from her, but he knew that in a battle of that kind, her body, and his own weakness, would be the winner. He had been foolish to imagine that he would learn anything from this encounter. Katherine never changed and she never would.

Smiling at the thoughts she read so easily on Phillipe's face, Katherine realized that she had regained control. He was hesitating now, aware that he should not have met her, but she did not intend to let him go. She wanted him too much, in spite of everything—the rage, the treachery, the barrenness of her body for the past year. Her desire was agonizing, and the soft tendrils of his brown hair, the intensity of his blue eyes taunted her with the memory of what only he could do for her. "Phillipe," she said softly, "I don't want to fight."

"What *do* you want?" he demanded.

Her lips curved upward as she moved toward him, her gown like a pale green wave around her feet. "You know," she murmured. She wanted him to make her remember the pain.

Phillipe shook his head. She must be mad if she thought they could start again as if the very cliffs all around did not stand as a barrier between them. As if his pregnant wife were not waiting for him at home. But then Katherine's warm lips brushed his cheek, and he shuddered at the astonishing depth of his response. Backing away, Phillipe turned to go, but Katherine followed and locked her arms around his waist until he could feel the breathing presence of her body close to his.

"Don't go," she murmured huskily, as she traced a pattern on his neck with the moist tip of her tongue.

Although Phillipe's mind told him to push her from him and walk away without looking back, the crying need of his body held him immobile. "I can't—" he began in a last attempt to break free.

Katherine laughed and the sound of her mirth rang in his ears like an enticing invitation. "You can do anything you want," she replied. "You told me so yourself." She ran her hand lightly up his arm and smiled a smile that pierced the last of his defenses.

He had been too long without a woman—for Mianne had been unapproachable for months—and Kathcrine was far too beautiful to resist. Her hands wound their way into his hair, and his own arms locked around her as their lips finally met and the old fire raged between them as brightly as if it had never been extinguished.

Whcn she reached up to unbutton his shirt, Phillipe drcw in a ragged breath at the touch of her fingers on his skin. "Katherine," he warned.

She looked up then, smiling, her hunger lighting her face with its power, and he could not help but think how pleasant it was to look, for once, into eyes that were not cloaked with mystery and shadow.

"Yell if you need to!" Cassie instructed as she laid a cool cloth on Mianne's damp forehead. "It won't do you no good to keep all that pain bottled up inside. Give it a chance to escape, girl!"

Mianne lay with her lips tightly closed, and only the instinct of a long and difficult childhood kept her from taking the cook at her word. It seemed that she had lain like this for hours while the pain went on and on, ripping at her insides until she was certain they must be shredded and useless. As the time crawled by and the spasms of agony became more intense, the world began to slip away, as if it had been covered by a thin, gray haze that wrapped her in soft, cool fingers and released her mind to float toward the singing river for which she yearned.

She was tired—so tired that she thought she would no longer be able to feel the wrenching pain, until it came again, robbing her of will or reason. Through it all, Cassie's worn face had hovered above her, watching, waiting, twisted with sympathy for Mianne's torment. For a long time now, the younger woman had known that something was amiss. The cook had not quite been able to banish the worry from her face, and her concern communicated itself to Mianne through the mist that obscured all else from her sight.

"Don't worry, child," Cassie said soothingly when she saw the flicker of knowledge in Mianne's black eyes. "It should be soon now. They can't kick around in there forever."

Mianne reached out to grasp the cook's arm. "They?"

"That's right. You're carrying twins. And, if you ask me, they're a stubborn pair."

Closing her eyes, Mianne sank back against the pillows. Twins. She had suspected it from the beginning. Yet only now did she realize that the instincts she had been reluctant to recognize had been right once again. But she also knew that this birth would be more difficult than she had imagined. "What if—" she struggled to form the words that would not come. "What if—"

The cook snorted. "Between you and the others, I'm like to be 'what if'd' clear to death. Never you mind about anything at all. We've sent for the doctor, and I'll be right here watching until he comes. Who knows, maybe those rascals will arrive before he does." But Cassie knew she was lying. It seemed that things were all tangled up inside Mianne, and she could only hope that time would straighten them out.

"Oh!" Mianne whispered suddenly. Her fingers closed roughly around the cook's hands.

"That's it! Hang on!" Cassie cried. "And yell, dammit, before you explode with the pain."

"No!" Mianne hissed. "I can't. No, no." Her breath came in wrenching gasps and her voice rose with each word. "No!" she cried, in one last effort to defeat the rising terror inside her. Then she closed her eyes and screamed as if her heart were bursting inside her, and the sound of her voice rose like the wail of a cornered animal until it filled the house around her with the echo of her pain.

Anais burrowed deeper into the pillow she had pulled over her head.

"What is it?" Stephen asked, his pale blue eyes shadowed with concern.

"I can't bear it!" the girl replied, just as another scream reached her from the room down the hall where Mianne lay. Shuddering uncontrollably, Anais cried, "Make it stop!"

When Stephen reached out to draw her to him, she looked up at him with eyes wide with fear. "Mianne's so strong," she whispered. "She wouldn't scream like that unless it were so horrible that she couldn't—"

"Come on," Stephen said. "If the noise bothers you, we'll go."

Anais pulled away. "No. I have to stay."

"Why?"

"I can't—" she hesitated, stared at her hands and finally murmured, "I can't leave her now."

The tutor blinked at Anais in surprise. "You still love her," he accused.

"No!" the girl replied a little too quickly. "I don't care about her, or anyone else in this family. Why should I?"

"Then let's get out of here."

"I can't."

Suddenly the air was rent in two by a cry of pain that seemed to shake the very rafters, and Anais plunged beneath the pillow once again. "Oh, God," she moaned. "I can't bear it. I can't. I can't."

Stephen could not bear it either. All he knew was that they were hurting Anais again—it was all this family ever seemed to do for her—and he felt the pain as if it were his own. He swore more firmly that he would take her away from here when the time was right, but he knew that just now she was in need of something more than promises. "Anais," he said softly, "let me hold you." Tossing the pillow aside, he reached out for her, and she flung her arms around his neck as if he had offered her salvation.

They clung together and the tutor felt his body trembling in response to the quivering in Anais'. God, but he loved her. She needed him so much, so he had come to need her. Stephen leaned down to kiss the top of the girl's head, then, awkwardly, he shifted her weight away from him so that his lips could find her flushed face. "It's all right," he whispered, "I'll take care of you."

Anais heard the words, but she did not really understand them. She only knew that Stephen was here, holding her, and that she could not bear to let him go. She pressed her body close to his, and would have drawn him closer, had she had the power. The warmth flowed from his limbs into hers, and the comfort seemed to reach her through a haze of fear and insecurity. The brush of his lips on her forehead and cheeks was as light as the flutter of a bird's wings, and she crushed herself against him, wanting more—wanting anything that would make her forget the pain Mianne was suffering.

Slowly, slowly, Stephen began to run his hands along Anais' back and shoulders. As he did so, he could feel the desire that sprang half-grown out of her desperation, out of *his* wish to make her no more than an extension of himself. It was a hunger born of need that locked the two together in that moment, and they could no more have drawn apart than they could have ceased their labored breathing. The need to force back the torment of unshed tears was too great—so great that it swirled around them like a crashing wave that threatened to drown them with the force of its impact.

Night had fallen, dropping a shroud of darkness over the Chateau. The many flickering lamps were helpless against the somber atmosphere that hung in the drawing room like a thundercloud about to break. Phillipe paced before the empty hearth, his face a reflection of the dark night, and tried to make himself think rationally, but he knew it was no use. Mianne had been in labor for over twelve hours already, and every one of her cries seemed like an accusation. It was not only the knowledge that it had been too long or the look of disquiet in Cassie's eyes that haunted him now—he knew Mianne was in danger, though the cook had not told him so—it was the weight of his own cloying guilt. He had spent the morning in Katherine's arms while his wife had been suffering with the birth of his child. It was his fault she was in pain at all, just as it was his fault that he had not been beside her when she needed him. He had let her down again. Phillipe looked up when Cassie entered the room, a worried frown between her brows. "How is she?" he asked.

The cook considered for a moment, then shook her head wearily. "Not good," she admitted at last. "Are you sure there's no chance the doctor will get here tonight?"

"He's in Mandan for a few days. I'm afraid that's too far to get him back in time." Phillipe suppressed a deep spasm of fear. "Has she asked for me?"

"Mianne asks for no one," the cook responded. "I think she believes she can do it all alone."

"But *you* don't believe it?" Johnny asked from the corner of the room where he had been following the exchange in silence.

Cassie sighed heavily. "No, to be honest, I don't. Mianne is carrying two babies in there—"

"Two?" Phillipe interrupted, incredulous.

"Don't pester me with questions now," Cassie warned, waving him away. "I've got enough on my mind. The thing is, there's something wrong with the position of the babies. They're twisted around somehow and they just won't come out. I don't know what to do for the poor girl, but I'll tell you this much—she's bleedin' pretty bad, and if those kids don't decide to be born soon, I'm going to have to cut her open and lift them out. I wish to God that doctor hadn't chosen this week to abandon us."

Before Phillipe or Johnny could recover from their astonishment enough to respond, a high piercing cry reached them from above. "Cassie!" It was Mianne's voice, ragged with exhaustion and pain. "I need you."

The cook nodded and reached out to grasp Phillipe's hand. "Pray that this is it," she told him. "I've plumb run out of breath, and I doubt if God can hear me anymore, anyway." But as she turned to find her way up the dark stairs, she closed her eyes and whispered under her breath, "Please. I don't think that girl can take much more, and that's the truth, whether you want to hear it or not."

Mianne sank back against the pillows which had long ago been soaked with her sweat. The faces came and went above her, but she could not bring them into focus. It was as if she were wandering in a world full of strangers and the only reality was the slow, steady seeping of her own blood from her tired body. It was a relief, really, to just lie back and stop the constant struggle; the children had finally fought their way from inside her, but somehow she could not make herself care. She only knew that the pain was over at last, that now she could close her eyes and let sleep overcome her. The hovering faces, twisted and frowning, would take care of themselves. She wanted only to surrender to the creeping mists that had clung to the edge of her thoughts for hours, tempting her, promising welcome numbness. Mianne let her eyelids flutter closed.

"No!" Cassie cried as she grasped the younger woman by the shoulders. "You're not going to give up on me now. Not if I have anything to say about it. And since I delivered your son and daughter, I guess I have the right to an opinion."

Mianne heard the voice above her and felt the pressure of fingers digging into her skin, but she wanted to shake them away.

"Fight! Damn!" the cook snarled. "Here," she said over her shoulder, "you talk to her. Keep her awake any way you can while I see to the children."

An arm slid softly beneath Mianne's shoulders and a voice whispered in her ear, "The Mianne I know wouldn't give in so easily. She's a fighter, not a coward."

The warmth from a hand on her hair was strangely familiar, but she could not remember when she had felt it before. And the voice—a memory teased at the edge of her mind, just out of reach.

"Forgive me, Mianne, for everything. But I can't make it up to you if you leave me now. Please do as Cassie says—Fight!"

She knew that voice, knew that it was dear to her. Suddenly, she wanted to open her eyes and see to whom it belonged. But the effort was so great, the oblivion of sleep so tempting.

"Mianne! Listen to me! Listen. We need you here. Your children need you. Please."

The sound of that voice was the loveliest thing she had ever heard, and she knew, all at once, that she had to fight to keep it near her. Drawing on the last of her depleted strength, Mianne forced her eyelids open and found herself staring into Phillipe's troubled face. She did not understand what had upset him; she only knew she wanted more than anything else on earth to smooth the wrinkles from his brow and the darkness from his eyes. "Don't," she whispered in a voice that was barely audible.

Phillipe did not realize he had been holding his breath until it escaped in a rush. When he reached for his wife's hand, he closed his eyes in gratitude when her fingers entwined themselves with his and clung, as if drawing the life from out of his blood and into hers. Phillipe could only smile in return and hold Mianne's cool hand a little tighter.

Chapter 26

With the sound of the water running in her ears, Katherine hovered at the edge of the trees and watched the early morning movement around the Chateau. She had been waiting for an hour already, but she would continue to wait all day if necessary. She had to see if it was true. With her own eyes she had to verify what she had heard just after dawn, when the cool mists of morning had still clung about her, touching her cheek with a cold, vaporous hand. It must be a lie, she had told herself over and over again. But she had to know for certain.

Katherine glided back into the shadows of the ceiling of leaves that danced and wavered in the breeze. She was waiting for Cassie to appear. She must not reveal her own presence until the old cook was in sight. Katherine knew that no one at the Chateau trusted her, but Cassie had always had a soft spot for the woman she had known as a girl. The cook was the only one who might let Katherine in, and it was so important that she go inside and see them. They were waiting for her, she was certain, and nothing would stop her from doing what she must.

Katherine was not even aware that her hair tumbled loosely over her shoulders in disarray or that her hands were weaving and unweaving a senseless pattern against the front of her gown. She did not know that her eyes were wide and dark and lit by a strange glow that flashed her wild and rootless thoughts like a beacon.

Phillipe pushed open the study door and found Medora sitting at the desk with the books spread open before her. "What are you doing?" he asked, forgetting his own exhaustion in his concern for her.

Medora smiled at him over her shoulder, but she was careful to move only her head. "The wound doesn't bother me as much anymore," she said. "I just decided it's time to get back to work."

"You shouldn't push yourself," Phillipe admonished her, although he could see by the fresh color in her cheeks that leaving her room at last had been good for her.

"And *you* should be asleep, after the long night you've had."

Phillipe clasped his hands together behind his back and shook his head. "I'm too restless to lie down."

Surveying her stepson's pale, shadowed face, Medora felt a sudden twinge of hopelessness. "Mianne's all right, isn't she?"

"Yes. She finally fell asleep about an hour ago, and Cassie said to leave her be for the rest of the day. She just needs time to get back her strength."

"Good." Medora sighed with relief. "And what about the children?"

"Cassie has them with her in the kitchen. She says it's the warmest room in the house and certainly the cleanest." Phillipe smiled at the memory. He had offered to help her care for the two tiny babies, but she had laughed and told him to go to bed. The cook had informed him pointedly that he would be of no use to her at all, and, besides, she herself would not be able to sleep until nightfall anyway.

"I suspect she'll be an excellent temporary mother. We're very lucky to have her, you know."

But Medora was not really listening. Her eyes had grown distant, her face suddenly soft. "His first grandchildren," she murmured. "And twins at that. Have you named them yet?"

"No. I want to discuss it with Mianne first. She couldn't even speak her *own* name when I left her."

Staring blindly down at the ledgers that were scattered across the desk top, Medora swallowed the lump in her throat and said softly, "You did the right thing in marrying Mianne. You can see that now, can't you?"

Her stepson opened his mouth to reply, hesitated, then muttered thickly, "I hope so." But he didn't believe it. He had done nothing but cause Mianne pain from the moment he had asked her to be his wife. Since last night, his doubts had become a kind of creeping darkness that poisoned his blood. In the long, sleepless hours of waiting and fear that had stretched through the black night, Phillipe had come to despise himself for his weakness. He wanted more than anything to make things right for his wife, but he did not know how to begin.

Medora looked up in time to see the inner struggle that was reflected in Phillipe's eyes, but she could not tell what it meant. She realized that, for the first time, he had closed his thoughts against her, and she felt all at once as if the winter wind had swept through the room, taking all the warmth and light with it when it disappeared. "Is something wrong?" she asked, although she knew he would not answer.

"Nothing," Phillipe replied. "I'm just tired. And I'm worried about you. Are you sure you should be working so soon?"

Medora forced a smile to her lips and turned back to the cluttered desk. "I couldn't let it go any longer," she said stiffly. "Besides, William has been doing all the bookwork by himself for too long, and I'm tired of being idle. I had to get up and do something." She paused while the rows of figures blurred before her eyes. "Tell me, Phillipe," she added after a moment of thought, "have you noticed if William seems unhappy lately?"

Phillipe shook his head. "No, but then I haven't really thought about it. He's always quiet, you know."

"Yes, but he seems different to me." Her brows came together in a thoughtful frown as she remembered her husband's rigid features. "Something has changed him and I don't know what it is."

"Don't worry," Phillipe advised her. "William has always taken care of himself in the past. I'm sure he'll get through this, too. If I've ever known a man who's in complete control, it's William."

"I suppose so," Medora agreed doubtfully. "But it worries me, just the same." It seemed that now not only was she losing Phillipe, but William as well. It wasn't fair, she ranted silently. She had lost so very much already. When would it finally stop?

"Could I talk to you, Cassie?"

The cook looked up in surprise at Katherine's anxious face. Cassie had not seen the younger woman for a long time, and just now she had crept up so silently, like a mountain lion stalking its prey. "I've only got a minute," the cook said. "I have to get back inside to—"

"See to the babies. I know," Katherine interrupted, glancing around to see that no one was watching. "That's what I want to talk about. I wonder if you wouldn't let me see them, just for a moment."

Blinking at the harsh sunlight which framed the younger woman in a false radiance, Cassie considered the request in astonished silence. Why was Katherine's face so flushed and eager, and, even more important, how did she know about the twins already? The babies were only a few hours old.

When Katherine sensed the cook's hesitation, she put a pleading hand on Cassie s arm. "It's been so long since I've seen a newborn child. I promise I won't get too close. It means so much to me, Cassie. Please."

At the look in Katherine's eyes, the cook felt the familiar tug at her heartstrings. Ever since she had tended Katherine as a girl after one of her father's dreadful beatings, Cassie had felt a certain sympathy for the unhappy woman. The cook knew that a Pendleton was a Pendleton, no matter how you looked at it, but she could never quite bring herself to hate Katherine as she knew she should. "All right," she murmured, surprising even herself. "But just for a minute."

Smiling her gratitude, Katherine followed the woman into the kitchen, her heart pounding wildly in her chest.

"The babies are over there in the basket on the table. I do believe they've finally gone to sleep," Cassie observed. "That's the boy on the left and the other is a girl. They don't have names yet."

Katherine nodded, but she was not listening. She stood immobile, fascinated by the tiny, wrinkled, red beings whose faces and hands were visible above the carefully wrapped blankets. She could feel the regular throbbing of her temples and the rush of her blood sounded like the river when it ran with the madness of the melting snows and overflowed its banks. William had told her, but she had not really believed it until this instant when the evidence lay before her eyes. Two—the number echoed in her mind with the monotonous drone of a hollow church bell. Two tiny, perfect babies, and neither of them hers. Dear God, how insensitive he was, how infinitely cruel to do this to her. With fingers that shook just a little, Katherine reached down to touch the girl's cheek. The baby awoke with a wail that pierced the fragile silence and shattered it into tiny, glittering fragments . . .

. . . . October, 1885—The scream rose in the still, cold air with the impact of stone on thin carved crystal, and Katherine twisted wildly, searching for the source of the heartrending cry. Make it stop, she pleaded desperately as she closed her eyes and fought against the growing terror. Dear God, please make it stop! But the tortured voice continued to groan, until the tiny clearing was full of the pitiful screams that reached beyond the boundaries of the naked branches, abandoned so recently by the colorful autumn leaves.

Katherine lay with one hand in the water of the pond where she had met Phillipe so often, the leaves dried and scattered around her writhing body like layers of skin she had shed and discarded. Through the haze of pain that blurred her vision, she reached out blindly to silence the hoarse cries which only increased her misery. It was only when she opened her mouth to gasp for breath, and the cries ceased at last, that she realized they had come from her own raw throat.

Help me, she pleaded silently. Make the agony stop, at least for a moment. But the wrenching spasms of pain tore at her, shattering the clearing into disconnected fragments of dried grass and water and barren, black branches. The world was a blur of gold and brown, like the packet of herbs she had swallowed hours ago. She had gotten the herbs from an old, grizzled Indian woman who had assured her they would not fail. She had had no choice, Katherine cried inwardly. Phillipe had taken the choice from her when he left her alone with his bitter memory.

With her arms wrapped tightly around her body, Katherine doubled over again and again with the wracking torment. She had not known it would be like this—the blood and the pain and the blind rage of terror. She had begun to think it would be with her always. She would lie here like a helpless child as the blood flowed out of her body a little at a time, leaving her hollow and empty—a broken shell. The Indian woman had warned her not to wait too long into the pregnancy, but Katherine had not listened. And now she knew it was too late. She opened her eyes wide in an effort to locate something familiar, something that would remind her that the rest of the world existed and that she was not alone. But there was no comfort in the blur of branches and broken grass. Even the image of Phillipe's face had left her.

Katherine sucked in her breath when she felt the spasms pushing her insides outward. She knew it was out at last, but she turned away from the puddle of red that had formed a second pond between her legs. Then, from somewhere far away, she heard the sound of an unfamiliar voice. Struggling to make herself turn to look upward, she bit her lip with a violence that brought the taste of blood to her mouth. A flash of hope lit her face with momentary relief. Was it Phillipe? Had he come to her after all? But then, through the fog that wrapped her in a blanket of confusion, she recognized her father's sneering face.

"So," Greg said, his mouth twisted with disgust, "Phillipe left his mark after all."

Katherine wanted to turn away, but her muscles would not answer her will; she was frozen with the shock of horrified discovery. Then she felt the pressure of the object between her legs and she could not stop herself from looking, for an instant, at the burden she had fought so hard to lose. Shuddering at the sight of her own weakness, Katherine drew her knees up to her chin and rolled away. "Get rid of it!" she cried raggedly.

Greg shrugged, too disgusted to argue, and bent to pick up the unwanted baby.

"Wait!" Katherine said. "Tell me what it is!"

"A girl," her father hissed. "A perfect reflection of everything you've ever done to make yourself a fool."

Katherine closed her eyes, overcome by nausea at what she had done. The sickness washed over her in waves, shaking her sweat and blood-soaked body from head to toe. She had no choice, she repeated in a silent litany. No choice at all. *But when she heard a splash and knew the child was gone forever, Katherine rose to her knees against her will, braiding her hands together in an iron band to keep herself from reaching blindly outward. . . .*

. . . . The baby's hand closed tightly around Katherine's extended finger, and the woman fought to suppress a shudder of despair. A girl, Cassie had said, a tiny living reflection of Mianne. It wasn't fair that the other woman should have two and Katherine none. For she had gone back to the Indian woman after it was over and been told that she had waited too long; the abortion had damaged her insides, and she would never have another child. She was barren.

It was for that, more than anything, that she hated Phillipe Beaumont. She had ripped the memory of him from her body, but she had not been able to forget. And now he had given Mianne what Katherine would never have. He had given another woman the child that should have been hers. Just then the girl opened blue-veined lids and gazed at Katherine with Phillipe's blue eyes. Katherine stood hypnotized, not daring to breathe, and then she knew what she had to do.

Cassie was worried by the intense absorption on the younger woman's face. It made her uneasy somehow, and she was relieved to see Anais enter the room. "Good morning," the cook said with forced pleasure. "I suppose you've come to see your niece and nephew."

Anais eyed Katherine with suspicion, then shook her

head violently. "They don't belong to me," she declared. "I hate them."

"You won't say that once you see them," the cook informed the girl. "No one can look at those dear little faces and not be moved."

"Well, I don't *intend* to look at them," Anais replied firmly. "They're Phillipe's problem, not mine." The girl was only half listening to Cassie; her attention was focused on Katherine as she backed away from the basket that held the babies.

"They belong to Mianne, too," the cook reminded Anais gently.

"I don't care!" The girl whirled to face Cassie, her eyes blazing with sudden fire. "I don't care who they belong to, and I don't want to see them. Can't you understand that?"

Katherine pursed her lips thoughtfully as she watched the girl's outburst with interest. "I should go now," she said suddenly.

Cassie reluctantly looked away from Anais and nodded her agreement.

"You won't tell them I was here, will you?" Katherine added. "I don't think they'd understand."

"Of course not," the cook replied with a sidelong look at the girl who was still seething with her anger. "Anais?"

Anais shrugged. "I don't care if she was here or not."

"Thank you," Katherine said as she headed for the door. She had to get away to think. Smiling to herself as she remembered Anais' anger, she stepped out onto the porch. She had recognized the girl's dislike for those babies the instant she entered the room, and Katherine would not forget.

As she watched the younger woman disappear over the hill, alone, her wildly dishevelled hair trailing over her shoulders like a long-forgotten banner of defeat, Cassie shook her head, sighing. And for some reason which she could not name, her insides twisted with a sudden stab of pity for Katherine Pendleton.

"You ready to talk business?" Johnny asked. "It's time we got back to our other problems for a while."

Phillipe nodded and settled himself on the drawing room sofa. He had finally fallen asleep late that morning. After a three-hour nap, he was wide awake and ready to face the many aspects of the meat packing business which had not really had his full attention since the attack on Medora over a month ago. "Good afternoon, William," he said as the secretary joined the other two men. Remembering Medora's concern, Phillipe decided to try and draw the man out. "You were out early again this morning, I noticed. You must have developed a recent affinity for the morning mist."

William shifted uncomfortably under Phillipe's searching gaze. "I like to walk while it's still cool," he responded, as if choosing his words with great care.

Eyeing Van Driesche narrowly, Johnny decided it was time to change the subject. He did not know what it was about the secretary that had begun to make him uneasy of late; he only knew he didn't want to look too far to find the answer. In fact, Goodall had decided it would be best if he didn't look at all. "How's Mianne doing?" he inquired, turning his attention to Phillipe.

"I looked in on her before I came down," the young man replied. "She's still sleeping and she looks more peaceful now than she did this morning."

"I imagine that's because Cassie's the one dealing with the squalling babies," Johnny observed. He was unable to suppress a gleam of delight for a moment, but then he forced all thoughts of Mianne and his grandchildren to the back of his mind. "We've got to make some decisions," he said, including William in his sweeping glance.

"While we've been busy with personal problems, the Pendletons have kept the game going. They've bribed some of the icemen along the railroad route to stay away again, and I don't need to tell you we can't afford much more of that. One carload of rotten meat is quite enough. I suspect they've even gotten to the plant on occasion, haven't they, Van Driesche?"

For the second time, William hesitated before answering. "I suppose it was them. A couple of the boilers have been acting up, and some of the machinery has been tampered with."

"Why didn't you tell me?" Phillipe demanded.

"It was nothing I couldn't handle. Besides, you had problems of your own, what with trying to get that railroad rates legislation passed."

Phillipe had to agree that the politics had kept him busy for the past few months. Then, in the end, his work had all been for nothing. The legislature had defeated the measure by a wide margin. "I hope you've had better luck than I did at stopping the trouble before it really got started," he muttered.

"The *Pendletons* are the ones who've been having all the luck," Johnny pointed out. "It's time we started to fight back."

"I still can't believe how much they've accomplished," Phillipe mused. "It seems odd that they suddenly have so much power all over the state. I don't understand it."

"Well, we can't know everything," Johnny said. "But I'm thinking the Pendletons must have some important connection we haven't thought of."

Phillipe looked from Johnny to William and back again. "If they do, then the only way we can fight them is to find out who it is."

Swallowing nervously, William managed to ask, "How will you do that?"

"I don't know," Phillipe responded, "but I'm sure we'll think of something."

Johnny rubbed his chin and suggested, "What about Paul? Do you think he could tell us anything?"

"Maybe, but he won't." Phillipe shrugged hopelessly. "He seems to become more stubborn as time goes on. I can tell he's pretty badly frightened, and if it's the Pendletons who scared him, they've done a thorough job. Besides, I doubt if Paul noticed anything anyway. All he can really tell us is who asked him to give Medora that message. We'll have to look elsewhere if we want any real answers. All we can say for sure is that they're getting desperate. That means we'd better work fast, before they *do* kill someone."

"I don't think—" William began, but then he stopped abruptly.

Neither Phillipe nor Johnny seemed to hear him. "Our one advantage is that contract with Swift," the younger man said. "As long as we keep producing cut beef at the rate we are and Swift continues to buy it, the Pendletons won't be able to stop us."

Goodall nodded enthusiastically. "I promise you, we'll stop them first. We just have to out-think them, that's all."

With a sigh of regret, Van Driesche sank back in his chair. He knew now without a doubt that Phillipe and Johnny's confidence was little more than an illusion, but he also knew that, no matter how much he wanted to, he could never tell them so. He had already gone too far to turn back now.

Chapter 27

The azure summer sky was half-hidden by the dark, threatening clouds which foretold a leaden afternoon, but to Cory the cool air was a relief. She had grown to hate the gloomy stillness of the house, which she feared had settled permanently into the dark, empty places of her mind in the last few months. Now the feeling of free, open air and the brush of her hair against her face was precious to her beyond words. It had been so long since she had seen the trees and cliffs and sweeping prairies except through the thick glass of her bedroom window, and the shadows of the clouds that lay scattered across the land only added depth and meaning to the unrestrained beauty, at least in Cory's sight.

David St. Clair smiled and followed as his mother-in-law led the way across a thickly carpeted field to the edge of the copse, which the morning shadows had transformed to a forest-green bower touched with an unearthly light that set the leaves quivering. Then, suddenly, Cory grasped his hand and pulled him downward, her finger pressed in warning to her lips.

"Shhh," Cory whispered. "I don't want to disturb the buck standing among the trees there." As they crouched in the tall, waving buffalo grass, she pointed. "Look, David."

With a tiny smile, David raised his head slowly, expecting to see anything from a prairie dog to a grazing buffalo. He had listened to Cory's fantasies long enough to know that her mind was not restrained by the conventions of reality. But this time she was right. A magnificent stag stood poised among the overhanging trees, his pale brown head raised so that his antlers stood in relief against the background of shifting greens. The stag's body was poised, ready for flight, while he listened intently for the sound of an intruder.

"Isn't he beautiful?" Cory breathed. "Wouldn't it be wonderful to be like him, even for an instant?"

David gazed at her searchingly. When he looked back at the regal animal, he could only nod in mute acquiescence.

"Mama!"

The sound of Katherine's harsh voice exploded in the hushed stillness, and the stag turned and fled into the shelter of the trees. Her eyes brimming with disappointment, Cory looked away, and David wondered if he would ever cease to feel that sudden stab of pity that pierced his heart whenever he saw that look on his mother-in-law's face.

"Mama! What are you doing out here?" Katherine demanded as she stopped before the crouching pair, her hands poised threateningly on her hips.

"David said we could go for a walk," Cory explained. "He said it would be all right, since I've been feeling so well."

Katherine considered her mother's flushed face, the light of intelligence that flickered in those almost colorless eyes, and she drew her breath in sharply. She had noticed that Cory was improving under David's constant care; she had even had occasional moments of lucidity in the past few weeks. But not until this moment had Katherine realized how far her mother had come. Still, the madness must not be allowed to disappear altogether, at least not yet. For Katherine had plans for Cory, and once she was sane, her daughter would lose the only power she had ever had over her helpless mother.

Katherine could not afford to set Cory free; she needed her too badly. So she must make certain that her mother's recovery was incomplete. "Leave us, David," she said, without taking her eyes from Cory's face. "I want to talk to Mama alone."

By now, David had learned that it was useless to argue with his strong-willed wife. He knew that he would not have had the strength or the will to defeat her anyway. She did not love him, but he was wise enough to realize that she was still the only constant light in his bleak world. With her beauty and her confidence and her inner strength, she held him in the palm of her hand, but he knew there was nowhere else on the face of the earth that he would choose to be. "I'll be waiting at home," he told her, but it was as if he had not spoken. With a sigh, he brushed the leaves from his pants and left them alone.

"Mama," Katherine snapped when David was gone, "you know Father doesn't allow you to go out."

Cory's mouth thinned into a stubborn line. "It was only a walk. We didn't hurt anything."

"But Father will be angry. You know he will."

A flicker of distress lit Cory's gray eyes at the memory of Greg's anger. Katherine saw it and knew she had won before the battle had even begun. "You don't want to make him angry, do you?" she said. "You remember what happened the last time."

Cory fought to keep down the panic that clogged her throat at the memory of her husband's voice. *I'm sorry, but I can't leave you free to threaten everything I hold dear.* "It's different now," she declared obstinately, but her voice trembled a little, betraying her uncertainty. "I've gotten better."

"Have you?" her daughter asked. "I wonder how quickly you would recover if you could remember what you did in the past. Convenient for you that you've forgotten, isn't it?"

Shaking her head wildly to dislodge the shadows she felt creeping out from where she had them hidden, Cory clenched her hands into fists at her sides. She would *not* think about the past, no matter what Katherine said. She would just feel the present. She would not remember Greg's face distorted with hatred and fury or the guilt and despair that had begun long ago to eat away at her sanity. She would not! "Leave me alone," she gasped.

"But I can't, Mama," Katherine murmured with false sweetness. "Because even though you don't remember, *I* do. I know the truth about you, you see. I know what you've done and what you might do in the future, and I'm not likely to forget any more than Father is."

"You hate me!" Cory accused. "Just like he does. You *want* to see me suffer."

"Don't be silly. If I hated you, why did I go to all the trouble of forcing Father not to put you in an institution?"

Cory winced as if her daughter had struck her. "I don't know why! And I don't want to think about it."

"You'd better," Katherine hissed. Now all the softness had fled from her tone and her eyes were hard and cold. "You'd better not make *me* angry too, Mama. Because I'm the one who kept you here and I'm the one who can send you away. You know very well that if I hadn't fought for you, Father would have gotten rid of you a long time ago."

Trembling visibly now, Cory realized that she could no longer keep the fear at bay; it was gnawing at the edge of her thoughts like a hungry rat, and she had no more power to banish it. "You won't let him do it, will you?" she whispered in a strangled voice.

"I don't know," her daughter replied stiffly. "It depends on how hard you try to appease me."

"I'll do my best," Cory choked. "Only please don't send me away." Her eyes were full of wavering darkness and her stomach was roiling with the terror that washed over her in waves. It did not matter if Katherine hated her. Nothing mattered, so long as she could stay here, where it was safe, where she could see Greg's face now and again and remember that she had had him once, a very long time ago. "You won't do it, will you?" she pleaded.

Katherine smiled slightly, then reached out to take her mother's cold hand in hers. "Not if you do as I say, Mama." The sense of satisfaction was almost overpowering. Her plans were safe after all. "As long as you do what I ask, you'll be safe," she murmured. "I promise."

The early afternoon sunlight that filtered through the thin lace curtains was muted and softened by the darkening clouds which had reached nearly across the broad Badlands sky, and Anais stood facing her mother with the cool touch of approaching rain on her back. "What do you want?" the girl demanded.

Medora paused for a moment as she closed the door behind her. She was surprised by the lovely picture her daughter made poised before the window with the lace curtains like a softly woven veil around her face. Anais' thick black hair was tied back loosely with a velvet ribbon, and the curls fell in disorder across the front of her beige silk blouse with its fashionably puffed sleeves and delicate lace trim. As always, she was wearing the heavily carved gold locket her father had given her long ago, but today she looked older somehow. Even the swirl of her skirt where it clung to her hips and legs proclaimed that Anais was becoming a woman. With a stab of dismay, Medora realized that her daughter had grown up and her mother had not even noticed that it was happening. "You're old enough now to make yourself a part of this family," she said softly.

A tiny smile of disdain twisted Anais' lips. "It's too late for that."

"What do you mean?"

"I haven't been part of this family since—" The words caught in her throat and she found that she could not say them.

"Since your father died?" her mother finished for her. "But that was your choice, wasn't it?"

Anais held her breath and turned to stare at the swelling, changing clouds that made a threatening wall beyond her window. They were, she realized, no more than a reflection of the constant storm that wreaked its havoc inside her. "No!" she cried suddenly, surprising even herself. "It was *not* my choice!"

Distressed by the pain that brimmed unexpectedly in those deep, black eyes, Medora took a step forward. "You moved beyond my reach," she murmured, "but I've tried to talk to you—"

"Not very often. You were too busy with other things," the girl accused.

"Don't start blaming Phillipe again," Medora warned.

"I won't," Anais assured her, "because it doesn't matter anyway. I don't care anymore." She could not look at her mother's face as she uttered those words; her eyes were fixed with longing on the dismal scene beyond the window. "No one cares about me, so I don't care about them. It's really quite simple."

Medora swallowed the angry denial that rose to her lips and said instead, "Perhaps if you made more of an effort to befriend us, we would respond. You've always chosen to be off alone somewhere or with your tutor. You have to reach out if you want an answer."

She had done that once, Anais thought bitterly, and it had brought her nothing but pain. She was not likely to do so again, except with Stephen. Stephen was different from them. She knew he was the one person on the earth who she could really trust. "How would you suggest I do that?" she asked idly, just to see what her mother would say.

This was the opening Medora had been waiting for, the reason she had come to her daughter's room in the first place. She thought she had finally discovered a way to force Anais to leave her private little world and join the real one. "You could, for example, help Mianne with the twins. You were her friend once and she needs you."

Anais clutched the windowsill until the wood grated painfully against her fingernails. What kind of lie was her mother trying to pass off on her? She knew very well that Mianne needed no one now that she had Phillipe. "No," the girl said firmly.

"Why not?"

"Because I don't want to."

Medora suppressed a sigh of exasperation. "Anais," she said warningly, "listen to me—"

But the girl shook her head and continued to look out the window at the lowering sky. She found that she was weary of the conversation; it had grown too dangerous.

"Anais!" Medora spoke more sharply than she had intended, but she had begun to discover that there was no other way to speak to this moody girl.

Whirling to face her mother, Anais rasped, "You'd better not let yourself get upset. Your wound might re-open, you know." She drew a deep breath and forced herself to go on. "How *is* your wound, Mama? Is there still much pain?"

Medora took a step backwards when she saw the softly pulsing light in her daughter's eyes. There was something vaguely threatening in those dark velvet depths that had once been so like her father's. Medora felt a chill run down the back of her neck. All at once she was remembering Paul's pinched and colorless face and his stubborn refusal to give them the name they needed to hear. It was then that the horrible question formed itself on her tongue, but she found that she could not ask it of the girl who stood silent and hostile before her, because she knew, suddenly, that she could not bear to hear the answer. "I'm healing nicely," she lied, "but that's not what we were discussing. The point is that Mianne needs your help just now. Whether you give it willingly or not, you *will* give it to her. The time has come for you to pull your weight as the rest of us do. I'll have no more argument on the question." Then, before she could change her mind, Medora rotated on her heel and left the room without looking back.

Had she done so, even for an instant, she would have been horrified by the look of hatred on Anais' face—a look that would have made the girl unrecognizable to the mother who had never even begun to understand the weight of the burden of pain and anger her daughter carried inside her like an open wound.

The notes from the fiddle spilled across the drawing room to mingle with the dancing flames of the red-gold fire. With a sigh of contentment, Mianne rested her head on the wing of her chair and smiled at her father, who sat playing his fiddle before the hearth. "Look," she murmured, "you've put the babies to sleep." But then, before Johnny could answer, she closed her eyes and let the music wash over her like the soothing babble of the river she had not seen in so long. The notes touched her eyelids, her cheeks, her long, slender fingers, and the curve of her arm with a caress like the flutter of a bird's half-open wings, and she felt herself relaxing for the first time in the three long weeks since the birth of Antoine and Kira, who lay wrapped in warm, clinging blankets in the basket at her side.

"Maybe I should stop before I wake them again," Goodall suggested in a voice barely above a whisper.

Mianne looked up in time to see the proud smile that touched his lips. She shook her head. "Your grandchildren have learned already that your fiddle is the best lullaby. If you stop, they'll only awaken and beg for more. You've charmed them into silence for the moment. Don't spoil it."

With a pleased grin, Johnny settled back against the arm of the sofa and coaxed the music from his old fiddle. Mianne listened as he played songs she remembered vaguely from her childhood, and a smile curved her lips.

"Are you happy?" Goodall asked.

"Yes," his daughter replied, realizing as she said it that it was true. Even the overcast sky and the unexpected chill in the middle of the afternoon could not dim her pleasure. She gazed fondly at the tiny sleeping forms of her son and daughter. She had been surprised by the intense love she had felt for them the first moment she saw them, for she had not expected to care for them so much. But she knew in her heart that the children would love her back without thought or reservation and that made them precious to her. There were times, when she looked at their wide, watching eyes, when they reminded her painfully of Phillipe, but she loved them for that too.

"I'm glad," Johnny said, interrupting her thoughts. "I've been worried about you."

"There was no need," Mianne assured him, though she knew it was not entirely true. She had been disturbed by her husband's strangely stilted behavior toward her since the birth of their children, but she had learned long ago that there was nothing she could do to change Phillipe.

He was beyond her reach, and she had come to accept that knowledge, though it never stopped hurting her. But she would forget her husband for the time being and enjoy the intimacy that had grown up between herself and her father in the past two weeks. She had never in her life felt so close to him, and in this instant the image of his lined and sunburned face was dear to her beyond words.

Leaning back with one hand resting on the warm, breathing body of her daughter, Mianne sank slowly into the spell of the music that spoke to her of the irresistible pull of the rushing river which she thought she had lost so long ago.

Katherine drew her cloak more tightly around her as the wind came whistling up from the rock like a high, piercing warning of the storm to come. She was mad to stand here like this in the deepening darkness of the afternoon; she knew that as certainly as she knew that she could not turn away. The sky could open its heart and bleed its lifeblood upon her but she would not care. She had to see Phillipe once more.

Her plans were already well laid and she was ready to carry them through, but she had realized suddenly that she could not do it without one last look at his face. That single moment of weakness had brought her here, to the stone maze where they had met so often, because she knew she had to be certain. The choice, if there was one, belonged to him now. It lay in his open palms like a piece of fragile crystal, only he did not know it. Katherine smiled to herself. That was the cleverness of her plan—to give him the choice without telling him so.

Her heart beat out a deep and wild tattoo against her ribs as she waited for Phillipe to appear. She knew he would come, there was no question of that, because, quite simply, he could not help himself. Therein lay her power and the certainty of her eventual victory. The clouds, the cold, the hint of night in the middle of the day would only add to the moment. Katherine was not afraid. She was afraid of nothing but the pulse of her own desire. Then she heard him coming and the breath stopped in her throat. It would not be long now. Then she would know the truth—finally.

Phillipe rubbed his arms to warm them as he climbed upward, wondering how long it would be before the rain began to fall. He had been waiting all day for the storm to break, and it had held off so long that he had begun to fear a flood when the clouds finally released their dark, heavy burden. But it was Katherine's urgent message that disturbed him the most. He had come, although reluctantly, remembering their last meeting with grim despair. Surely this time she had some important news to tell him, for even Katherine would not choose to have a rendezvous on the sandy cliffs while the rain streamed down around her.

Then he saw her waiting with her dark cloak whipping about her legs in the angry wind, and the expression on her face made him pause for a moment in wonder. "What is it?" he asked as she approached him on feet that never seemed to touch the rocky ground. "What do you want to tell me?"

Katherine's lips twitched into a smile, and she tossed her head so that the hood fell back, revealing the brown, gleaming waves of her hair. "I have no information to offer you," she said in a throaty whisper. "Only myself."

Phillipe was taken aback by the unconcealed desire in her eyes, and he knew that he should not have come. "Katherine—" he began.

Shaking her head in warning, she touched a finger to his lips to stop him from saying any more. "I want you," she said.

Phillipe took a deep breath and turned away, though

her body called to him and the wind in her hair sent a flicker of response dancing along his spine. He would not betray Mianne again. "I can't," he told her firmly. "Not this time."

"You can't," she repeated. "You mean you won't." When Phillipe did not raise his head or turn to look at her, Katherine felt her stomach tighten and the trembling began as a tiny flutter at the base of her spine. She needed no more than his silence to tell her that this was the last time for them. If she turned away now, she would lose him forever, if she had not already done so long ago. He would force her to destroy him, and she could not let that happen. The need for his destruction would tear her apart.

Only now, as the first few drops of rain escaped at last from their cloud prisons, did she realize how much she had depended on his need of her. She had believed, in spite of all that had come between them, that he was incapable of turning her away. He, who was the very breath of her body, and whose loss would be to her worse than death. It must not happen. For, no matter how much she hated him, she loved him more.

The rain began to fall more heavily, until it pelted them with drops that seemed to be made of brittle glass. And, while the water drenched her, turning her hair into long, dripping strands that clung to her shoulders, Katherine made her decision. With a last deep breath that could not even begin to dislodge the lump that had formed itself in her throat, she fought her way through the rain until she stood face-to-face with Phillipe once more. "Please," she begged him.

Phillipe felt as if she had struck him just below the heart. Even through the curtain of water that came between them, he could read the love that burned in her eyes. It was the last thing he had ever expected to see there. Dear God, what had he done? Katherine Pendleton had never pleaded with him before, and he knew instinctively that she never would again, but he could not let the passion flare again, not with the memory of Mianne's fathomless eyes to stand between them. "No," he said.

Pressing against him, Katherine threw her arms around his waist. "But you want to. I can feel it."

He thought the blood had ceased to flow in his veins as he fought to make his body obey his will. He was stunned when, for the first time in his memory, he won the battle against his desire. "No," he said gently as he worked himself free of her arms. "I'm sorry." But his words were drowned in the pounding of the unfriendly rain.

Katherine looked up at him then, and her heart stood still when she saw what was in his eyes—pity, and a little regret, but nothing more. Swallowing the agony that rose in her throat, she turned away and began to run. With the unforgiving rock beneath her feet and the unrelenting rain against her back, she ran blindly into the darkness. She knew, in the deep center of her being, that as long as she lived she would never be able to rid herself of the memory of the pity she had seen in Phillipe's eyes. For that, more than anything else, she would never forgive him. She could not. Phillipe had made his choice, and one day he would learn to regret it.

Chapter 28

Night had fallen, deep and dark, enfolding Cory in its velvet blackness, and she stumbled as she walked with nothing but the stars overhead and a tiny lantern to guide her. Raising the lantern a little higher, she felt the chill wind crawling beneath her collar and wondered what she was doing here, alone in the night when the rest of the world was sleeping. It was madness—it must be. Cory smiled tightly at the irony of her wandering thoughts. For this time it was Katherine's madness and not her own. She would have turned back long ago, abandoning this terrible errand, if it hadn't been for the knowledge that her daughter was waiting at home.

Cory shuddered as Katherine's face rose before her and the memory of her cold warning rang in her mother's ears. *You'd better not make* me *angry, too. I'm the one who kept you here and I'm the one who can send you away.* Suddenly overcome with dread, Cory realized that she was shivering uncontrollably. Why was the night so cold, when it was mid-August? Or was it just prickles of fear that raced along her skin? Help me! she pleaded silently to no one. Tell me what to do! But her only answer was the keening of the wind, so high and piercing that it might have been a cry torn from a human throat. And far, far in the distance was the threatening echo of Kathcrine's voice. Cory knew she had no choice but to go on.

Stopping at the foot of the hill, she searched for a flat area where she could leave the lantern. Katherine had warned her not to carry it beyond this point, where the light might be seen from the house. Obediently, Cory bent and set the lantern on a patch of dew-wet grass, then stepped away from it into the encircling darkness. She stopped for a moment, waiting for her eyes to adjust to the gloom, and her body began to shake with a terror that began in her fingers and crawled like a poisonous snake up her arms and down her back. I can't do it, she cried desperately, but the words never left her mouth.

What was she more afraid of, Cory asked herself, the crime she was about to commit or her daughter? The answer came to her in an instant on the back of the wind—Katherine. *As long as you do what I ask, you'll be safe. I promise.*

Cory stiffened her spine with new determination. She couldn't let them send her away. Especially not now, when, with David's constant attention and kindness, she had just begun to crawl out of the black hole where she had crouched, unnoticed, for so long.

Then she realized that the darkness had fallen back, revealing the Chateau at the top of the hill. There, just as Katherine had promised, was the tiny light burning from somewhere within the back porch. Cory took several deep breaths and began to move forward slowly. "I'm sorry," she murmured to the sleeping house, but the sound was lost in a whisper of wind that disappeared into the glittering heart of the deep night sky like a single, sighing breath of soft regret.

As she approached the silent house, Cory saw that the door was ajar, and her blood began to race in her veins as she stepped up and pushed it open with a trembling hand. Let nothing go wrong, she prayed. Don't let them find me here. All at once she was afraid that Katherine had made a mistake, sent her on the wrong night. Perhaps she had come for nothing at all. But then she moved inside and saw the basket waiting, just where her daughter had said it would be.

Leaning over with her breath held back in her throat, Cory looked inside. There, lit by the wavering light of a lantern hidden away in some corner, lay the two tiny babies. Cory stood with her hand extended toward the handle of the basket, but suddenly she found that she could not make herself move. She should not have looked at the children; they were too vulnerable and their fragility twisted like a jagged knife in her chest.

Then Katherine's voice came to her from out of the shadows, as clearly as if her daughter stood before her. *You know very well if I hadn't fought for you, Father would have gotten rid of you a long time ago.* Cory swallowed her doubts, though they threatened to choke her, and grasped the handle with fingers that trembled just a little. Then she lifted the basket, took one last wrenching breath, and turned to make her way out the door and down the steps. But all the while the blood was singing, screaming in her ears like a bitter accusation.

As the woman moved away, hunched with the weight of her burden, Anais came forward out of the shadows which had hidden her. With the muted light of the lantern at her back, she went to stand at the half-open door, and her fingers closed tightly around the cool knob. She had not dared to breathe in the past few minutes for fear that something would go wrong, but now she sensed that she was safe. The babies would not betray her with their cries, she knew, for she had given them a liberal dose of laudanum before she wrapped them in their blankets and brought them here. No doubt they would sleep for hours.

Closing her eyes with a sigh of relief, she leaned against the door and smiled to herself. When Katherine Pendleton had first approached her, asking for her help, she had been uncertain. But her mother's stubborn refusal to understand her problems, her enforced care of the children over the past three weeks, had changed her mind. She hated them, Anais told herself. To her they were just another proof of Phillipe's unbreakable power over all she had once held dear.

But tonight she had broken that power, and she had done it alone, without even Stephen to guide her. This, she had decided, would be her triumph, unmarred by the knowledge of any strength but her own. She, and she alone, had beaten Phillipe. But as she watched Cory disappear into the waiting darkness at the foot of the hill, Anais wondered why she shuddered all at once, as if her heart had been frozen by the touch of an icy hand.

"Are you awake?"

Phillipe's voice came to his wife like a whisper of longing, and she answered, "Yes." She knew before he even moved that he was going to reach for her, though he had not done it for so long. Closing her eyes in expectation, Mianne held her breath as her husband's fingers brushed her cheek, then found their way down across her throat to the open buttons of her nightgown.

"Are you sure it's all right?" Phillipe asked as he shifted his body closer so that his lips hovered just above hers.

"It's been six weeks since the babies were born," she told him softly. "I'm fine now." Besides, she thought as the warmth of his body penetrated the thin material of her gown, she could not have turned him away, not while the touch of his hand burned along her skin, leaving a trail of goosebumps behind. As his fingers moved along the curve of her breasts beneath the fabric and his mouth met hers in a long, searching kiss, she felt that it was like the first time he had touched her, as if there had not been those long and barren months in between.

Phillipe raised his head, the blood running hotly in his veins, and he realized it had been too long since he had last claimed his wife. His hunger now was like a fire that burned out of control inside him and his body trembled with the force of his desire. But he knew he must go slowly just the same, for Mianne had been unwell, and even before her pregnancy, she had seemed to him more fragile than the strong and spirited Katherine. In the blackness, all he could see was the outline of his wife's face and the rise and fall of her chest beneath the thin sheet, but for this he was grateful.

It had always been so with Mianne; he chose to make love to her only in the darkness. Never once had he taken her in the daytime, nor even with the soft light of the lamp on her face. He needed the shadows to hide her dark, glowing eyes. He knew that he would not be able to touch her if he ever again saw the tearing sorrow that had lit those eyes on their wedding day, so he took refuge in the blanket of the night.

With hands that were infinitely gentle, he explored his wife's body as if he had never known it before, tracing the curves and hollows while his own skin tingled with the soft flow of warmth that Mianne's seeking fingers created on his naked back. He had forgotten the sudden rush of pleasure that the touching of hungry flesh could bring, and when they lay together skin to skin, he smiled and drew her so close that he thought for a moment her blood began to flow through his veins.

Sucking in her breath at the sudden overpowering pleasure of his nearness, Mianne clasped her hands around Phillipe's neck and brought his head down until his warm, wet lips moved against hers and his tongue probed her mouth, soft and hungry and searching. More than anything, she wanted to see the flush of desire on his face, but she knew it was impossible. From the beginning, she had sensed his distaste for the light. Never once had she seen his naked body without the shadows of night to cloak it in mystery. It was as if he did not want to see the woman—his wife—who moved beneath him, answering the call of his body with her own. Perhaps he was pretending she was someone else, and the lamplight would have shattered his fantasy. No! her heart cried out in protest. Just then, Phillipe entered her, and her thoughts were swept away in the swirling river of warmth that engulfed her. In this moment there was no room for doubts or worries—there was only Phillipe and his hands and the rhythmic movement of his rocking body that filled her head with wonder and her eyes with blinding color.

When at last they were still, Phillipe reached over to draw Mianne's head against the hollow in his shoulder, and they lay unmoving while the first fingers of dawn crept through the slightly parted curtains. He had not realized how much he had missed her in these past few months until tonight, and now he was reluctant to let her go.

"Mianne," he whispered.

But all at once his wife sat up sharply, her eyes wide and staring. "Something's wrong," she gasped. "I know it."

In the new light of morning, her face was oddly shadowed, and Phillipe felt her agitation run like fire through his own body. "What is it?" he asked.

"I don't know." Mianne turned to look at him but she did not really see him. "I'm going to check Antoine and Kira." Without waiting for his response, she rose from the bed and found her robe in the half-darkness.

Phillipe watched her go, unable to dismiss the feeling of alarm her expression had created in him. He had just raised himself on his elbow, ready to follow her from the room, when Mianne appeared again in the doorway.

Her black hair and eyes were lost in the darkness behind

her, so that only the pale, shining oval of her face was visible, and he saw that the last drop of color had drained from her cheeks. "What—" he began.

"They're gone, Phillipe," she cried, her back against the doorframe. "The children have disappeared."

"Where's Katherine?" Cory demanded of her son-in-law.

David looked up in surprise at the pale, distraught woman who stood before him. "She left a little after dawn," he said, then added kindly, "Don't you think it's time you got some sleep? You don't look as if you got much last night."

"Not now," Cory insisted, waving his concern aside. "Where did Katherine go?"

Perplexed by Cory's agitation, David nevertheless told her, "The last time I saw her, she was heading toward the river with a large basket over her arm."

"Oh, no!" Cory wrung her hands, long, bony fingers woven together like the pliant fibers in an Indian basket. "I have to find her, David. Will you let me go?"

"If it's so important, *I'll* do it."

"No! You don't understand. I must go alone. Please. Greg will never know. And I've been getting better. You know I have."

David sensed the panic that made the color rush to Cory's cheeks, then disappear, and he sensed also that the time had come to let her make her own choice. She had come a long way with his help, but now she had to begin to learn on her own, although he was reluctant to let her go just now.

"Please," she repeated. "Wait for me here. I may need you when I get back."

"Are you sure you have to do it alone?"

"Yes, yes. It's the only way."

"All right then," David agreed. "But be careful."

"It's too late for that," Cory cried as she threw the door open and ran outside. Too late for a great many things, she thought, as her feet flew over the still wet ground, but, please, God, not too late for the children. She was running again, fleeing as if the nightmares were still at her back, but this time she knew where she was going. She must get to Katherine before she did something dreadful.

Cory had seen the look in her daughter's eyes when she held Phillipe's baby girl for the first time, and it had not been a pleasant one. In fact, for an instant, Cory had recognized madness there, and it had shaken her to the very core. She had to get to her daughter. Cory knew that as certainly as she had ever known anything in her life. She only hoped she would find her soon enough.

When she reached the trees that guarded the river, Cory darted beneath the branches, searching frantically for a flash of brown hair among the green leaves. But the cottonwoods seemed determined to deter her; they swayed and crowded before her like the ranks of an enemy army. Yet she knew she had to push her way through, though by now her hair was full of twigs and leaves and hopelessly tangled by the low-hanging branches. Then she found what she was seeking. There, in the clearing by the deep, still pond, Katherine knelt near the waters where the soggy dampness of the bank had already begun to stain the soft blue fabric of her gown. Beside her lay the basket and in her arms she held one of the babies, whose blanket trailed pitifully into the water.

"No!" Cory gasped as she dropped to her knees beside her daughter. "What are you doing?"

Katherine turned to stare at her blankly. "Go away," she said, as if speaking to a small, annoying animal.

Cory saw that the children were still sleeping; they must

have been given a great deal of laudanum the night before. "What are you doing?" she repeated stubbornly.

With the baby clutched to her chest, Katherine turned back to the smooth surface of the pond. "I'm sending the children back where they belong," she said in a voice that was oddly empty of emotion. "To the water."

Cory fought off a wave of nausea. "You're mad," she whispered, and she realized, all at once, that it was true.

"Don't say that!" Katherine growled threateningly. "Don't ever say that to me again!" Her eyes were glassy and the yawning blackness gaped just behind them. She put the baby girl back beside her brother and turned to face Cory.

Cory's hand clamped down on her daughter's arm. "Give me the children," she demanded, ignoring the fluttering of panic that had begun in her stomach. She could not let the fear overtake her now. She had to have enough strength for both of them. "I took them for you," she said, "but you promised they wouldn't be hurt."

Katherine threw back her head to laugh wildly. The sound sent a chill down her mother's spine. "What did you think," the younger woman demanded, "that I wanted to hold them for ransom? No, I don't want their *money.*" She spoke the last word as if it were poison.

"I can't let you do this," her mother declared.

"Maybe you don't want to, but you're too feeble to stop me." Katherine smiled wickedly. "No one can stop me. Not even the all-powerful Phillipe!" she crowed.

Rising to her feet slowly, with infinite care, Cory reached in her pocket. "*I* can," she said. "Get away from those children, Katherine."

Katherine glanced up and froze when she saw the tiny revolver that gleamed in her mother's hand.

"I'll shoot you before you can breathe if you hurt either one of them," Cory threatened.

For a moment, Katherine hesitated. It was all the encouragement her mother needed.

"You know I'll do it, don't you?" Cory asked. "You know I can. I'm warning you, Katherine, I mean it this time."

The flame that blazed in her mother's eyes was familiar to Katherine; she had seen it more than once before. And she knew quite well what Cory was capable of when this mood overtook her. She was, at times like this, a woman without fear, and a woman unafraid of dying is also not afraid to kill.

But Katherine could not give in to the vision of death that rose from the gray barrel of the gun. "Go away, Mama," she hissed. "I have things to do." Then she leaned down toward the basket at her feet.

Cory saw before her the remembered image of those tiny sleeping faces, and her hand tightened convulsively on the revolver. "Katherine!" she warned. But Katherine ignored her. With a sudden surge of strength she had not known she possessed, Cory pointed the gun at her daughter's shoulder and pulled the trigger.

Katherine was stunned as much by the explosion as by the tearing pain in her arm and the blood that began to seep through her blouse. Then she looked up and saw her mother bearing down on her, the gun still in her hand. "Mama!" she cried. "Don't—"

"I told you," Cory said. "But you wouldn't listen. I have five bullets left, Katherine. And I don't think you really want to die. So let the children be. I won't tell you again."

Wincing at the agony that burned across her shoulder and down her arm, Katherine pressed a hand to the deep red stain that spread quickly beneath her wet fingers. And, as she faced her mother with the tiny gun between them, she knew that this time she had lost. Cory had been right; she did not want to die. She could not—not until the debt had been paid and the score with Phillipe made even once and for all. "Take them!" she snarled. "But don't be so naive as to think this is the end. I'll just have to find another way, that's all. And next time you and your little gun will have no power to stop me."

Phillipe and Johnny sat on horseback, concealed by the drooping green leaves of the cottonwoods, watching as Katherine, Cory and Greg Pendleton mounted their horses and left the ranch house behind.

"Where do you think they're going?" Phillipe asked tensely.

"Don't know," Goodall replied. "I just hope they stay away a good long time. This way, we've only got St. Clair to deal with."

Phillipe nodded. "We can handle him, but are you sure this is where the children will be?"

"Where else would they be? Who in this valley but the Pendletons would dare kidnap your children? Who but the Pendletons would want to?"

"I suppose you're right." Phillipe's eyes narrowed as he watched Katherine's hunched figure shrink until it disappeared.

When all three Pendletons had vanished, the two men made their way slowly and carefully down the hill to the silent ranch house. "You go around to the back," Phillipe murmured, "and I'll take the front."

Johnny nodded and slid from the saddle, motioning the horse to wait where he stood for his master's return. Then, walking as if on a floor covered with broken glass, Goodall disappeared around the side of the house. Phillipe waited until the foreman had had time to find the back door, then, with his revolver clutched in his hand, he tried the knob, found that the door was unlocked and pushed it open.

David St. Clair sat on the couch with his head resting in his hands. He looked up, astonished, when he heard the threatening click of the hammers on two revolvers. Then he saw who stood before him, and the surprise in his eyes turned to bleak despair. "I thought you'd come," he said, speaking to the empty air between Johnny and Phillipe.

"Will the others be gone very long?" Phillipe demanded.

David did not hesitate before answering. "They're on their way to Dickinson to see a doctor. It'll be late afternoon before they get back, assuming they catch the late train."

"Where are the children?"

Shrugging in resignation, David pointed toward the back of the house.

"Have they been hurt?" Johnny hissed. "Because if they have—"

It was then that the wailing cry reached them, and David realized the babies had awakened at last. "No," he said. It seemed to be the only word he was capable of uttering at that moment.

"Did you know anything about this?" Phillipe demanded.

"If I had, I would have tried to stop it. I hope you believe me."

There was no mistaking the sincerity—or the misery—in the other man's eyes. "It depends," Phillipe said. "Johnny and I are going to take the children home now. I don't suppose you'll try to stop us?"

Shaking his head, David sank back against the sofa.

"Still," Johnny said thoughtfully, "I guess we'd better tie him up, so it looks like we had to work at getting his cooperation."

David smiled slightly. It was true that the Pendletons

would have been enraged to find that their guard had given in without a fight. "Thanks," he muttered.

While Phillipe went to get the children, Johnny set about tying David's hands tightly together behind his back. Then, for good measure, he bound the man's feet, just as Phillipe reappeared with the basket in his hands.

"Let's get out of here," the younger man said. "I don't want to be around if they decide they forgot something and come riding back." But, despite his concern, the tension had left his voice for the first time in what had already been a long day, though it had only begun a couple of hours ago.

"Nope," Johnny declared. "You go on ahead. While we're here, I want to do some investigating of my own."

"Now wait—" David cried.

"Not now, Johnny. It's too dangerous," Phillipe interrupted.

"I've never seen a better opportunity," Goodall grunted. "You said you want to find out the truth. Well, here's our chance."

Phillipe considered this argument in silence for a moment, then he nodded slowly. "All right. But I'll stay and help."

"Hell!" Johnny laughed. "I'm not going to get anything done with those two babies wailing like the bell on the town fire engine. You take them and get out of here. Besides, Mianne will want to hear from you. It wouldn't be fair to make her wait any longer than necessary."

Reluctantly, Phillipe admitted that the foreman had a point, but he didn't like leaving the old man alone here. "If you're sure," he said.

"Positive." Johnny waved a hand in dismissal. As he moved off down the hall, he listened closely for the sound of the front door closing behind Phillipe. Now that he knew the children would get home safely, he could get down to business. Goodall whistled as he looked into each room he passed, searching for the study. He had a feeling in his blood that this was his lucky day. Phillipe wanted the name of the Pendeltons' contact, and Johnny intended to present his employer with the information before the sun had reached the middle of the sky.

Smiling in satisfaction when he finally found the study, Goodall closed the door behind him. There were papers strewn everywhere across the desk and tabletops, so he'd have to work fast. Even he wasn't fool enough to tarry for long. Johnny seated himself behind the huge oak desk and the blood began to pound in his ears as he rifled through the pages scattered in disarray before him. Somehow he knew that the information he wanted was here; he only had to find it, and quickly.

He shuffled through rental agreements, letters to and from the railroad officials, and several business agreements, but the papers he sought were not among them. Then he tried the center drawer and when he realized it was locked, his heart speeded up in his chest. This would be it, no doubt, where all the important papers were kept locked away. Johnny worked at prying the lock open with the letter opener, but it was several minutes before the mechanism gave way under his assault. Then, with hands that trembled with expectation, he reached inside the drawer and withdrew the contents.

This time he saw that his haphazard search had come to an end. Here was everything he needed—checks, letters, written agreements. But when he came to the name scrawled across the bottom of the first page, his breath lodged in his throat and the racing of his heart slowed to a crawl. It couldn't be, he objected silently. There must be some mistake. But as he thumbed through the rest of the pages, he saw that there was no mistake. It was true. "Holy Christ!" Goodall's breath escaped in a long, low whistle, and the flash of realization was like an explosion inside his head. Now that they knew, he thought, how in the hell were they going to fight back? What defense did they have against something like this?

It was then that he heard the door squeak on its hinges, and he looked up in horror at the man who faced him across the room. "So now you know," Greg said softly—so softly that his words were little more than a deadly whisper. "But I'm afraid, Mr. Goodall, that this time you've stuck your nose where it doesn't belong once too often."

Only then did Johnny see the long, sleek rifle that Greg Pendleton cradled threateningly in the curve of his arm.

Chapter 29

While the sun burned overhead like a demon that obliterated the wide blue sky with its white-hot glow, Phillipe slid from the saddle and approached the Pendleton house for the second time in a single day. He glanced over his shoulder to see that William and the other men were behind him, rifles held ready in their hands. It seemed that the time had finally come to confront the enemy face-to-face.

Johnny had been gone since early morning, and the atmosphere at the Chateau had become more and more charged with tension as the hours crawled by and still he had not come. It was now mid-afternoon. Phillipe had sent one search party into the countryside while he and William and a few men made their way to the Pendleton ranch where he had last seen the foreman. This time Phillipe did not even bother to turn the knob, gathering all his strength, he kicked the door in and found himself in the midst of a startled ring of too-familiar faces.

His glance moved quickly over Cory, who sat knitting in the corner, her fingers moving wildly even as her eyes widened in fear at the collection of threatening rifles. Then there was Katherine, her expression unreadable, her left arm cradled in a sling. But Phillipe did not take time to wonder about the heavy bandage on her shoulder. Instead, he turned to David, who would not meet the intruder's gaze at all. Finally, Greg stood leaning against the mantel with one booted foot poised on a low stool. Despite his casual attitude, his steely eyes were wary.

"Where's Johnny Goodall?" Phillipe demanded. His voice fell like the report of a rifle into the taut silence.

"I have no idea," Greg replied. "Why should I?"

Phillipe held his rifle steady, although his body trembled with anger at Pendleton's careless tone. "Because I left him here this morning."

Raising one eyebrow a fraction of an inch, Greg said, "That was foolish, don't you think?"

Suddenly William came forward. "Where the hell is he?" But he was not looking at Greg.

Katherine stood unmoved under Van Driesche's accusing appraisal. She was surprised by the aggressive tilt of his chin. "My father told you, we don't know," she maintained, her eyes transmitting her own silent warning.

"Then you won't mind if we search the house," Phillipe said. He sensed that William's hostility was about to explode and he did not want more trouble than they already had.

Greg shrugged, as if he were no more than slightly annoyed at this invasion of his privacy. "You have the guns," he observed. "I don't suppose we can stop you."

Although he knew they would not find anything, Phillipe motioned two of the men to look in the other rooms. Greg would not have been so accommodating, he knew, if Johnny were still here. But if he wasn't here, then where was he? The answer that came to him shook Phillipe to the core and he suppressed it ruthlessly. They would find the foreman, he told himself. They had to.

Just as the men came back to say they had discovered nothing, Phillipe heard a shot from somewhere in the distance, followed by another. He exchanged glances with

William and hurried to the door. This was the agreed-upon signal from the other group of searchers. As he ran outside, a man came riding forward and gasped, "We found Goodall's horse near the north cliff face."

"Any sign of Johnny?"

"Not yet, but he must be nearby."

Phillipe swallowed once and nodded. "Rest a minute while we mount up, then we'll join the others." While the man attempted to catch his breath, his employer went back inside to find that no one had moved even a fraction of an inch since his departure. "We're going," he announced, waving the men out the door; then, just for a moment, his clear blue eyes met Katherine's wintry stare. "But don't think we won't be back."

The men filed out one by one. William was the last to go, but when he reached the door he turned back and hissed softly, his eyes fixed on Katherine's face, "Johnny had better be all right."

"It's not our fault," the woman said coldly, "if he refused to play by the rules."

Van Driesche's heart turned to lead in his chest as he went to join Phillipe. But this was only the beginning of an afternoon that seemed to stretch into a long and pitiless week of frustration and discomfort. Phillipe rode before the other men with the sun beating down on his head like a determined enemy. Despite the protection of his hat, his eyes were burnt nearly blind with the pulsing heat and the sweat ran in rivers down his dusty face. But not once did he reach up to wipe the moisture away; all his attention was focused on looking for signs that Johnny had been here before him.

When he reached the edge of the cliff where Johnny's horse stood grazing peacefully, Phillipe dismounted and made his way to the narrow stone opening that led among the multicolored rocks. His jaw set in a grim line, he began to wind his way upward. All at once, it was as if the men behind him did not exist. This was his battle, not theirs, and he knew that no matter how many others came behind him, he was alone as he had never been before in his life.

Phillipe's body was soaked in sweat and his breathing was no more than a ragged stabbing in his chest when the formation of the rocks began to look familiar. When he realized why, he stopped as if someone had struck him a forceful blow to the heart. This was the edge of the twisting stone maze where he used to meet Katherine. Surely they would not have brought Johnny here. Raising his arm at last to wipe the moisture from his forehead, Phillipe forced himself to follow the tortuous path to the center of the maze, while the heat clung around him and would not let him be.

Then he turned the final corner and came face-to-face with the nightmare that had plagued him from the moment when he learned that Goodall had not returned. The body lay stretched facedown across the rigid stone, and the puddle of bright red blood that surrounded the head had begun to seep into the patterns of the flat rock beneath, creating a strange, rippling pattern of its own. With a deep breath that echoed hollowly against the carved stone walls that closed in on him like the bars of a bleak prison, Phillipe moved forward and gently turned the corpse over. With a tremor of horror, he found himself staring into Johnny Goodall's wide, blind eyes and the dark, ugly bullet hole through the center of his head.

Mianne climbed the stairs with unaccustomed weariness, welcoming the cool shadows that closed around her in the upper hall. Without thinking, she made her way to her father's bedroom door and stood uncertainly before it, as if waiting for the blank face of the wood to give her the answer she sought. But when the silence of the hallway swelled into a hollow crashing in her ears, she pushed the door open and stepped inside. Like a blind woman, she walked slowly around the empty room, trailing her fingers over her father's possessions—the white cowboy hat he treasured, the stuffed wildcat he had killed with his own two hands, the dried, brittle flowers from her own wedding.

Closing her eyes, Mianne stood absolutely still, as if the very absence of movement would keep the dreadful knowledge away. Phillipe had not yet returned from the search, but his wife already knew what he had found. She had known since morning when her father's face had risen before her, then disappeared in a rush of bright water. Even though she knew, these hours of waiting had been a kind of hell that she hoped she would never have to live again. For until she heard the truth from Phillipe's lips, she could not accept it.

Then, again, Medora had spent the day questioning everyone at the Chateau about the kidnapping of the children. No one seemed to know anything, or so they said, but Mianne knew as well as Medora did that one of them was lying. It was another frightening fact that Mianne could not even begin to contemplate. This day had been filled with tragedy from the beginning and she had begun to think she would crack under the strain. But then the numbness had come to enfold her in blessed oblivion. She was grateful, though being here in Johnny's room brought occasional sharp pricks of pain that she forced to the shadowed edges of her mind. Then she saw her father's fiddle lying on the seat of a chair in the corner and for a moment she was blinded by a despair so deep that it turned her insides into charred and blackened ashes.

Mianne bent to pick up the well-used instrument with hands that were oddly steady, then she sat on the edge of the bed with the fiddle resting on her lap. She cradled it as if it were a baby that needed comfort, her fingers strumming gently at the strings. Each wavering note shot through her like a needle heated until it was red, but she could not make herself stop—this unbearable torture was why she had come here, after all.

"Mianne?"

She looked up to find her husband standing in the doorway. She needed no more than a single glance at his eyes, clouded with grief, to tell her what she wanted to know. "He's dead," she said dully. It was not a question.

"Yes." Phillipe's fingers tightened convulsively on the doorjamb when he realized that there was nothing more he could say. Medora had offered to break the news to Mianne, but Phillipe had insisted it was his responsibility. Now he was sorry. He hadn't expected to find her here, of all places, her dark head bent over Johnny's fiddle. Phillipe himself could not even bear to look at the objects in the room—they were too painful a reminder of the dead man—so he had to look at Mianne, but that was no easier. He could not bear to meet her deep black eyes, which revealed a depth of pain she would not even recognize.

"How?" Mianne asked, her voice still expressionless.

"I don't think—"

"How?" she demanded.

She was far too cool and calm, Phillipe thought. "He was shot through the head."

Mianne nodded and her eyes never wavered in their curious regard. "Do you know why?"

With a sharp breath, Phillipe forced himself to look away. How could he answer that? Could he tell her it wouldn't have happened at all if he hadn't insisted they find out who the Pendletons' contact was? If Phillipe himself had stayed at the ranch this morning, or if he had insisted that Johnny leave with him? Should he tell her about the knowledge that had burned through his body all day—that her father would have been alive right now if it hadn't been for Phillipe? But he couldn't say that.

She had already suffered enough. "Johnny was looking for some important information at the Pendletons' this morning."

Mianne sat up precipitously, suddenly alert. "He must have found it, don't you think, or they wouldn't have killed him."

"He probably did, but we'll never really know. The Sheriff from Mandan has come to see what he can do, but I'm sure he won't be able to prove anything. The Pendletons are too clever for that."

"Yes," his wife murmured softly as her hand strayed across the strings of the fiddle that still lay in her lap. Then she drew back as if it had burned her, as if she had only just realized what she was doing. A momentary flash of horror crossed her face but she quickly wiped it away. Without looking at the wooden instrument again, she pushed it onto the bed and stood up. "Well," she said briskly, "there are lots of arrangements to make before the funeral, I'm sure, and we might as well begin now."

Phillipe looked away, unable to listen anymore to the bright, brittle quality of her voice. "Mianne," he whispered, "please." He did not even know what he was asking for. Perhaps it was forgiveness. Without thinking, he reached out to lay a hand on her arm.

Mianne stopped, frozen by the touch of his fingers which sent a shock through her body strong enough to crack the protective wall she had built so carefully around herself during the long hours of waiting. Suddenly, though she struggled against it, the tide of pain and loss washed over her, sweeping her defenses away in a rush of swirling foam. Mianne felt her insides crumbling and she looked at her husband for a blind instant. Then, as the tears spilled over onto her cheeks, she let him draw her into his arms.

While Mianne clung to him, gasping and choking with the force of her weeping, Phillipe closed his arms around her and prayed that he would have the strength to continue standing upright. For, even to him, the pain was too much to bear. He had hurt this woman, his wife, more than even she could understand, and he realized then that it didn't matter if she forgave him—he could not forgive himself. She should hate him, yet she had looked up at him a moment ago with no trace of accusation in her eyes, only bitter grief and a plea for his comfort. As if he could ever comfort her again.

This woman, who should have turned away from him in horror, now clung to him as if she might fall if he let her go. He thought, in that instant, that the intensity of her need hurt him more than her anger or rejection would have. And he knew then that the tragedy of it all would break him, sooner or later, just as it had broken her.

The stars were glimmering like jewels scattered across a wide, dark sky—David St. Clair was sure of it, though all he could see in the window glass was a distorted image of his own face. The sight disgusted him, but he found that he could not look away.

"Come to bed, David," Katherine said petulantly from behind him.

He looked down and saw that his hands had been gripping the windowsill so tightly that every last drop of blood had drained away, leaving the fingers long and white and stiff. "Goodall is dead, isn't he?"

Pausing with the belt to her robe in her hands, Katherine surveyed her husband with a strange glint in her eyes. "How would I know?"

"Answer me, damn you!" David hissed. "Is he dead?"

It took Katherine a moment to gather her thoughts, so taken aback was she by the threatening tone in her husband's voice. She found she rather liked the change; it intrigued her. "Yes, he is," she said.

"Did you kill him?"

Katherine's eyebrows came together in a frown. "No. My father did."

"You didn't try to stop him?" David spoke into the cold glass, where he could see his wife's reflection, wavering and white.

"What did you expect me to do? Knock my own father unconscious?"

David ignored the note of irritation in her voice. "Goodall found what he was looking for, so you killed him."

"He had no right to be here," Katherine pointed out.

"And *you* had no right kidnapping those two babies."

Stiffening perceptibly, she breathed, "It was Mama—"

"Liar! You made her do it and that's why she shot you. What I can't understand is what in the hell you hoped to gain." For some reason, David could not make himself turn away from the window to face his wife. He suspected that it was because he couldn't bear to look at her anymore, knowing what he now knew.

"Revenge," Katherine murmured in a voice that was dangerously soft.

"What about the attempt on Medora's life? Was that another form of your 'revenge'?"

"I don't give a damn about Medora!" his wife snapped. Suddenly she had grown tired of the game.

David drew in a long, painful breath. "No, I suppose the only person you *do* give a damn about is Phillipe Beaumont." He waited for her answer with every muscle in his body tensed and rigid, then he realized, too late, that he did not want to know.

Katherine recognized her husband's fear and smiled crookedly. "You're right," she said. "On this whole earth, as my father says, the only one I care about is Phillipe. And I *hate* him."

Now, at last, her husband turned to look into her eyes. "Love and hate are very close to one another," he murmured.

Katherine shrugged. "How can *you* judge? You don't know anything about either one."

The pain of her derision stabbed him as it had a hundred times before, yet even through the torment he realized that she had avoided answering his question. But that didn't really matter, because there was another, more important question that had been eating away at his insides for the past two months, and he knew in a moment of utter panic that he was going to ask her now. "Your father said I would never have children. Why?"

Quirking an eyebrow, his wife regarded him with mild amusement. "Been listening at doors again, my dear? You must have been saving that question up for a long time but perhaps that's because you don't really want to know the answer." She smiled and took a step toward him. "Which is exactly why I'm going to tell you." Katherine could see that he was waiting with his breath held back in his throat, and she busied herself with tying her robe awkwardly with her healthy arm just to prolong the torture. "You see, David," she said, "when I was seventeen, I ruined myself by waiting too long to abort Phillipe's baby."

The color drained from David's face and his jaw muscles tightened until the skin was stretched unnaturally across his cheekbones.

"Poor David," Katherine murmured. "Have I shocked you? You'd think you would have learned all about me by now."

With a great effort of will, David dragged his voice up from the bottom of his belly. "Why are you so evil?"

Katherine tossed her hair back over her shoulders. "Why are you so weak and stupid? If you want the truth so badly, why don't you shake it out of me? Why don't you ever demand instead of pleading? Why don't you just hit me if I sicken you so much?"

Her eyes were lit with a taunting challenge and David

saw that she really wanted him to do those things, but he couldn't. "Why did you marry me?" he rasped.

Shaking her head in disgust, Katherine told him, "Because I couldn't have Phillipe. And because I knew that of all the men who ever courted me, you were the only one who would never have the strength to turn against me."

David rotated on his heel before the nausea could rise in his throat and choke him, then he started for the door.

"Where are you going?" Katherine demanded imperiously.

"Out." He paused for a fatal instant with his hand on the knob.

"I don't think so," his wife said, "because I want you to stay."

David closed his eyes and took a deep breath. "You can't stop me anymore."

"Can't I? Let's just see." Before he could escape, she had thrown off her robe, revealing the naked flow of her skin underneath, which even the heavy bandage on her shoulder could not truly mar. With practiced ease, Katherine pressed her unclothed body against her husband, and her free hand began to trace a sensuous path across the chest hair exposed by the open collar of his shirt. "I want you with me tonight, David," she whispered huskily.

David clutched the doorknob and refused to look at his wife.

Katherine insinuated herself between her husband and the door, then she reached up to touch his face. "David," she murmured, "look at me."

He could feel her swaying before him, her hand like a burning brand on his skin, and in a single moment of weakness he opened his eyes. Katherine smiled and leaned forward until her breasts whispered against his shirt and her glorious hair fell all around her shoulders in silken waves that glistened when they caught the light.

He knew then why he had stayed so long at the window. He had been afraid to turn around and see his wife in all her glory, because she was, quite simply, too beautiful to resist. It had always been this way with him, and Katherine knew it.

He might hate her for what he had learned tonight, but he knew that in one thing at least she was wrong—love and hate were so close sometimes that they were indistinguishable. He had known *both* in the space of a single hour. He despised her, even feared her, but he could not leave her, for he despised himself even more.

"Are you coming to bed?" Katherine asked as she nibbled provocatively at his earlobe.

Though he would have given anything to have it be different, David knew that his answer would be yes—now and always.

Chapter 30

Leaning out the window as far as she could, Cassie gave the rug a vicious shake. She had to draw her head inside quickly to escape the choking cloud of dust that escaped from among the brightly woven colors. "If you ask me," she said as she waved a leathery hand in front of her face to dispel the clinging particles, "the Badlands in late summer is no place to keep a clean household. I could shake the rugs once a day and the dirt they collect would choke me every time."

When Mianne remained silent, the cook glanced back over her shoulder. "You sure you're all right?" she asked suspiciously.

The younger woman smiled and nodded. "I'm fine." With a grunt of doubt, Cassie turned back to her dirty rug, and Mianne found herself wondering what she would have done without the cook in the two weeks since Johnny's death. Cassie had also been deeply moved by the loss, and the two women had found that only constant action kept the grief from overpowering them. Together, they had begun a concerted campaign to clean the Chateau from top to bottom, and now, except when she was with the children, Mianne could always be found with a mop or a dust cloth in her hand. The mindless work had saved her sanity and she knew it.

"I'm glad the Marquise took the children again this afternoon so we could finally get to the nursery," Cassie observed. She was tired of the morbid silence. If Mianne couldn't talk, at least the sound of the cook's own voice would break the monotony.

"Yes," Mianne replied, but her attention was focused on dusting the babies' wooden crib and she did not look up.

"She sure does love those children," the cook continued, unabashed. "I guess she sort of looks upon Antoine and Kira as her own grandchildren."

Mianne paused in her furious dusting. She suspected Cassie was wrong; Medora loved the children because they were a part of Phillipe. On them she could lavish the affection she could never show the man himself. As it always did, the thought of Phillipe brought a flash of bright pain. Since her father's death, he had been there whenever she needed him and his touch had been comforting, but she sensed that now he was even more distant than he had been before. She did not understand why, but she knew she was losing him, and that extra pain of loss only made her grief for her father more intense. But she would not think about that. She had work to do.

Grasping her dust rag with new determination, she reached down to lower the side of the crib, but the smooth, cool wood refused to move. "Cassie," she said, "could you help me with this?"

The cook ambled over and tried to work the side free, but soon her brows were furrowed in frustration. "It's stuck. Here, you work at the top while I try the bottom." Although the wood rattled, it didn't really move. "There's somethin' jammed down here," the cook said finally. "Tangled in the mechanism." With her lip held between her teeth, she jiggled the bottom of the crib until the obstruction came loose in her hand. "I'll be damned," she exclaimed. "Don't that just beat all!"

Mianne looked down and her fingers clenched on the railing when she saw the heavily carved gold locket with the broken chain that lay in the center of Cassie's reddened palm.

Rubbing her chin thoughtfully, the cook asked in bewilderment, "That's Anais' necklace, ain't it? How do you s'pose it got stuck here?" But then she looked up and saw the disquieting answer in Mianne's troubled gaze. "Dear God!" Cassie cried. "You don't think—"

"Think what?" Phillipe asked, appearing suddenly in the doorway.

Mianne bit her lip and controlled an urge to reach out and hide the necklace whose presence here could only be incriminating. Her eyes, when they looked at the cook, were full of some dark plea, but Cassie either did not see it or did not choose to acknowledge it.

"We found this jammed in the bottom of the crib," she said as she rose to her feet and extended her hand to Phillipe.

When he saw what lay there, glittering in the bright September sunlight, Phillipe's jaw clenched and he murmured harshly, "So she finally made a mistake. I wonder how Anais will talk her way out of this one?" Then, without another word, he took the necklace and turned to go.

"Phillipe, please!" Mianne cried, crossing the room to place a restraining hand on his arm.

But her husband merely shook his head. "I'm sorry, Mianne," he told her, "but you can't protect her anymore. We have enough enemies *outside* our house. We can't afford to harbor another within."

Medora stood staring out the French doors of her private study, but the leaves which, in early September, had already begun to turn golden, made little impression on her tumultuous thoughts. Behind her, where the blazing sunlight did not reach, sat her daughter Anais, waiting in silence, her hands folded in bored indifference against the crisp folds of her gray linen skirt. Medora realized that she might never have met the girl before in her life, so little did she know her. What had started as a small rift between them had somehow become too wide ever to cross. The woman's fingers closed around the cold metal chain in her pocket and the view before her suddenly blurred, transforming itself into a searing memory of the Marquis' face. How could it be that this man's daughter had inherited her father's features but not even a hint of his good, giving heart?

Medora had seen this coming for a long time, she had to admit, but now that it was finally here, she could not really believe it was true. Perhaps it wasn't. Perhaps there had been some mistake after all. Rotating so that her soft red gown made an unexpected murmur in the still room, Medora said, "Tell me again, Anais, if you had anything to do with the Pendletons' abduction of the children."

"I've already said it a hundred times," the girl replied fretfully.

"Did you or didn't you?"

Anais kept her eyes focused on the window at her mother's back. "No, I didn't."

With a sigh of deep weariness, Medora took the necklace from her pocket. "Were you aware that you had lost this?" she asked.

Anais' fingers tightened their hold on each other. "Yes."

Her mother heard the tiny quaver of nervousness in her daughter's tone and she knew that her wild hopes had been mere fantasy. She had to fight back a storm of outrage before she could force herself to continue. "It was found in the babies' crib. Apparently it got caught on the edge and the chain broke," Medora said, her voice taut with suppressed fury that clamored to be released.

Anais regarded her in silence, but the twitching of a muscle in her cheek betrayed her agitation. "How did that happen?" Medora persisted.

Shrugging, her daughter replied casually, "I don't know."

"You're lying again." Medora's patience had run out. "Everyone knows you hate Kira and Antoine and that you never go near them of your own free will. You made it quite clear that you wanted nothing to do with them. So how did your necklace find its way to their bed?"

Anais bit her lip nervously. "Someone must have put it there."

"Who?" Her mother wanted to believe, but she could not quite make herself do it.

"Phillipe! He hates me. He'd do anything to hurt me."

Medora was shocked at the wave of anger that engulfed her at this absurd accusation. "I got the impression it was the other way around. That you'd do anything to hurt *him*. Even kidnap his children, perhaps?"

Rising precipitously from her chair, the girl shook her head as if to free it from a demon who would not let her rest. "Just leave me alone," she rasped. "I don't want to—"

"Not until you give me an answer. Did you help the Pendletons or didn't you?"

"Go to hell!" Anais hissed.

With fingers that had turned to stone, Medora closed one hand down on her daughter's shoulder. "Did you do it?"

"Yes!" Anais flung the word at her like a crumpled banner of triumph. "And I'm glad!"

Fingers digging deeper into Anais' flesh, her mother cried, "How *could* you?" She thought she would choke on the bewildered disbelief that had lodged itself in her throat. "The children could have been hurt or even killed. Don't you care about that?"

"No," Anais spat. "I've told you before, but you wouldn't listen. *I don't care!* Can't you understand that?"

Medora drew back at the venom in her daughter's tone and the barely healed wound in her chest began to throb. "Why do you hate me so much?" she whispered at last.

"You know why."

Shaking her head in denial, Medora struggled to make her voice remain steady. "Tell me," she demanded. "Tell me what could make you bitter enough to risk the lives of two six-week-old infants. How could you do something so hurtful to us?"

Anais folded her arms across her chest, hoping that it would disguise the ragged pounding of her heart. "You did it to us," she countered.

"What?" Medora felt that she was trying to swim in water that grew ever deeper and more violent.

"You brought us here to please yourself, and you didn't give a damn what *we* wanted."

"We came here for your father's sake."

"Now *you're* the liar. It was for your own sake, and Phillipe's and no one else's. You never loved Papa. You thought we were too stupid to realize that you came here to forget him."

Medora caught her breath and turned away. She could no longer bear to look at that lovely girl's face, twisted with hatred and the wish for revenge. How foolish Anais was to believe that her mother could ever forget Mores, here, in the house he had built for her. Every moment in this place was full of some bitterly painful memory. It had taken every shred of will she possessed to come here at all. "You're wrong," Medora breathed.

Anais smiled crookedly but her eyes were lit with the full force of the raging anger she had kept inside for so long. "No," she insisted. "You came here to make Phillipe a king over Papa's kingdom, and every day that you look at my half brother with love in your eyes, you betray my father a hundred times over. Don't you think it would have sickened him to see you defile his house with your disgusting obsession for his son?"

"Stop it!"

"I won't!" Anais shrieked. "I don't know why you didn't just marry Phillipe. Papa couldn't have been any more disappointed in you. He's dead, after all. And incest is no worse than murder."

Bewilderment turned to rage and something inside Medora snapped. She flung out blindly to strike her daughter across the face. The sound of her hand as it hit Anais' cheek seemed to shatter the last remnant of restraint that had kept them apart. The girl clenched her hands into fists and began to beat on her mother's chest.

"I hate you!" Anais screamed as she struck Medora again and again on the raw area where the gun shot had ripped open her mother's chest. "I'd kill you if I could!" she cursed wildly, unaware of what she was saying. Just now she knew only that the fury and hurt had finally come to the surface and spilled over. Her limbs and her mind would not answer her will, for the anger was controlling her now, and she cared for nothing else. "I hate you so much that I wish you had died!"

Then, suddenly, she felt her body encircled by two arms that might have been made of iron, so tightly did they hold her.

"Stop it!" Phillipe warned. "Are you utterly mad?" He spoke through teeth clenched with the force of the anger that had arisen out of his fear for Medora's safety.

"Leave me alone!" Anais shouted. "I hate you! I hate you as much as I hate her!" She struggled like a trapped animal, but Phillipe did not release her.

"Get her out of here," Medora hissed when she had caught her breath enough to speak. All at once she was overcome by rage and hurt and desperation so intense that they filled the room like a physical force. "Lock her in her bedroom until we decide what to do with her." She did not add that she feared that, in her momentary madness, she might hurt Anais more than she intended if the girl stayed.

Phillipe nodded, then dragged Anais from the room while she spat and kicked at his unprotected legs. But when she realized that the drawing room was full of the other members of the family staring at her in astonishment, some of the fire went out of her blood. Then she saw Stephen standing with one hand on each of the boys' shoulders, as if to protect them from her wrath. When her eyes met the tutor's, she realized with a rush of despair what she had done.

Although he was aware that the girl was struggling no longer, Phillipe's own anger kept his arms locked around her in an unbreakable grasp. Never, as long as he lived, would he forget the blind rage that had risen in him when he saw this girl attacking Medora, and never would he be able to forgive her for the things he had heard her say as he wrenched open the door at the sound of her wild screams. Anais had hurt Medora and somehow she would have to pay. With the anger like pulsing fire in his throat, he pushed the girl into her room and turned the key in the lock with grim finality.

In the darkness of her room, touched with only a glimmer of moonlight, Anais lay perfectly still while the shadows hovered above her, somber and vaguely threatening. Even the warmth from the pot-bellied stove in the corner could not penetrate the chill that had settled in her bones, and she shivered now and then as if the winter snow, and not the autumn leaves, covered the ground outside her window. She had been locked in her room since late afternoon and it was now deep night, but she had heard nothing from those who had the power to decide her fate. She knew that they had gone to bed long ago, and that of all the people in the house, only Mianne had paused outside her door to reassure the girl that she had not been forgotten.

Wrapping the covers more tightly around her, Anais suppressed a fresh surge of fear. What would they do to her, now that they knew how much she hated them? She closed her eyes and wished again that Stephen would come to her tonight. She had given him the key to the back door long ago, and there were times when he crept upstairs to her room when the shadows were heavy and the hush of deep sleep was upon the house. They had learned to come together silently, clinging to each other in the stillness; the touch of his hands had given her great comfort. She had come to need him so much that his absence was like a kind of hopeless exile and the nights without him cold and empty. Only Stephen understood the cravings of her soul, only he could stop the anguish. Please let him come tonight, she prayed.

Then she heard the muffled turning of the key in the lock, and she knew that Stephen had come to set her free.

He stepped into the room, as soundless as a wraith accustomed to prowling in the night, then closed the door behind him. He did not even speak her name, but came to the side of the bed as if he knew she had been expecting him. "What's the matter?" he whispered when he realized she still lay unmoving beneath the covers. "Aren't you ready?"

Anais reached out to brush his hand in a mute plea. "For what?"

"To leave here, of course."

Now she sat up abruptly. "Tonight?"

Stephen sat on the edge of the bed and took her hands in his. "Now is the time," he murmured. "They know about you and I'm afraid if you stay they may do something drastic."

Shivering, Anais moved closer to him. "I don't know—"

"Do you think they'll be satisfied with locking you in your room for a week or two? This is serious, Anais, and they know it as well as we do. I don't see that you have much choice."

The girl knew he was right but she was suddenly afraid.

"Listen to me," Stephen said, sensing her hesitation. "We've been planning to go anyway. This just forces us to do it sooner. And don't worry about the future, little one. We'll get married the minute we get away safely and I'll take care of you." He smiled into the darkness as she rested her head on his chest. He was glad this had happened, because now Anais would be his absolutely; she had already learned that she could depend on no one else. "Come on," he insisted. "We haven't much time. The longer you think it over, the more chance we have of being discovered. Are you coming with me or not?" But he already knew the answer. She was no more capable of sending him away alone than he was of leaving her.

With the image of her mother's horrified face burning across her inner sight, Anais nodded; she could not speak just then because of the growing lump in her throat.

"Good." Stephen rose, moving on silent feet to get a small suitcase from the bottom of the wardrobe. He had memorized this room in the darkness, just as he had memorized the contours of Anais' smooth, white body. "You'd better decide what to pack, and just take the things that are most necessary."

Fired by a sudden urgency which she could not explain, Anais threw the covers off her and went to rummage through her wardrobe. But when she came to the sketch book full of her own drawings, she paused to look up at Stephen. "What should I do with these?"

As he knelt beside her and shuffled through the drawings, his jaw tightened in irritation. "They're all of this place and the people who live here. You want to forget them, don't you, Anais? You want to break every tie that holds you here."

"Should I just leave them?" the girl asked regretfully.

All at once, she sensed that Stephen was smiling in the darkness. A moment later he whispered, "No. We'll burn them." Before she could protest, he had grasped the pages and crossed the room to the stove. "Block the crack at the bottom of the door so they won't see the light or smell the smoke," he instructed.

It was as if the commanding tone of his voice had hypnotized her, and Anais did as he told her without stopping to question him. But she could not help but wonder. Why was he so intent on burning the drawings? Did he want so much to destroy her past?

"You finish your packing," Stephen told her.

Again, she moved to follow his instructions without question.

Stephen heard the girl moving about behind him and a slow, dangerous smile spread from his lips to his pale blue eyes. One at a time, he inserted the end of each page into the fire, then dropped them on the floor to watch them burn. It was not long before he was mesmerized by the crackling orange flames that danced along the paper, consuming, destroying as it went. The destruction itself was so incredibly beautiful—more beautiful by far than the charcoal figures Anais had created. He thought he would never see anything more lovely than the golden-red curls of glowing heat that licked and wavered at his feet.

It had been too long, he realized. Too long since he had felt the surge of power that overcame him when he made the flames dance to his will. Yet the fire on the floor was no more than a pale reflection of the flames that lit his eyes in that instant, giving them an almost satanic gleam. The other fires had been magnificent, he told himself, but they were too far in the past. Even the last, which had nearly destroyed both the Pendleton ranch and this one.

Stephen smiled more broadly when he remembered how easily he had had them all befuddled. Never for an instant had they suspected it was him. And, oh, the excitement of working side by side with those desperate men to put out the blaze he himself had created. He had enjoyed it more than any other moment in his life. They had even been stupid enough to believe in those matches he had put in Cory Pendleton's basket. They had blamed her—poor, mad Cory who did not even know what world she lived in. They were hopeless fools, all of them. He had proved it time and again.

The last page turned to blackened ashes and Stephen became aware of Anais behind him. Only *she* was not a fool, he thought. He would take her away so that the others could not hurt her anymore.

Leaving the ashes as a smoldering monument to his achievements, he turned to put out his hand. "Are you ready?"

Anais nodded dumbly and, when his fingers closed around hers, she followed him to the door. "We'll have to go the back way to the study," he said. "I've managed to find the combination to the safe. There'll be enough money there to keep us happy for awhile."

"Are you sure we should risk it?" the girl breathed while her heart thudded hollowly in her chest.

"We have to. I haven't enough to keep you comfortable otherwise. Besides, they made the choice for us, didn't they?"

Gulping down her objections, Anais clung more tightly to his hand as he led her into the black hallway. She trusted him, after all. She had to—there was no one else.

When they had crept through the leaden silence at the back of the house and found their way to the study, Stephen carefully closed the door behind him. "Don't make any noise," he warned. "Just wait there until I have what we need. Or maybe you should leave them a little note."

He knelt before the safe and lit a tiny candle. Because she could not bear to watch him, Anais found a scrap of paper and a pen and scrawled a brief message. By now, the deepening shadows had begun to press in on her and she felt that in a moment she would not be able to force the breath through her throat anymore. Dear God, what was she doing? What had she already done? Only when Stephen looked up to smile at her did her fears dissipate a little, but even then they lurked above her, hidden in the encroaching darkness.

Then, at last, Stephen motioned for her to follow, and she dropped her note into the open safe just as he opened the door and drew her out onto the porch. It was then, when she saw the pale image of Medora's bedroom door before her, that Anais suddenly stopped. Even the pulse of her blood seemed to cease. Stephen pulled at her hand, but she could not force herself to move.

"What is it?" he whispered hoarsely.

Anais felt her stomach tie itself into a hard knot and she found that she could not breathe. "I want to say goodbye," she murmured raggedly.

"You're mad!" Stephen hissed. "Once they see you, they'd never let you go."

Anais stared at the closed door before her as if he had not spoken. Her eyes widened with a blaze of pain and she whispered desperately, "But I can't go yet. I have to say goodbye." . . .

. . . . May, 1897— "Aren't you going to say goodbye to me?" the Marquis murmured, unable to mask the hurt in his voice. With one finger, he tilted his daughter's chin upward until he could see her eyes—an exact reflection of his own.

Anais pushed her father's hand away and refused to look at him again. "No," she muttered obstinately.

"I'm going on a long trip, you know. I won't be back for quite awhile."

The pain twisted inside Anais and she turned her back on her handsome father. "I don't care," she said. Closing her eyes, she tried to pretend that she was anywhere but here with her father kneeling beside her just before he went out the door. He was leaving her again. It seemed he was always leaving. Sometimes she thought she would spend the rest of her life saying goodbye to a man who didn't even care enough to stay with his family where he belonged. And she hated him for that.

"Anais," the Marquis said softly, "I *have* to go. I've explained all this before. The government—"

"I don't care about the government!" Anais cried. "Don't you understand? I don't care about you or the government or your stupid trip—"

Mores reached out and turned his daughter to face him, then left his hands resting lightly on her shoulders. "Please, try to understand."

Anais saw the hurt in those fathomless black eyes and, for an instant, she was tempted to give in.

The Marquis sensed her hesitation and pulled her closer. "Won't you even give me a goodbye kiss?"

Anais looked away. She loved him so much it was breaking her heart, but she could not let him see. He would only laugh at her and leave her just the same. She clenched her hands into fists and stood as still and cold as polished marble.

With a sigh of profound regret, the Marquis kissed his daughter's cool cheek, murmured, "I'll miss you, little one," and stood to go.

Anais turned her back on him, refusing to watch as he disappeared through the open door; she was too caught up with the sound of her own pain in the sunlight to think of the pain she had just caused him. *And she could not know that this time he would never come home again, so she didn't even raise her head to take one last look at the man who had shaped her life, and broken it, without ever knowing that he had. . . .*

. . . . "Come back to me, Anais. We have to go now, before they wake up and find us here," Stephen said.

Anais stifled a sob in her throat. "I can't do it," she murmured wretchedly.

With a sigh of exasperation, Stephen tightened his grip on her arm. "You're afraid, is that it?"

Anais shook her head violently. "No!" she declared. "But I was just wondering—" She broke off abruptly.

"Wondering what?"

Turning away, Anais took a step forward. She did not want to tell him what she was thinking. That she was wondering what the family would say when they read her note in the morning. No doubt it would only make them hate her more. Or perhaps they didn't even think her worthy of their hatred. She knew they thought she was mad, but it wasn't true. It was just that she had lived with the gnawing pain for so long, though she had tried time and again to make it go away. Only Stephen had been able to do that, and even then, only for a moment.

But her family didn't understand that. As Stephen had said, they didn't want to. Her eyes filled with bitter tears. She had told Medora she hated her, but it was a lie. The sad thing was that Anais loved her mother too much—just as she had loved her father. But neither the Marquis or his wife had ever cared to learn that small fact. Still, if only, just once, either of them had returned her love, then everything might have been different.

"Anais!"

Stephen's impatient voice brought her back to the grim

reality of the present. "Come on," he said. "Come be my wife instead of your mother's slave."

She needed no more than that. If she were going to survive, she would have to wipe all bitter memory from her thoughts, because she knew with a weary certainty that Stephen was her only chance for happiness. "I'm coming," she whispered. Then, with one last long look at Medora's tightly closed door, Anais turned with her hand in Stephen's to follow him into the deep black shadows of night.

Chapter 31

Mianne stood frozen for a moment on the threshold of the abandoned bedroom where the telltale ashes lay strewn across the floor in some primitive pattern. Wrapping her arms protectively around her body to ward off the sudden fears for Anais that ran across her skin, the woman turned abruptly toward the head of the stairs, though she feared it was already too late.

She was certain of it when she saw that Phillipe, Medora, and William were standing around the open safe as if disbelief had turned every one of them to stone. For an instant, Mianne wondered why Johnny was not there too, but then she remembered and the pain of her double loss wrenched the words from her raw throat. "Anais is gone, isn't she?"

All three of the others turned to gape at her as if she were an apparition, but Phillipe soon recovered himself and, taking a small piece of paper from Medora's stiff fingers, he gave it to his wife. "She left us a note," he said bitterly.

To Whom It May Concern,
   Leaving home to marry Stephen St. Clair. We have taken what we need. Don't bother to look for us, because we won't be found.   Anais.

Phillipe's wife swallowed with difficulty. "What did they take?"

Now, finally, Medora forced her frozen muscles into action and turned to face Mianne. "All the money from the safe, which, admittedly, was not a great deal, and many of our important business papers."

The younger woman took a step forward. "She probably just wanted to hurt you—"

"I don't think so," Phillipe interjected. "I think she took them to sell to the Pendletons. She's worked for them before, after all."

Medora clenched her fists at her sides and wondered why it should still hurt so much when she had begun to learn the truth a long time ago.

"Maybe if we went after them now, we could catch them before any more harm is done," William suggested tentatively.

Shaking her head firmly, his wife declared, "The harm has *already* been done. Anais has betrayed this family once too often. She chose to turn against us of her own free will, and I tell you now that I will never forgive her as long as I live."

She stood unmoving in her deep-green morning gown that set off the angry glow in her eyes. Her pale, finely chiseled face might have been cut from expensive crystal, so stiff and unforgiving were the lines across her forehead and between her nose and mouth. It was as if she had just pronounced her daughter's death sentence.

William shuddered inwardly. He knew that Anais was not the only one who had betrayed the family; the knowledge of his own guilt never left him, even for a moment. And if Medora would not forgive her daughter, how could she forgive her husband, were she ever to learn the truth? It was not until that moment that he realized the magnitude of what he had done. And for what? The Pendletons had failed to keep their word—Johnny's death more than proved that—and the family was no closer to leaving the Badlands, which William had come to despise with a deep intensity.

"We'll have to go after them anyway," Phillipe insisted. "We've got to get those papers back."

"If they haven't already sold them," Medora interjected. "I'm sure they made a stop at the Pendleton ranch on their way out of town last night."

"Still," her stepson said, "I've got to try. William, will you come with me?"

Mianne bit her lip and put a restraining hand on her husband's arm. "It's no use," she told him. "They're beyond our reach."

Phillipe rotated until he could see his wife's face clearly, and his eyes met hers with a little start of remembered guilt that always struck him when he looked at her. "How do you know?"

"I just—" Mianne drew her eyebrows together as she sought an explanation for the clear and vibrant premonition that had overwhelmed her in the instant when she discovered that Anais was gone—it was the same feeling that had come to her just before her father's death. "I just know, that's all."

For a full minute Phillipe stared into his wife's eyes as if he could read the secrets there if he only looked hard and deep enough, but, as always, he was disappointed. "I have to try," he repeated.

Mianne nodded her head in understanding, then, in an effort to combat the knowledge which she did not wish to recognize, she closed her fingers tighter around Phillipe's arm. "If you do find them," she murmured, "bring her back here—alone. Please."

"I'll do what I can." Then, very gently, with the detachment of a doctor who sympathizes with his patient's pain although he does not really know the person at all, Phillipe disengaged himself from his wife's grasp, turned on his heel and started for the door. "William," he called as he paused on the threshold to give Medora a fleeting smile of reassurance, "are you coming or not?"

William did not even look at his wife as he followed the younger man into the bright liquid gold of the September sunlight.

With Antoine and Kira in their basket beside her, Mianne sat on the sofa in the drawing room watching Medora, who stared blindly out the window at the empty porch. Although she knew that the older woman had made her decision, Mianne sensed that an imperceptible veil of taut expectancy had settled over the room in the past hour. When Mianne saw that Louis and Paul had entered the room, she was instantly alert. Even Medora turned away from her window.

The older boy stood with his hand on Paul's shoulder and for the first time since Medora had been shot, the younger boy's face was flushed with color. "Paul has something to tell you," Louis announced.

At the moment, he looked older than his thirteen years, Medora mused. The two boys, dark haired and dark eyed, made a handsome pair as they stood pinned in a shaft of sunlight from the open window. Sitting up straighter, she murmured, "Go ahead, Paul."

The child licked his lips nervously, looking up at his brother for reassurance. "Are they really gone?" he managed to ask finally.

"Yes."

Still Paul hesitated. "They won't be back?"

His mother sucked in her breath, then shook her head firmly. "No."

Mianne wanted to protest at this absolute rejection of Anais and her secret unhappiness but she understood Medora's pain too well, so she remained silent, though her eyes betrayed her inner doubts.

"You see," Louis said, "no one can hurt you now."

"Will we ever see Anais again?" the younger boy persisted with a lip that trembled slightly.

"Your sister chose to leave us," Medora said, "and I don't think—"

Before she finished her thought, Paul burst into a violent storm of tears. In an instant, Medora had left her seat to draw the shuddering child into her arms. She felt the full force of his anguish, but she could not tell if it came from relief or despair. When the wrenching sobs had begun to subside, she drew back a little and brushed the hair away from his forehead. Only then did she realize how great a burden the boy had been laboring under, and her voice, when she finally spoke, was unusually gentle. "You wanted to tell me who sent you to give me that message about Mianne's illness, didn't you, Paul?"

Paul nodded and made an effort to swallow his tears, but even now he seemed to be unable to escape the fear that had held him in its grip for so long; he could not force the words out of his mouth.

Medora glanced up at Louis, then she took Paul's shoulders in her hands. "It was Anais, wasn't it?"

Paul gaped at her in bewilderment. "No!"

"Then who?"

"Stephen St. Clair," Louis said before his brother could open his mouth. "Anais would never do something like that to you."

Now it was Medora's turn to stare and her eyes met Mianne's for a long, startled moment. It was the single answer they had never expected. "Stephen?" they both asked together. "Why?"

With the aid of a long breath, Paul found his voice at last. "I heard them talking once," he explained haltingly, "and Anais was telling him how—" He paused and looked to Louis for reassurance. When his brother nodded, the child continued. "She said you had hurt her, Mama, and that you were always watching for her to make a mistake. And Mr. St. Clair told her he would make sure that you never hurt her again."

In the taut, painful silence that followed, Paul was certain that his mother was blaming him for all that had happened. He was inexpressibly relieved when Louis said suddenly, "Paul wanted to tell you the truth right away, but Mr. St. Clair threatened him. He reminded Paul every day of the terrible things that would happen to him if he told what he knew. Can't you understand that he was too afraid to speak up?"

Medora choked back the agony of the knowledge that, although her own daughter had not tried to kill her, the bullet had nevertheless come from the heart of Anais' bitter anger. With her eyes closed tight against the image of the girl's lovely face, she pulled Paul back into her arms. "I understand," she told him softly. "It's all in the past now and we'll forget it. All right?"

Paul looked up at her in disbelief, but when he saw that she was sincere, he threw his arms around her neck and clung to her as if he had stood in the path of a deadly shadow and his mother had just turned on a long-awaited light. Above his head, Medora met Mianne's probing gaze. "Stephen must be mad, don't you think?"

"Yes, I do." The younger woman seemed to look beyond Medora to some private vision of her own, then she whispered raggedly, "Poor Anais."

Medora remained silent. There was no room left in her heart for pity anymore—only the horror was left.

While the clouds crept in to cover the sun with gray and white billows of spun glass, Phillipe shifted uncomfortably in his stiff, worn saddle. For two days he had ridden like this, harassed by the whims of the September sky, which was wide and blinding blue one moment and dark, heavy, gray the next. He had found that he preferred the clouds, which reflected his mood better than the azure sky, untouched by even a shadow of white.

It seemed he had begun this long and hopeless search weeks ago, and he was certain that, between them, he and William had covered every inch of ground from the Pendleton ranch to the town of Bismarck. But they had found nothing—not even a trace of the lovers who had vanished as if touched by the protective hand of some ancient magician. Wherever Anais and Stephen had chosen to run, they had been smarter than their pursuers and slowly, slowly, Phillipe had begun to realize that Mianne's prediction was true the lovers had disappeared entirely.

So, at last, Phillipe and William had turned toward home. They had ridden for some time in silence, as if the burden of defeat hung so heavily upon them that they could not find even idle words to pass between them. Phillipe was especially oppressed with the knowledge that he had failed once again. He had failed Medora and particularly Mianne, who alone of all those at the Chateau wanted to see Anais again for her own sake and not for the sake of the papers she carried. The business was continuing to do well, he thought, despite the inexplicable mishaps that had begun to plague the plant and the ice houses along the railroad route, but it seemed that everything else was falling apart. It was not only Anais' betrayal, or the kidnapping of the children, or even Johnny's death which haunted Phillipe just now, but the feeling that, once again, he was being propelled against his will into the center of a violent whirlpool that was likely to suck him into its murky depths. He felt that somewhere in the past few weeks he had lost his freedom of will. Now he was hurtling toward the unknown and he could not stop himself.

More weary than he remembered being in all his young

life, Phillipe dismounted when he and William reached the Chateau. Then, tying their horses to the porch railing, the two men went inside to find Medora.

She was bending over her desk with a pen held firmly in her hand, and Phillipe wondered if he had ever seen her in any other position since the day they had come here, but his thoughts were interrupted when Medora looked up, her eyes full of the question she could not bring her lips to ask. Phillipe shook his head, and his stepmother was silent for a moment. She blinked once— as if digesting Phillipe's response—twice—as if to file the information somewhere in the very darkest recesses of her mind—then she said firmly, "It's over now and we won't speak of Anais again."

Although he knew how much her daughter had hurt her, Phillipe was surprised by Medora's wooden expression and her complete dismissal of a girl who had been so much a part of her life until two days ago. But he knew without being told that she would not relent. Probably Anais herself would never ask it. He knew also that he still had to tell Mianne that the girl was lost to her forever, and though it would not be a pleasant task, he felt it would be best to do it now and have it done. "Where is Mianne?" he asked.

"One of the mares was having trouble foaling," Medora explained, changing the subject as easily as if her daughter's name had never been mentioned. "Mianne told me that Johnny used to help with those things. Now that he's gone, she wanted to do it herself. She should know how. She watched her father often enough."

"Thank you." All at once Phillipe felt as if he were moving through a nightmare and the people around him were no more than figments of his fevered imagination. The stillness was oddly fragile as he turned to leave the room, like the silence just before waking from a dream, and he wondered if he could not free himself from the horror simply by snapping his fingers. But somehow he could not make himself do it, and he moved instead toward the stairs. He would change from the clothes he had worn for two days, then go in search of his wife—the stranger, the focus of his curious nightmare, even though she was out of his sight.

Phillipe made his way to their bedroom and stepped into the cool, welcoming shadows that fell across the floor and touched the neatly made bed with fleeting fingers. Discarding his clothes, he pulled on a clean shirt and pants as quickly as he could. But as he started to turn away from the bed, he saw a piece of folded parchment lying half-hidden beneath Mianne's pillow, and his curiosity to know what she treasured like this was suddenly more intense than his own agitation. With one hand he reached up to brush the light brown hair back from his forehead; with the other he picked up the parchment and slowly unfolded it.

Even when it lay spread before him, it was a moment before Phillipe realized that what he had discovered was a drawing of Mianne by the river. He knew at once that Anais had done it, and he could almost see his wife staring at it in her grief, just as she had at Johnny's fiddle—in a flash of unusual perception he understood that it was the only link between Mianne and the girl who had left her behind. The drawing was very well done; it caught the mystery that was Mianne with great sensitivity. The woman stood in her bare feet on the riverbank in her beaded buckskin dress, gazing at the sun as if revelling in the feel of the warmth on her face.

Phillipe's heart turned over in his chest when he realized that he had not seen that look of joy on Mianne's face since that single brief instant on the day of their wedding. It was only then that he recognized at last that he had hurt her more than even he had known—he had broken the last remnant of the precious spirit that had once drawn him to her. He could never repay her for the loss.

Phillipe refolded the drawing and put it back where he had found it. Then, with a feeling of despair deeper than any he had known before, he went to find Mianne. She was in the barn, just as Medora had said, and Phillipe paused in the doorway, out of her sight, to stare at his wife in amazement. She wore an old, ragged skirt and a shirt that must have once been Johnny's. Her hair, which was always tightly braided, even when she went to bed at night, had begun to come loose. One fraying braid hung over her shoulder where it dragged now and then in the mud-covered floor on which she crouched. Her skirt was stained with mud and clinging wisps of straw and her hands were coated with bright red blood.

Yet Phillipe thought he had never seen a woman more graceful than Mianne when she leaned over the horse that struggled beneath her hands and began to speak to the animal in a soft, lilting voice. Phillipe could not understand the words, which were in Sioux, but he sensed that they flowed over the horse like a soothing balm and, at last, with its newborn colt beside it, the animal lay still.

In that moment, when Mianne's quiet song filled the stable and echoed rhythmically against the sky through the narrow window, the world stopped still for Phillipe, as if some ambitious artist had recognized the worth of that moment and frozen it in time in order to save it from destruction. Then, when the magic had seeped away, Phillipe turned and stumbled from the barn, gasping silently in an attempt to right his world, which had somehow turned upside down in less than an instant. He had never seen anything like it before and he knew instinctively that he never would again. It was toward this day, this hour, this minute that he had been moving all his life, but he had never known it until now.

He had to get away, he told himself, to think about what had just happened. It was too much to accept all at once.

When he found himself stumbling blindly toward the study, he realized what he must do.

"Medora," he said from the doorway, "I'm going away for a few days."

Both William and his wife looked up from their work to stare at him in surprise. "I've told you, it's over," Medora reminded her stepson. "There's no need to look for Anais anymore." She did not like the strange light in Phillipe's eyes and he was oddly pale and shaken—almost as if he had been touched with a moment of madness.

Phillipe smiled to himself at Medora's objection. She had given him just the excuse he needed to get away. "I don't want to lose those papers," he declared obstinately. "It's too great a risk right now. And I don't need to tell you that if they fall into the wrong hands "

"Which they probably have already," his stepmother interrupted.

"It doesn't matter," Phillipe told her. "I have to know what happened to them, one way or another."

Medora saw that he would not change his mind and, reluctantly, she bid him do as he wished. But when he had gone, she wondered if the man who had just stood before her was the same man she had come to know so well in the past two years. There had been something different about him—some minute change that had escaped her probing eyes, although she sensed that it was there. Her heart contracted painfully at the thought that she might be losing Phillipe, too.

So intent was she on watching the fading dust from the heels of Phillipe's horse that she was not even aware of her husband, who stared at her with all the secrets of his troubled heart in his light brown eyes. For he had read her thoughts as if she had painted them across the endless blue sky, and he knew now that the growing pain of his knowledge—and his constant, unfulfilled hunger—might easily destroy them both.

Chapter 32

Mianne bent over the crib, singing softly to the two children who had only just closed their eyes as the sound of their mother's voice soothed them toward sleep. She had come to the babies' room long after the night silence had settled over the house, not only because she had wanted to see Antoine and Kira and assure herself they were real, but also because she was restless and sleep had refused to come to her. It had been four nights since her husband had slept beside her and she did not even know where he had gone. She sensed that he was doing more than searching for Anais, but she cared not even guess what his purpose might be.

Turning her attention back to the faces of the children, more vulnerable in sleep than they had been while awake, Mianne watched the play of soft lamplight across their cheeks and her heart tightened with a rush of love that was undeniably tainted with fear. Then she heard the door open and the voice she had thought she might never hear again whispered, "Mianne?"

She looked up at Phillipe, who had appeared as suddenly as he had left, and for a moment she could not read the expression in his eyes.

Her husband did not even greet her after five days apart,

or tell her where he had been; he merely said in a stiff voice, "I want to talk to you."

In that instant, she saw the inner turbulence he could not quite hide and she knew. Her heart paused in its normal rhythm and with a last look at the sleeping children, she left the crib and murmured, "In our room."

Phillipe nodded and led the way down the hall to the open door of their bedroom. As he turned up the lamp and looked around the room with the eyes of a stranger, he did not even have to speak a word; she knew what he was going to say.

Mianne went to stand before the window and waited, staring blindly out into the night, but when the silence stretched between them like many brittle strands of woven glass, she turned to face Phillipe. In one brief glance, she recognized the battle that was raging inside him and she saw that she would have to begin for him. "You've made a decision," she said softly.

Phillipe seemed determined to look everywhere but into the heart of her eyes, and even after she spoke, it was a long moment before her husband answered, "Yes."

"Tell me." Mianne was amazed that her voice was steady when inside her world was spinning into the hungry center of a dark whirlpool.

At last Phillipe found his voice. "I want you to divorce me."

So she had been right. As the cold knowledge of reality burned across her inner sight, a deadly calm descended on her and she knew that, more important than anything else, she must not for an instant let him see what his cool announcement had done to her. "I know," Mianne said. "You've finally realized that you can't live without Medora, and I suppose you're too honorable a man to keep your wife and your mistress in the same house."

Phillipe was bewildered by his wife's explanation, and only then did he recognize that in all the wonder, pain, and heartbreak of the past few days, not once had he thought of Medora. Somehow she had become a shadow from his past and he knew the reason why. "You're wrong, Mianne," he told her, and he wondered how it was that he could speak at all.

"Then maybe you've decided you want to marry Katherine Pendleton after all."

Shaking his head, Phillipe swallowed deeply. This was not what he had planned at all. "No," he said, "it's not Katherine."

"But something must have changed," Mianne persisted, "to make you choose to end the marriage. What is different between us now?" She allowed a trace of desolation to creep into her tone, but Phillipe had turned away from her and she knew he had not noticed.

Her husband closed his eyes and took a deep breath. He had hoped he would not have to tell her the truth but he sensed that she would be satisfied with nothing less. "The difference," he said softly, "is that I have fallen in love with you."

Mianne recoiled as if he had suddenly wrenched the solid floor from beneath her feet. "If you love me," she murmured in a voice whose cool placidity was a lie, "then why must you let me go?" Her heart, her thoughts, the pulse of her blood were an agony more intense than any she had felt before, and she did not know why she stood and faced him. Why did she not run as far and as fast as she could go so that she need never again see the pain of regret in her husband's deep blue eyes?

Phillipe stood perfectly still, perplexed. He was not surprised that Mianne did not believe in his love for her; how could she, when all he had ever done was hurt her over and over again? But he did not understand why she did not thank him for setting her free. He had thought she would welcome the release from the living hell he had created all around her. And though he struggled to shroud his own pain in his concern for her, he found that the words would not come; he could not tell her about the tortured battle he had endured in order to reach this final decision.

"You tried once to make me go," Mianne reminded him as she wound her fingers together to hide their shaking. "What makes you think I'll let it happen now?"

For the first time her husband met her eyes and the shock of that meeting set her thoughts whirling. Even in the haze of her personal anguish, she could not deny the storm that raged in those twin circles of turbulent blue.

"Because," Phillipe murmured, "now you know."

"Know what?"

"That I love you, and that I can't bear to watch while the pain I caused destroys you. I may be a fool, but I'm not altogether blind. I've seen the shadows that cloud your eyes whenever you look at me. I've seen you grow more distant and more silent as the months go by." The words were wrenched from him as if from the heart of a deep well where he had kept them hidden for too long.

Mianne shook her head. "You don't know what I feel." She did not even know what she was saying anymore; she only knew she could not give in—not this time.

"No," her husband agreed, "I don't. I've watched the outward signs and though I've tried many times, I never could see inside you or really even begin to understand you. Maybe I was afraid to see the depth of the torment our marriage has caused you."

Only then did Mianne reach out to touch his shoulder and her eyes probed his, searching for the truth—or the lie he did not have the heart to express. But what she saw there was an exact reflection of her own devastating weakness, and with a flame that burned down the length of her body, she realized that he had told her the truth. In the instant of relief, a wash of anger doused the flame—anger for all the days and nights she had suffered in ignorance, for the agony of the last few minutes and, most of all, for the fact that he was willing to give her up. "You're *still* afraid," she cried. "You don't *want* to see inside me. Instead, you'll turn me away so you won't have to face the truth, ever!"

Phillipe took a step backward, as if he could not stand the warmth of her hand on his shoulder, but he knew Mianne was right, in a way. He realized now why he had loved Medora as he had; she had always been a light in the distance, untarnished and unattainable. He had chosen to love her because he had known, somewhere in the center of his heart, that he could never do more than worship her from afar. But the bitter irony was that now Mianne was the one who was unattainable. He could not close the gap between them, because he saw in her eyes that he had already hurt her too deeply. "I'm sorry," he told her. "But I can't keep up the facade any longer. I simply can't bear to watch you growing sadder and more desperate every day we're together."

Mianne had turned her back to him and when she did not answer, he took her shoulders in his hands and turned her to face him. When he saw that her eyes were full of tears, he thought the floor would give way beneath him. "Dear God," he whispered, "what have I done to you?"

Some slender strand which had kept her sane snapped, and she clenched her hands into fists and pounded futilely on Phillipe's chest. "Why are you so blind? So insufferably certain of your own rightness?"

Phillipe captured the flailing hands in his and whispered, "I know I've failed you—"

"You know nothing!" his wife rasped as she pulled free of his warm, binding grasp. "Nothing at all!" Then she whirled away from him and ran while Phillipe stood in stunned silence, watching until the sound of her retreating feet was no more than a distant memory.

* * *

Beyond the cold, thick glass of the window, the midnight world gleamed with soft moonlight and the radiance of the stars. But to Medora, with her forehead pressed against the glass, the light could not even begin to ease the stifling blackness inside her. She had seen Phillipe for a moment when he came in earlier tonight, and that moment had been enough for her to recognize the telling look in his eyes. But, unlike Mianne, Medora had interpreted it correctly. Phillipe had finally made his choice, just as she had always known he would since the day she had told him to make Mianne his wife. But having known for so long did not make the pain any less now.

This was what she had wanted, she reminded herself. Now, at last, Phillipe had a chance to be truly happy, perhaps for the first time in his life. And all she could do was open the palm in which she had held him fast for so long and finally set him free. But she knew that, in reality, even that was beyond her power—Phillipe had already gone. And he was not the only one. Anais was lost to her, too. When, she wondered, would God see fit to stop taking from her all the people she loved the most? It had happened so often that now she felt that every last thing of value was slipping from her grasp, like the brightly colored beads on a broken chain, and there was nothing she could do to stop it.

Behind Medora, William lay unmoving and watched his wife standing before the window, her long, red hair falling loose across her shoulders, her petite body in its simple white nightgown bathed in the soft moonlight. Despite the fragile beauty of her presence, he sensed that Medora was suffering. Van Driesche thought he knew why, and the knowledge held him frozen with the covers wrapped like a protective shield around him. She had stood so still for so long—a stiff stone carving that would neither bend nor break. But then she reached up to touch the glass beside her cheek and William flinched as though she had cried out. He wanted to comfort her so much, but he knew he dared not try. He no longer had the right to stand beside her, let alone touch her.

But when Medora shivered at a sudden chill, William knew he had to go to her. Pushing the quilt away, he swung his feet over the side of the bed and threw his robe across his shoulders. Then he crossed the floor on silent feet until he could feel the cold that radiated from the window and hear the regular rise and fall of his wife's breathing.

Medora half-turned to look at him. "William!" she said in surprise as if she had forgotten him.

Her husband did not turn away, for it had always been this way between them and he knew it always would be. But Medora surprised him when she took his hands and, holding them tightly in her own, murmured, "I'm glad you're here."

He could not mistake the sincerity in her tone nor the hint of a deep, consuming need that flickered at the back of her eyes.

"Hold me!" she whispered urgently and, without thinking, William closed his arms around her.

Only when her hands had locked together behind his back and her head was resting on his chest did he feel the dampness of her cheek and realize that she was weeping. His arms tightened convulsively, as if he would draw her into himself, as if he wanted nothing more on this earth than to make her pain his own. He had not seen her weep since six months after the Marquis' death; he had honestly come to believe that tears were beyond her. He had wanted to know she was human, begged to know it, but the knowledge of her weakness paralyzed him, and he could do no more than hold her while she wept her sorrow out onto his chest.

"Maybe you were right," she said at last, raising her head a little so she could see her husband's face. "Maybe we should never have come here."

He had wanted her to say it, had waited what seemed like a lifetime for her to realize her mistake, but suddenly the victory seemed hollow. With a strength of will he had not known he possessed, William shook his head. "Whatever has happened here was meant to happen and you know as well as I do that you could not have stayed away. You *had* to come to the Badlands, Medora. We all did."

His wife looked up at him in gratitude. "Thank you," she murmured. She had heard only his effort at reassurance and not the note of desperation in his tone. "Let's go back to bed," she added, shivering. "The night's too cold."

Together they turned away from the window, still luminous with moonlight, and made their way back to the bed with the red velvet canopy that dominated the room. And when they lay silent beneath the heavy covers, William, disturbed by the unnatural hush of night, reached out to brush a finger across his wife's cheek. It was still wet with her falling tears, but before he could think of a word that would offer her comfort, Medora's arms came up around him.

"Hold me, William," she said. "I need you tonight."

Her fingers wound themselves in his hair as he drew her tight against him and he realized she was clinging to him as if to keep the ugliness of the rest of the world at bay. This, too, was something he had always wanted, but not now, not like this, knowing what he had done to the woman whose arms sought him as a blind man seeks the sunlight. But when Medora swept the covers from between them and stretched her body full-length against his, he knew he could not pull away.

He could feel her trembling in every nerve and pore, and when she cried out to him, he felt his body begin to answer her plea. With hands that quivered with the sudden need that drove him, he tilted her chin upward and his searching mouth met hers. The impact of that kiss rocked through him with the force of a violent shifting of the earth, and he pulled her nearer and nearer still, until only the thin fabric of her gown came between them.

Medora's hands moved up and down his back and her fingers seemed to burn the skin from his body. Never before had she clung to him like this, pleading with every movement of her hands for him to take her. William's senses swirled and eddied, blended and parted as an answering passion raced through his blood. She needed him, she wanted him, and the swell of her breasts, her belly, her thighs, were an invitation he could not resist. He turned at last and braced himself above her, and when he entered her, slowly, gently, she moaned his name. The emotions that swept through his body in that instant were a joy beyond words and an agony beyond description. Then all the brooding frustration of his years of hunger exploded within him and his world shattered into a blind confusion of rainbow fragments that he knew would never come again.

"Hold me," Medora whispered again when at last they lay still and the night had settled back into darkness.

William buried his hands in her luxuriant hair and pressed himself against her. He could not have let go in that instant even if he had wanted to. He held her in silence, for what seemed like hours, until the tears had dried on her cheeks and the tremors in her body had subsided. He knew that what had just happened between them had been the single moment for which he had waited all his life, but the knowledge of his betrayal had somehow made it into a mockery.

"William?" Medora murmured. "Do you know, I could never have let another man see me like this. But I'm glad you were with me, because you're not like other men." She had not realized until tonight how true that was, nor how much she had come to depend on her husband's steadying presence.

William closed his eyes so he would not have to see the blind trust in her gaze. This was Medora, who had always seen so much, who had always known the truth, even when others could not recognize it, and her faith in him was like a burning brand that turned his insides to hot, red ashes.

Oblivious to his silence, she touched his cheek gently and said, "Thank God I have you."

But William knew that she did not have him. She had lost him long ago, in the instant when he had lost sight of himself, denied his integrity and succumbed to his frustration. William Van Driesche had died that day as surely as if he had slit his own throat, and there was no way on this earth to bring him back.

The sputtering light from the single candle pierced the deep shadows around Mianne and sent them scattering to the dark edges of the hallway. She held the candle high and moved silently through the house, seeking Phillipe. She had had two hours alone to think about her husband's disturbing discovery, and she knew now why she had run from him, though he had said twice that he loved her. She had finally realized that, like him, she was afraid. She had turned him away just as she had accused him of turning *her* away—because her heart was too vulnerable and she did not want him to know he had the power to break it. But she also knew now that the fear of someday losing her husband would be easier to bear than the knowledge that she had never had him at all.

So she had come looking for him, though she did not know what she would say when they stood face-to-face at last. Her pulse began to throb rhythmically in her throat when she saw that he sat in the wing-backed chair in the study, the flickering lamplight above him and his head resting in his hands. Everything was just as it had been on the night of their wedding, except that this time the half-empty glass of liquor at his elbow was whiskey instead of brandy. Odd, she thought, that they should have to live it twice—then, as now, he had wanted to leave her and she had known that she must somehow make him stay. The memory closed around her heart as if bound by an invisible thread that had been pulled too tight, and she recognized that even then she had loved him.

Mianne restrained herself from running her hand through his brown hair, touched by the wavering fingers of lamplight, and went to kneel before her husband, just as she had once before. When he did not look up, she put one hand on his knee and murmured, "Forgive me. You did not deserve my anger."

Phillipe wanted to pull away from the warm touch of her hand, but he knew she would not understand. She could not know that he desired her so much that his head was reeling at her nearness, the rise and fall of her breasts and the clean scent of her hair. Yet he must not touch her. If he did they would both be lost. "You had the right," he told her wearily.

Aware, all at once, of the torture he had endured, Mianne reached out to touch the strong line of his cheek, which he had turned away from her. "No," she said simply.

He was forced to look at her then—at her beautifully chiseled nose and cheekbones, softly parted lips, and sleek black hair—but he would not meet her eyes. He knew too well what he would find there. Even so, he was deeply struck by her loveliness, which only seemed to have grown more intense in the last year. This woman, this stranger, had become more precious to him than anything else in his life, and Phillipe found that he had to look away. If he continued to watch the lamplight play across her warm, brown skin, he would never have the strength to let her go.

But in the moment before he turned away, Mianne read

his thoughts in his eyes and her heart contracted with a flash of joy unlike any she had ever felt before. "You're not the only one who ever made a mistake, Phillipe," she said.

"What wrong have *you* ever done?" he groaned.

"I did not tell you the truth."

Curious about the vibrancy in her voice, Phillipe looked at her once more. "What truth?" he asked. He did not understand why hope flamed bright and shimmering in his chest.

Mianne took a deep breath. It would not be easy to destroy the barrier she had hidden behind all her life. By letting her husband see inside her, she would rend to shreds her last surviving protection of the fragile spirit that had dwelt for so long behind a silken veil. But for this man alone of all the man who peopled the earth, the risk would be worth it. Only now did she see that that single veil had kept not only the pain away, but also the joy.

At long last, she opened her eyes and looked directly into Phillipe's, and, for the first time since she was five years old, she opened her mind, her heart to another. Even Phillipe, blind and passionate with guilt though he was, could not fail to see the depth of emotions that swirled in those deep brown eyes, and he held his breath while the wave of recognition washed over him. She loved him after all. And only he, of all who had ever known her, realized what it had cost Mianne to let him see the truth. He opened his mouth to tell her how much she had just given him, but the words caught in his throat and he said only, "I—"

"Love you," Mianne finished for him and they smiled. She had thought she would never say those words to another person, but she was surprised at how easy it had been.

"Come," Phillipe said, closing his hand over hers.

"Where?"

Her husband leaned forward and whispered against her lips, "To walk by the river in the last of the moonlight."

Mianne followed him out into the night and they walked, wandering with the river beside them through the myriad songs of the waning darkness. Hand in hand they wandered together like children who had never before had the chance to be young. They had grown up too fast, but the night and the song of the water and the fading magic of the moonlight brought their childhoods back and they stopped, leaning body to body, in the place where he had first made love to her so very long ago.

Mianne wound her hands into his hair as his lips found hers and the press of his body was warm and taut against hers. For the first time, she felt the power of the touch of his hand on her skin, and she knew that she had been thirsty for many years and that Phillipe had finally brought her the clear bright water she craved. His lips trailed a path from her ear to her throat to the tingling skin above her gown and then, abruptly, he backed away.

"Look," he murmured, pointing to the orange flicker of sky that stained the grayness with vibrant color. "It's almost morning. I want to wait till dawn, so I can see you. Every part of you."

Mianne smiled up at him and her last fear vanished into the heart of the laughing river. She knew then that the last wall between them had finally fallen away, to be crushed beneath their feet on the red riverbank.

Chapter 33

William had lain awake for hours, staring at nothing, while Medora slept uneasily beside him. He had just seen the first glimmer of dawn through the window when his wife turned over, reached out to touch his hand and murmured his name. Van Driesche closed his eyes against the pain that pierced his heart in that moment. Even half-asleep, Medora knew he was there. It was *his* name she had called and no other. The knowledge was an agony that tore him apart, and the guilt which had been eating him alive for the past month finally reached every inch of his protesting body. She lay there with her hand in his, believing herself safe and secure, unaware that in reality she was alone, lost, betrayed.

When Medora had finally slipped back into deep slumber, William bent to kiss her forehead and he thought the lump in his throat might easily swell until the breath was stopped there forever. He knew now what he must do. He was not certain when the idea had come to him; he only knew that it had worked its way into his thoughts with grim determination and that, slowly but surely, he had come to see that there was nothing else to be done.

Moving carefully so that Medora would not awaken, he slid his hand from beneath hers and rose from the bed.

Let her continue to sleep deeply, he prayed. Don't let her awaken before I've finished my task. Then he found his clothes from the night before and carried them with him into the study. He paused in the doorway, just to look at her, and the disordered strands of her red hair seemed to him to be the most beautiful sight he had ever seen. She was a wonderful woman—a treasure more precious than any man deserved. With eyes as dry as the windswept cliffs all around him, William pulled the door closed and stood for a moment, unable to move, the knob smooth and cold in his hand.

But then he forced himself to turn to the tumbled pile of his clothes and he began to dress with infinite care, from the hat on his head to his leather boots, as if this were every other day. But it wasn't, he thought. Nothing would ever be the same for him since the moment when Medora had turned to him with tears on her cheeks and whispered, "I need you."

When he was ready, Van Driesche went over to the desk and lit the tiny lamp that sat there. Then he pulled the chair forward, found a piece of paper and a pen, and bent his head over the letter which would be the most difficult he had ever written. While the shadows moved across his face, emphasizing the dark hollows in his cheeks and the deeply chiseled lines in his forehead, William struggled over words which he knew would never be adequate to explain what he must do. But he also knew he had to try.

He had covered several sheets, discarding them one at a time, before he was satisfied. The last one he folded carefully and put it into an envelope on which he scrawled Medora's name. Then he set it gingerly in the center of the wavering pool of lamplight. The six black letters swam before his eyes and he looked back longingly at his wife's bedroom door, but he did not rise and go to her. Her name, in his own handwriting, was all that was left him now;

one more look at her sleeping face might just destroy the last fragments of his resolve.

William left the letter beside the burning lamp and went to open the French doors that led onto the porch. Then, with the cold morning air bringing the false color to his hollow cheeks, he began to walk toward the river. The pale pink haze of dawn lay over the world like a softly woven veil that muted everything, gently curving the sharp edges. Glancing up at the distant cliffs, Van Driesche was surprised at how beautiful they were in this soft light. The reds and browns and oranges had run together and the carved stone had taken on a magical intricacy that made him pause in wonder.

Only then did William realize that in spite of all that had happened here, he had come to love the Badlands. Slowly, unconsciously, the affection had crept into his blood and he had not even noticed. Not until now, when it was already too late. It seemed that his whole life had been cursed with the same blind fate. He had fallen in love too late, married Medora too late, realized she needed him too late, and made long and lingering love to her—far too late. It seemed that fate had ordained from his birth that he would follow in the footsteps of other men whose strength and shining merit could only eclipse his dull, steady character.

He had tried, in final desperation, to dissipate the haunting shadows of Mores and Phillipe by saving Medora from destruction at the hands of the Pendletons, but, instead, he himself had nearly destroyed her, just as he had destroyed himself. When he came to the soothing whisper of the river that passed undisturbed at his feet, William looked back to see if he was far enough away from the house. He did not want Medora to hear. That was one horror she did not deserve. Then, with the breath held prisoner in his raw throat, William reached into his pocket and took out the small revolver he had put there as he dressed. For the first time in his life, he knew he had made the right decision. His heart raced for an instant with a brief rush of joy that at last he could give her something she would value as he valued her—her precious freedom. But as he raised the revolver to his chest, just over his heart, the blood slowed in his veins and his hand began to shake.

"Stop it," he hissed. "For once in your life, do exactly what you believe in." Then, because he hated the world he had made for himself and he knew that Medora would hate the man he had come to be, if she only knew, he pulled the trigger once and released them both from their agony.

The leaves had begun to turn to yellow and red and orange, but the sun itself was as bright and golden as it had been in early spring. Medora stood on the porch and let the warmth seep into her chilled skin. With the regal, striped cliffs in the distance and the rush of the river below, she could almost make herself believe that life was worthwhile after all. But she wished William would come back from what she assumed was one of his usual early morning walks. She had been surprised to awaken and find him gone, but she had not gone after him, for she had learned in the last few months that her husband needed a great deal of time to think. He was always considered and careful in his actions; it was one of the things she admired most about him.

But for some reason, her thoughts were unsettled this morning and she waited anxiously for William to appear. She had to talk to him. There were things that must be done. Medora saw a movement on the hill below and she was just going down to greet her husband when she realized that it was Phillipe and Mianne who were emerging from the confusion of cottonwood leaves by the river. The older woman tried to smile, but when she saw the expression on Phillipe's face, she froze with her hand held out before her.

The young man was pale, his skin had a grayish cast that she had never seen before, and his eyes were a turbulent blue. Beside him, his wife was stiff and silent, obviously deeply shaken. "What is it?" Medora demanded when they reached the end of the porch.

Phillipe stared at her as if he had never seen her before, then recognition turned his blue eyes ashen gray. He swallowed several times before he could make a sound and then, finally, he rasped the single word, "William—"

Clutching the railing with cold fingers, Medora asked thickly, "Is he hurt?"

When she saw that Phillipe was struggling for words, Mianne moved closer to him and murmured, "You can only tell her the truth."

He nodded blindly and turned back to Medora. "William—shot himself. He's dead."

In the stunned stillness that followed, only the droning of a tiny bee was audible—even the river had ceased its song—while the memory of the night before rose in Medora's mind and called Phillipe a liar. It could not be true. Not after what they had shared. "Why?" she breathed raggedly.

"We don't know," Mianne said gently. "We just—found him."

Medora stood up straighter and demanded, "Where is he? I want to see for myself."

"You don't have to do that," Phillipe objected.

With a gaze as steady and bright as emeralds, Medora looked her stepson in the eye. "Yes, I do."

"Go with her," Mianne said to Phillipe as the older woman moved past them. "She'll need you there."

Phillipe reached out to touch her cheek so lightly that his fingers might have been no more than a breath of air, then he turned to follow Medora. They walked together without speaking but he could feel the tension building inside her with every step they took. He wondered how long it would be before her icy astonishment melted into burning grief. It was not fair, he thought. She had already lost so much.

When they reached the edge of the trees, Phillipe took his stepmother's arm but she shook him away as she stepped under the golden canopy to the place where her husband had chosen to die. William lay sprawled on his back with one hand floating in the water and Medora knew in the instant she first saw him that he was quite dead. The blood lay all around him; it had spread from the gaping hole in his chest to the marshy grass and even into the river itself, though the moving water had long ago swept that crimson evidence away. But it was the look on his face which held her transfixed while the moisture seeped into the hem of her gown. His lips were curved in a half-smile, the lines of his face relaxed, almost as if his last emotion had been profound relief that he had finally escaped. Escaped from what? Medora wondered. Had he hated her so much?

Phillipe came up behind her to put one arm around her shoulders. "We should go," he said.

"But the body—" She heard her voice, steady and strong, but somehow she could not believe it was her own.

"I'll come back for it," her stepson assured her.

As they turned away, it occurred to Medora that this man was not really William at all, but a stranger whose pain she would never understand. The walk back to the Chateau seemed to last an eternity, but when they stood once more on the porch outside the study, she rotated on her heel until she could look Phillipe in the eyes. "Why?" she repeated. "I just don't understand."

"Perhaps this will explain." Mianne came to stand beside them, carrying a letter in her hand. "I found it on the desk. I think perhaps he meant you to find it before—"

She could not bring herself to finish the sentence. It was as if she and the others were moving in a world of emotions that no longer existed. The pain had not yet come through the haze of bewildered realization.

Without a word, Medora took the letter and went inside to read it, but when Phillipe started to follow, Mianne put out a hand to stop him. "This she has to do alone," she said.

Medora sat in the wing-backed chair, staring at the envelope in her hands. William was dead, she told herself over and over; her last hope was gone. But still she could not believe it. Surely there must be an explanation that would make this last death seem less pointless and cruel. William, of all people, could not have done this thing carelessly. And yet he had. Damn him! she cried without making a sound as she tore open the envelope and spread the pages on her lap.

Dearest Medora,

I realized last night that the time had come to tell you the truth. I'm sure our enemies will come to you soon, but I would rather you hear it from me, and then, perhaps, there will be a chance to make you understand. I have been working for the Pendletons for some weeks now—I give them minor facts about the weaknesses in the business and they give me money (which you will find in a bag in the bottom desk drawer. Somehow I could never bring myself to touch it).

I ask you to believe that I did not do this out of hatred but out of fear for your well-being, which they promised to protect if only I would cooperate. They told me no one would be hurt. They lied, of course. I believed them only because I had to, and when Johnny was killed, I refused to give them any more information. But that did not bring Johnny back.

I would have you understand that I did this because I loved your life more than my own honor. I wanted to get you away before it was too late. I did not realize until tonight that it had been too late from the very moment of the Marquis' death. There can be no excuse for the damage I have done, and I know now that the only way I can begin to make it up to you is to free you from the shadow of my betrayal. I must leave you alone to pick up the pieces, but I know that you, of all women, will be strong enough to do so.

It is my fault alone. Everything comes back to me, though I tried, for a while, to blame it on you and then Phillipe. I was a bitter fool and I will not ask forgiveness for that. I ask only that you forgive me for never having been the man you thought me to be. And that you try to understand that my weakness sprang, not from an evil nature, but from loving you too much. For that, I see now, was my greatest sin.

I love you more than this pen without heart or soul can ever express, and I only regret that I waited so long to tell you so. God bless you, Medora. You should know that every moment of joy in my long and empty life has come from you. I only wish that I might have had the chance, just once, to give you back a little of that joy.

I'm sorry, but I've lost the right to call you my wife. I love you.

Forgive me, for you must know I will never forgive myself.

Yours ever,
William Van Driesche

Medora dropped the last page from nerveless fingers. William had loved her and she had never even known. She buried her face in her hands and, for the second time in twenty-four hours, she found that her cheeks were covered with tears.

The group that sat stiffly around the drawing room was oddly silent while they waited for Phillipe to appear. Paul and Louis and Mianne watched the doorway but did not speak and even Cassie had nothing to say. The cook focused her attention on Antoine and Kira, who lay in the basket beside her, for only the babies seemed unaffected by the string of tragedies that had beset this household in the past two months.

It was as if the life and energy had begun to ebb away from the members of the Chateau. Johnny had taken a little with him when he died, Anais had stolen a little more, and now William had swept away the little that had remained. The people left behind were like ghosts wandering in the present because they had lost their way in some life long past, and the air of unreality had infected their spirits with a strange lassitude. When Phillipe entered the room at last, he felt that he was walking into an old, yellowed photograph whose subjects were frozen forever in the bleak, distant past.

But then his wife looked up at him and he saw that her eyes were still alive with the battle between her new-found happiness and her sorrow over all that they had lost. "Medora and I have talked it over," he said, "and we decided it might be best if we left for New York early this year."

"How early?" Cassie asked, suddenly alert.

Phillipe smiled reassuringly at the cook; he knew she was lonely during the long winter months when the family was away, and now that Johnny was gone, Cassie would find herself even more isolated. "Right after the funeral," he told her. "But you needn't worry. We'll be back even earlier next spring. It's just that we thought in New York it might be easier for all of us to forget what has happened here." As if we could ever do that, he added silently.

Cassie nodded, but when she looked down at the twins, she felt a deep wrenching pain in her chest and she wondered why it was that, despite Phillipe's reassurances, she believed she would never see these beloved children—or their parents—again.

Greg Pendleton slammed the ledger closed with a weary sigh, and when he turned at last to look at his son-in-law, his expression was distorted with a hopelessness he could not hide. "That's it, then," he said.

For the first time since he had known Greg, David almost pitied the man. "What are we going to do?"

"I don't know," Greg replied. "I have to think."

"Will you tell Katherine?"

The older man shook his head vehemently. "No, not yet. I may have one alternative left." It was a slim hope, he told himself, but, at the moment, it was all they had. He had already found himself wondering more than once if it was even worth continuing the struggle. The Vallombrosas were near the breaking point, it was true, but Greg had begun to believe that they would never really go over the edge. Still, Van Driesche's suicide had been quite a blow and they *were* leaving the Badlands early this year. But the business was thriving, despite all the Pendletons' efforts to make it fail, and the Pendletons themselves had not gained much from the battle.

At least Medora was still alive; to lose a woman like that would have been too great a tragedy. And maybe she would stay whole and healthy now that Cory was recovering from her long, debilitating madness. Funny, Greg mused, that Stephen St. Clair had been the one to come closest to killing Medora, when Cory had been trying so hard for so long to eliminate her rival. He wondered if Phillipe and the others would be surprised to learn that it had been Greg's mad wife, and not Greg himself, who had made those attempts on Medora's life last year. No doubt they would not believe it; they could never hope to understand the obsessions that clouded a Pendleton mind.

Medora, he said silently. The name still had the power to move him, even after all that had come between them. He had caught a glimpse of her in town the other day. She had moved slowly and regally, as ever, but her skin had been nearly translucent and the sadness had been like a wash of deep blue in her clear green eyes. Greg's heart— which he thought had turned to stone long ago—had twisted at the sight and he had quickly looked away. He had had enough of pain for one lifetime, and enough of pity too.

"Father," Katherine said imperiously as she swept into the room, her cashmere skirt undulating about her legs, "I want to talk to you." Her eyes rested briefly on her husband, then she added significantly, "Alone. Maybe you could go and talk to Mama or something, David. We have business to discuss."

David stood up without a word and started for the door, but when he reached the threshold, he stopped and turned to glare helplessly at Katherine's back. She despised him—she had made that perfectly clear—and he had begun to wonder how long he could continue to exist with that gleam of disdain from her mocking eyes always before him.

Greg saw the look on his son-in-law's face. When David had gone, he warned, "I'd take more care with your husband if I were you, my dear. The quiet ones are often the most dangerous, once they're truly angry."

Shrugging indifferently, Katherine said, "I've told you

before, David is *my* problem. Besides, we have something important to discuss just now."

Let her be a blind fool, if that was what she wanted, her father told himself. "Well?" he asked aloud.

"The Vallombrosas and Phillipe are leaving for New York next week. What are you planning to do about them?"

"I'm planning to try to run our ranch—"

"They won't give up just because they're having troubles now," Katherine interrupted. "We can't give up either."

Greg crossed his arms and leaned back in his chair. "No doubt you have a plan that guarantees their ultimate destruction?" he observed caustically.

"I wouldn't go that far. But I can make certain that they never come back to the Badlands. Isn't that what we really want?"

"I suppose it is," Greg murmured, and he knew it was true—in every way but one.

"Then we must follow them to New York. Not just yet, but later, after I've had time to make some plans."

Greg knew he should ask what her plans were but, at the moment, his thoughts were concentrated on the idea of going to New York. He did not care what Katherine intended; he had reasons of his own for wanting to be in the city. He could plead his cause in person then and make it very clear that it was time to repay a debt long overdue. "What about Cory?" he asked.

Katherine smiled a lopsided smile that her father was too preoccupied to notice. "We can take her along. She's much better, you know, except when anyone talks about the past." Besides, Katherine added silently, I need her there. She might just prove useful in the end.

"I don't know," Greg said cautiously. "I'll have to think about it." But he knew already what his answer would be. He looked up at his daughter curiously. "I don't see what

you hope to accomplish. In a city that big, the Vallombrosas won't even know we're there."

Katherine's slow, languorous smile crept into her eyes
and gleamed there, dark and threatening. "You're wrong,"
she whispered thickly. "When the time is right, they'll
know."

Part V

New York:
New Year's Eve, 1900

"I believe in the protection of God and hope in the future."

—Marquis de Mores
May, 1897

Chapter 34

Von Hoffman, Gretta, and Medora sat huddled around the drawing room fire in the New York house. Outside the snow swirled and eddied, cloaking the world beyond the windows in a soft, pure cloak of untouched white. Medora stared vaguely out at the dancing snowflakes and shivered, for she knew that soon the white would be stained with the scars left behind by many muddy feet, and then it would be as if the perfection had never been.

Rubbing his chin thoughtfully between two fingers, Louis Von Hoffman wondered at his daughter's strange expression. He was glad Phillipe had been called out of the room to receive an important letter, because now the older man had a chance to really watch Medora and try to read her thoughts. Not that that was very difficult. She was in mourning again; he did not need to see her black crepe gown to know it. Ever since her arrival here three months ago, her face had never once ceased to reflect a deep and constant grief. He had not seen her cry, but he knew the gnawing pain was there inside her, just the same.

Unconsciously, Von Hoffman clenched his fists as the old anger turned his rosy face even redder. All Mores and his family had ever brought Medora was sorrow. He hated them for that—every one of them. And the violence of his hatred had not dimmed over the years; it still glowed within him, as bright and intense as the day it had been born.

The door swung open and Phillipe stepped back into the circle of firelight with several pieces of paper clutched in his hand.

"Well?" Von Hoffman demanded. He was annoyed to see that Medora looked up with a flicker of curiosity in her eyes.

Phillipe went to stand before the fire where the chill of the old house was not quite so bad, and his eyes went from one expectant face to the other. "It's from Swift," he announced in a voice oddly devoid of emotion. "He has offered to buy out the business in North Dakota—the plant, the land, the cattle, everything. And he's willing to pay a great deal of money.

Von Hoffman rubbed his hands together in delight. "At last!" he crowed. "We're finally a success." His eyes narrowed as he scrutinized the younger man's face with care. "You've proven your point, haven't you? Obviously, it's time to sell if the price is right, and I suspect it is."

"But, Louis," Gretta objected, brushing futilely at a fly-away curl, "I don't think you can make the decision for them. Shouldn't you ask what *they* want?"

Clearly annoyed at the interruption, her husband turned cold, brown eyes on his ineffectual wife. "One thing you can be sure of," he said. "Nobody is interested in *your* opinion. You'd think you would have learned that by now." Then he turned away as if she were no longer worth his notice.

Gretta shrank back, surprised that Louis still had the power to hurt her, even after all these years. But perhaps it was because lately he had become so thoroughly cold to her. She knew he was suffering for Medora's sake, but it was something more than that. It was almost as if he had become obsessed, and he was no longer as clever at hiding his feelings anymore. She did not know exactly why; she only knew that her husband made her more and more uneasy of late.

"Papa, really!" Medora cried. "Mama was only making a sensible suggestion." The younger woman rose as if to follow her mother from the room but Gretta waved her away.

"This offer won't stand forever, you know," Von Hoffman said to his daughter's back. "We need to discuss it. Are you willing to sell or aren't you?"

Medora turned to find that Phillipe, too, was watching her with the same question in his eyes. What could she tell him? Six months ago, her answer would have been a firm no, but now she was not so certain. In a way, her father was right; Swift's willingness to spend a small fortune on the business meant that they had succeeded. They had finally proven that Mores' plans for the meatpacking business were not just one man's empty fantasy. But they had lost so much in proving it.

As long as she lived, Medora would never forget the look of glowing hatred in her daughter's eyes or the image of William's still body on the blood-stained grass. The acrid odor of death still followed her like a restless ghost. She did not know if she could go back to the Badlands again and face so many bitter memories. Not this time.

Von Hoffman saw her hesitation and realized that she was finally willing to abandon her stubborn loyalty to a dead man's schemes, so he murmured gently, "No need to decide right now, as long as you're thinking about it. I want you to enjoy the party tonight, my dear. It's to be the biggest I've ever had. But then, it's New Year's Eve and the turn of the century as well. No party could be too big to celebrate that. And now we have even more to celebrate."

Phillipe could not bring himself to share Von Hoffman's enthusiasm. The 1800s might be coming to an end, but there was so much he had not accomplished. It was true that, together, Medora and he had finally made the Marquis' dream come true. They had shown that the man had not been a failure after all. But as the flames leapt and spat behind him without easing the coldness that had settled in his heart, Phillipe suddenly realized that it was not enough.

For this one dazzling night, the crisp electric lights had been left off. Instead, the soft light from several chandeliers of candles played over the shifting crowd below. Already the snow had melted from the hems of the vibrant, swirling gowns and the cold outside had been forgotten in the warmth and excitement of rotating dancers and expensive champagne. The turn of the century did not come every day, and the guests at Von Hoffman's party intended to celebrate to the full. After all, tomorrow would be the first day of 1900; at midnight the world would change forever.

Katherine Pendleton St. Clair stood at the edge of the crowd, smiling contentedly to herself. It was a magnificent party and a magnificent night; she could feel it in the warm center of her bones as she watched the jeweled and glittering dancers. No doubt, she thought, Phillipe and Medora would be astonished to find that the Pendletons were here tonight, but that was part of the fun. She had known that the Vallombrosas and Beaumonts always stayed with Medora's father, so Katherine had approached him at the bank one day and wangled an invitation. She had explained that the Pendletons were the most prominent family in the Badlands and that, since they were in New York, it was only right that they should be invited here. Von Hoffman had agreed readily enough, but Katherine had suspected that the old man disliked Phillipe so much that he was rather looking forward to a dramatic confrontation.

But there would not be one—at least not the kind Von Hoffman might have imagined. No, tonight Katherine would stun them all with the very last thing they had ever expected. Peering anxiously through the crowd, she sought the blue-gowned figure of her mother. That was one person she must not lose sight of this evening. Katherine smiled when she saw Cory hurrying toward her daughter, clearly upset.

"Oh, Katherine!" Cory cried as she held a trembling hand to her throat. "Thank God I found you. The most dreadful thing has happened. I just can't believe it. She's here, at this very party. I saw her."

"Who?" the younger woman asked with casual interest.

Cory moved closer, whispering, "Medora de Vallombrosa. She's not dead at all. I saw her."

"Of course she's not dead. You tried to kill her but you failed, remember?"

Shaking her head to clear it of the cobwebs that had begun to weave themselves across her thoughts, Cory murmured, "But I thought—" She was so confused and she knew that soon the shadows would come and she could lose her way altogether. "I don't know," she wailed. "I just don't know."

Katherine gazed at her mother with sparkling eyes. "Yes, you do," she insisted. "If you try very hard, you'll remember why Medora isn't dead."

Aware of the warning lurking at the back of her mind, Cory raised her hands before her like a protective shield. "No," she rasped. "I don't want to remember." She dared not. With a deep, ragged breath, she started to move away but Katherine stopped her.

"You must, Mama. You'll never escape your fear if you don't." She put a hand on her mother's shoulder and guided the woman into a nearby empty room.

"No! Don't make me think about it. I can't bear it. You know I can't!"

Katherine forced her mother to meet her eyes. "You can and you will."

"I have to find Greg!" Cory cried, her face drained of all color. "I have to get away and find Greg."

"That's what you said that day so many years ago," Katherine breathed. "Don't you remember? You'd been cold all that night and you didn't know why. Remember?"

Her daughter's voice droned relentlessly above Cory's head as she made one last desperate effort to break free. "I don't want to know, Katherine," she whimpered. "Please."

"I'm sorry, but it's time, Mama. You've hidden from the truth for too long. Try to remember how you felt when, after tossing and turning all night, cold and frightened, you finally awakened to find that Father was gone. . . ."

. . . . *August, 1885—The light from a new summer dawn fell with pitiless radiance on the empty pillow beside her; Cory closed her eyes against the blinding light.* But she knew, though she tried to tell herself it wasn't so. Greg had not slept in this bed because he had found another that was warmer—Medora's. Cory had never doubted that her husband loved the other woman. From the first moment she saw them together, she had known.

Rage swept the bright morning light from her mind in an instant, replacing it with threatening shadows. She was losing him at last, just as she had always feared she would. But she must not let it happen. She would stop it. She knew just how to do it.

When Cory had dressed quickly, she found the rifle on the rack in the study and cradled it carefully in her arms. She would find them, she promised herself. Then she went to get her horse and discovered she was lucky. There were clear hoofprints leading directly down to the river. With the knowledge of her sudden power pulsing like a second heart in her chest, she rode after them. She knew that this time she would put a stop to the affair once and for all.

She saw them from a long way away—Greg on horseback with Medora before him in the saddle. They must have left the other horse behind. No doubt they could not bear to be apart, even for the length of the ride. Blinded by the fury that blotted out the morning sun, Cory clutched the rifle tighter and rode forward until the leaves of the cottonwoods hid her from sight. Then she called out once, hoarsely, without even knowing what she had said.

Greg turned, startled, and in that instant the woman pulled away from him and jumped down to the marshy riverbank. Cory sat perfectly still for a full minute, watching Medora run. She must be afraid to run so fast from an enemy she could not even see, but that was good. With a grim smile, Cory raised the rifle, aimed carefully for the center of the other woman's back, then pulled the trigger.

She felt an overwhelming surge of triumph chase the cold from her blood as the woman staggered, then fell, while the blood flowed freely from the gaping hole in her back. Greg would come home to stay now; she knew it. Now that Medora was finally dead.

Then Greg came up behind his wife, his voice taut with rage as he hissed, "I thought you were no more than a fool, but now I see that you're a lunatic as well."

Cory followed the direction of his cold silver gaze. Only then, as she stood within the grasp of the concealing trees, did she see that the woman who lay covered with her own blood wore a buckskin dress instead of a shirtwaist and skirt. And her hair was coal black, not thick waving red. The woman was not Medora at all. From somewhere at the back of her mind a name Greg had used rose before Cory's eyes. Ileya. She had killed Ileya and she didn't even know her. *Suddenly the terror washed over her in waves, and she began to tremble violently as Greg's unforgiving hands closed around her in a choking hold. . . .*

* * *

. . . . Katherine's fingers dug cruelly into her mother's upper arm and she whispered thickly, "You remember now, don't you, Mama? You know now that you're a murderer."

Cory gasped and shook her head, too blind with fear to respond, but Katherine persisted with her questions. "Do you know that Phillipe has been looking for Ileya's killer? He won't stop till he knows who it is."

This threat brought Cory's voice up from inside her in a cry of terror. "What if he finds out? He could have me hanged."

Pursing her lips thoughtfully, Katherine pretended to consider this for a moment. "Maybe not," she said at last. "Maybe if you go to him yourself and explain how it happened—well, he might even be moved to pity you."

Cory was too afraid to move. "Do you really think so?"

Katherine shrugged. "I don't know, but it seems to me that that's your only chance." And if she knew Phillipe, he was just fool enough to really feel sorry for a desperate Cory.

"Then"—Cory paused in an effort to force the spectre of the nightmare back so that she could move on her own again—"then, I'll do it. Now. Before it's too late."

"Good." Katherine guided her mother to the door and watched as the tiny woman wound her way across the crowded floor. Cory did not see that her daughter's eyes were glistening with self-satisfaction, nor did she get a glimpse of the imperceptible movement that curved those full, red lips into a smile of pure evil.

Phillipe rotated on the dance floor with Mianne in his arms, intensely aware of the press of her body against his and the whisper of her breath against his cheek. Tonight she wore a deep orange gown of flowing satin and her beautiful hair had been swept into loose curls at the back of her neck. She was so lovely that, despite the troubling thoughts that had plagued him all day, he was enjoying himself at Von Hoffman's incredibly extravagant New Year's Eve party. Everywhere he looked he saw tables laden with delicacies of every kind, and the champagne never ceased to flow. But Phillipe did not care about those things. He cared only that Mianne was with him and that, when she glanced up now and then, he could see the affection shining in her eyes.

"Damn!" he muttered when he saw Cory Pendleton coming toward him with a wild look on her face. He was not surprised to see her here, for he had learned early in the evening that the Pendletons would be attending. But he had sworn to himself that he would avoid any contact with them. Tonight, of all nights, he did not want to remember how much they had done to hurt him.

Mianne raised her head curiously to see what had upset Phillipe. Then, in an instant, Cory was upon them, grasping the young man's arm with bony fingers.

"I must talk to you," she whispered urgently. Then her gaze fell on Mianne and she added, "Alone. It's very important."

"I don't—" Phillipe began, but his wife had recognized the desperation in Cory's eyes and she urged him to do as the woman asked.

"I'll wait for you in the drawing room," Mianne told him.

Phillipe suppressed a sigh of annoyance. He wanted nothing to do with the Pendletons anymore, but he, too, could see that Cory was deeply troubled. "Let's go in here," he said, indicating a small room off the central hall.

When he had pushed the switch so that the harsh glare of the electric light captured them in its grasp, Phillipe turned to face Cory. "What did you want to talk about?" he asked.

Cory licked her lips nervously, then murmured, "I want to tell you the truth—about an Indian girl named Ileya."

Stiffening imperceptibly, he wondered what this half-mad woman could possibly tell him that would mean anything, but he sat down to listen just the same as she told her long and agonizing story. He realized then that, in the turmoil of his last days in the Badlands, he had forgotten the Indian girl, and he felt a pang of guilt, as if he had somehow let her down.

Cory told him everything, from her early suspicions about Greg and Medora to that final morning when she had ruined her marriage forever. Phillipe could see from the tortured look in her eyes that she was telling the truth. He did not wonder what had made her come to him here tonight; his mind was too busy sorting out the new facts he had learned. So it had been poor, mad Cory who had killed Ileya. But now that he finally knew the truth, why didn't he feel quite satisfied? Why had he sought so hard and so long only to discover that bitter jealousy and a dreadful mistake had taken that girl's life? There must be something more, he thought. There *must* be. "Will you tell me something?" he asked.

Cory had already recognized a flash of sympathy in his eyes, so now she leaned forward eagerly. "Anything."

"Everyone blamed Greg for that murder. I know that much. If it wasn't his fault, why didn't he tell us the truth?"

Clasping her hands together in her lap, Cory squinted in an attempt to dredge up what remained of the past she had tried for so long to forget. "I think," she said slowly, "that it was because Mr. Von Hoffman told him just to let things be. He said he didn't want a lot of questions being asked."

Phillipe blinked as if he had heard her incorrectly. "Von

Hoffman?" he repeated. Suddenly his mind was whirling with disconnected thoughts and he had to force himself to think clearly. "Are you sure it was Louis Von Hoffman?"

Cory nodded tensely. She was frightened by the new expression on his face.

But Phillipe was hardly aware of the woman. Why had Medora's father told Greg to keep the truth hidden? More important, why had Greg obeyed him? The old man had not even been in contact with the Pendletons—then or ever—as far as Phillipe knew. Yet they were here at the party, were they not?

Suddenly Cory's claw-like fingers pressed into his arm. "What are you going to do with me?" she asked, but her voice shook so badly with fear that her words were hardly recognizable.

With an effort, Phillipe dragged his mind back to the present. What *could* he do? It was no secret that Cory had been mad for years. No doubt the fear and the violence had arisen from the troubled center of her weak mind. Besides, he sensed that this poor, broken woman had suffered enough for her sins. "Nothing," he told her gently. "It was a long time ago and you were ill. Why don't we all just try to forget it?"

Cory smiled for the first time that evening as she rose, murmuring, "Thank you. Oh, thank you." Then she left him.

Phillipe watched her go but his thoughts were already far away. *Had* Von Hoffman been in contact with the Pendletons all along? And *if* he had, what did it mean? There was only one explanation that Phillipe could see and that explanation made the blood freeze in his veins.

Chapter 35

"I want you to open the safe for me."

Gretta stared at Phillipe in bewilderment. He had come looking for her in the midst of the crowd, then drawn her aside to ask his question in the half-darkened hallway where others could not hear them. "Oh, no!" she cried, "I don't think I could—"

"You know the combination, don't you?" Phillipe's voice was steady only because he kept it rigidly under control. He knew he was about to explode but he was also aware that he must not. Not until he discovered the truth.

Twining her hands together nervously, Gretta nodded. "Yes, but—"

Phillipe put his hands on her shoulders and looked directly into her gray eyes. "It's important," he told her urgently. "More important than you can imagine."

"It's Louis, isn't it?" she asked as a spark of intuition lit her plain face. "He's done something dreadful." She realized then that she had been waiting for this moment for a long time. She had begun to wonder more and more often lately if her husband was up to something. Now she saw from the look on Phillipe's face that he had begun to wonder, too.

"I don't know," Phillipe said. "And I won't until I see

what's in that safe. It would be easier if you helped me, Gretta, but I intend to do this, one way or another. I have to know."

His desire to know the truth was something Gretta understood. She had always wanted to know, but she had never had the courage to find out. The young man before her had that courage. "All right," she whispered, glancing over her shoulder as if Louis were hovering there, watching. And she knew as she led Phillipe toward the study that she was doing this for herself as much as she was for him.

When the study door was safely closed behind them, Phillipe waited impatiently while Gretta stood awkwardly before the safe, turning the dial in stiff fingers. The young man sensed that he was on the verge of answering all the unanswered questions that had haunted him for so long, and his heart pounded raggedly as the heavy metal door finally swung open and Gretta stepped back out of the way.

The woman stood with her hands clasped tightly before her, fear mingled with curiosity in her eyes. Phillipe tried to nod reassuringly at her, but he knew he was only delaying the task ahead. Finally, he moved in front of the gaping darkness of the safe and began to sift through the papers he found there. At first he could see nothing out of the ordinary, but then he discovered a bundle of tightly wrapped pages hidden clear at the back and he drew it forward with trembling hands.

Suddenly his labored breathing seemed to swell until it filled the quiet room with pulsing expectation as he slid the string from around the bundle and let the papers fall open in his hand. He saw at once that he had reached the end of a long and painful journey, for what he held was an incriminating record of checks, letters, and intricate instructions from Louis Von Hoffman to Greg Pendleton. Most surprising of all, they dated back to 1883, the year the Marquis had first arrived in the Badlands. There could no longer be any doubt.

The blood in Phillipe's limbs seemed to drain away, leaving his body numb and leaden while the horror of his discovery ran through his empty veins. He thought he might never be able to move again, but when he saw one more paper folded and placed carefully at the very back of the safe, he reached for it automatically. He did not think there could be anything worse than the pages he held limply in one hand, but some instinct made him spread out the new paper with special care.

When he saw what was written there, Phillipe had to brace himself against the desk to remain standing. In that instant, he felt that the walls were closing in on him, squeezing the breath from his lungs with an iron hand. He realized then that Ileya, the mysterious Indian girl who had haunted his dreams for so long, had indeed led him here to this moment—to a truth so devastating that he could not even begin to recognize it.

"What is it?" Gretta asked in a hushed whisper. Her voice, soft though it was, shattered the stillness like the report of a rifle.

Phillipe swallowed twice before he could find the strength to reply and even then his words seemed to come from the mouth of a stranger a long distance away. "It's a record of payment. Twenty-five thousand dollars from your husband to a French colonel named Rebillet."

"Who is he?"

"The man who we believed engineered my father's assassination."

Gretta gaped at him in confusion. "But if Louis paid him, it means—" She paused and Phillipe looked up to meet her gaze for the first time. The answer she sought burned furiously in his eyes. "No!" she cried. "Dear God, no!"

"Yes, my dear," a new voice said from the threshold. "I'm afraid that for once you've guessed correctly."

Phillipe and Gretta whirled toward the door where Louis Von Hoffman stood watching them, his brown eyes glacial, a revolver held tightly in his steady hand. Pointing the gun threateningly in Phillipe's direction, the older man smiled grimly and said, "Put the papers back in the safe."

Phillipe did so willingly; he had seen quite enough and he wanted nothing more than to rid himself of the evidence of this final betrayal.

"Now, Gretta, I want you to leave us alone while I try to decide what to do about Mr. Beaumont," Von Hoffman instructed.

Only then did his wife finally find her voice. "You really had Medora's husband killed?" she asked incredulously. Her fingers were braided so tightly together that the knuckles were white.

Annoyed at her outburst, Von Hoffman snapped, "I did what I had to do. Now be quiet and leave—"

"Why?" Phillipe demanded suddenly. He could not keep silent anymore.

The older man raised the gun a little higher and a muscle in his jaw began to twitch, though Phillipe could not tell whether it was with fear or anger. "I wanted my daughter back," Von Hoffman explained. "There was no other way."

"But she didn't *come* back," Phillipe reminded him foolishly.

"No," Von Hoffman hissed while his finger toyed with the trigger. "She chose to go with you instead." Then, for the first time, he let the young man see the full force of his hatred.

But Gretta had seen it, too. "Louis!" she wailed, "you can't—"

"I *can*," Louis spat. "I've done it before. Now, get out! Unless you want to get hurt, too."

With downcast eyes, Gretta moved toward the door, but when she reached the point just behind her husband, she swung around unexpectedly in an attempt to knock the gun from his grasp. That was the opportunity Phillipe needed. He crossed the room in an instant and lunged for the older man, locking his gun hand in a steely grip. For what seemed like an eternity to Gretta, who stood by helplessly, the two men struggled for control of the revolver.

They staggered toward the desk, Louis puffing for breath while Phillipe tried to pry the gun out of the other man's fingers. As they toppled backwards onto the floor, they knocked the lamp over and it shattered into hundreds of tiny, glittering fragments. Louis grunted when he rolled onto some of the glass and his arm began to bleed, but still he would not give up the gun. As Phillipe attempted to draw away from the broken fragments, Von Hoffman broke the younger man's grip and struggled to his feet. "Now," he said, grasping the revolver with both hands and pointing it toward the center of the young man's chest. "Now we will see who is stronger."

Then the door swung open and a breath of cold winter wind seemed to freeze the combatants in their places. "Papa!" Medora gasped. "What—" But the rest of the words stopped in her throat when she saw the wrath that had turned his red face nearly blue and pulled his lips across his teeth in a grotesque grimace. "Put that gun down!" his daughter cried.

It was as if the sound of her voice had struck a chord buried deep inside him that her father had long ago forgotten. "Medora!" he said as he straightened up and turned toward her. "Go away!" he insisted. "This is between us. It has nothing to do with you."

"Liar!" Gretta shouted. "For you there is nothing else *but* her and there never has been."

Medora glanced from one to the other and all at once

she could hear her heart throbbing. "What happened here?" she demanded.

Phillipe rose from the floor, brushing ineffectually at the tiny pieces of glittering glass that clung to his shirt and pants. "I broke into your father's safe," he explained stiffly. "And I found —"

"Medora," Von Hoffman interrupted.

But Medora's attention had been caught by the look of utter defeat in Phillipe's eyes. "You found what?" she prompted.

Suddenly Phillipe wondered if he had the strength to tell her the truth when he knew it might very well destroy her. But he also knew that Medora was the kind of woman who would ask until she got an answer. "I discovered evidence that proves your father has been working with the Pendletons to get us out of the Badlands ever since Mores first went there. Von Hoffman was the connection we suspected for so long. And—" His voice suddenly failed him and Gretta came forward to take her daughter's arm.

"And he found that your father paid to have the Marquis de Mores killed in northern Africa."

For a moment, Medora felt that she might fall; the room swayed dangerously around her and she closed her eyes in an effort to fight off the dizzying waves of horror that shook her body from head to foot. When she could breathe again, she turned to Von Hoffman and whispered, "Why?"

The old man took a step toward his daughter. "I knew from the beginning that Mores would ruin you. You can see now that I was right. He only brought you pain and confusion and hopelessness."

"How can you think that?" Medora gasped in horror. "He made me happy—while he was alive." What madness had so distorted her father's view of her marriage? Had it somehow been her fault? No, she thought, he had *chosen* to be blind—always. Appalled at the realization of what he had done, she stood unmoving, her hands clenched stiffly at her sides.

Von Hoffman continued as if she had not spoken, for he did not wish to hear what she had said. "At first, I only wanted to prove to you what a fool he was. I hoped when his ridiculous schemes failed to succeed that you would recognize—"

Medora shook her head blindly. This could not be happening.

Swallowing convulsively, her father put out a hand to touch her, but she shuddered and shook it away. "I thought I could make you leave him and then you would come home where you belonged. But when I saw that you would stay with Mores whatever happened, I knew he had to die. I couldn't let him hurt you any deeper; don't you understand that?" His voice rose in desperation with every word.

"No!" his daughter choked. "I *don't* understand."

"Medora," Von Hoffman groaned, his hands outstretched in a silent plea, "you're the only person in my life who ever meant anything to me. Everything I did was for you alone. The money I made, the work I did, the hours and hours of time I spent trying to make you into a person I could be proud of."

"A person like you?" Medora hissed. She could no longer keep the growing revulsion out of her voice. She felt that at any moment her insides might explode with the realization that this man, whom she had believed in, even when they fought each other, had taken her fate in the palm of his hands and crushed it like the body of a helpless gnat.

Von Hoffman recognized the cold rejection in his daughter's eyes and he felt the earth rocking beneath him. "Why did you have to marry that man at all?" he rasped finally.

The icy numbness began to course through Medora's

veins, dulling the pain for the time being, and she was grateful. She was sickened by her father's confession of his unnatural affection for her and, although she knew she should pity him, there was no pity left in the ruins of her charred and battered emotions. She had already borne too much. Medora gathered her strength around her like a torn cloak, looked her father in the eyes and said, "I married Antoine because I loved him, but even more than that, I married him because he was everything you had ever taught me to despise."

Then, before Von Hoffman could find a response, Medora reached for Phillipe's arm. Closing his hand over hers, he guided her through the door. From the other side, she paused and, with a last tortured look toward Gretta, Medora said, "We will leave your house in the morning. I promise you, Papa, that I will never cross this threshold again." Then, in a whirl of black silk, she was gone.

Von Hoffman stood paralyzed where his daughter had left him. He had failed after all. He had lost her. If only he had planned more carefully. If only Phillipe had not been so foolish. But then he heard the clock in the hall begin to chime midnight and in the last few moments of the century, he recognized that the end had finally come. He could not even bear to look downward, where he knew he would see the last trampled fragments of every plan he had ever made and every dream he had ever dreamt.

At the first stroke of midnight, the excitement that had been building all evening suddenly threatened to explode, as if every person in the room had been touched at once by an unseen hand. Hearts raced faster and faces flushed with expectation as the hollow notes of the grandfather clock boomed out across the crowded dance floor. It was almost time, and everyone who waited with the breath held back in his throat knew that never again would he see the turn of a century.

Greg stood at the edge of the collection of tense celebrants, an outcast who did not share the vibrant sense of anticipation. When he heard a soft rustle behind him, he turned without hesitation to see Medora coming toward him with her hand resting in the curve of Phillipe Beaumont's arm. She held her head high, as always, the intricate woven braids curving around her head and down her neck like a caress. Her simple black silk gown was more magnificent than all the multicolored velvets and satins of the other guests; its very plainness gave Medora a regal look that no other woman there could claim. She might have been a queen or a high priestess. Greg could not make himself look away.

He could guess what had just happened in the study down the hall where the light from the open door spilled onto the Persian carpet. Cory had told him everything a few minutes earlier. His rage had been short-lived, and now, as Medora approached, it faded altogether. It was too late now; there was nothing to be done. Besides, Medora was so much more than he remembered. Her small body radiated strength and determination and all that was good in this world. But as his eyes met hers, he realized that she did not even recognize him.

He would never forget the look in those eyes—an agony so deep that she might just have lost the only man she had ever truly loved. With an insight that was clear and piercing, Greg realized that that man was not him and never had been. As he watched her disappear down the hall, the last reverberating stroke of midnight seemed to foretell his final doom.

The room erupted into raucous shouts, blasts from tin horns, and the popping of champagne corks, but Greg did not hear the joyful celebration. He heard only the fading memory of the rustle of Medora's heavy skirts and he knew that single everyday sound would be with him forever.

"Greg?" Cory touched her husband's arm tentatively. He turned to gaze down at her in astonishment. "It's time," she said softly. "1900 has finally arrived."

Greg was amazed at his wife's clear eyes, untouched by the shadows of madness for the first time in fifteen years. It seemed that her confession had somehow banished the fear from her mind; the process of recovery which had begun under David's tutelage was now complete, at least for the moment. It struck Greg then that he might have helped her overcome her afflictions sooner with a little care and a little time, but he had never even tried. He had been too full of hatred, too busy blaming her for causing Medora to leave him. But now he knew that he had been wrong even about that.

On an impulse, he pulled Cory into his arms and her timid smile cut him more sharply than a knife blade. While the world exploded with happiness all around them, he remembered what Cory had said. "1900 has finally arrived." Yes, he thought bitterly, and with it our last hope has died. But he did not say it aloud. Let his wife have this moment of pleasure for all the years of misery she had endured. One moment before the world crumbled finally at her feet.

Chapter 36

David St. Clair slammed the bedroom door behind him and saw that his wife was already releasing the fastenings on her gown. "What in the hell did you hope to accomplish with your little performance tonight? I know Von Hoffman is an evil man, but he's been your ally for so long."

Katherine shrugged. "I do what's best for the family and alliances be damned, especially when they've grown old and stale over the years. Besides, it turned Phillipe's attention away from us."

"Only for the time being," David objected. "He's too shocked to open his eyes right now, but he will eventually."

Turning her back on her husband, Katherine began to pluck the pins from her hair. "He may, but then I know Phillipe well. He can never go back to the Badlands now; it would be too painful for him."

David almost said icily, "Neither can we," but he caught himself in time and instead concentrated on taking off his shirt. "You're pleased about what you did to Beaumont, aren't you?" he asked incredulously.

Katherine smiled at her reflection in the mirror. "Yes, I am."

Sickened by the casual tone of her voice, David backed away. He saw now that Katherine would stop at nothing to get what she wanted. She had used Cory and William and Von Hoffman, even David himself, all to break the man who had once abandoned her. This beautiful woman who stood before him so cool and detached must be incapable of love—hatred was the only thing she knew. "Nothing matters to you but hurting Phillipe," he groaned. "You're obsessed with him, aren't you? And you'd do anything to destroy him, even if it meant destroying the whole world along with him."

Katherine stepped out of her gown and petticoats until only her chemise covered the inviting curves of her body. "It's true," she hissed, smiling crookedly. "But at least Phillipe Beaumont is a man worth hating. He has courage and spirit and determination that makes you look like nothing more than a spineless puppet."

Her husband had been in the act of unfastening his belt but now he paused. All at once he wanted to hurt her back, to make her wriggle and squirm with agony as she had done to him so many times. He knew he would feel no remorse; she had burned his heart, his sympathy into ashes long ago. "I hope you're happy with your petty little revenge," he snapped. "Because the memory of this night is all you'll have tomorrow."

Katherine stared at him in surprise. His voice was taut with anger and she saw in his eyes that he wanted to bring her to her knees, but she only smiled. This was only David, after all, and David was a fool. "What are you talking about?" she asked coolly.

"The ranch," her husband replied. "It's in deep financial trouble. To put it simply, there is no money left. Your father has already made inquiries about selling, but he came to New York to make one last attempt to save it. There is only one man who might have given us the capital we needed, and that man is Louis Von Hoffman. He wouldn't let us approach the front door now, so we'll have to sell. Because of you."

"No!" Katherine cried in disbelief. She flew at her husband, fists clenched and eyes blazing. "You're lying!" she shouted. "It can't be true. We have to win, don't you understand? We *have* to!"

David pushed her away with hands that trembled at the realization of what he had done. "Not this time," he said.

"Then it's *your* fault," his wife railed. Before he could stop her, she struck him hard across the face. "You've ruined us with your snivelling and your goddamned righteousness. I hate you! Your very presence makes my skin crawl. I hate you, do you hear?"

At some point David had removed his belt and now he looked down at the wide leather band in his hands. He stared as if he was not certain what it was, and his thoughts seemed to fade into oblivion as a new white-hot fury raced through his veins.

When her husband did not move, Katherine struck him again, then reached out, her nails poised, ready to tear the skin from his face. "You sicken me," she sneered. "You're nothing, not even half a man."

"No?" David said, as something inside him screamed to be released. The last vestige of his control snapped, and he pulled the belt taut, then sent one end flying with a force that struck Katherine's shoulder and sent her reeling.

She stood for a moment, too astonished to move, wondering where this madman had appeared from, then he came forward and flung her face-down on the bed. "if you hate me," he said, "then I'll give you a reason." Folding the leather double, he struck her again and again while she tried to struggle free of the weight of his knee in the center of her back. For a full minute, he was deaf to everything but the hiss of his belt as it split the air in two.

The force of his pain, bottled up for too long, gave him a strength that even Katherine could not break.

But then his wife moaned, a long, low growl that hit him like a blow across the face, and he paused, clutching the leather band in frozen fingers.

"Please," Katherine rasped in a voice David had never heard before.

He dropped the belt abruptly and moved his knee so he could turn his wife to face him. Her hair fell in disarray across her shoulders and her eyes were two flaming wells of darkness in which he could see her pain—the torment *he* had caused her. He knew then that, in spite of all the anger, the disgust, the deep, searing hatred that had consumed his soul since he had met her, he wanted this woman more than any other. And the knowledge of his weakness sickened him more than her evil.

With one hand, he held her shoulders still; with the other, he ripped the chemise free of her body so he could look at the pale, soft skin beneath. Seeing his intention, Katherine began to claw and kick, struggling to push him away, but David was determined, this time, to take what he wanted before it was offered like a bone to a wayward dog. He flung his body on top of hers and they rolled across the bed wildly, thrashing, spitting, growling their hatred for one another.

David's hands on his wife's skin were rough and uncaring and his lips on her breast bit down too hard, so that she struck his back again and again in protest. But then, at last, he entered her and her cries turned to moans as his fingers dug brutally into her shoulders.

The scent, the power, the excitement of his body seemed to fill her, and her nerves screamed out their pleasure as they struggled, skin to skin. Then suddenly, Katherine stiffened as the explosion shook her body again and again. She clutched her husband to her and moaned his name aloud.

David collapsed beside her, his hand still tangled in the warm disorder of her hair. He knew that this had been the first time for her, at least in his arms. He had satisfied his wife at last. This was the answer to his touch that he had sought from the first moment he met her. Yet it had taken a moment of madness, despair, and violence to bring Katherine to this. And now, even as his body cried out for him to take her again, he could not help but wonder if it had been worth the bitter cost.

Downstairs, the party was still going on, though not one of the members of the Von Hoffman household was there. They had retreated to the solitude of their rooms, every one of them seeking escape from the harsh reality that was 1900. Phillipe turned and opened his arms to his wife as she climbed into bed beside him, her flowing white gown just visible in the moonlight that spilled through the unshuttered window.

"The children are asleep at last," she murmured as she rested her head on Phillipe's shoulder.

For a moment they lay together in silence, letting the warmth of their bodies chase away the chill of the night, then Mianne whispered, "What are we going to do?"

Phillipe shifted slightly, so that he could look into her lovely, shadowed face. "We've decided to sell to Swift. Somehow neither Medora nor I could face going back."

Mianne nodded. This was what she had expected and she knew her husband had made the right decision. It was time to leave the Badlands behind. "But what about Von Hoffman? Are you going to have him prosecuted?"

"We can't," Phillipe said bitterly. "Remember that Rebillet had the assassins killed long ago. They were the only link between my father and his real murderers. We can prove that Von Hoffman paid the colonel a lot of money, and the Pendletons as well, but that's *all* we can prove. It seems Medora's father has been too clever for us from the very beginning."

Aware of the self-disgust in his tone, Mianne moved even closer to her husband. "That doesn't make you any less a man," she said.

Furrowing his brows thoughtfully, Phillipe said, "I feel like such a fool. I should have guessed that Von Hoffman was the one but I didn't even suspect. I feel that I've failed Medora—"

"No," Mianne interrupted. "You haven't failed anyone. Don't you understand that you made your father's dream come true, in spite of all the problems? You did something for him that he could never have done for himself. No matter who betrayed you, no one can change that fact. Von Hoffman is the failure, and the Pendletons, but not you."

Phillipe cupped his wife's face in his two hands and murmured, "You believe that, don't you?"

"I believe it because it's true. Do you think that because one man is weak and evil, you have nothing to live for? Do you think for one moment that your father would not be proud of what you have achieved? It hasn't been easy, but you did what you set out to do, and now you can leave the burning memory of your father behind you. You'll find peace eventually, though you don't believe it now."

But as he looked down at her in the half-darkness, he realized that he *did* believe it. He would find peace with this one woman, because it had to be so. And if the agony of the past two years had brought him here, then he could only be grateful, because in Mianne alone he found the fulfillment he had sought so futilely all his life. "I love you," he murmured. "I don't think you can even begin to know how much."

"I know," his wife told him softly. "It took me a long time to learn, but now I know."

Phillipe leaned down to brush her lips with his, and

Mianne's arms came up around him, warm and inviting and infinitely safe. He realized that he needed her tonight as he never had before and the hunger that suddenly flamed in his blood was deep and strong. But her hands, as they moved over his naked skin, promised to assuage the ache in his body, and he pulled her to him so tightly that the fire on his skin seemed to melt into hers. The night was cold and black around them, but the warmth of their clinging bodies reached out boldly to obliterate the haunting shadows with a flame of bright, pure light that blazed for that one instant, then faded back into the waiting darkness from which it had come.

Medora sat alone in her room with the flickering fire to warm her and the flame of a lamp to show her how empty her world had become. She had refused to turn on the harsh electric lights her father was so proud of; they were too cold, too efficient, too much of all the things she had always thought she wanted to be. But the members of her family had proved to her, one by one, that she was not immune to human emotion. They had torn out her heart in order to show her that she had one, and they hadn't even known that that was what they were doing. But it was over now. Her body had been wracked with every pain and torment man could create, and she knew that her nature had been altered forever.

Today she had learned that she had finally fulfilled a promise to Antoine, who even in death had reached out to guide her in his path. But now that he was vindicated in the eyes of the world, she realized that she had nothing left to fight for. She had lost him; she knew that now with a knowledge more deep and painful than even his death had brought to her. His battle was won, and he had withdrawn the comforting hand that had kept her sane through all the anguish that had beset her in the Badlands. She was, for the first time in her life, finally and truly alone.

"Medora?" Gretta Von Hoffman stepped into the room and closed the door behind her. "I knocked, but you didn't answer."

"It's all right," her daughter assured her. "I was just thinking."

Gretta sat on the edge of the bed facing her daughter, her eyes full of regret and sympathy. "You think too much," the older woman murmured. "It's not healthy."

Medora winced. If nothing else, her father had taught her that fact tonight.

"I'm sorry," her mother said, fluttering her hands before her face as if to ward off her ill-chosen words. "I just came to ask if you still intend to leave us in the morning."

"I have to, Mama. Papa has given me no choice. But you don't have to stay behind. I want you to come with us."

"Oh, no!" Gretta cried. "I *do* have to stay. Your father needs me now, for the first time in a long time, and I couldn't bear to leave him behind."

"You love him?" Medora asked in bewilderment. "After everything he's done?"

"Yes," her mother answered simply. "And I pity him. Someday perhaps you'll find it in your heart to do the same."

Medora reached out to take Gretta's hand. "Do you blame me for going? I know it isn't fair to leave you alone."

Smiling sadly, the older woman shook her head. "You do what you have to do. You've always known what was right." Gretta wrinkled her brow as she thought of a disturbing question. "Where *will* you go?"

"Not back to the Badlands. For now we'll just find a hotel while we negotiate with Swift. That will give us time to make plans. I'll let you know when we decide. And I'll write to you, Mama."

Suddenly overcome with sadness, Gretta squeezed her daughter's hand and rose to go. "I'll miss you," she said, "but I'm used to that. Take care, Medora, and don't ever forget your poor father. Even if you hate him, please remember that it was only because he loved you too much." Then, before Medora could respond, her mother turned and fled.

He loved you too much. Wasn't that what had destroyed William, too? The words of his last letter came back to her in a rush. *Try to understand that my weakness sprang, not from an evil nature, but from loving you too much. For that, I now see, was my greatest sin.* If love had been her father's weakness, and William's, then what was her own? The answer came to her before she could stop it— Antoine. He alone had been the cause of all this agony. But Medora realized that even that knowledge could not make her regret her marriage. For fourteen years it had been the most precious thing in her life and she saw now that nothing would ever replace it.

All at once the door swung open and Paul and Louis came into the room wearing their long white nightshirts.

"We couldn't sleep, Mama," Louis hurried to explain, "so when we saw your light, we thought maybe you couldn't either."

"You don't mind if we keep you company, do you?" Paul asked as he laid one warm hand on top of his mother's. "It can't be any fun to be alone on New Year's Eve. Louis and I thought—"

"Be quiet," his older brother admonished. "Can't you see that Mama's upset? She doesn't want to listen to children chattering." Then he turned and knelt beside Medora's chair, "What is it, Mama? You can tell me, you know. I'm thirteen now, practically a man."

Medora felt that she was wandering in a dream. It

seemed to her that she had never before seen these two scrubbed, innocent faces with their thatches of light brown hair. She knew they had been there—they had touched the periphery of her life many times—but never until this moment—when she saw the concern, the desire to comfort mirrored in two pairs of brown eyes—had they touched her heart. She realized with a shock that in some fundamental way, she had been ignoring her children. She had never known quite how to reach them. Especially Anais.

Closing her eyes against the disturbing thought that suddenly plagued her, Medora pulled her sons closer. Perhaps, after all, Anais had been right; perhaps Medora had never really tried hard enough to understand the girl who so closely resembled her father. She had been too busy with her own pain to recognize how much her daughter needed her. And maybe Anais had been hurting too. But it was too late now—too late to apologize and try to start again. After all, Anais was gone. She had turned away without a backward glance and left her family behind. Had that been Medora's fault too?

"Mama?" Paul said, when she did not answer Louis. "Are you all right?"

Medora opened her eyes and looked into her son's troubled face and she smiled. The past was the past, she told herself. And now these two boys, whom she had hardly known existed, stood beside her, offering their comfort, their eyes clear and honest—untouched by the shadow of past betrayal.

"We can go now if you want to be alone," Louis said.

"No!" Medora cried. "I want you to stay." How arrogant she had been just a few minutes before, how blind to think that she had nothing else on this earth worth fighting for. If she thought her world empty and cold, it was only because she had not yet opened her eyes. But now she had done so, and she knew that the sons she had nearly forgotten for so long had just given her a miracle.

The Marquis' battle had been won, but now she was beginning a struggle more painful, more uncertain and more difficult by far—the battle against her own stubborn blindness, which had almost cost her all that she held dear. "Sit down," she told the two boys. "I'm glad you're here. It will make the hours seem shorter."

"You're sure you don't mind?" Paul asked.

Medora turned to him and smiled. "I'm sure."

When they were seated on the floor beside her, she put a hand on each boy's shoulder, listening to the sounds of the party that still filled the house with the joy of a rare celebration. Louis and Paul would never know another night like this in their lifetimes, Medora thought; nor would she. But, for the moment, past and present alike would be forgotten as the three sat together in silent expectation, watching for the first dawn of a new century.